"It takes a skilled and intelligent imagination to seamlessly blend history and fiction. Rose doesn't gloss over the brutality of the period . . ."

– 5 Stars *ForeWord Clarion Review*

5-Star Amazon Reviews for Chatelaine

"I love this book! I found it difficult to put down. The characters were so real and gave me a wonderful glimpse of the times. To see their lives unfold from beginning to end was so well done."

"Wonderful research – learned a lot about the time period."

"Once I started reading it, I could not put it down!... This book is so well written that I was not only drawn into the history of the time, but I also fell in love right along with Judith and Raoul, sharing in their joys and struggles."

"One of the true tests of an excellent book is whether or not the characters become friends to the reader. Judith and Raoul quickly become those friends... It was a difficult book to put down and I was sad when it ended."

JAI ROSE

ISBN: 978-1-943492-82-4 (Hardback)

ISBN: 978-1-943492-83-1 (Soft Cover)

Book design by 

Castle photograph © Mick Prodger

Medieval woman photograph ©Artycrafter | Dreamstime.com

ELM GROVE PUBLISHING
San Antonio, Texas, USA
www.elmgrovepublishing.com
Elm Grove Publishing is a legally registered trade name of Panache Communication Arts, Inc.

AUTHOR'S NOTE

Dear Reader,

This story and the time in which it is set have been carefully researched. Medieval attitudes and behaviors, especially toward women, are different than those of today in many respects. Yet with all the limits placed upon women in that time, history shows here and there a woman who rose above the expected and did amazing things.

Please put aside preconceptions of time and gender, and prepare to enter another world.

Sincerely,
Jai Rose

ENGLAND CIRCA 1065

OAKWELL CASTLE

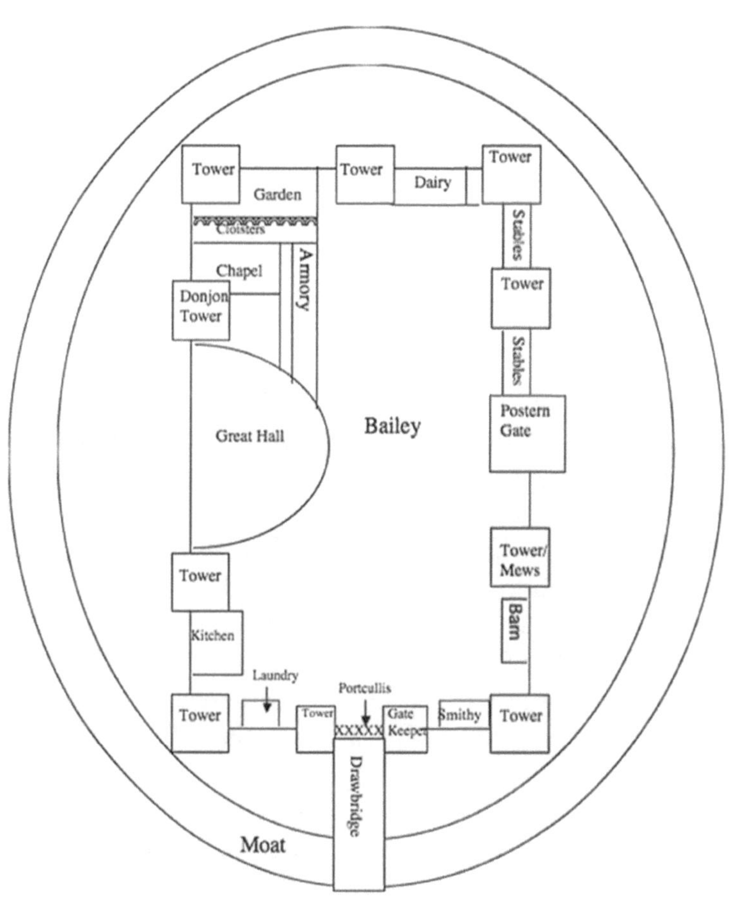

PROLOGUE

England

In 1060, her mother died in childbirth, a messy, heart-breaking business. Aged 7, Judith was there to see it all, as she was being instructed in medicine by her nurse. Her father beat her afterward, because she could not save the babe.

It was some time later, in the year 1063, that her father remarried. This time, unlike Judith's Saxon mother, he wed a widowed noblewoman from Normandy. Thus she acquired a stepmother and a stepsister, both as vicious as her father, and neither of whom with a desire for the tasks necessary to run a Saxon thane's household. Judith kept house and filled the duties of lady of her father's hold, although she received none of the privileges.

In 1066, her father was killed at Hastings, when the Normans invaded England. The new Norman lord of Oakwood, Judith's home, arrived the following year.

CHAPTER 1

erdic, Thane of Oakwood, heaved himself astride his shaggy dun and observed the straggle of folk that had ventured forth to bid their lord Godspeed upon his journey. Shivering in the course, gray trulls commonly worn by the servants of the hall, the people pressed close together for whatever warmth might be found against the December winds. Here and there in the press, Cerdic noted a spot of brown, or faded red or green, indicating to his jaundiced eye that some of the villagers, at least, knew the observance due to their lord. He spat in disgust, for in truth it was a poor showing. Pulling his cloak of wolfskin closer, he adjusted the brass circle pin, which held it in place. Things had come to low ebb indeed, he reflected sourly, if his villeins kept themselves clustered about their fires when duty bade them attend upon their thane.

Oakwood Hall was an ordinary Saxon hold, a two-story wooden building with a courtyard in front and outbuildings to either side. The courtyard of packed dirt had been turned to mud by the weather and then frozen. As a result, dips in the ground were covered by thin, brittle patches of ice. It made for villainous standing. The folk gathered before the hall carefully shifted their feet often, either to escape the cold or to stamp feeling back into limbs held too long in one position.

It was time to be off, yet Cerdic made no sign to his men. They sat motionless, obedient to his will. Their ponies, however, showed resentment with constant stamping and jingling of harness and bit. Cerdic enjoyed his power and fluffed out his long, blond beard as he ignored the questioning look of his second-in-command. Deliberately, he let them await his pleasure. It was no bad thing to remind his hotheaded warriors who ruled here.

Shifting in the saddle to ease his gouty leg, he glimpsed a small, blonde girl at the edge of the crowd. Dawn lent a slivery gleam to her fair braids, but Cerdic was far from pleased with the sight. He sent a stream of spittle in her direction and scowled.

"Strong sons I wanted," he muttered to himself, "and instead I got that pale, puling she-thing!" He felt that particular injustice strongly. A man needed sons.

Sir Hugh moved his pony forward. "You said something, my lord?"

Cerdic waved him away. "You, girl!" he called, pointing a rough finger. "What do you here?"

The peasants, among whom Judith was huddled against the biting cold, prudently withdrew from her vicinity, exposing her to the elements and her father's scorn. She flinched, swallowed uneasily, then raised her chin and forced herself to meet Cerdic's gaze. She had done no wrong, she knew, but that meant less than nothing when her father was in such a mood. "I came but to wish you a pleasant journey and to pray for your safe return."

"I want none of your pious wishes, you stupid cow!" he sneered. "Get your ugly face from my sight! And take that idiot in monk's clothing with you!" he added, jerking a thumb at the cleric who stood a few paces to the girl's left.

Cerdic watched, smiling unpleasantly, as the girl moved through the common folk. He laughed aloud when she reached the door, for Agnes, daughter of his second wife, put her foot in Judith's path to send the smaller girl sprawling across the threshold.

"Yon's a clumsy creature," remarked a voice at his knee.

The thane glanced down knowingly at his wife. "Aye, well, my lady, that's as may be. But I've no use for that wench an' she's dead. I've more than half promised her to Sir Hugh to bind him to my service. See she doesn't break her skinny neck while I'm gone." Cerdic's French, learned at King Edward's court, was excellent.

"Oh, as you wish," pouted Lady Bertha, with a careless shrug. Her dark hair was coiled and pinned, in the Norman manner, under the rose scarf that covered it. Her gown, a good red wool, showed signs of wear but was still serviceable. "Though she tries me sorely, so sullen as she is."

"I'll have naught to say to a beating or two," Cerdic added with a wink. "She's an ungrateful brat and needs the schooling. But there is Sir Hugh, my lady, and I have need of his skills. Take care, lest by some mischance lasting damage is done. The man might well refuse to take a cripple to his bed!"

Lady Bertha laughed ruefully, careful not to show her bad tooth. "Your word is law, my lord. But I vow, at times her long face and scholar's ways are more than I can bear!"

He responded to the pony's toss of its head with a vicious jerk of the reins. "Bid you farewell, my lady."

"A safe journey, my lord," she replied, lowering her voice huskily and gazing up at him through her lashes.

His eyes slid to her full breasts. "And a speedy return," Cerdic murmured meaningfully. "God's Beard, but I shall miss your warmth at Thorney! I've half a mind to take you with me to the King's assembly!"

Lady Bertha shivered in the icy cold. "You know I have no love for travel, husband. And would you have me embark upon so rough a ride when we know not yet whether I may be with child?"

"Think you 'tis true?" demanded the thane eagerly.

She knew it was not, but leaned forward so that he had a better view down her bodice. "Perhaps. And t'will not be so long 'ere your return," Lady Bertha said, resting a hand upon his thigh. She felt the muscles tighten under the heavy leather of his breeches. "Do you remember, my lord, when you bed some wench at that Saxon court of yours, that I have yet to show you all the tricks we Norman women know to play."

"There are no wenches at King Edward's court, you recall. He wouldn't know what to do with 'em an there were," he returned with a wolfish grin. But he had spent enough time in dalliance, especially with his own wife, and so turned his pony's head toward the ford, feeling already the quickening in his loins Lady Bertha's touch aroused. He gave a last look back from the other side of the water. Then he moved off at the head of his band of housecarls to join the annual Christmas meeting of the witan, to be held this year at Thorney Island, due to King Edward's poor health.

‡

Gytha, the dairymaid, pushed back her long mop of hair. "Now we'll see some sport!" she whispered to the sewingmaid.

Redheaded Edwina grinned. "Aye. Do you think she'll wait until her lord is out of sight?"

"A brazen whore like her? Why should she? Hasn't she bedded half the hall servants in the master's chamber with her lord sleeping in his chair below?"

"But he's dead drunk, usually," objected Edwina. "He'd not wake in that condition, even if St. Peter himself appeared before him!"

"True enough," the other woman conceded. "And he's in a bustle to get himself to Thorney. He'll not stay for naught; mark my words. 'Tis a wonder to me, though, how yon lady shames him so boldly before his folk! There's surely some rumor will reach his ears soon or late."

The sewingmaid gave her a knowing glance. "No woman's tale would be believed by the thane; he'd count it as jealousy and a desire to supplant her. No man would dare whisper of what happens behind his lord's back, since he's sure to have had his fun with the lady himself."

"Not all of 'em have been beneath her skirts," Gytha objected.

"Wouldn't matter. I've been in her service since Normandy," retorted Edwina. "She can twist the words of anyone, noble or commoner, to suit her purpose. I've seen her in many a scrape and come out with nary a mark to show for it."

"Is it true she lived in a grand hall with stone floors and a household of fifty knights, like they say?"

"Who says? She lived there, in a fine tower with stone floors and a moat, but she was not chatelaine, if that's what you heard. Christ's Wounds, her last lord, God rest him, was a landless knight! If I'd not lost my own man and child to the bloody flux, I'd not have lowered myself to serve the likes of her! But at the time I was that close to starving, I'd have served the Devil himself!" Edwina sniffed and tossed her head. "Still, we did alright until her brother bade her join him in England."

"Aye, we were at court," she added at the other woman's questioning look. "There's lots of Normans with the King. Any road, her brother sent her the passage silver, and we came." The redhead quirked a shoulder. "You should have seen her face when the thane brought her here that first day! Him being received at court and having pennies enough to buy her what trinkets caught her eye, she thought he'd be a great lord like in Normandy, with a castle and the rest! 'Tis a bit of a comedown from fancies like that to this place. A swine shed, she calls it, when Lord Cerdic's out of hearing."

"No!" The shock was genuine. Gytha, born and raised at Oakwood, had never left the holding. She could not imagine anything grander than the Saxon stead. "How could anyone say such a thing?"

"Each to his own taste, is what I say," shrugged Edwina, mindful of her doubtful position as an outsider. No good would come of offending the natives. "It's better than some I've seen, and at least it keeps the rain from our heads."

"My lady doesn't *like* it here?" repeated Gytha, uncomprehending.

Edwina realized she must go carefully with this. It would not do to be too closely connected with the behavior of her mistress. "Well, she doesn't speak the language, but for a few words. Puts you off a bit, not understanding folk about you. I'd a Saxon granny, so the tongue came easily enough to me. Lady Agnes learned it readily, too. Her mother has no gift for it. But then, Lady Bertha has no need, really, what with Lord Cerdic's brat to run the household for her and tend to things."

Gytha bristled. "Lady Judith is one as knows her duty to her folk," she said repressively.

"Oh, of course!" Edwina said hurriedly. "Of course! I meant no disrespect!" Knowing she had overstepped the bounds, she moved away as if to watch the small cavalcade, now barely visible in the distance. The serfs of Oakwood and their fondness for Lady Judith! She could not understand it. Of course, she was better than Lady Agnes, one had to admit that. Edwina sighed. She would never find a way back to Normandy, and the sooner she was accepted here the better.

‡

By the palisade, Lady Bertha watched as her lord disappeared into the wood. *Dirty Pig!* she thought. *Good riddance!* Really, she deserved better. Lady Bertha sighed. She glanced to her left and caught sight of Ethelfrith, the groom, standing with the other stablehands in the crowd. Her face brightened. Ignoring the whisperings she could not understand; she smiled seductively and pushed out her breasts until they strained at the bodice of her gown. An irritating whimper caught her ear. She turned to find her daughter, who had been well enough earlier, with a hand clamped to her jaw and a piteous expression on her pimpled face.

"Is it your tooth again?" Lady Bertha asked, keeping her impatience in check. "Never mind, loveling. Go to your chamber and Mama will attend upon you in a moment."

Hell's Gate! she thought in annoyance as the girl left. If Agnes' teeth rotted, Cerdic would have ill luck in getting her suitably wed, and they must do that within the next year, or else, she'd be on their hands forever. She thought spitefully of Cerdic's daughter, with her fair thick braids and perfect teeth. Why could *she* not have been the one with the toothache, that insolent whelp? Well, what could not be mended must be endured.

She pushed such bothersome musing from her mind and eyed the groom afresh. What a lusty lad he was! Those broad shoulders and a lean belly made her think of other parts of him. A loud cough made her aware of her surroundings and the witnesses.

"You!" she called out to him, pointing. "Come in here!" She knew the crowd snickered at her grammar, but that couldn't be helped. "I must tell you something about my mare!"

This form of address fooled no one as the grinning Ethelfrith followed his lady up the broad stairs. One old crone laughed aloud. This brought bawdy jokes and murmurings at such shamelessness, and ribald speculations in regard to Lord Cerdic's lack of prowess, which caused his lady wife to seek a companion in bedsport so soon after his departure.

Finally the crowded dispersed. The women returned to their looms and querns, where they made woolen cloth or ground corn. The men wandered down the track to the village alehouse for a judicious sampling of the new Christmas brew.

‡

Within the hall, a fire burned fiercely upon the hearth. Dogs lay huddled close for warmth and a few half-frozen birds rustled among the rafters. On a low bench drawn a little to one side to escape the searing heat of the flames sat Judith and Brother Plegmund, the monk.

Judith was a small girl, seeming little more than a child, but her face was grave as she plied her spindle, fingers working rhythmically to twist the woolen fibers into thread. She ignored the entrance of her stepmother and the groom, the subsequent rustlings of the straw bed in the chamber at the head of the stair, and the moanings as well. Her attention was focused instead upon Brother Plegmund's voice, discoursing upon the important events of the day.

"'Tis a sad thing, the King's illness," he sighed, his brown eyes on the flames. "T'was Tostig's exile began it, but only the Good God knows how t'will end." His round face was stern and his voice took on the teaching tone he used with her from the time eleven years before, when Lady Milburga, perhaps sensing her own early demise in childbed, had commended to him the education of her beloved daughter.

"Tostig, you will recall, is Lord Harold's younger brother, and was a great favorite of the King. He is a poor leader, however. The people of Northumbria rejected his rule, as is their right under law. Even Lord Harold had to acknowledge the lad's cruelty as senseless. So, the King was forced to send him into exile and to set young Morkere, brother to the Earl of Mercia, in his place as Earl." He eyed her profile. "You say nothing. Do you not remember speaking of this before?"

"Certainly," she replied, glancing at him from clear, blue eyes. "I always remember your lessons. But I like to hear you tell it again, for your voice is so deep and strong."

The monk flushed with pleasure, mentally took himself to task for the sin of vanity, and continued. "It is not what one would have wished, but one is forced to admit that Morkere, young as he is, must be better suited to rule than Tostig." Pale light came from the door in a long beam, dust motes dancing. It touched the top of his shaven head, making it seem almost as if the middle-aged man had a halo.

He sighed again, and Judith, who knew that he was related by blood, however distantly, to the Godwinesons, England's most powerful family, smiled with real sympathy. "And Tostig's exile affected the King's health?" she prompted.

"Um, yes, yes," Brother Plegmund muttered, trying to recall precisely the gist of a communication he had lately received from a brother of his order who was, in a humble capacity, attached to King Edward's court. "The Northumberians were, in effect, defying the King, you understand, to reject the earl set over them. In another land, France say, or Castile, the King would simply send an army to punish the folk, and there would be an end to it. But here in England, even a king may be dethroned under Saxon law." He spoke with a touch of disapproval. Although he was a Saxon by birth, the monk had spent more of his life in Normandy and France than his native country. The uncertain sort of rule favored by the English seemed not at all to his liking. Judith smiled again and bent her head over her spinning.

"It was all most distressing for the King," he went on, hands folded at his lean waist. "And since there was nothing for it but to accede to their wishes, the King was in a terrible rage. Indeed, one cannot wonder at it. It brought on some fever of the brain, I think, and fits. In any case, he has been ailing since, poor man. Truly, I fear this witan assembly is an error in judgment. He should be resting in his bed, not arguing with hotheaded nobles. Lord Harold could have deputized for him."

"Will he die, think you?" Judith asked curiously.

Brother Plegmund shrugged, spreading his hands. "I am no physician, child. But the King's illness is come at a bad time. A very bad time. And for a childless king to refuse to name a successor . . ." His voice trailed off and he shook his head, affecting not to hear the rhythmic grunting which assailed the ear from the direction of the lord's chamber.

Judith moistened the woolen fibers trailing from her spindle with spittle to make them adhere more firmly. "Still," she said. "The King may not be in so serious a case as you suppose. He has recovered from his seizure, has he not?"

"Oh, aye. He's recovered. But he may have another. Then where would we be? And after all these years, 'tis doubtful he'll get the Queen with child. Her whole family is prolific, so she cannot be barren. I fear it is some weakness in the King."

"Mayhap he is under some vow of chastity," suggested the girl, who also believed in legends and heroic deeds.

"However that may be," returned the monk severely, "the witan is only a ruling assembly. Without the God-given right of a king, it is left with the task of choosing a ruler should the King die of a sudden, which God forbid!"

"And they would choose . . .?"

Plegmund smiled, for this was a subject he thought upon often. "T'would be best an he named an heir, but he will not. In the event of his death, there are certain names that leap to the mind. Were I asked, I would have to say that the Earl of Wessex is by far the wisest choice."

"Lord Harold?" Judith fitted the distaff more snugly under her left arm, her brow creased in thought. "He's able enough, I grant you, but not of royal blood. And if the witan should look outside the bloodline, would they not consider Tostig? He is, after all, the King's favorite, and may have mended his ways."

"No! Never!" he snorted. "Tostig has proved he is as unsuited to rule as his eldest brother, but the less said about Svein Godwineson, the better!"

She hid an impish smile. Even *she* knew the story of Godwine's eldest son, who had shamefully seduced an abbess. He had been exiled for it by the King, but upon his return had turned against and murdered his cousin, Beorn. The original scandal had rocked even the nobility, more used to impiety than lesser folk. Her father had been disgusted by the second exile, but then, Beorn was his friend, and Cerdic wanted justice for his murder. Most nobles had felt differently.

Brother Plegmund frowned and went on. "Should they bring Tostig back, Northumbria would revolt. The nobles would never risk it. As for royal blood, what choice have they? Edgar is the only male left of Ethelred's line, and he is rumored to be a weakling of a lad. Think you the witan would call upon King Swein of Denmark or King Harald Hardrada of Norway? Hah! Foreigners!" The monk smiled. "My dear, Harold Godwineson is the obvious man. Has he not ruled wisely under King Edward all these years?"

"That's truth," she conceded. "But was there not some rumor you once mentioned in passing that King Edward did promise the throne to William of Normandy?"

He beamed his approval. Always the child had been an apt pupil. "It has been said that something of the sort was spoken of many years ago when King Edward was very young, but there is not a shred of proof such a pledge was made. And in any case, of what worth are promises made between stripling lads? Even if there were an arrangement of this sort between King Edward and William the Bastard, the witan would never approve. He is of foreign blood and a Norman." He smiled tolerantly. "No, child, I feel it is safe to say that the Norman Duke will never rule in England."

"Bastard though he may be, Duke William is at least honorably wed in the Holy Church to the mother of his sons," remarked Judith pointedly.

The monk's cheeks reddened, but he was staunch in defense of his kinsman. "There are many such unions among the people, girl. I do not approve of a marriage not blessed by the Church, but doubtless when he wears the crown, Lord Harold will be properly joined to Edith Swan-Neck." He was clearly nettled that the girl should find a flaw in his hero.

"Have you consulted the stars, then?" she inquired with interest.

He nodded. "Be sure. T'was my first action when I heard of the King's ailment. The stars do not lie, Lady Judith. Harold will be King of England."

As she considered the matter, the spindle, with its heavy clay weight, twirled against her right leg. Her fingers moved ceaselessly. "'Tis said Lord Harold is a comely man and rich. Mayhap he will take some earl's daughter to wife or make a foreign alliance. T'would be wise policy, surely, with so many across the seas keeping a watchful eye to our shores. Has not King Swein a daughter of marriageable age? What do the stars indicate?"

"I . . . I had not thought to look for that," he admitted, startled. "I sought only kingship, which I found. I looked no further. Hmmmmm. I must consult my charts again."

"When you do, could you look at my chart, also?" asked Judith in a small voice.

He looked at her anxious eyes. "Something troubles you, my child?"

Judith nodded. "My father has made mention of Sir Hugh's need for a wife. I believe he means to give me to him and I . . . I had hoped the stars might indicate marriage with one other than Sir Hugh." She blushed and looked away, biting nervously at her lip.

The monk's face was compassionate. Sir Hugh, a vicious bully of a man, was well known to him. The fellow had been away in Normandy for many years and returned with the Norman title of knight. Desirable on one's side in battle he might be, but there could be no doubt of his unworthiness to be husband to the gentle Lady Judith. "It has been years since I cast your horoscope," he said, voice soft. "I will look again and see what the stars have to tell."

She smiled gratefully. "Do you visit in the village this day, Brother Plegmund?"

"Aye," he grunted, rising. "Old Egfrieda has asked for Last Rites. She's had them once before, but this time I fear she will finally be called."

"I shall pray for her," murmured Judith, saddened.

He patted her shining head, gave her his blessing, and departed, the skirts of his dark habit brushing the rushes as he left.

‡

From her father's chamber, a deep-throated cry gave evidence that Lady Bertha had found satisfaction in her encounter with the groom. Judith bundled up her spinning and mounted the narrow stair to her own chamber.

As a result of her lowly status in Cerdic's hall, Judith's chamber was placed under the eaves and was also the room used for drying and storing medicinal herbs. Since, under the tutelage of her old nurse Arnhilda, Judith was responsible for the tending of whatever ills befell the Oakwood folk, this was no great hardship. Of course, during the season for gathering elder leaves and flowers it was well nigh unendurable. Both women would suffer headaches and occasional dizziness, which might last for days on end, but usually it was not so bad.

Entering the chamber, Judith found Arnhilda, an aging woman with a cheerfully homely face, carefully warming a stone vial on the tiny hearth.

"Lady Agnes has the toothache again," grunted Arnhilda. "I told her t'would be few moments 'ere I'd send a draught to bring her ease, but she's in mortal agony if that mewling is aught to go by. I've heated oil of cloves, what precious little we have left. A bit of poppy juice in a horn of warm ale might not come amiss," she hinted.

"Tis not Lady Agnes howling like a bitch in the briars," returned the girl dryly. "Lady Bertha and Ethelfrith are discussing matters of importance in my father's chamber." She raced briefly down the stair for the horn of ale and returned, breathing hard.

"Lady Bertha about yet?" asked the older woman anxiously.

"Nay, I was fortunate. But I pity the serving wenches. They will be the ones to pay for her sin." Judith sighed, propping the drinking horn carefully on the hearth. "Why is it, I wonder, that she must needs inflict pain after she enjoys pleasure?"

Arnhilda grimaced. "I think it is she's like Eadgytha in the vill, and secretly yearns to have women's caresses. Also, there's an evil in her loves to see another's pain. Some demon rides her, and I praise God your lady mother is gone from this place and cannot see what has happened to us."

"If my mother were here," remarked the girl with a smile, "Lady Bertha would not have happened to us at all!"

"Hah!" Arnhilda spat into the rushes. "Don't be so sure. You've seen how lightly she regards her own marriage vows. Think you she'd be overly concerned for the sanctity of vows made by another? A shameless whore, that's what she is!"

"True," Judith agreed, stirring the veriest hint of a brownish powder into the warm ale. "But she *is* lady of this hall, and you'd best keep your tongue between your teeth lest you lose it. Even last night she was pressing my father to have one of the kitchen wenches whipped. Thirty lashes, she says, for spilling the juice from a platter of meat and ruining a new gown. God save us, but she's vicious!"

"As you've reason to know," muttered the servant angrily.

Judith shrugged and regretted it. "Aye, my back still smarts from the last beating I received at her hand."

Arnhilda's eyes were concerned. "Does it pain you so, dearling? Shall I rub in more salve to ease it?"

"Nay, let be," she replied with her enchanting smile. "I'll heal soon enough. As for the beating, why, t'was well worth a few stripes to tell that Norman bitch's whelp all know her for a liar and a whore." She nodded her satisfaction. Then she picked up both vial and ale horn and moved carefully along the gallery to where Agnes lay in a comfortable chamber, moaning her pain. Judith ministered gently to the suffering older girl, not through fear, but because she felt it her duty to bring ease to those in agony, and because she believed firmly that God would be disappointed in her if she inflicted needless pain on one in her care.

‡

News traveled slowly. It was not until well into the New Year that Oakwood learned of the death of King Edward and the coronation of the new king. It came as a shock to the village folk. Not that they felt any great affection for the priestly King Edward, with his scholar's ways and his Norman friends, but over the years they had grown accustomed to him. None of the peasants had ever seen him, of course, but the thought of King Edward as ruler had seemed right. However, Lord Harold was, so they said, a big, strong man and a handsome one, who would look well in a crown. Naturally, none of them had seen Harold, either. Still, the Godwinesons were a powerful family, long associated with the throne, and the people trusted Lord Harold to care for them in much the same manner as King Edward had done. He would make a good king, they decided. He would not interfere with his people and life would go on as it always had at Oakwood. They were content.

If the peasant population was satisfied with its prospects, there were those in Oakwood Hall less optimistic about the future. Cerdic, just returned from the witan gathering, sat in his massive wooden chair with his bad leg propped upon a stool and stared moodily into the fire.

"The King, God rest his soul, fell ill on Christmas Eve," he told his audience of warriors and retainers. "His physicians and priests could do nothing. The queen was at his side always, and Lord Harold, as well. Archbishop Stigand attended upon him constantly, and that Robert FitzWimarc, the King's Norman toady, was there also."

"FitzWimarc is none so bad," remarked Lady Bertha, gesturing one of the wenches forward to fill Cerdic's silver goblet.

"I've no patience with foreign influence at court!" snapped the thane.

"Well, what would you, my lord? The King's lady mother abandoned him to the rearing of his Norman cousins so that she might be free to wed the enemy of the poor King's dead father. Surely 'tis only natural he should feel more at home with his kinsmen at hand."

He grunted in answer, his thumb moving absently over a small dent in the goblet's side. "Remember, lady wife, you yourself are a Norman. Doubtless you have a fondness for your own folk. Yet many a Saxon, such as myself, is wearied of the Norman influence surrounding our King. 'Tis a fortunate business that Lord Harold has come into the crown and will put an end to that nonsense."

Lady Bertha smiled sweetly and patted her husband's hand. "Doubtless you are correct, my lord. I am only a female and know little of weighty matters. But pray tell us, what of the late King's illness?"

"King Edward roused on the tenth day, or mayhap the eleventh, I forget. They say he spoke of a strange dream of destruction, but Archbishop Stigand vows he was raving. Then he had a few words for his lady wife, and lastly, he named Harold heir to the kingdom. He was dead soon after." Those assembled before the thane made the sign of the cross, and he echoed their motion somewhat belatedly.

He drained the mead from his goblet and held it out wordlessly to be filled again. "We, the witan, confirmed King Edward's choice that same day, as was right and proper to do," he declared. "King Edward was buried in the abbey the next morn, and Lord Harold crowned there that day." Cerdic belched.

"There are those who say t'was a mite hasty, but I believe we acted in the best interests of our fair land. In any event," he added, "the new King rode later to York and was again confirmed by a gemot of the earldoms." He took a draught of the heady mead and sighed deeply.

Lady Bertha frowned. "But what is there in all this to so distress you, my lord? You have said often enough how brave a warrior is Lord Harold, and I believe you are not displeased with his kingship. Were you then so affected by the death of King Edward?"

"My concern is not for King Edward's passing," muttered Cerdic impatiently. "He was sickly always and less king than cleric. Nay, it is rather something I heard when I rode to London to make those purchases you requested, my lady. T'was not a fortnight after the crown was placed on Harold's head that there were rumors of threats to our King from William the Bastard."

"Threats?" she repeated in a startled voice.

"Aye." The thane belched again and wiped his beard. "This mighty Duke of Normandy whose mother sprang from a tanner's loins! 'Tis said he calls King Harold traitor and false, and swears the crown of England belongs by right to himself! Well, Brother Plegmund had this day a message from a priest, or some such, who sought me out in London, and mayhap t'will bring some light to bear."

Lady Judith, of little consequence in her father's hall aside from the day-to-day running of it, did not possess a coveted stool like Lady Bertha or Lady Agnes. She stood in a chilly corner, intrigued by the tale. What the monk had foretold had indeed come to pass, but that which she had sensed was true, as well. All who spoke of William of Normandy agreed upon his strength, justice, and determination. To her, it seemed clear that Duke William believed in the promise that King

Edward was said to have made him and that he intended to be King of England, or at least to try. Else why bother with threats? It was possible he might expect to be bought off with gold, but somehow, she doubted he was as easily dissuaded as a Viking might be. Judith wondered if he had ever failed to attain that which he desired, and whether there would be war in the land. King Harold's confirmation by the witan or no, William of Normandy sounded more the type to be bound by no man's decision but his own.

" . . .the insolence to challenge our King!" Cerdic was shouting, strong drink having magnified both feelings and voice. "T'will be known all over Christendom that he has grossly insulted us! All England will be shamed before that world!"

"Mere words," soothed Lady Bertha. "And spoken in the heat of anger, too. What does it matter *what* Duke William says, now that Lord Harold wears the crown?"

"Oh, aye, you think this Duke William of yours a saint!" Cerdic sneered, casting his lady a rare public glance of disapproval.

But Lady Bertha was too clever to be caught in *this* argument. "A man like other men," she said with a wink. "Indeed, he may be a brave knight and a just ruler in Normandy, my lord, but I vow he makes use of his chamber pot of a night like any other."

Cerdic was surprised into a laugh.

"Think you there will be trouble over this?" she asked after a moment. "I would not like to see England and Normandy at odds."

"Perhaps. That does not worry me. 'Tis the sound of the ugly rumors riles my guts. Aye, insults of the sort a man may not stomach without bloodletting to wash them away!"

"Whence come these tales?"

"Started by the Norman Bastard, no doubt," Cerdic muttered. "He thinks to divide us with foul lies." He drank deeply and peered about the hall with bloodshot eyes. "Where is that damned monk? Someone fetch Brother Plegmund! We'll hear what he has read concerning these slanderous Norman claims!"

"I am here, my lord," spoke the cleric from his place near the door. He appeared paler than usual, and although he maintained an air of calm, Judith saw that he was deeply disturbed. She wondered fearfully just what it was he'd learned from his far-away friend.

The monk approached the thane's chair and held before him a single sheet of parchment, much creased and closely covered with writing. He offered this for Lord Cerdic's inspection with a shaking hand. "See, my lord!"

Few warriors learned to read, and Cerdic was far from scholarship. He was reluctant to admit this, however. He took the paper, glanced at it with some embarrassment, and then returned the thing. "My eyes are not what they once were," he announced. "Read it for us all. Has it some reference to King Harold?"

"Aye, my lord," said the monk stiffly. He licked his lips, and his eyes darted briefly about the hall as if seeking allies.

Judith, who could read and write in Latin, Greek, Saxon, and French due to Brother Plegmund's zeal for education, slid unobtrusively behind him. She peered around his shoulder without shame, absorbed in the epistle.

"It is a communication addressed to me from Brother Seul in Rouen and writ in the Latin tongue," he informed his audience. "He writes that our Abbot has informed all members of our Order concerning the truth of the legal succession to the English throne, which matter is now in question. In the Year of Our Lord 1064, Earl Harold Godwineson did sail to Normandy upon order of King Edward, may God give his soul absolution from sins, and there, upon Holy Relics of great sanctity and power, did Harold give allegiance to William, Duke of Normandy, and did swear fealty to Duke William as heir to the throne of England. Thus, is William of Normandy true King of England, and Harold Godwineson a usurper."

Cerdic's face was alarmingly red, blue eyes bulging. He glared at the hapless cleric. "Tell us, monk," he invited softly. "Do you believe this Brother Seul of yours has writ you the truth? That Duke William is true heir to the throne and that King Harold has stolen it from him?"

Even an idiot would have scented danger at that moment, and Brother Plegmund was not a foolish man. He licked his lips nervously. "I do not know, my lord."

"Well, then, you must know whether your friend is a reliable man," remarked Cerdic, still in that soft, deadly tone. "Could he be mistaken?"

It was a way out, yet the monk felt Lady Judith's eyes upon him. If he took the safe path, the coward's path, and said that Seul was incorrect, she would know it for a lie. In all her life he had been her only model of truth and integrity, save for a peasant maidservant. To fail her now was to fail in the oath he had made to Lady Judith's dying mother, as well as his duty to God. He could not do it.

"I have known Brother Seul from boyhood, my lord," admitted Brother Plegmund, "and have never known him to speak less than the truth. So, if he says that King Harold gave such assurance to William of Normandy, there must be some proof. Perhaps a misunderstanding is at the root . . ."

"Lies!" screamed Cerdic, starting from his chair in one of his sudden, dreadful rages. "Filthy Norman lies! How dare you come before me to speak vileness of our King! Slanderer! Traitor! Nithing!" He gestured to two of his armed housecarls. "Remove this . . . this foulness masked in holy orders from my hall!" he thundered. "Take him out and give him twenty lashes for daring to profane our noble King Harold with his evil!"

The men hesitated, as was natural since the Holy Church reserved to herself the right of trial and punishment of erring clerics. Men had been excommunicated for just such thoughtless acts as this, and they hoped against hope that their thane would think better of his hasty words. However, he gestured impatiently for them to carry out his command. They glanced briefly at one another, shrugged, and then moved forward to take the shaking monk in charge.

"Father, you must not!" cried Judith, slipping past several people to the front of the crowd. All eyes turned in shock to the slim, pale girl who stood trembling in fearful defiance.

"By the Beards of the Apostles!" roared the thane, heaving himself upright to face his daughter. "Am I to brook rebellion in my own hall?"

Judith felt sweat start upon her forehead and run down to her neck. She willed herself not to run from the hall in fear. She longed to do just that, but Brother Plegmund belonged to God, and was not her father's to use as he saw fit. Her duty was clear. She stretched out her hand pleadingly. "Think what you do, my lord. It is for the Archbishop to rebuke his monks. You risk grave displeasure. And in truth, Brother Plegmund did but read to us all what was written by another and not words of his own choosing. The guilt is not his."

"Enough!" he shrieked, his fists raised, his face almost purple in his rage.

The girl fell silent. She had seen him like this before and knew him to be past reasoning. If she had been frightened a moment ago, she was terrified now. Her own life was in jeopardy along with the monk's. Only the fact that fear had frozen her limbs kept her knees from buckling.

Cerdic pointed violently toward the door, and the housecarls dragged the cleric away. After a second's hesitation, the folk rushed after them into the courtyard. A whipping was a form of entertainment few cared to miss. Soon only Judith, her father and Lady Bertha remained in the hall.

The thane stared at his daughter. She had grown in the past months, her rounding breasts strained at the bodice of a gown too small for her ripening body. He removed the heavy leather belt from round his waist and beckoned to her, a strange excitement building inside him. And when she approached cautiously, knowing what was to come, he grinned as he lashed out with the belt.

His arm rose and fell with a regular motion. The girl had turned, stood with her back to him, arms wrapped around herself, bent over slightly at the waist. Her acceptance angered him, and he swung harder. Judith cringed away from the heavy blow and then screamed in shock and pain, as hurt came from an unexpected direction. Before her stood Lady Bertha, holding a riding crop in one hand, and wearing an expression of unwholesome delight.

They beat her mercilessly. Cerdic's blows fell at random, mostly upon her buttocks and thighs, but Lady Bertha aimed for her breasts and belly, laughing wildly when the girl's gown ripped from a particularly vicious blow. Finally, Cerdic cast his belt aside. His face flushed with exertion, he caught at Lady Bertha's arm. "Enough, my lady. We don't want to kill the wench." He stared down at his daughter, ogling one pink-tipped breast clearly visible through the rent gown. He nudged her lifeless form with his foot. "She has swooned." A glance about the hall showed him the maidservant, Arnhilda, who had retreated only as far as the door when the others had left.

"Remove her!" he ordered. "See to her wounds, and warn that stupid sow that if I have any more of her insolence, there'll be more of the same."

The thane watched as Arnhilda grasped the girl in her arms, and half-dragged, half-carried her up the stair. He was breathing heavily, his heart pounding. He noted with some surprise that his hands were shaking.

Lady Bertha sensed the fever in him and approached, venturing to slip an arm about his waist uninvited. "Is all well with you, my lord?"

For answer he placed her hand upon his member. It was as rigid as an iron bar. "T'will burst, I think," he said wonderingly.

She closed her hand firmly about him and smiled into his eyes. "Not before it fills my need, I hope." She giggled as he pushed her in the direction of their chamber.

CHAPTER 2

efore Eastertide there came word throughout southern England that the fyrd had been called to attend upon the King, who feared a Norman invasion. Cerdic's land was well to the north and west, and he certainly ridiculed the idea of a Norman landing in any case. But he was a poor farmer at best, and a call to arms fired his blood. He gave careless instructions for the spring planting, orders to sell as slaves two kitchen maids he had got with child during the winter, and once again rode off to enjoy himself, leading his tiny army of housecarls. If there was to be fighting, he welcomed the prospect, and if not, he could always fill the time with wine, wenches, and conviviality.

No one took seriously the threat of invasion, and it was an easy time at Oakwood. The village women tended the fields or weeded the bits of garden about their huts, while young boys herded cattle and pigs, and little girls kept geese and hens in order. In the hall, Lady Bertha spread her legs for a lad from the village, who had replaced Ethelfrith while the latter followed his thane to join the fyrd. The winter's spinning and weaving were considerably advanced, so the hall women replenished the old year's rushes with new cuttings from the riverbanks. Judith and Arnhilda, as they had always done at this time of year, searched the fields and woodlands for fresh herbs with which to treat the sick.

Often Brother Plegmund, his back hideously scarred but whole once more, accompanied the two women upon their expeditions. He had a mild interest in sketching medicinal herbs, but his real purpose was accomplished when, under the shade of some convenient tree, the women rested briefly from their labors. At those moments, the monk would produce from his capacious pouch a slate and chalk to continue his instructions in the art of mathematics. Sometimes he would unroll a map drawn on leather and test Judith upon her knowledge of places both in England and abroad. She particularly liked the images of dragons in the seas but was not allowed to dwell upon them. Dragons had little to do with proper domestic management or conversation at table.

Brother Plegmund had not spoken again of political issues to Judith. When she inquired about his study of the stars on her behalf, he replied brusquely that there had been no indication of a marriage with Sir Hugh, and so severe was his tone that she did not dare to question him further. His renewed insistence that she perfect her knowledge of the French tongue told her enough. He considered the possibility of a Norman invasion likely. Although he had some whispered conversations with Arnhilda, to Judith he said no more than that her studies must continue.

The monk was not her only tutor. Again and again Arnhilda stressed the duties of a lady to her people, training which she had received from the same source since her earliest childhood. She knew already all the things a lady must be and do, but daily Arnhilda emphasized the needs of the common folk and what she might do to ease their sufferings were she but a great lady in the land. There was no surer way to God's salvation than to aid the weak, Bother Plegmund told her, and Judith tiredly agreed. The people lived to work, and suffer, and die, Arnhilda declared, and must somehow be given a chance for more than that pitiful existence. Judith was often bored and resentful of such familiar litanies, but since these two were the only people who took her welfare to heart, the girl listened obediently and absorbed their lessons.

By no means had all the thanes been moved to join the fyrd, as was discovered when Lady Bertha took a small cavalcade through the lower bog to visit Deerfield, less than a day's ride to the north. Lord Hywel informed them that he and several other local lords were preparing to leave for the Easter witan. There was no fear of attack, he said, and made a poor joke about some comely wench in London or Pevensey who doubtless had taken Cerdic's eye. A Norman army set to invade the English coast? Sheer and complete rubbish, fit only for the dungheap! T'was a skirmish of quite another sort that kept Cerdic so long away!

Deerfield was a smaller place than Oakwood. It boasted a triple-storied wooden tower, with each floor containing a single large room, except for the third. There, the area was divided into three chambers, separated by wooden partitions and heavy cloth hangings. Visitors were housed in a chamber hurriedly vacated for their use. The tower was well kept, with clean rushes and whitewashed walls, and the fire pits generously supplied with wood.

The Oakwood party stayed several nights, Lady Bertha gossiping with Lord Hywel's lady, using Brother Plegmund as interpreter, while Judith played chess with her host. Agnes, her afflicted tooth blackened and no longer painful, disappeared into the shadows with a plump, hot-eyed youth who was Lord Hywel's youngest son.

On the night of the Tuesday after Easter, however, there was an omen so terrible that even Lord Hywel was shaken, and it sent the visitors racing for home. A monstrous light appeared in the sky. It moved silently across the heavens, followed by an ominous trail of fire.

At home on the following night, the entire population of Oakwood, both village and hall, was gathered on the common to witness the sight. The crowd was evenly split into two camps, one of which believed that the heavenly apparition was a dragon come to devour their young, the other holding it to be a demon escaped from the gates of hell and bent upon devouring them *all*. No one, however, hid themselves or their offspring.

"Nonsense," said Brother Plegmund quietly to Judith. "'Tis a comet. These things are not unknown to men of science, my child. It is a star which is not always visible but appears only upon those occasions when God wishes to warn mankind."

Judith's wide eyes followed the trail of fire across the dark sky. "But what does it mean?"

"Destruction," replied the monk, a tremor in this voice. "If it had shown itself with a crown of shining rays, it would portend the death of a king. But when a comet appears to streak across the sky with a tail of fire, it warns us of the destruction of a country."

Judith saw the fear in his eyes and asked no more questions.

For eight days the star glowed its evil message across the heavens. It was visible all over England, and the folk were afraid. Those at Oakwood had heard the monk's discourse. Brother Plegmund's explanation of the comet as a portent of doom, a sign of God's displeasure, and a warning of wrath and fire to come was more real than a dragon, so the people believed him.

Just as he predicted, scarcely had the malignant glare vanished from sight when a strange fleet of ships was sighted off the Isle of Wight. Fierce foreign warriors waded ashore. At their head, shockingly, was not the feared Duke of Normandy but Tostig, exiled brother to the new ruler of England! His army was pillaging towns and villages along the southern coast, between Lymington and Sandwich.

King Harold marched his small force from London to Sandwich, tight-lipped but firm, wishing that more of the fyrd had seen fit to obey his summons. When Tostig, happily burning and ravaging his own countrymen like the Norse invaders of old, heard of his brother's approach, he retreated like a mongrel cur to the north and begged refuge of King Malcolm of the Scots.

Peddlers and chance travelers brought the news to Oakwood, and folk smiled again in their relief. Had they not said all along that there was nothing to fear? Only a fool like Tostig would attempt such a ridiculous undertaking. The Normans? Duke William was too wise a man to lead an invasion clearly doomed to failure. The people voiced their satisfaction and proposed to think no more about it.

Cerdic sent no messenger to tell of his safety, but in any case, he was not much missed. Lady Bertha, who had missed her monthly cycle, had to promote her courses with a dangerous potion of pennyroyal. She exchanged the village lad for the attentions of one of the kitchen wenches, made willing enough by the promise of a new gown and continued patronage. Agnes, meanwhile, rode off in the direction of Deerfield whenever weather permitted, her maidservant in attendance, until the departure of Lord Hywel and his sons for the King's court.

For Judith these were happy weeks, a marvelous time of quiet pursuits, with not even the petty annoyance of Agnes and Lady Bertha to distract her from her labors. From April through July, once the orders for meals were given and household tasks assigned in the hall, she and Arnhilda roamed the countryside. There was watercress to be found in cold, swift-running brooks, feathery horsetail, chamomile and tansy, which liked waste places. There were long evenings in which she plied her needle and conversed with Brother Plegmund and Arnhilda in French, or with the monk alone in Latin and Norse and even, occasionally, in Flemish. She went out to the kitchen at times, concocting new dishes for her own amusement. Sometimes they were successful, and Cynefred, the cook, watched her closely; like Arnhilda, he liked to learn anything useful. And she went among the serfs at Arnhilda's suggestion, studying for long hours how the burden of their meager lives might be lifted. She tended the wounded and ailing as she had always done, washing rheumatic joints in wolfsbane and cocklebur, dousing internal bleeding, broken bones, and the bloody flux with comfrey tea. Arnhilda watched approvingly.

Brother Plegmund spoke often these days of his travels in Normandy, describing large castles and households supporting many knights, squires, pages, and ladies-in-waiting. He related the various distractions devised by anxious chatelaines to avert domestic crises during the long, inactive winter months. Once he told in intimate detail of a visit by the Duke William, who had come to stay in the household of a baron near Brother Plegmund's Order. And so, her lessons continued unabated.

‡

The license now permitted under Lady Bertha's slack governance was spoken of in disgust and contrasted with the harmony that had prevailed when Lady Milburga had lived. Lady Bertha's cruelty toward her dependents and her appalling lack of piety were ruthlessly condemned. Piety, charity, chastity, justice, and cleanliness, the cleric told her, were the virtues by which God judged a lady. Her own people, her peers, and most importantly, her husband, also judged her conduct as it accorded well or ill with those principles. Lady Judith could do no better, he informed her, than to follow the example of her late mother, who had been so saintly a lady that surely God had taken her straight to heaven upon the instant of her demise.

Sometimes as Judith lay awake in her chamber at night, she listened to the sound of Arnhilda's inspired snoring from the pallet on the floor and pondered these lessons. More often, though, she thought of Agnes and her new peasant lover. Brother Plegmund said that Agnes would burn in hellfire for her sins, and Judith believed him. All the same, she wondered how it would be to lay with a man. She thought about it more and more. T'was shameful, of course, but a riveting subject. All the women said it hurt the first time, but Judith was not concerned with that aspect of the matter. It was what happened *after* the pain that excited her curiosity.

Once, when she was eleven, Lord Hywel had come to visit her father. His eldest son had hidden behind a tree and grabbed her as she walked past. He had kissed her before she could break loose and then had run away while she stood staring after him, puzzled. It had been an unpleasant experience. The boy had frightened her with his roughness, and his mouth, as she recalled with distaste, had been sloppily wet.

She never thought of Sir Hugh, to whom she feared she might well one day be wed, despite the monk's assurance to the contrary. Instead, she imagined a stranger, a knight of the Norman sort. He would be young and handsome and well made, and he'd ride through the north wood, close to the sea. He might be on his way to serve the King. He would see her gathering herbs (Arnhilda having wandered away, of course) and stop to stare at her beauty, for she had somehow become the kind of belle about whom the minstrels sang.

So taken with her was he, that he would insist upon being taken at once to her father. He made an offer for her hand, and they were wed. Then she would pretend it was her wedding night, and her hands would stray to her rounded breasts or slide between her thighs. Her breath would catch in her throat, and then, ashamed of her actions, she would pray passionately for forgiveness.

‡

In September, at the time of the harvest, Cerdic returned to Oakwood. The fyrd, he told them, with its provisions exhausted and its stipulated period of duty long since ended, had left the Isle of Wight on the nativity of St. Mary. With the single exception of Tostig's abortive raid, no hint of a possible enemy had been sighted, and seafaring, as even a hillman knew, was a summer occupation. No, the Normans would not be foolish enough to brave the ferocious winter gales, declared Cerdic with certainty.

Thus, the fyrd had come home. England was safe until the spring.

Why, even King Harold was so little concerned that he had ridden painfully to London and put himself to bed to ease a rheumatic leg. Cerdic planned to make the most of the winter to get his lady with child.

But several days later, a belabored pony splashed through the ford in the stream and skidded to a halt in the muddy courtyard before Oakwood Hall. The messenger was a lad of no more than twelve summers. He plunged into the hall without so much as a word for the astonished housecarl on duty at the door, and raced to the high table where Lord Cerdic sat gnawing at a mutton bone (and fondling his lady's knee under the table).

Panting, faint with fatigue, the boy fell to one knee before the thane. "My lord," he gasped. "The King has sent me to rouse the western parts! He bids you assemble what men you can and join him on the road to York. Harald Hardrada and Lord Tostig have taken Scarborough and laid it waste!"

For a moment Cerdic sat stupefied. "I don't believe it!"

"'Fore God 'tis true, my lord! King Harold is even now on the march. They say the marshes are so strewn with the dead that the Norsemen ford the streams upon the bodies of fallen Saxons!"

Doubting no longer, Cerdic leapt from his chair, screaming for his sword and shield. Within minutes the hall was a scene of frenzied activity. Servants scurried to gather provisions for the march; housecarls ran to collect villeins, armaments, and mounts. Cerdic bellowed hurried commands regarding completion of the harvest. The hall dogs, excited by the uproar, added their shrill voices to the already deafening din. Unnoticed, a pig wandered into the hall, rooting noisily among the rushes for scraps, as Lady Bertha ran to and fro, harrying the folk with contradictory orders.

Judith drew the messenger aside to a bench at the lower end of the table. She motioned Arnhilda to fetch ale, while she herself filled a trencher with venison and placed it before the tired lad. "Eat," she told him quietly, "T'will give you strength." She did not speak again until he had taken his fill. "I will find you a quiet chamber where you may sleep," she said then.

"I must go on!" he protested wearily.

"You will do no good if you topple from the saddle for lack of rest. You can make up the time easily enough when your mount has rested as well."

The boy nodded, his face grim beneath the dust of the road. "Aye. But for a few hours only, lady; I've others to warn."

"I shall waken you myself," she promised. "First, please tell me what happened with Lord Tostig. We thought him beaten earlier in the year."

"Who did not? Yet King Malcolm succored him well. The invaders burned Scarborough," he related in a soft voice. "Aye, and used the old Viking trick in the doing. They built a bonfire atop the hill that overlooks the town and then pushed it down on the village roofs below. When the people ran out to escape the flames, they were cut down."

Judith knit her brows, remembering her lessons. "I'd not have thought Scarborough was worth taking. It's a small place, surely."

"No more than a fishing village," agreed the boy. "I've seen many such on the King's service; poor folk with no loot worthy of mention. But when have *Vikings* ever lacked for an excuse to ravage an English village? T'was done for the sport of the thing, no doubt, or mayhap they felt some of the younger men needed practice. Who knows the workings of the Viking mind?" He sagged over his empty trencher of a sudden, too tired to go on.

Between them, Judith and Arnhilda guided the exhausted lad to a chamber at the far end of the gallery and left him deeply asleep upon the bed. With a damp cloth, Judith wiped away what grime she could without disturbing him. It was not the traditional bath due a guest, but it was the best she could manage.

Within the space of a few hours, the messenger was gone, and Cerdic as well, flatly refusing to leave so much as a single housecarl for the protection of his people. If Tostig were defeated, said Cerdic, his people needed no protection. If not, a few housecarls could not stand against a Viking horde. The women watched stoically as their men set out, the thane followed by his mounted housecarls. There were also upwards of twenty villeins afoot, some bearing only scythes and pitchforks, walking behind. A few were from the fishing village on the coast, which owed fealty to Oakwood, and those men had only their gutting knives to defend them.

The women, children, ailing, and elderly stared at the valiant army, many mumbling prayers and making surreptitious signs for luck with their fingers. This time it was no idle threat of unnamed invasion forces but an actual landing, and the years had not dimmed memories of Norse ferocity in the past. All were fearful as their men faded from view in the distance. And surprisingly, Lady Bertha took charge. She turned briskly to Gwenddyd, her favorite.

"Fetch the women from the vill and the fishwives, as well," she commanded in her poor English. "I will meet with them in the courtyard very soon."

"Aye, my lady." The wench sprinted off, skirts flying.

Lady Bertha turned to Judith. "I cannot speak your heathen Saxon well enough, so you will have to speak for me. Tell them that the harvest is nearly in, and what is left to do, the remaining men can see to with the help of the women and children. Make arrangements for the slaughtering, for I doubt the men will return in time for Martinmas." She paused, shuddering.

"If the Norsemen come here, we must be prepared. See to our defenses. Something must be devised if we are not all to be raped and murdered in our beds! Lord Cerdic would leave no housecarls, and even Ethelfrith is gone! Christ's Holy Sepulcher, I have never even seen a battle, much less directed one! Ask if any of the older women remembers what should be done." She cast a disparaging eye about the courtyard. "Had we a decent castle or a tower, mayhap things would be different, but we're like to have the hall burnt down about our ears! Damn Cerdic for deserting us!"

She covered her eyes with a shaking hand. Why had she let her brother talk her into traveling to England upon her first lord's death? Cerdic's reception at court had led her to believe him a powerful Saxon noble, and she willingly wed him in the hope of security for herself and a wellborn husband for her daughter. All her fine wishes had brought her to this, a probable death at the hands of a Viking barbarian in this Saxon pigsty! Life was so unfair!

Judith had never seen her stepmother so shaken, but then, she was frightened herself. "Lady Bertha, in all honor, my father had to go when summoned by the King. I am sure he would have stayed to protect us if he could." This was patently a lie, but Lady Bertha, she thought, would want to believe it. The important thing to do was to calm her; the good of all the folk depended upon sensible leadership. Lady Bertha could not go to pieces before them now!

The older woman took a deep breath. "Well." She looked about her again, at the wide courtyard surrounded on three sides by the wooden palisade, at the shabby hall, the stream still muddied by the hooves of horses and the feet of men, and at the servants standing awkwardly about, nervous and pinched-looking in the chill.

Lady Bertha glanced at Judith. "Certainly, the palisade must be repaired," she declared, jutting her chin toward the straggling line of wooden poles surrounding the court. "Have them double the number of stakes. It won't buy us much time, but if it is only a small party sent to take this place, we may be able to hold them off." Her shoulders slumped wearily. "If aught else occurs to you, do it at once." Having turned the matter over to Judith, she withdrew. The girl could explain without her presence.

‡

After the initial shock, life continued with astonishing normalcy that autumn. The harvest and winnowing were accomplished with a minimum of fuss. A new palisade was erected, shutters constructed for the windows, the food grains parched and stored. Fruit was gathered against winter's austerity.

Certainly, vague rumors reached them of a battle at York and an English victory, but September drew to a close without word of Cerdic's return. A query sent to Deerfield proved that there, too, no message had been received, so the women settled down to wait with what patience they could command.

The fall slaughter was always a messy business, more so that year with fewer men to handle the rough work. Yet somehow the folk managed, with a multitude of bruises, to be sure, but only a few broken bones. Meat was salted, smoked, or packed in heavy brine to preserve it. Fish was smoked and dried. Earthenware jars of vinegar and honey were stacked in the cavernous cellar beneath the hall, along with barrels of cider, stacks of new cheese, and wooden tubs of butter layered with salt. Ropes of onions and garlic festooned some rafters; ropes of apples or pears hung on others. Bags of lentils filled the corners, and small bundles of arrows and new-made bows lined the walls. What few spices Cerdic had been able to purchase in London were locked away in a wooden chest.

Since there was yet a goodly supply of soap, sheep's tallow was boiled down with beeswax to make candles for hall and church. The breeding pigs, reserved from the slaughter, were driven from the fallow to the relative safety of the palisade, where they would survive the winter on scraps.

Judith, in happier days, had been tutored in the use of the bow and arrow by kindly housecarls. She set up rude targets in the courtyard, where several women who wished to learn joined her. Arnhilda and three fishwives daily demonstrated the art of self-defense by means of the gutting knife and spindle. And Lady Bertha, bored and resigned to the futility of it all, retired to her chamber with Gwenddyd and taught her a few tricks of her own, which just might conceivably be used to good effect for survival if any invading Norseman had an eye for a likely woman.

Spinning and weaving were chores never truly ended, and the women busied themselves with those when not practicing warriors' skills outdoors. Lady Bertha labored briefly upon a tapestry planned to depict Cerdic in pursuit of a stag, but interest waned as time passed with no word of his return. Even Judith grew short-tempered with the uncertainty of their situation.

Finally, Brother Plegmund, perhaps wearied in this house of women, certainly as anxious as any for news of the battle at York, if battle there had been, took leave of Lady Bertha. Mounted upon his aged and reluctant donkey, brown skirts and cloak firmly wrapped about his spindly shanks, he journeyed away to the east.

‡

Winter brought a peddler, who had heard rumors from a woman, who had heard from a priest, that a great battle had taken place at Hastings, far to the south. King Harold was dead. None knew the fate of the men from Oakwood, and the peddler was unclear as to the nationality of the victorious army. The woman from whom he had first heard the tale declared it to have been William of Normandy who defeated Harold in battle, but an innkeeper he had met a fortnight later had insisted the Viking host had returned after King Harold chased it from York. It might, as a farmer had hinted, even have been King Malcolm of the Scots who had killed King Harold. It was agreed by all, however, that neither young Edgar nor any of King Harold's sons had been crowned.

So far as he knew, England was without a king. The women grew more frightened, and none slept without a weapon of some sort close to hand.

‡

On New Year's Day, two young boys, who had been set to watch for intruders, raced into the hall with excited cries. Behind them, Brother Plegmund's donkey limped wearily into the courtyard. A stable lad took the reins of the mount and moved off. The women rushed to meet the monk and lead him out of the sharp winter wind. They settled him on a stool by the fire with a horn of hot, mulled cider and the leg of a fowl, patting his thin shoulders or touching the sleeve of his habit for reassurance.

Lady Bertha sat in the thane's chair, controlling herself with an effort. When patience waxed thin, she gripped the carven arms of the chair and demanded, "What news bring you?"

Judith translated the French so that the listening Oakwood folk could understand both Lady Bertha and the monk.

"You must be brave, lady," he said, gray eyes sunken and red-rimmed with wariness. "Lord Cerdic is dead, fallen at Hastings." Face still, she made no comment as Judith's voice murmured in the background. After a moment the monk continued. "Many are dead, our noble King Harold among them. Of those who followed Lord Cerdic, most were slain. The Oakwood men, who still live, are a few hours' march behind me on the road. All of the housecarls, certainly, are no more. Ethelfrith the groom, Ossa and Eadric of the fisherfolk, and the villeins Wulfric, Aeden, Burgred, Cynric, Guthlack, Giso, Wiglaf, and Tatwine are all numbered among the dead." Shakily, he made the sign of the cross.

Some of the women who had crowded eagerly into the hall began to moan and weep. Others led them gently away so that their grief might not disturb the Lady Bertha and the others of the hall, who had their own dead to mourn. A small girl, who had been standing near the door, ran for the village to bear the dread news, and one of the boys sped to inform the fisherfolk.

Judith was stunned. So many dead! She crossed herself and said a quick prayer for the repose for all their souls. It did not seem possible to her that her father was gone. She stared at the monk for a moment, and then the realization came that never again would Cerdic return to abuse and berate her. For a brief space, she was filled with a shamed relief, but that sensation was drowned by the understanding that she was now completely in the power of Lady Bertha, her father's widow. It was a chilling thought. Life would be impossible under such circumstances, she thought fearfully. She remembered all too clearly Arnhilda's relaying that the brutal Cerdic had been the one to call a halt to the beating that Lady Bertha would have continued, and other times he had shortened punishments meted out by his wife that he felt too dangerous.

She toyed with the notion of seeking the aid of Lord Hywel, did he survive the battle in which her father had died. If he would not accept her into his household, perhaps he could be cajoled into providing her escort to London or some other large place. There she might find an order of holy nuns who would consider admitting into their ranks a dowerless girl, for she did not doubt Lady Bertha's refusal to part with the smallest part of her inheritance.

The monk sighed deeply, jarring Judith out of her morbid reflection. She moved quickly, refilling his drinking horn with a steady hand. Her blue eyes softened with compassion for his spiritual agony.

She said calmly in English, "We know naught of what has occurred since my father left our hall. Will you tell us what you have learned on your travels?"

He nodded and sipped at his cider, relishing the warmth. "Aye, it is my duty to do so, child. We have fallen upon evil times, as the warning star foretold. For our sins, God has hidden His Holy face from us; we are a defeated people."

Now Judith translated his tale into French for Lady Bertha.

"Earl Edwin and his friend Earl Morkere, were both in York when Harald Hardrada set Scarborough ablaze. Each was young and untried in battle, yet they found what men they could raise and marched on the invaders."

"My father arrived in time?" questioned Judith.

The cleric shook his head. "Nay, child. The force from York met Harald Hardrada at Fuldord 'ere even Lord Cerdic heard the call to arms. T'was a bloody business, and our own Saxons broke and ran before the fury of the Norsemen."

Of those remaining in the hall, many wept or hid their faces in shame at such cowardice. The Saxons were a proud people, with a history of staunch courage. Even to a lowborn serf, a retreat before the enemy was deep disgrace. Judith bit her lip, eyes burning at the thought. She, a female, was willing to stand and fight the Vikings when they came, despite her fear. How could warriors, trained from birth to battle, turn and run? But then, she told herself, she had never been in a battle. Perhaps things reached a point in battle where men could bear no more.

Brother Plegmund continued. "York surrendered, having no defenders, and sent hostages to Hardrada, named from a list supplied him by Lord Tostig. Then for four days and nights the Norsemen were encamped near their ships, feasting and rejoicing in their victory. They asked of York half a thousand hostages more, which the city did agree to, and set the exchange for the Monday at Stamford Bridge." He actually smiled then, albeit grimly, for the first time in his narration.

"T'was a fine morning, they tell me, the sun shining and warm, so that the Norsemen left off their mail and padding. Merry, they were, and some vow that they sang as they came to the place of meeting. Whatever the reality of it, they'd no hint of danger 'til they stood upon Stamford Bridge and saw King Harold's army upon them. And with them," he added, "fresh from York, were the men of Oakwood." He drank deeply, set his horn aside, and clasped his hands almost in an attitude of prayer. His listeners leaned closer.

"They tell me t'was a hideous battle. I'd trouble enough finding men to speak of it, God knows. I heard that one of Hardrada's men, a big fellow with thews of iron, held Stamford Bridge alone for hours. 'Tis said of him that he slew forty Saxons. Finally, a housecarl, one of Harold's own men, drifted downriver with the current in a swill-tub and speared him from a gap in the planking. Then our army swept across the bridge, and the fighting was awful indeed.

"Harald Hardrada was killed by an arrow in the gullet, and when men saw that he was dead, the battle stopped. We'd have been done then, with no more losses, but that nithing traitor, Tostig, held aloft Hardrada's fallen standard, that which men call 'Land-Ravager.' Although King Harold offered truce, the battle raged again. The river flowed red with the blood of the fallen, folk do say, and as the sun began to set, Lord Tostig was slain. At last, with the darkness to cover them, the Norsemen fled."

"Where was Lord Cerdic in the fighting?" asked Lady Bertha.

"I know not, lady. Upon the morrow, Lord Cerdic stood with the King when the Norse leaders came to lay down their arms. The King, ever gracious, bade the Norsemen swear an oath never again to touch our shores, and he spared them. Under his truce, they sailed down the River Ouse and were gone."

"A valiant victory for the King," murmured Judith in the hush.

"Also his last," returned the monk, his voice heavy with pain. "For seven days the army rested. They made a feast to celebrate their victory. And then, upon the eighth day, word was brought from the south that Duke William had landed a mighty army at Pevensey."

The small crowd of women hissed indrawn breaths. Now it came . . . the deaths of their men, and the truth of what lay in store for themselves and their children. More than one woman reached for the hand of another, either to offer strength or to ask for it.

"No one believed it at first," he went on. "A sea voyage in winter seemed too incredible to be true. But the Norsemen had done it, so it was not completely discounted. And there was need of some haste if it *were* true, for our forces were all at York, and this left none to oppose William of Normandy at Pevensey or any other place."

Judith protested. "Surely the local people must have resisted the Normans!"

"One or two, mayhap. But my child, we speak of Norman archers and scores of mounted knights. Be reasonable; what chance would pitchforks and meat hooks have had against the likes of those?"

"The knights fought *mounted?*"

"Of course," interrupted Lady Bertha, with contempt for such ignorance. "Norman knights always fight a-horse. I told Lord Cerdic so half a hundred times, as did Sir Hugh, but the old fool was too stupid or set in his ways to change. If he'd heeded me, I doubt I'd be a widow today." She shrugged. "But then, I may be wrong. The Duke of Normandy is the greatest warrior in all Christendom. Lord Cerdic could never have held out against him," she added, clearly identifying with the victors.

Glances aplenty were exchanged among the listeners, but none dared to speak. The monk, fingering his beads, and lowered his voice so that they had to strain to catch his words. "The Bastard quartered his army near the manor of Rameslie, which was given in the time of King Edward to the Abbey of Fécamp. Along the line of march as they moved out later, many towns and villages were ravaged. Most were laid waste."

Those gathered in the hall were familiar with tales of rape, pillage, and indiscriminate slaughter, but they had heard those stories from their parents or grandparents. The events related to them now had happened in their own time, and might well be repeated here at Oakwood. Their eyes grew wide with fear. Only Ladies Bertha and Agnes, Norman-born, seemed unaffected by the grisly account, as if nothing could touch those lucky enough to share common blood with the conquerors.

"T'was on the fourteenth day of October that the battle was fought near Hastings. Lords Gyrth and Leofwine, King Harold's own brothers, were slain early in the fighting. Thousands died that day. The Normans sent archers, then mounted knights, then archers again. The range of their arrows had great effect, and our men, brave though they were, could not hold.

"King Harold was slain near the sun's setting. Some say t'was an arrow, which pierced his eye. Others tell of a group of craven knights, mounted while the King fought afoot, who butchered him cruelly. I do not know the truth of it; no man does, save perhaps Duke William. It matters not. Edith Swan-Neck came later, when the fighting was done, and did swear that the body they buried was that of the King, so there is no doubt of his death.

"Lord Cerdic was stuck down as he led the men of Oakwood toward the wood when it was seen that Harold's standard was fallen, and that the King was no more. He made a stand there, and died bravely; may God have mercy upon his soul."

He said no more and the folk stared, wondering, until at last Judith put their unspoken questions into words. "What will happen now that the Normans have gained victory over us? Who will rule? And . . . and what of Oakwood? What comes to us here?"

"What comes to us is that which I read in the stars many months ago, my child. We are ready. As to who rules," he said grimly, "why, it is William, of course, Duke of Normandy, and now, King of England. He was crowned in London on Christmas Day."

"A Norman to be King of England?!" exclaimed a voice from the crowd.

Lady Bertha flung up her head in an arrogant gesture, the gauze scarf she wore over her hair flaring in a cloud of blue. "And why should he not?" she challenged, skimming the crowd with her eye. "Surely he has earned the right in honorable combat! As for the safety of all here, I see no cause for alarm. I, myself, am Norman-born. Certainly our new king will see to my widow's rights as mistress of Oakwood."

Brother Plegmund let fall his beads and cleared his throat. "You have been too long in England, lady. Only under Saxon law do you have rights as Lord Cerdic's widowed wife. We live now under Norman law, which you will remember, makes no such provisions. I fear you must take up the question of your future with the new lord of Oakwood."

"The new lord?" she echoed, her brown eyes momentarily blank.

"Aye. When I was in London, I learned that Oakwood has been given to one of the youngest of the new King's most favored knights. The lands extend, as I understand, north to the end of the marshes, along the sea coast to the west, east past Deerfield, and south to the road that leads to the mountains in Wales."

Judith was thunderstruck. "But those lands belong to Lord Hywel and to. . .

"They are lords no more, Lady Judith. The only lord here is Lord Raoul, the one men call Hawk."

Lady Bertha bit the tip of her thumb and thought. "I believe I've heard tell of such a one, from Lord Hywel. A well–favored man and a most valiant knight." Then, suddenly, she smiled. "When does he arrive?"

"To take possession of his new lands? In the spring, they said." The monk shrugged. "Doubtless the King has need of him yet awhile, until the countryside is settled."

Lady Bertha stood. She ran her hands along her flanks, pressing and smoothing the blue wool against her body. She smiled again. "Well," she said smugly. "Bridals are best planned for the spring. I am most pleased that William has chosen for me a lord worthy of my rank."

The women whispered and gasped as Judith translated, shocked beyond measure at such shamelessness, even from Lady Bertha. Why, she had only just learned her lord had died!

Brother Plegmund was no less astonished. "But, my lady, how can you speak of a match at this time? Lord Cerdic is but three months dead, and you've only just heard the tidings! 'Tis not decent!"

She ignored him, stretching and purring like a great hungry cat.

"I heard no mention made of bridals, lady," he said.

But Lady Bertha smiled. Almost, she licked her lips. "Believe me, sir monk, you will. Oh, yes, most assuredly you will."

CHAPTER 3

udith picked her way around the rocks scattered here and there across the waste, holding a skirtful of leaves with both hands. Behind her the wide area showed only a few plants retaining foliage, and those were left deliberately to ensure a healthy crop next year. She emptied the leaves into her basket and scratched absently at a fleabite on her arm. The basket was heavy, but she smiled as she lifted it, satisfied with the pile of leathery leaves it held. Properly dried and stored, coltsfoot could be used to treat St. Anthony's Fire, or, as was far more common, stuffed noses and chest complaints, frequent ailments in any hall during an English winter.

The clearing in which she stood was a large one, where a flash of lightning had caused a fire a few years back. For some reason the forest had not reclaimed it. A couple of yards away, the ancient trees grew thick and tall in all directions. A glance at the sky showed the sun had moved to the west. Dusk was not far off, she realized. She had best find Arnhilda.

A short walk brought her to the curve of a hill, where she could see the maidservant gathering violets beside a stream. She called out and waited patiently for the ageing woman, shifting the rush basket more comfortably on her hip. Against her will, she remembered an incident from the day before, when she had come unexpectedly upon Agnes and her lover, hidden in the tall grass of a meadow. They had not sensed her presence and she had left quickly, but the scene was fresh in her mind.

Agnes lay on her back, eyes closed tightly, while the boy had slammed himself into her with such violent force that she cried out. She had clutched at him even more tightly then, and Judith, slipping away unseen, had been disgusted. She had seen such things before, crossing the floor of the hall in the early morning hours, for the servants slept among the rushes all in a group, without regard to gender. It mattered not if a serf's daughter lost her virginity, but the daughter of a noble was a different bucket of washing. No matter how detestable she was, Agnes' actions condemned her to God's sure and just punishment. What troubled Judith most was her stepsister's lack of concern in the matter. The pits of slime, lakes of fire, and tortures of demons Brother Plegmund described had no effect upon Agnes other than boredom.

Judith's cheeks reddened as she recalled her own activity of the night before, when she pretended a man's hands explored the secret places of her body. Gratefully, she looked up at Arnhilda's approach.

"Tired, dearling?" asked the older woman with a keen eye to the girl's face. "Ah, well, 'tis a goodly harvest this season. A few more baskets and we'll have enough to see us through. T'would go a mite easier, though, an Lady Bertha allowed us a wench or two for help. More hands make lighter work."

"If you'd leave the violets and aid me with the coltsfoot," Judith began.

Arnhilda snorted. "The violets are for your complexion, girl. Unless you'd look like that Lady Agnes, all spots, you'll use the lotion I make and say no more about it."

They began to walk along the pony track, which led to Oakwood Hall.

"Lady Bertha needs all the women to get the hall in order for the new lord," remarked Judith with something very like a sniff. "I suppose she thinks to prove herself a careful housewife."

"Hah!" Arnhilda smiled dourly. "She'll need to go a long way beyond a clean hall to make herself acceptable to the new lord," she replied, not without smugness. "Our gracious mistress has at least seven-and-twenty years to her credit and only one child for all of them. A man will look for more than bedsport in his bride, especially since he's gained new lands. He'll want strong sons to inherit and hold the land. A ready wench can be had anywhere."

"Then, you think Lord Raoul will wed Agnes in her mother's place?" Judith inquired, shocked.

"'Tis not for me to say," Arnhilda told her austerely. "But I *will* say that Lady Bertha leans a bit heavy on a promise never made. Ye'll recall our monk said no mention was made of weddings. For all we know, this new lord of ours could be already wed. I'm not saying he is, mind, but that would make Lady Bertha look uncommonly foolish after all her boasting."

Judith hopped over a wagon rut and shrugged a careless shoulder. Lady Bertha's possible future did not concern her. "Will our people suffer overmuch under this new lord, think you? The Normans are a cruel race."

"You say so because they are invaders and because the only Normans you've known are Lady Bertha and Lady Agnes. 'Tis true, they are enough to give anyone a dislike of the whole folk," returned Arnhilda coolly. "Yet you've heard Brother Plegmund say often that he met with much kindness in Normandy. We shall see what is to be seen when Lord Raoul arrives."

"Think you the new lord will find a husband for me, Arnhilda?" the girl questioned after a moment.

"Would you be wed, child?" the woman smiled tolerantly. "Aye, you're full old enough, I reckon. T'was near fourteen years ago I held you in my arms for the first time, still wet with birthgrease. And you've the right shape for childbearing," she added, glancing at the girl's rounded hips. "Doubtless when our new lord sets eyes upon you, he'll see you're ripe for the marriage bed."

"I should not say it, I suppose," sighed Judith, "for he died defending our land, but it is *such* a relief to know I'll not be bound to Sir Hugh! I've heard tales of his conduct amongst the kitchen wenches! Ugh!"

"And how often must I tell you not to gossip with those strumpets?" demanded the older woman crossly. "'Tis unseemly for you to have speech with those feckless sluts other than to give them orders for service."

"Oh, Arnhilda!" Judith murmured. "How else can I answer their questions about the day's chores except to listen to them?"

Arnhilda pursed her lips and narrowed her eyes. "Now, you know very well what it is I mean, child. See you behave yourself properly. Gossiping with the kitchen wenches! I never heard the like! Why, your sainted mother, God rest her, would spin like a top in her grave did she but have a suspicion of such conduct in her daughter! Are you listening to me, child?"

"Yes, Arnhilda."

As they stepped from the shelter of the wood into the cleared fields of the village, both women came to an abrupt halt. On the high ground between the vill and the ferry landing at the river's edge was an army of multicolored tents. Silhouetted against the darkening sky, men hurried about to direct the unloading of oxcarts, belonging to the fishing village, and piled high with blocks of gray stone. As the carts were unloaded and moved off, others took their place.

There were several villeins armed with shovels, who seemed to be digging a wide trench at the base of the hill, and the soil they removed was being added to the top of the hill to make it taller and wider. A number of fishermen were busy carrying tools and rolls of parchment. All were overseen about their chores by a fierce-looking man armed with a crossbow.

The women looked at one another. Shakily Judith made the sign of the cross. "Normans!" she whispered.

Arnhilda nodded and pulled her back into the cover of the trees. Her wrinkled face was grim. "Heed me well, child. These Normans will think you a peasant for the ravishing an they find you now. Go back to the Roman road. Find the grove, and hide yourself in the old oak folk call Sacred. Stay there until I come for you, or men from the lord, who will know where you are and protect you."

"But what of you?" protested the girl. "Surely you will not be safe, alone and unprotected!"

"Now, who'd rape an old woman?" she demanded, chuckling to ease Judith's fear. "It's been so long since I had a man, I might give 'em a surprise or two. In the end the ravishers'd be too weak to stand, and I'd escape a lot stronger than when I was caught!" Then she looked deeply into the girl's eyes, and her smile faded. "I swore to your lady mother I'd protect you, child, with my own life if need be. And you mean more to me than any of those I bore and lost when I was young. You understand me? Good," she said at Judith's nod. "No more arguments. Now, give me your basket and be off. Don't forget to say the charm when you get to the oak grove, and keep to the cover of the trees."

Arnhilda watched Judith glide away through the foliage and prayed to the Blessed Virgin for the child's safety. Just to be on the safe side, she whispered a petition to an older feminine deity, as well, as she stepped into the clearing. One could not be too careful in these matters, she thought with a sniff. She headed straight for the soldier.

‡

The sun was almost gone from the horizon when Judith, sitting quietly upon a wide branch, heard approaching hooves. She clung desperately to the trunk of the oak as the horse, a huge Flemish bay stallion, halted directly beneath her. Its rider was a Norman. He was helmless, wore only a hauberk for protection, and his knight's spurs glistened. He looked upward, and although he did not smile, Judith knew he was mightily amused. She felt an odd surge of annoyance war with her fear.

"You are the Lady Judith?" he inquired politely in French. His teeth and eyes gleamed in the half-light.

The girl clutched the tree more tightly but replied in the same tongue for politeness' sake. "I am Judith of Oakwood," she replied.

"I am Lord Raoul, the new Baron of Oakwood, whom men call Hawk. Your woman sent me to fetch you since she feared for your safety with so many of us dangerous Normans roaming over the countryside."

Her chin went up at the jibe. It was important to be dignified in the face of the enemy. "You think, my lord, she was a fool to harbor such fears?" she demanded icily.

"Nay, Lady Judith," answered the knight, amused anew by her indignant air. "So much faith had I in her judgment that I sent none of my men but rode out to collect you myself. Will you be pleased to descend?"

"I fear I cannot, Lord Raoul," she said, acutely conscious of her skirts and the height of the tree. "Unless you would add to your kindness by turning your back?"

He complied wordlessly and at once, although Judith was certain she had heard a chuckle, quickly stifled. Truth to tell, she did not know what to think of this strange lord. His hair was cut too short, in the Norman manner, and he was clean-shaven. His hair and eyes were dark. It appeared strange to her after a lifetime of longhaired, bearded Saxons. His shoulders were broad, and she had noted well a most determined chin. Probably, he was stubborn.

His courtesy puzzled her, for he was lord here and conqueror, and she one of a defeated race. Yet he treated her respectfully and as an equal. His manner, amused and polite, confused her. When at last she stood upon the ground, she stared at him with curiosity. He turned 'round and stared back.

Raoul sat unmoving in the saddle. He saw a small woman, still part child, with thick, flaxen braids and enormous blue eyes. Under the right circumstances, a man could lose his bearing in eyes like that, he mused. Her face showed no hatred, nor fear, nor coquetry, any of which he would have considered normal for the situation, and understood. Instead she was obviously perplexed by him. Perhaps she'd been prepared for him to run her through with his sword. The Norman chuckled. "Think you, *demoiselle,* you have studied my features enough to commit them to memory for our next meeting?"

Judith was grateful for the growing darkness, which hid her scarlet cheeks. "I crave pardon, my lord. 'Tis only that I have never before seen a Norman knight."

"Well, you shall see many more in the future," he replied, extending a calloused hand. "Mount up behind me, little girl. 'Tis late and I want my supper."

The horse was frighteningly tall after the hill ponies Judith had seen all her life. It had an easy gait, but Raoul set it at a fast pace, forcing her to hold onto his belt. His back was very broad and hard. "My lord," she ventured after a moment, "I saw many tents and men near the ferry. For what purpose are they there?"

"Why, those are my masons, *demoiselle.* King William has ordered me to build a castle to hold these lands and to protect the people."

"Oh," said Judith. "I have never seen a castle. Will you live there with your lady wife?"

Again, the knight chucked. "I have no wife."

"Then. . . then 'tis true that you will wed the Lady Bertha?"

"I plan no bridals yet awhile," he said with a tone of finality that warned against further questions. The remainder of the ride to the hall was accomplished in silence.

‡

Judith was astounded at the condition of the hall; everything had been transformed. Large tents were pitched along the stream beyond the palisades, and scores of men moved to and fro among them. She opened her eyes at the sight of Cynefred, running back and forth between two huge cooking fires, over each of which he was roasting a whole bullock. Men and women, dressed in rags and clearly Saxons, moved about carrying stacks of wood, provisions, and clothing chests. She recognized none of them.

So, she mused, the new lord had brought with him serfs to work the lands. By the look of them, these folk were from ravaged towns in the south. They appeared tired and defeated, no few of the men bearing marks of recent wounds. The sight saddened her. None of them appeared to be severely abused, though, which gave her some hope for her own folk.

"I must see to my destrier," said the lord as he swung his leg over his horse's neck and slid to the ground. He reached up, grasped her slender waist, and lifted her to the ground beside him. "You'll be safe enough here." And with those carelessly spoken words, he led his destrier off toward the stables.

She stared about her, a little frightened. Should she go inside? The courtyard was abustle with folk carrying baggage and arms. She had felt secure enough with Lord Raoul, but now she was alone amongst scores of strangers. These unknown folk eddied and swirled about her and all with that odd short hair. Many men eyed her covertly whilst they worked, sizing her up for bedsport. She kept her hand close to the eating knife she wore in her girdle. She had never had to defend her virginity in her father's house, but she was prepared if it proved necessary. In her mind she reviewed Arnhilda's lessons with painful intensity as she entered the hall.

Indoors was even more confusion. The long trestle tables were being arranged for the evening meal. Someone had tied the dogs in a corner, from which they snapped peevishly at passersby. Making her way carefully past what was clearly a group of knights, who crowded near the door to watch two serfs wrestle among the rushes, Judith slipped to the stair and sought the refuge of her chamber.

The long drying frames were still in place, but her clothing chest was gone. Even as she wondered, a villein entered, pushing past the leather curtain in the doorway to drag Lady Bertha's chest across the floor. He placed it at the foot of the bed beside that of Lady Agnes, already in position. Nothing of her own remained. After a moment she retreated to the stairhead to consider the matter. Where should she go? Was she now to sleep with the serfs? It was possible.

She peered over the gallery railing into the hall below. The knights had moved to the fire. Among them were two ladies, one plump and small, the other tall and gaunt. Both of them were dark of hair and eye. Beyond them in a corner, strumming idly upon a gittern, sat a jongleur. She knew he saw her, and her cheeks flushed as she drew hastily back into the shadows. Aubrey!

Of a sudden, a hand gripped her arm. "Why, what have we here?" drawled a male voice teasingly. "A little yellow kitten lost its mother?"

She whirled to face him, a big sly-faced knight with a grin that brought to mind a wolf regarding its prey. He raised one hand toward her breast, smiling more broadly at her surprise and fury. "Christ's Nails!" he murmured to himself. "A jewel in this dungheap! I shall ask Raoul to give you to me as a prize of war. He owes me that much!" He broke off with a yelp of shock as her dagger slashed at the caressing hand. Blood dripped to the rushes. The knight clenched his teeth in anger. His eyes blazed. "By God's Teeth, you bitch! I'll teach you to . . .!"

Before he could rush her, as he obviously intended to do, a slim form stepped between them. "I see, Sir Eustace, you have already made yourself acquainted with the Lady Judith of Oakwood," said the jongleur clearly.

"Judith of Oakwood?" Sir Eustace paled and swallowed convulsively. He looked from the jongleur to Judith. "I crave your pardon, *demoiselle*. I did not know! I hope I have not inconvenienced you unduly." For a quick moment, he seemed not to know what to do. He made a quick recovery, however. He bowed mockingly and glanced at her knife, still held at the ready. "If you would accept the advice of a stranger, lady, I would suggest you clean your blade at once. Blood pits the steel, you know." He bowed again, then turned and sauntered away, wrapping a cloth about his injured hand and grinning back over his shoulder.

The jongleur turned back to the girl. "You must forgive Sir Eustace. He is sometimes a bit hasty. I do not think he'll come nigh you in future."

"I've to thank you for a most timely rescue, Aubrey," she said calmly enough, although her heart still raced. She took a small rag from the purse at her girdle, wiped her blade as the Norman had suggested, and replaced the knife in its sheath. "What was it turned Sir Eustace from his purpose? I saw naught in what you said to give him pause."

Aubrey smiled easily, charmingly. It was, after all, his stock in trade. "Oh, t'was simply that he knew himself to be in the wrong. Lord Raoul gave orders that no one was to be harmed unless there was resistance to his coming, and on no account does one disobey Lord Raoul's commands. Not even his younger brother."

Judith knit her brows. "Sir Eustace is the lord's brother? Strange, he has not much of a look of him."

"You've met Lord Raoul?"

"In the wood," she explained. "He came to fetch me, for Arnhilda was feared to have me come without protection." She looked at her hands. "She has always taken the greatest care for my well-being."

"Yes," said Aubrey in a dry voice. "That I recall quite clearly."

Judith hurried into speech. "You look very well. Did you return to England in the Norman Duke's train?"

"Aye. I traveled with his minstrel, Taillefer. He became a tutor to me and was a friend. Poor fellow! I don't suppose you've heard, but he fell at Hastings."

"A minstrel?" she inquired. "How is it he was involved with the fighting?"

"He'd taken a good deal of teasing from the knights about his bravery and pleaded with William as a boon to be allowed to strike the first blow at the Saxons." Aubrey grimaced. "He killed two men before he was stuck down."

"God requite him," murmured Judith, crossing herself reflexively.

Aubrey followed suit. "Aye." As an entertainer, he was banned from the Church, but that did not mean he could afford to ignore its forms. He studied her face intently in the ensuing silence. "You've changed."

She raised her brows. "How do you mean? I've grown up, you know. Once does not remain a child forever."

"Nay, 'tis not that alone. You seem colder. Once when you looked at me there was warmth and trust in your gaze. It's there no longer. Do you feel that I am an enemy because I am a Norman and have come this time in the new lord's company?"

"Now, Aubrey." She smiled with cool kindness, as she would at one of the grooms. "How could that be so? Were we not friends, so long ago? 'Tis merely that you've grown older, too, a man now, and different from the boy who visited my father's hall with a traveling troupe. You intend to work alone now?"

The minstrel ducked his head with a half-proud grin. "I am become something of a personage: Aubrey the minstrel, Aubrey the juggler, Aubrey the jongleur. I learned a great deal from poor Taillefer, and the noble lords like my work. They pay well for songs of love and tales of war these days. Soon I hope to have a troupe of my own." He shrugged. "About your father's death," he added. "I'm sorry. It must have been difficult."

It was Judith's turn to shrug. "I naturally regret the manner of his passing, but I cannot feel his death a great loss. I suppose 'tis unChristian of me."

"No. He was not a very good man." There was an awkward pause. "Lady Judith, ever since my visit here, I have wished to speak with you again. I wanted to explain . . ."

"I crave your pardon," she interrupted hurriedly. "I must go to assure Arnhilda of my safety." And before he could seek to detain her, she was away down the stair.

Halfway down she was met by her maidservant, who was on her way up, elbowing her way past others. Her eyes were alight with excitement and good humor. "All's well with you, child? Lord Raoul found you safely?"

Judith nodded. "Yes, he was most kind."

"I imagine he was," agreed Arnhilda, smiling and patting her hand. "Come. See where my lord has quartered us!" She grabbed Judith's wrist and dragged her back up the stair, babbling all the way, leading her charge past Aubrey, who stared after them.

"They say Lord Raoul sent no warning, but rode himself into the courtyard, the first of all of them to arrive. T'was at midday, when Lady Bertha retires to her chamber with that worthless Gwenddyd, and the serfs lose themselves, so that none was there to greet him but Cynefred, who himself related all this to me only a short time ago." She took a deep breath, full to bursting with gossip.

"You may imagine the lord's anger!" exclaimed Arnhilda happily. "None to greet him, no one about, no work being done. Cynefred says he walked straight into the master's chamber, and caught Lady Bertha and Gwenddyd in their guilt!" Arnhilda chuckled, a wicked glint in her eye. "Busy as ants in a honey jar, they were," she declared as their path was momentarily blocked, "and knew naught 'til Lord Raoul, himself, pulled them apart and had at them with a stick from the corner! Gwenddyd'll be black and purple for a fortnight. As for Lady Bertha, well, she'll not be lady of the hall now," declared the maid smugly. The crowd eased, and they moved forward once more. "She can't sit down too well, and never mind *what* he said afterward. T'was not meant for the ears of a young girl. Imagine! Lady Bertha no more in the thane's chair! And she's to remain on sufferance 'til she has proved her worth. She's at the loom even now, working like a demon! To think I missed the whole thing!" she exclaimed regretfully, with a shake of her grey head. "Ah, well. Must be punishment for some sin I'd forgot."

"What has Lord Raoul done with Gwenddyd?" Judith asked apprehensively.

"Gwenddyd? Oh, he gave her a choice of being a woman to one of his men-at-arms or work in the fields. Gwenddyd's no fool. She chose the man-at-arms and is probably unpacking his belongings right now in one of those tents. She's to work in the kitchen again, which'll keep her out of the hall since she's been given orders not to serve at meals. Lord Raoul said if she comes into the hall or nigh Lady Bertha again, she'll find herself in the fields with a raw back and a serf as master."

"But that's justice of my father's sort!" cried Judith, eyes flashing. "It wasn't Gwenddyd began . . ."

"'Tis fair enough," interrupted Arnhilda placidly as they made their way past more servants crowded in the passageway.

"Was it not you who taught me that the welfare of all folk was my responsibility?"

"Yes, indeed. But there's no use blinking at facts. Gwenddyd was willing enough when Lady Bertha beckoned. And the Holy Saints know how meanly she flaunted her new status in the faces of the other wenches while Lady Bertha held the reins! I think you know what Brother Plegmund would say of their conduct together. Although," she added thoughtfully, "had Lord Raoul not found the hall empty of serving folk, he might not have been so angry. But enough; there's no need to dwell on that pair! Lady Bertha and Lady Agnes are to sleep in your old chamber, and we sleep here!" She led Judith into a wide, comfortable chamber previously reserved for the rare guests that visited Oakwood.

Judith was incredulous. Her battered chest stood at the foot of the bed, which itself was covered with a worn but clean woolen cover of faded blue. A massive table had been set against one wall, littered with vials, pots, and jars containing medicines of her making. Space had been cleared on a corner of the table for the two leather-bound books that had belonged to her mother, several scrolls of parchment, her quills, inkpot, and stone bottle of sand. Bewildered, she stood staring in the middle of the chamber floor while Arnhilda chattered on gaily.

"My lord says the old chamber is to continue as the drying room. T'will be a penance and more for Lady Bertha when the elder flowers are in bloom. The main thing is that we are not to be crowded here.

"Saw you the ladies in the hall?" inquired Arnhilda. She went on without pause. "The plump one is Lady Edith, wife to Sir Tancred, who is to be bailiff here. He prefers managing things to fighting, and the lord trusts him. The other is Lady Blanche. She's wed to Sir Robert, who owes fealty to Lord Raoul and will live at Deerfield. T'will be hard on Lord Hywel's lady, but she's widowed now, and mayhap Lord Raoul will give her to one of his knights. There's many a lusty-looking fellow among them, and the poor lady was wed so long to Lord Hywel, that dried up sack of bones, she'll likely welcome a change from abstinence."

"It is possible, you know," commented Judith sternly, "that Lady Margaret was fond of her lord and will want no other."

The maid snorted. "Been listening to love songs again, have you? There's rarely love in marriage, girl, which you well know. And Lord Hywel was not a loveable man. He had a face like a mangy boar and the table manners of one, too, if you'll care to remember. T'was why he and your father got on so well."

"But, Arnhilda . . ." Judith spread her hands. "He was no different from *any* of the men we know."

"Exactly my point! There are, although you've never met any, men who don't make your stomach heave when you watch 'em eat. Besides, although Lady Margaret was a chaste and faithful wife to Hywel of Deerfield, t'was often enough her eyes followed one comely young man or another when she thought none saw."

"Three young sons she lost at Hastings," mused Judith. "A grievous blow."

"She's young yet; she'll breed more," Arnhilda returned stoutly. "Grief don't kill; and to live with your thoughts on the past is the road to madness. Give her a husband can swell her belly, and she'll find solace."

As she spoke, Arnhilda slipped the worn gray gown and ragged kirtle from Judith's body. She took a cloth and began to wash her from a basin of sweet-scented water, which had been waiting for her arrival. "I've learned much this even," she said thoughtfully. "I bless the day that Norman whore wed your father and forced me to learn her heathen tongue! Lord Raoul is a baron's son. The second-born, to be sure, and the elder brother has heirs. For his service, Lord Raoul has been given Oakwood and more by King William, and been made a baron himself. Also, he took plenty of loot from somewhere, for he has three squires of good birth and twenty knights to serve him. 'Tis no small measure of a man's worth to see an army of that size guarding his back!"

Arnhilda paused significantly. "Hear you that hammering, child?"

"Who could miss it?" And indeed, the heavy blows of hammer on wood overrode even the babble of voices and the movement of furniture in the hall below.

The maid lowered her voice. "T'was from one of the squires I heard what's toward. They're making a door for the lord's chamber!"

"A *door*!" repeated Judith, astonished. "Why?"

Arnhilda's eyes twinkled. "Ah! While I watched, two big men-at-arms carried in a chest. Small, it was, no bigger than a year-old babe, but heavy, and guarded with a lock. That Aubrey said t'was filled to the top with silver pennies!"

Judith grimaced. "Jongleurs will say anything!"

"What? Does it still bother you, what happened when he came to entertain us in the winter of '64? You can put down your arm, now," she added as she tossed the wet rag down beside the basin.

"It does not trouble me the way you mean," Judith replied, lowering her arm. She wrinkled her nose at the memory. "I've to thank you for your warning then, no matter how much I resented it at the time. You were right. Had I listened to him and his pretty words, I'd have come to a bad end." She flushed and cast down her eyes. "I was a fool to think he loved me."

"Now, child," admonished the maid gently. She dried her mistress with a soft cloth. "He was the first man ye'd ever seen with a pretty face and manners to match. A young girl, t'was only natural you'd be dazzled. And it ended with but a few tears shed. No need to dwell on it."

"I still can't believe he'd do something like that, to bed Lady Bertha after he's told me he'd never love another."

Arnhilda grunted. She said nothing, however. She knew that Judith would likely be furious did she suspect her servingmaid had arranged that fateful tryst between Cerdic's lady and the handsome jongleur. It had been easy enough to do, with Lady Bertha liking what she saw and the lad so hot for a woman he hadn't cared *who* it was so long as she was willing.

What he'd felt for Judith, and likely still did, could not be allowed to influence events. A jongleur could never aspire to a noble's daughter. Arnhilda had seen her chance to put a stop to Lady Judith's infatuation and acted accordingly. Now, observing the girl's set face, she held her tongue. Better that Judith despise the young man undeservedly than complicate all by falling in love once again with his comely face.

Deftly, she dressed Judith in a fresh kirtle and a blue velvet gown, which the girl recognized as having belonged to her dead mother. Arnhilda combed and plaited Judith's long, golden hair and smiled mistily. "You'll do, child." And then, because she wanted to take Judith in her arms in a loving, maternal gesture, she sniffed and added, "That's real ermine for the trim. It's held up well after so many years packed away. T'was a gift of Lady Milburga's father, your grandsire."

"It's beautiful," whispered Judith as she ran her hands lovingly from her waist to hips, luxuriating in the feel of the velvet. "I've never worn anything so wonderful!" The fur at her neckline was soft.

There came a voice at the portal of the chamber. Arnhilda poked her head around the tapestried curtain which afforded what privacy existed, and almost immediately popped back in. "'Tis a squire," she announced importantly. "Until the monk told me, I'd never heard of them. This one says you're to go with him."

Lady Judith settled her leather girdle firmly about her hips and stepped past the curtain to confront a smiling young man, only a year or so older than herself. He wore a tunic emblazoned with a hawk, and his eyes were respectfully admiring. "Lady Judith, I am Louis d'Ouvremont. It is my honor to lead you to your place at table."

She laid her hand lightly upon his proffered arm, and went with him down the stair and through the milling crowd.

The trestle tables had been set up on their supports in the same pattern as usual, with the table for the highest of rank at the head of the room and the other two tables at right angles, forming a u-shape. She did not, however, occupy her accustomed place with the servants. Indeed, the servants had no place at Lord Raoul's table. Ladies Bertha and Agnes, she noted, were being seated ignominiously below the salt, between the knights and men-at-arms. But Judith was led to a place near the high table. She had as her dinner companions Sir Tancred, of whom she had already heard, and a fat priest whom the squire introduced as Father Hubert.

The priest smiled upon her in a paternal manner. "So, my dear. You are the lady of whom I have heard so much." Judith looked puzzled, and his smile broadened. "Brother Plegmund and I conferred together all afternoon," he explained. "He has warranted you virtuous, industrious, pious, and learned. Most commendable, my child."

"Brother Plegmund is too kind," Judith replied shortly. She was nettled. It seemed to her they'd gone over her good points like buyers at a horse fair!

"Then the good brother did not mention that she climbs like a monkey, has the courage of a lioness, and chatters, as well," put in a deep voice behind them.

All at the tables came to their feet, and Judith, rising also, turned to face Lord Raoul, whose stern expression did not mask the twinkle in his brown eyes. His hair was darker than his eyes and thick with curls. His mouth was thin-lipped, his cheekbones high. "You find your chamber to your liking, *demoiselle*?" he inquired.

Judith flushed, lowering her eyes. "Yes, my lord. It is most comfortable, I thank you."

He nodded carelessly and moved to the solitary chair placed at the high table. Sir Eustace, his brother, was seated in the first place of the table across from Judith's. Only after Lord Raoul was seated did the company resume their places. Father Hubert blessed the meal, and at a slight gesture from Lord Raoul, the first course was set forward.

Father Hubert placed the slices of meat in cinnamon sauce Judith had selected in their shared trencher and spoke of the political situation. "The Pope, you know, was himself in favor of the invasion."

"No, I wasn't aware," she murmured, lifting a piece of meat with thumb and two fingers only, in the most approved style of elegance. "He took Duke William's part?"

"Yes, yes," the priest assured her happily, helping himself to the largest slice and smacking his lips. "Gave the King a Papal banner to carry with him into battle, too. Even had the contest gone against him, Duke William would still have won, having God on his side."

She saw the force of that argument and questioned him about the banner, and why the Holy Father had decided in favor of King William. Father Hubert explained at some length but had questions of his own.

"The battle has been won, of course," he said, deftly plopping into his mouth the last of the meat. "But there is always the possibility of trouble with the common people. Think you they will choose to benefit by William's rule or resist and make trouble?"

"How can I speak for all England?" inquired Judith, half laughing. "Indeed, I have not traveled much and have little knowledge of folk outside Oakwood." This was a time for circumspection. She was conscious of the many eyes upon her, curious and intent.

Father Hubert pressed, "But you may make an educated guess, surely. You know your people."

"I think that the peasants, certainly, would not wish more blood spilled," she said with some confidence, for she did know country folk. So long as things did not interfere with the daily round of their lives, they had no interest in politics, and one king was much the same as another to them. "But," she continued, "there are those who have taken to the woods after Hastings, and they may well cry out for vengeance. What man would not fight, whose land was taken away by force?"

"True, true," responded the priest. "I suppose one must allow for the emotions of warriors left after battles. They cannot hope to prevail against King William, however."

"It is very sad," she murmured tactfully.

Father Hubert nodded and expounded his views on the situation, while Judith chose to partake of eels in puree for the second course, and to listen with a dignified air. Modestly, she tried to avoid the curious glances of the knights and their ladies, and wished the meal at an end. And where, she wondered, would the servants eat? In the kitchen? She would have to check to be sure they were taken proper care of under the new system.

Ignoring her stepdaughter completely, Lady Bertha chatted with a pleasant-faced knight. Agnes, however, watched her stepsister with increasing bitterness as the third course began and the priest placed choice morsels of roast boar before Judith, encouraging her to eat.

From behind her husband's ample form, the Lady Edith peeped shyly at Judith, flushing and smiling when their eyes met. While across the room, Lady Blanche stared at the girl in frank curiosity. Once Lady Blanche leaned past her husband and smiled in so condescending a manner that Judith was offended.

In her father's time, only just past, Oakwood had been a haven for younger sons with little dignity and less politeness. Conduct at table had been casual to the point of slovenliness. These new folk, however, behaved as Brother Plegmund had related to her from his travels. The conversation was polite, with no lewdness spoken, and none became so full with wine that they vomited upon the table or slid to the rushes in a stupor, actions to which Cerdic and his housecarls had been much addicted. She noted with approval that the knights and men-at-arms refrained from openly fondling the serving wenches. Gnawed bones were not returned to the serving platters, but tossed properly under the tables for the dogs, now loosed from their confinement. Between courses servants went from one diner to the next with a basin, ewer, and towel, that one's fingers might be clean for dipping into the platters of the following course. Judith had cause to be grateful for Brother Plegmund's tutelage, more especially when she overheard Sir Tancred remark to his lady that this Lady Judith of Oakwood had very pretty manners.

Sometime after the meal was ended and the tables dismantled and stacked against a wall, the same squire led Judith over to the great hearth, where Lord Raoul sat in what had been the thane's chair. Earlier, she had seen Agnes and Lady Bertha stand before him, listening to his commands, she presumed. They had retired to their shared chamber now, however. She joined the group of three who awaited their lord's pleasure, wondering what he meant to do with her.

Arnhilda, Brother Plegmund, and a strange Norman man-at-arms stood with her. None of them seemed to be in the least nervous, which reassured her greatly. Also impressive was the fact that, although the hall was crowded to overflowing with people, a considerable area about

Lord Raoul was now cleared, and none ventured close enough to disturb the lord's privacy unless specifically called upon. As the lord conferred privately with the man-at-arms in a voice too quiet to be overheard, Judith began to grow restless and anxious. It occurred to her that Lord Raoul held them all in the palm of his leathery hand. What did he mean to do with her? Uncertainty spurred fear, but fear always made her angry. Her chin came up and her blue eyes glinted.

Raoul glanced over. The corner of his mouth twitched, but he did not smile. In the light of the fire, his eyes had almost a golden hue. Of the men she knew well, Brother Plegmund was pleasantly homely, her father had been definitely ill-favored, and Aubrey almost girlishly handsome. The Hawk was like none of them. His face was rugged, with a hard strength. The brow was wide, the jaw firm. There was no visible sign of weakness or gentleness. No, Judith decided, it was not a pretty face, but she rather liked it. Perhaps he could be trusted; she would see.

His voice sliced neatly through her thoughts. "I am lord of these lands, Lady Judith, which I hold for the King. As daughter of Cerdic, late Thane of Oakwood, you are orphaned and my ward. You understand this?"

"Yes, my lord," she answered calmly, wondering at his apparent need to state the obvious. What did he want of her?

He grunted. "'Tis well. Your maidservant tells me you tend the sick and wounded. This is so?"

"I have always done so, my lord."

"Then you shall continue in your efforts," he said firmly. "There are those of my men who have sustained injuries in the late fighting. You will see to them. Also, I am told you are accustomed to order the meals and oversee the daily workings of the hall. These tasks you will continue to perform. Lady Blanche saw to the meal this eve, but she will be gone to Deerfield soon, and things will go more smoothly if the serfs take their orders from you as they are used to do.

"The quartering arrangements will, of necessity, be difficult to manage in so small a place. My knights and men-at-arms are at present sleeping in tents, and my masons tell me that the castle will not be completed in time to shield them from winter's cold. Thus, when the weather changes, many of them will be forced to make their beds here in the hall. T'will be your responsibility to see that all are situated as comfortably as possible."

She swallowed. Dear Heaven! "We. . . we will be very crowded," she ventured.

"I am sure you will handle the matter to admiration." He cut her off. "Sir Tancred and his lady will occupy the chamber previously used by the girl, Lady Agnes. You will keep for your own use the chamber now assigned to you. Arnhilda will continue to share it." He waved a casual hand in the direction of the man-at-arms who stood before him. "This man is Conan. He is to guard you and will sleep on a pallet outside your door."

"I . . ." said Judith.

"Your good Arnhilda has expressed certain fears for your safety," he went on smoothly. "There are a great many men about, not all of them, perhaps, as trustworthy as one would hope in matters of so delicate a nature. Therefore, by tomorrow, there will be a door for your chamber such as the one the carpenter has made for mine." He frowned. "At no time are you to venture forth without Conan's attendance. Is this perfectly understood?"

"Yes, my lord, but . . ."

"Do not argue with me!" snapped the Hawk. "You will do as you are bid! There are always reasons for my orders, as those who disobey them discover to their cost!"

Judith clenched her hands in anger. How dare he speak to her as if she were the village idiot! "I was not going to argue!" she protested in some heat. "I merely wished to ask, my lord Hawk, if I am in such danger that I must needs have a guard set over me like a . . . a spice chest!"

There was a pause during which Raoul seemed to choose his words. "A pretty maiden is always in danger amongst so many men," he finally replied, quite mildly. "You might prove too great a temptation. Conan will provide a discouragement while the need for it exists."

She thought about that. "Then, you plan to have me wed, my lord?"

"Does the idea displease you? Had you a wish to join a nunnery?"

"No," she replied shortly. "I have no such vocation."

He smiled. "Then, you might consent to marry. When you come of age for it," he added with a twinkle.

"I am near fourteen," said Judith, drawing herself up with dignity.

"Ho! So great an age!" He studied her for a moment in amused silence. "You will study with our good monk here, as you have in the past," he said then. "I cannot read, and can write only my name. T'would be wise to have several here with the skill. I wish also that you would make friends with Lady Edith, who is new to England and unhappy so far from her home.

"I will have conveyed to your chamber several lengths of cloth, from which you will have fashioned new gowns. My ward will be expected to dress accordingly with my rank. You will not wear that gray monstrosity of a gown again. And if you are a good girl," he added, seeing she was about to protest, "if you fulfill your duties and give me no cause for complaint, we shall speak again of this business of marriage again. *After* the harvest!"

And with that she had to be content.

‡

Usually Judith was so weary from her labors at night that she fell into bed with no thought for conversation. On this night, however, she seethed with excitement.

"Arnhilda," she said with a laugh in her voice. "Did you hear? Lord Raoul says I am pretty! Am I? Truly?!"

"I suppose so," returned the maidservant, shifting to find a more comfortable spot on her straw pallet on the floor.

"Am I as pretty as Lady Edith?" she persisted.

Arnhilda sighed and raised herself on one bony elbow, "You've as much as she to commend you, I reckon."

"Oh, well." Judith hugged herself. "Where did you eat?" she asked, belatedly recalling her duty to provide for her servant.

"The new rule is all servants of the hall eat in the kitchen. Makes it cozy-like, if a bit crowded. Nice to get food hot for a change," Arnhilda muttered, yawning. "Can we get to sleep now?"

But Judith was thinking. "Am I honestly as pretty as Lady Edith?"

"Prettier, mayhap. She's a shade too plump for real beauty, and your eyes and hair are better. Are you not tired, child? You've had a long day."

"And he promised to see to my marriage! Is it not exciting?"

"No, that he did not!" returned the woman sleepily. "What he *said* was, he'd discuss it again after the harvest. Holy Mother, I'm weary!"

"Well, that means the same thing, doesn't it? At least he's *thinking* about it. I wonder if he plans to have Agnes wed one of his men or if he plans to wed her himself. Do you think he knows she's not a virgin? They say a man can tell just by looking at a girl. But mayhap he cares not. And you should have seen how Agnes looked at me while we ate. You'd think they'd served her green apples; she was so sour! If her eyes had been poison, I vow I'd have been dead upon the rushes! 'Tis jealousy, of course. Arnhilda? Did you hear?"

Her only answer was a contented snore.

CHAPTER 4

ave you heard?" whispered Edwina excitedly as she reached out to snatch a piece of fish from a platter carried into the kitchen. Other hands grabbed at whatever scraps they could find as servers returned from the great hall with leavings of more noble diners.

"Heard what?" Gytha demanded around a mouthful of pickled egg.

"Lady Judith went to the vill this morn and had words with Mildred. Seems one of those masons came out of her house still fastening his hose, right in front of Lady Judith!"

"No!" gasped Gytha. She tore a piece of bread from a half sodden trencher on another tray. It seemed fairly dry. The serving wench carried them past and tossed the discarded trenchers into a basket, where they fell with a series of damp plops. These were for distribution to the poor. Gytha's strong teeth crunched though the crust of the bread. "What happened then?"

"The way *I* heard it, she sent the fellow back to his work on the castle, then went inside to speak to Mildred." A half-slice of ham caught her eye, but one of the grooms was faster, so Edwina made do with a mangled fowl's leg.

"She didn't offend Lady Judith, did she?" asked Gytha anxiously. "Mildred's got a fearful temper when it's roused," she added. A craving for vegetables was satisfied by handful of lettuce sautéed in broth. She wiped her hands surreptitiously on a discarded cloth from the hall.

"No," Edwina returned in a mildly disappointed voice. "It seems that she, Lady Judith, I mean, asked Mildred why she betrayed her man with another, and why she did not let herself be guided by the teachings of the Church in such matters."

"Jesu! You tell me *that* did not anger Mildred?"

"Not according to Wiglaf, which is where I heard it. And he should know, since he stood outside the door to hear the whole of it."

"Well? What did Mildred say?" demanded Gytha, rubbing absently at the mound of her belly, where her babe kicked strongly. Her appetite was gone, a sure sign that the babe would come soon, since that had been the way of it with her first.

"Mildred told her that she has no milk for her babe, and that it's mortal hard for a poor woman to find a wet-nurse. With what the masons pay, though, she earns enough to get food for the little one, and even to save enough coin for the purchase of a cow if the masons keep up an interest in her."

"And Lady Judith said?"

"Wiglaf said she made no reply at all but came back to the hall, all thoughtful-looking as she walked." She shrugged. Edwina herself scarcely left the hall and its closest environs. "Doubtless t'was a new experience, talking with the poor in the village."

Gytha's eyebrow rose. "Lady Judith speaks with her folk often, even the poorest of the poor. I should know," she added with a sigh. "I was one myself before the lady made me dairymaid when the last one died. Put her trust in me, she did, and I've never let her down. She even got permission from Lord Cerdic for me to wed my man!"

Edwina perceived her error and made amends by offering her friend a pastry from a huge platter.

"No, you go ahead," said Gytha, with a rueful shake of her head, for the delicacy looked good! "The babe's moving too much for food to settle." She sighed. "You know, that meeting my lady had with Mildred might no be too bad a thing," she opined softly. "She's been sheltered, has Lady Judith. Now, mayhap, she'll understand better why some folk, as are looked down on, do what they do."

"Are you sure you don't want this?" asked Edwina, hefting the pastry, "How about just half?"

Gytha looked at the honey-coated treat. "Well, mayhap I was a bit hasty. One small bite shouldn't hurt. . ."

‡

Judith wiped her unguent-smeared hands on a clean rag and smiled to reassure the man before her. "T'was a deep wound, but the rib is not touched. Now it's been cleaned and dressed, it should heal swiftly. I must change the dressing twice each day. See to it you keep it clean," she admonished. "Evil humours in certain elements could cause it to turn green."

"Eh? What evil humours?" demanded the man, alarmed.

"I am not certain," she admitted.

"Well, then, how do you know?" inquired the man-at-arms reasonably.

She smiled at his suspicious nature, so like the Saxon peasants among whom she usually worked. "Our Brother Plegmund received a scroll from a priest he knows, who traveled to the Levant and there attended a great university where he studied the sciences. You know," she added at his blank stare, "medicine, astrology, and mathematics."

"Oh, but of course," he murmured, assuming a knowledgeable look.

"Well," she continued, "there are five basic elements: earth, air, fire, water, and mist. Of these, mist is the most dangerous, for it may combine with earth, air, or water unseen. And it often contains evil humours, which can produce illness, deformities, and turn wounds septic. To avoid this, it is necessary to keep earths from foodstuffs and cuts, and to bathe after a sweat. One must also avoid the north wind, which everyone knows is harmful."

"One good sweat washes away an old one, is what my father used to say," the man remarked challengingly.

She nodded, a rueful smile creasing the corners of her mouth. "Mine said the same. But sweat is a form of water, and if, as the priest suspected, an evil humour can use it to enter the body. . ."

"If that is true, all the saints protect us!" gasped the man, seriously shaken by the new idea. He crossed himself for luck. "But, my lady, my companions would laugh if they saw me bathe that often!"

"Better the butt of jokes than dead of a fever," she countered.

"There's God's Truth in that!" He slipped his overtunic down to cover the bandage. "My thanks, lady," he murmured. "You've a light touch, if you don't mind my saying so."

"'T'was nothing."

"Nay, Lady Judith. Some I've known made the treatment worse than the getting of the wound!" He sketched a half-bow and left.

She looked about expectantly, but the chamber was empty now of the crowd that had collected earlier.

"He was the last, my lady," said Conan standing quietly in his corner.

His black eyes had no expression, but his tone was not hostile. Judith had given up trying to discover what he thought about anything. She nodded at him and began to cover pots and jars, replacing them in her tray.

Arnhilda appeared in the doorway and gave Conan a sharp look, which he ignored. She did not dislike the man. How could she, when he protected the child of her heart as if she were more precious than gold? But he would not acknowledge Arnhilda's superior claim to that role, which vexed her intolerably. Her glance turned to Judith. "You're weary, child," she declared, moving to take the tray from her hands. "Why not go take a walk in the sunshine? T'will refresh you."

"You're right." She touched the maidservant's hand in thanks, took her woolen cloak from its peg, and left.

Brother Plegmund met her on the stair, and they walked outside together, Conan stalking impressively at Judith's heels.

Mid-morning sunshine warmed them as they headed down the track to the village. The Normans had been at Oakwood only a few weeks, yet already the tenor of life had changed remarkably. Small parties of men worked here and there, their tasks varied. A few cut hay, while others bound it ready for the carts. Still others sharpened wooden stakes to reinforce the palisade, cleaned weapons, or rode off on mysterious errands for Lord Raoul. Occasionally, a voice would be raised to shout orders or ask a question, usually in Norman French.

"Is it not a wonder how different things are?" murmured Judith, hopping over a rut in the path.

"Aye, that it is. Have you learnt to recognize the villeins without their long hair and beards?" he teased.

"More to the point, have their wives and children? Remember the cries and moanings the morn t'was accomplished? You'd have thought they'd been slain!" She laughed, but at the time there had been a nagging worry, for shearing and shaving had brought the closest thing to hostility she had seen from those in the vill since the Normans' arrival.

"They're used to it now," the monk said gently, understanding her concerns. "It might have been different had not the robbers not been about to take their minds off the outrage of bare necks and chins, though."

"They were Saxons, did you notice?" she muttered shaking her head. "I'd never have believed such a thing a year ago. But when they lined up the bodies there, outside the vill, there was no denying it."

The monk sighed. "And two of them, at least, were nobles. I'd seen them, father and son, just after Hastings, when I was in London. Their lands must have been given to some Norman baron or other, and they'd no other choice than to take to the woods."

"Or to turn themselves into serfs," said Judith bitterly, thinking of Lady Margaret of Deerfield, now a servant in her own hold. She wondered how many others across the land were similarly situated. There must have been many who fled into the hills. Had she been Cerdic's son instead of his daughter, she might be dead on the field of battle herself or living wild in the forest and plotting revenge. Or, she thought suddenly, set herself up as a scrivener in some large town. What an interesting idea! A pity she was female.

"'Tis best not to dwell upon unhappy memories, my dear," murmured Brother Plegmund. "Think instead of the wellbeing of our people. Did not Lord Raoul vanquish the band of men attacking the vill? Aye, and the folk are not ungrateful. It was, in a way, a proof of the rightness of his rule, that he defended the land and his folk."

"I suppose," Judith agreed. "Certainly things are better here than at Northwatch, where Lord Edward now rules. Dear God, I *knew* some of those people! Limbs hacked off for resistance and babes dead in the fired huts! 'Tis almost more than the mind can bear!"

"Hush, now, hush! My child, you know how things are in wartime," he admonished. "'Tis never pleasant. Yes, there are killings and woundings, huts fired, children who scream in the night from evil dreams, and those who lose their reason. But at least here, under Hawk's eye, life is safe enough. And look you at the new fields he has opened for planting, the new huts in the village to replace the ones lost when Dunna's brewhouse burnt down a fortnight past. The lot of our folk is better than before, you must admit the truth of that."

"Even mine is changed for the better," she acknowledged, remembering the abuse and misery of her father's reign only too well. Then she shook off her dark mood.

"'Tis a good thing last year's harvest was a fine one," Judith said, lifting her right hand to flip one golden braid behind her shoulder. "The grains should feed us all, even if we have to dip a bit into the seed stock. The additions to the stables are near to finished, too. I shall be able to quarter in the loft the men-at-arms who won't fit in the hall this winter."

"True, true; your plans are excellent." The cleric glanced at her from the corner of his eye. "You are still concerned over the beating of Endelbright?"

She sighed and then smiled reluctantly, for the case of the lazy groom had caused considerable friction between herself and the new lord. "No, I reckon Hawk had the right of it, much though it pains me to admit it. I thought five lashes was a bit harsh for that offense of sleeping the afternoon away. But since that incident, not one serf has been caught idling when he should be at work, and the whole of Oakwood is in much better stead than I would have thought possible."

They walked past the new fields as they spoke. Lines of hedges, newly planted, marked off the division between one large plot of land and the next, in the Norman manner. Here and there men and women labored, bent over, pulling at weeds that threatened the new rye and barley. It looked to be a good crop.

Brother Plegmund cleared his throat uneasily. "There is one matter which does not sit well with me."

"Oh?"

"The knights and men-at-arms spend entirely too much time both here in the vill and in the fishing village," he declared, his cheekbones red and gray eyes flashing. "As you may suppose, with their men off in the fields or out to sea with their nets, the women, well. . . um, I think you know what I mean," he finished lamely, not wanting to put words to a situation he found extremely unpleasant.

Judith thought for a moment. "Well, you know how it is. The women are poor, and the knights have coin enough to pay for their pleasures." She shrugged. "I do not approve, that goes without saying, but what can one do? The knights have no women of their own. At least there have been no cases of rape, what with the Hawk's threat to castrate the first man who tries it."

"Yes, yes, Lord Raoul is to be commended for defending the chastity of the womenfolk. The problem is that so few of them are *chaste*. It is a grievous sin, and I positively shudder to think of their punishments in hell!"

Judith made soothing noises, but she was amused. The cleric clearly blamed the women. She was inclined to blame the men just a bit more than he seemed to do. After all, without the promise of those seductive, jingling coins, many fewer would be tempted to dally with a man not her own, no matter what his social status in the hall! She said so and watched the monk struggle with the concept, adding after a few moments, "And the masons are even worse. They've more coins than the poor knights and men-at-arms, and their food is much better. I couldn't believe the stipulations in their contact when Sir Tancred showed it to me! Why, I can't imagine that the King eats better than they do! I know *we* don't!"

"Unfortunately, they show entirely too generous a spirit when it comes to sharing it with the girls of Oakwood in return for favors of the most shocking nature!" he snapped. "Have they not listened to a single one of my sermons?"

"I suspect they have not been as attentive as they should," she agreed. "But so long as neither the girls nor their fathers complain, I don't see what can be done about it."

Brother Plegmund grunted his disapproval but said no more.

They rounded the corner into the village, and the track widened into something approaching a heavily rutted road. It was lined on either side with mud huts, some thirty in number, the thatching dropping gently over their eaves. Smoke circled up from the exhaust holes cut in ceilings and drifted slightly to the east in a middling breeze, which came off the western sea a few miles distant. Judith fancied she could smell the salt tang in the air.

They visited the sick and aged, as Judith generally did when she was in the vill, exclaimed over new babies, and remarked upon the growth of older ones. A woman whose child Judith had saved the previous winter from an ague rushed to present a garland of flowers, hastily twisted into shape. The alewife dragged them off, not entirely against their will, to the table outside the new brewhouse, where they were honored with a sample of the latest brewing. Judith, blossoms in her hair, sipped raw ale from the leather tankard, and listened to the pleasant sounds of Saxon gossip from the women crowded round them, and the laughter of children still too young for work in the fields. She smiled her contentment. Conan, who declined all refreshment, looked on impassively.

As usual, the walk back to the hall seemed to take less time than the trek to the village. Judith thought about all that she had seen and heard. Oakwood was an orderly place these days and industrious. Cerdic had been a bad thane, and his people had felt no love for him. While Lord Raoul was unquestionably a foreigner, part of a conquering horde and a hard master, the folk seemed to feel that he was a fair one.

Their acceptance of their lot in life, which bound them to a master and to the land, led them to accept their new situation without visible protest. Then, too, the people contrasted the indifference of Lord Cerdic's rule with that of the Hawk. Cerdic had spent an inordinate amount of time wenching and drinking. While the men of the vill saw nothing *wrong* with those activities, Cerdic had not found time to attend to more important matters, as well. The new lord saw to it that Sir Tancred, his bailiff, kept an eye upon labors of the peasants, provided what tools and instructions were needed, and protected them from harm. Sir Tancred was not, as Cerdic's housecarls had been, averse to plunging knee-deep in mud to help rescue a lamb or to put a shoulder to a cart that needed righting. Lord Raoul, himself, led his knights into the woodlands and marshes to patrol the land as a warning to potential robbers and to hunt for game. He began to be known in the land and to know it. Always, he supervised the training of the squires, who practiced their skills daily within the palisades of the hall, or in the fallow if horsemanship or archery were involved. They would one day be knights, and his life, as well as the safety of Oakwood, might well depend upon their abilities. And, of course, the new policy of allowing the villagers to approach Cynefred, the cook, for kitchen scraps, was one that met with approval in many quarters.

Judith approached the hall, her steps slowing as she gazed at the encampment of the new serfs who had come from the south with the Hawk. For the people born at Oakwood and bred to its marshes and hills, life was better, but her heart was wrung by the misery of these new folk. They were from villages laid waste the previous fall and had lost what little they owned. Most had lost entire families; many wore iron slave collars. Despised by the Normans, looked down upon by the native serfs of Oakwood, they sat huddled about their open fires each night in the chill air. Even the infants had no shelter other than their mother's breast from the gentle, treacherous spring rains.

She could never afterward account for it, but at that moment, as she passed a group of women bent over their querns, painfully grinding corn into flour, a fury possessed her. Enough was enough! She had seen this spectacle once too often! Without a word, she turned and marched out to the fallow, where Lord Raoul stood watching his squires and knights at practice. Brother Plegmund was left standing openmouthed in mid-noun behind her. Conan kept pace, as always, at her right heel.

Raoul was not a tall man, but her head reached only to his shoulder. That, for some reason, added considerably to her anger. "My lord," she declared loudly as she drew near, "I would have speech with you."

The Hawk did not turn his head. "Not now, girl. I'm busy."

"It must be now," she insisted firmly. "Unless, of course, you enjoy the vision of corpses strewn about the campfires?"

Raoul sighed. "This has to do with the serfs, I presume?"

"It does." She squared her shoulders, prepared for a battle of words and determined to prevail.

"I will not have them quartered in my hall!" he snapped, eyes on the young Odo, who was doing remarkably well controlling his mount while practicing with a broadsword.

"My lord, I did not suggest they share your chamber," she returned more calmly. "I do feel, however, that unless they are sheltered from the elements, many will sicken and die."

He shrugged. "Life is always hard for them; they are used to it, *demoiselle*."

With great difficulty Judith refrained from kicking him. Causing this insufferable beast of a man even momentary pain would have given her great satisfaction she decided, but it would not help the peasants. God, she felt certain, depended upon her to aid them. She must not fail Him or them. She thought furiously and then said, "Lord Raoul. The new serfs do not work well. I have noticed they do far less than our own folk."

The Hawk turned, patently suspicious. "I beg your pardon?"

"'Tis not that they *will* not, but fed as they are, upon scraps of the meanest kind, and sleeping in the damp air, which everyone knows saps the strength, well, what can one expect?" She tried for a causal tone. "It is a great pity. They will be needed for the harvest, but living as they do, the few who will be left by that time will not have the strength to do the work."

His lips twitched. "I see. Tell me, *demoiselle*, have you a remedy for this tragic situation?"

This time Judith was not fooled. She smiled eagerly. "Each evening, when work is done in the fields, all the serfs, both old and new, may gather at the far end of the vill. In a short time, a new hut can be built, for 'tis only wattle plastered over with clay. There would be a new cottage each night or two, think you, and no time lost in the fields or in digging out the castle moat. The women and children can make the wattle or dig the clay during the day. All could be safely housed in a fortnight, my lord," she pleaded, her eyes locked to his. "Oh, please, my lord! Think of the babes who sleep now in the rain!"

Raoul had been staring into those clear, blue eyes, which he had known were dangerous from the start. Suddenly, he leaned forward, grabbed her shoulders with both hands, and kissed her hard on the mouth. Her lips, parting in surprise, opened under his, and for a moment he gripped her strongly, pressing her tightly against his firm, lean body. Then, just as she felt a faint tingling deep in her belly, the Hawk moved away. If his chuckle was more than a bit unsteady, Judith did not notice. She was too busy remembering how to breathe.

"If it will give you pleasure to house these vermin, *demoiselle*, then do so by all means," he said. "But I think you will find the other serfs less than willing to assist you." He glanced at Conan, standing rigidly behind the girl, his eyes fixed at some point in midair. "See that all comply with some enthusiasm to Lady Judith's request."

"Yes, my lord," said Conan.

"Thank you, Lord Raoul. . ." Judith faltered, shaken and unnerved by that unexpected and bewildering kiss. But Hawk was already striding toward that section of the field reserved for archery practice, shouting advice to Louis about the proper angle for an effective drop shot.

‡

If the housing problems were thus easily solved, other matters went less smoothly. Lady Agnes, for instance, loomed large as an irritant. She openly sulked and brooded, jealous of Lady Judith's new status and unquestioned authority over household matters. It was not that she wanted to take on Judith's tasks, but her elevated position rankled. She was also embittered by her own relegation to the rank of unofficial lady-in-waiting to her stepsister. Her stitchery improved; her manner deteriorated. When ordered by Raoul to learn from Lady Judith the skills involved in competent handling of wounds and physical ailments (which her mother, had she cared, should have taught her years before), she sat with smoldering resentment while Judith explained procedures. She then yawned elaborately and refused to participate in caring for those who came to them for aid. Having lived with Judith for several years, Agnes knew the other girl would not tell tales of her to the Hawk. She felt nothing but contempt for Judith and her so-called virtues. Besides, why should she bother with something in which she had no interest?

The enforced chastity under Lord Raoul's orders made Agnes' tongue even more acid than usual, and she constantly jibed at Judith for her work among the people. If Lady Judith preferred the company of Saxon swine in the village, she declared in a bitter tone, then the Hawk should settle her there permanently. She also set her mind to the destruction of the tentative friendship between Judith and the Norman woman, Lady Edith. She whispered to Lady Edith that it was said that Lady Judith shared her favors between the jongleur, who, as anyone with eyes could see, felt a great partiality for the Saxon girl, and the man-at-arms, Conan. Then Agnes told the kitchen wench, Gwenddyd, that Lady Judith had said in her hearing that all the wenches of the hall were whores and worse. The tales circulated rapidly. It was only when Arnhilda finally brought the matter to the attention of the Hawk that the situation was resolved. By then, Lady Edith, believing Lady Agnes, had spread the word of Judith's supposed indiscretions so far afield that Raoul had to call all the knights, men-at-arms, servants, and serfs into the courtyard before the hall. He told the embarrassed, and embarrassing assembly of Lady Agnes' spite. He declared Lady Judith innocent of all charges, exonerated Conan, and sentenced Lady Agnes to five lashes and six months in her chamber on half rations.

Although vindicated, Judith was appalled by the severity of this punishment. And, since she felt it to be her duty to remonstrate with him, did so.

The Hawk listened courteously, and when she was done, said, "It *is* a harsh judgment, Lady Judith. I agree with all you have said. Nevertheless, she defamed you and cast doubt upon the integrity of my most trusted man-at-arms, to say nothing of what doubts she cast upon my own judgment. She also made trouble for us all by her slanders; for the kitchen wenches worked poorly, and you will admit that conversation at table flagged somewhat while all were aware of the breach between you and Lady Edith. I am lord here. I will *not* permit anyone to disrupt what harmony we have achieved by our labors. Lady Agnes harbors no love for you nor for me either now, but she will think twice before she attempts to make mischief again. So will anyone else. The matter is closed."

And so it was.

‡

Lady Bertha maintained her recent attitude of cool indifference toward her stepdaughter, which Judith found preferable to the open enmity of old. Still, her malice was nonetheless active for that, and Judith knew it. There was no question that could Lady Bertha but find the means, she would do her best to see Judith suffer for both her elevated status and for Agnes' beating. She also blamed the girl for her own failure to win the interest of Lord Raoul as a possible wife, which rankled most of all.

Lady Bertha kept mostly to her chamber or worked in quiet corners at her embroidery. She spoke graciously when addressed and in general behaved as one expected from a well-born lady. However, Arnhilda had seen her on occasion slipping out to the cow byre to meet with Gwenddyd. Lady Bertha was often similarly occupied in the stable loft with one of the knights. Judith wondered where the older woman found the energy for such activity. She also wondered if Lord Raoul knew and what he would do if Lady Bertha were indiscreet. Then, remembering Agnes' punishment for offense against propriety in Hawk's household, she decided it would be better never to know.

‡

On a particularly fine summer's eve, as she sat quietly upon her own stool by the fire, Judith became aware of someone standing over her. Her eyes lifted to behold Aubrey, gittern in hand, gaze intent upon her face.

"May I sit at your feet and entertain you with a song, my lady?" he asked. His dark eyes sparkled with admiration and something deeper, which disturbed her. His smile was charming, though, and his lifted brows begged an answer.

"That would be pleasant for us all," Judith replied, conscious of the wider audience in the hall. She bent once more over her embroidery, needle flashing in the light from the fire.

Aubrey sang of a lovely princess locked away in a tower and of a fierce dragon, which guarded the maiden. While his lips told of a handsome prince who proposed to rescue the royal maiden from her predicament, his eyes promised a similar devotion. Judith, however, refused to meet his stare. She pretended total absorption in her needlework, for while she did not fear the jongleur, neither did she trust him. And there were those still who, while they no longer completely believed the tale Agnes had told weeks before, were not wholly convinced of her innocence, either.

Then too, twice that spring Aubrey had attempted to have speech with her when none were about to see or hear, as Arnhilda had warned her men would do with a girl when their intent was not virtuous. Both times Conan had stepped between Judith and Aubrey, silent but menacing. The young jongleur had moved regretfully away, but it had made Judith wary. It appeared to her that now she no longer felt a desire for his companionship, he could not cease wishing for hers. Arnhilda had been right, it seemed, when she spoke of the fickleness of men. Offer a thing freely and a man would push it away, bored. But the very same object, firmly denied, became a prize of the greatest desirability. She found it more irritating that anything else that this should be so.

"What is it which claims your attention to the exclusion of all else?" asked Lord Raoul, who had been watching the scene from a few paces away.

Judith looked up sharply, startled. Seeing his curiosity, her eyes warmed, and she smiled. "New bedcurtains, my lord."

Hawk came forward. He reached out and picked up a corner of

the linen to better regard her design. "This is quite good," he said, impressed. "I had no idea you possessed such skill. It puts me in mind of the work done by Lady Matilda." He scanned the overall picture she had sketched in charcoal, then looked back at her intently. "What is the part you are working on? I seem to recognize that."

"'Tis the old oak by the Roman road," she murmured, lowering her lashes shyly. "It is one of my favorite places."

"Ahhhhh," he sighed, letting go the fabric. "There should be a mounted knight on the ground before the tree, *demoiselle*, and a lady on that branch, *hein*?" He pointed. "Her gown should be gray. See to it."

Small prickles raised the hair at her nape and her breath was unaccountably short. "As you will, my lord."

"Oh, always," he agreed sardonically as he moved away to where a group of knights were dicing.

Aubrey stared after him a moment, then looked back at Judith. "What meant he by that?"

"Why, nothing. Merely an improvement upon my design," Judith answered innocently enough, ignoring her rioting pulse. "What should it mean?" She blushed.

The jongleur smiled crookedly. "Naught. As my lord says, you work well. When will it be finished?"

"Sometime in the fall, I suppose." Judith began picking out the threads on one part of a wide branch, leaving just enough room for a lady. He waited, but seeing that she meant to say no more, Aubrey moved away to sit staring at her from across the hall. Soon, when he realized that Conan was watching him with a narrow interest, the jongleur took up his gittern, looked away, and strummed a tune.

Shortly thereafter, both Conan and Judith were summoned to the lord's side as he sat in this chair. Hawk's brother, Sir Eustace, was there also, as was a knight who was his friend.

A manservant placed Judith's stool before the lord. She thanked him, but gazed up at Raoul inquiringly. "My lord?"

"If you would be so kind, Lady Judith, tell us of the wooden tower beside the river."

She sat, placed her embroidery basket on the floor beside her, and smoothed the skirt of a new dark green gown, Hawk's bounty. "It is called Danesford Tower, my lord. T'was first built in the time of my mother's grandsire, Wolfhere, to warn of Viking raids. I believe it has been rebuilt several times since then."

Hawk looked thoughtful. He leaned forward upon his right elbow in her direction. "One may assume they named the place for more than simply a vague fear?"

"Aye. The Norsemen had in the past a certain preference for sailing up the river and coming ashore at that point. They'd creep through the marshes and attack the village and hall. Even my father, God requite him, was used to keep it manned the year round."

"I'd not have thought even loot-hungry Norseman would bother to sail clear around the kingdom to come at it from the west," remarked Sir Eustace disdainfully. "I don't believe it; the place is worthless."

Hawk's eyes chilled. "There are redheads enough in the village to give credence to Lady Judith's words," he replied. "To say nothing of the stories I've heard from Gundrun, who is nigh a hundred years old and remembers the last few raids from his youth. T'was his own father who was head of the fishing vill before him and was slain in the last raid, if I remember the tale correctly."

"You believe the word of a Saxon swine?" scoffed Eustace.

"I'm willing to accept the warning of a man who cares whether or not his family is chopped into blood eagles before his eyes," stated Raoul coldly. "In any case, why would he lie?"

"Why not? We're Normans, you and I, for all you may be lord at last. Is it likely a Saxon will tell the truth to us about anything?" Eustace asked, brown eyes mocking.

Raoul grunted. "Nevertheless, I have seen the land about Danesford, and were I a Viking, I'd choose that area above all others to tie up my vessel for a raid." He turned his eyes upon Judith. "How many men did your father keep there?"

"A dozen, usually, in shifts. They took their supplies with them, though I'd often thought the area north of the marshes fertile enough for farming," she answered.

"Yes, I thought the same myself. There may even have been farming done there at one time, for the sides of the hills show only new growth. Shouldn't be too hard to clear. Yes." He was silent for a moment, his brow furrowed in thought. "Eustace, I've made up my mind. I want you to take a few men and fortify Danesford Tower."

"What?!" exclaimed the lord's brother, his face full of vexation and incredulity. "I'll be thrice damned if I will!"

"You'll be damned if you don't," returned Hawk amiably, his eyes twinkling.

"Send someone else! I have no intention of mouldering away in some damned wooden tower by the water's edge!"

Raoul grinned. "I suspect you'll find plenty to keep you occupied. And it really is necessary, brother. Like you, I've no real expectation of waking to find Vikings in the courtyard, not after the debacle at York! Still, it's an approach that leaves us vulnerable here, and in case you'd forgot, there are men enough left who fled Hastings would like to burn a Norman's keep down about his ears. And not a few of our own, to whom King William saw fit to grant no lands in England. Unless, of course," he added cunningly, "you are afraid?"

"Afraid!" roared Eustace.

"No, I thought it could not be so. Let us consider the matter settled, then. Now, 'tis too late in the year to do more than clear the land and plow under the grasses, but we've serfs enough to do the job. Oakwood will keep you supplied, naturally, and some of the serfs will stay on to work the land in the spring. Also, you'll be in need of a cook and maidservants." He looked at Judith pointedly. "You will choose the folk he needs, Lady Judith, an it please you."

She nodded. "Of course, my lord. Cynefred's chief assistant, Alfred, will manage Danesford's kitchen best. Ossa, the smith's son, and Svein the groom should go as well, and three or four serving wenches. There should be a double handful of the new folk to go and tend the land.

"As I recall, the Tower is furnished with tables and the like, but the bedding will be rotten by now," she added.

"Very well." He thanked her with his eyes. "We'll say twenty serfs to clear the land, and ten to stay, to work it, with their women and children. How say you brother?"

"It sounds a bore," replied Eustace succinctly. "I'd rather stay here. Why not send Armand or one of the others?"

"You refuse your own keep, then?" Hawk raised disbelieving brows.

Eustace's head snapped up. "You give me the land for my *own*?"

"If you will swear fealty to me for it, aye. Are you better pleased now?"

The younger man grinned. "Oh, aye." His eyes slid to Judith. "If I'm to have lands of my own, I'll need a wife, brother."

Muscles rippled an instant along Hawk's jaw, but he smiled pleasantly enough. "Well, time enough for that when you've cleared the land and the first harvest's in the threshing barn. Now, off with you, brother! You'll need to decide which of the knights you'll take, besides Evrard. Sir Tancred will spare you four men-at-arms. He and I have already discussed the matter, and he'll see to the details for you."

"Yes, of course!" said Eustace eagerly. "Shall I swear my oath now?"

"The morrow will be soon enough." Raoul watched, wordless, as his brother scurried to Sir Tancred's side. Then he sent a servant to fetch Arnhilda. Judith cocked her head, wondering.

When the maidservant was brought, Hawk turned to Judith once more. "This may be a trifle difficult, *demoiselle.* I beg you to know that I would not disturb you if t'were not of some import."

"What is it, my lord?"

He moved his eyes to his hands, resting on his thighs, and seemed to choose his words with some care. "My brother, Eustace, is often a bit rash. Being the youngest, he was somewhat spoiled by our father and mother. It, uh, it has come to my ears that he may have importuned you, Lady Judith."

"Oh, no!" she gasped. "Indeed, my lord, he has never said. . . not since first you came . . ."

"You misunderstand me," he interrupted quietly. "I speak not of the first meeting between you, which, I understand, you dealt with quite well. After that, knowing you are under my protection, Eustace is not foolish enough to say aught that could be repeated to his discomfort. Rather, it is his habit to plot and to cause the discomfort of someone else. I suspect that he has done this with you."

Judith stared down at the toes of her worn leather shoes, which peeped out from under her skirts. She said nothing.

"Come, my dear!" he teased, smiling a little. "Am I such an ogre that you think I'd turn on you for speaking the truth?"

"No, no, of course not, my lord. But . . ."

His eyes twinkled the more, "You think I'd turn on him?"

"Well . . ."

"I give you my parole, demoiselle. My scapegrace of a brother shall come to no harm," he swore. "However much he may deserve it," he added, half under his breath.

"All he does is look at me," Judith ventured.

"Ah? And where does he do this looking?"

She sighed. "Well, my lord, sometimes when I go into the meadows with Arnhilda and Conan to search out herbs, he will turn up there by chance, or if I go to the vill to treat the sick, I might happen to see him there."

"Almost as if he were waiting for you, I'll wager, or as if he'd sought you out," suggested the Hawk.

"Um, well, yes," she stammered nervously. "At times, it does rather feel like that. But all he ever does is smile and bid me good-day." She added in haste. "I suppose I am foolish to say that I do not like it, but he does make me uncomfortable, my lord. 'Tis a small thing, really."

He nodded in an understanding manner. "Have no fear, *demoiselle*. I know my brother of old, and this is his way. He enjoys teasing. He likes to hunt people and make them fear him. Rather like a naughty boy, in fact. Well, I beg you will forgive him, lady." His dark eyes sought Arnhilda's gray ones. "Is there aught in Sir Eustace's manner I've left out?"

"His lewd grin at my lady, for one thing!" snapped the maidservant, not at all intimidated.

Hawk coughed into his fist. "Yes, well . . ."

"Arnhilda!" cried Judith, mortified.

"Now, child, you've not enough experience in the ways of men to know the difference, but I have, and my lord knows quite well what I mean!"

"Sadly, yes, I do," Lord Raoul responded with a depreciating grin. "However, I am hopeful that now Sir Eustace is off to Danesford there will be no more such incidents. I had heard the stories, though. I wanted to be sure no insult had been offered that might require a more careful inquiry."

Arnhilda gave him a look that said Sir Eustace's ears pinned to the door of the stable might not be enough to soothe her sensibilities, but Judith was relieved. "Indeed, my lord, you are very kind. Please let it be forgotten. I assure you, I shall regard the matter as closed."

He smiled and took her hand, pleased that she gave it trustingly into his grasp. He had noticed in the past several weeks that she disliked being touched by men and avoided touching them herself, unless she was tending an ailment. "You are as kind as you are lovely, Lady Judith. On behalf of my brother, I thank you for your generosity."

Bemused, Judith watched as he kissed the tips of her fingers, and for once could find nothing to say.

Arnhilda sniffed, and Conan stared fixedly at the opposite wall.

CHAPTER 5

ore than once, as the summer deepened and young animals became confident enough to gambol away from their mothers' sides, Judith stumbled across lovers hidden in meadow grasses or under a likely bush. Each time, while Conan sent the idlers back to the field, village, or hall, Judith thought of her own reaction to Lord Raoul's kiss and then with shame to her fumblings alone in the dark. It was a sin she did not confess even to Brother Plegmund. Certainly, she could never tell Father Hubert, who spent his time in mediation at the church in the vill. Sometimes she wondered if Lord Raoul, who seemed to take no serving wenches to his bed, felt the same urgings as other men, and if he did, whether in his dark chamber of a night he found his hands wandering also. It was a novel idea, but she grew ashamed and pushed the thought away.

‡

The castle moat was completed by mid-summer, as were the deep cellars and massive drawbridge. The thick outer walls, over twice as wide as Judith was tall, took much longer, but grew steadily, day by day. The masons had no need to travel to find female companionship. They were now visited furtively and frequently by females of both the vill and the fishing village. Word had spread so quickly of their generosity that the women tended to find errands to run near the building of the castle. They were made more discreet, but no less enthusiastic, by Brother Plegmund's lectures and Father Hubert's sermons. Coins spoke.

The architects had devised a system by which water from an underground stream was brought to the surface and channeled into the castle moat and out again into the stream, making an island of the growing structure. Seen at a distance, it was less than impressive just now, but Judith discovered one afternoon its true size when she went out to inspect the cellars. It took her more time to walk the perimeter of the moat than it did to travel from the hall to the village.

"I had not realized t'was so grand an undertaking," she muttered to Conan. "This will be a very large place!"

"Yes, my lady."

"Why the moat?" she inquired, not liking the idea of all the damp walls she suspected it would cause.

"For defense, my lady."

"Hmmmmm," she returned, deep in thought. Yes, she could see the advantages. In event of attack, the serfs of the vill, as well as the folk of the castle, could be gathered inside the protective walls. Once assured that this was indeed the practice in Normandy, she gave the moat her unqualified approval. The Norman was not visibly gratified.

‡

Arnhilda, her mouth full of brass pins, bade Judith hold still for the final fitting of a gown fashioned out of a wondrous shade of blue, come, so Hawk had told them, all the way from the Levant.

"This is ridiculous!" the girl protested. "I've four new gowns already! That's two more than I've ever had at one time in my life! How many must I have until my lord feels I am adequately clothed to honor his rank?"

"Mphle grp," replied Arnhilda, twitching at a sleeve.

"What?"

The maidservant pulled the pins from between her lips and glared. "As many as he feels you need! Really, child! What ails you these days? I vow, you're as cross as a badger!"

"I don't know," sighed Judith, standing still as Arnhilda resumed her task. "I'm just... oh, restless, I suppose. I want to do something, yet I don't know what it is. That makes no sense at all, does it?" She sighed again.

Arnhilda smiled wisely but made no answer.

"Are you almost done?" Judith inquired.

"Almost." Arnhilda set three pins and leaned back on her heels. "Raise your arms." She eyed the set of the sleeves and nodded. "T'will do. You can take it off now."

Judith removed the gown carefully, mindful of her maid's work, and stretched. "It is very hot," she complained, pulling a crimson wool gown on over her head. She retrieved her girdle, also new, of fine silver, and fastened it. She then smoothed the long chain from which hung her shears and storage room keys. "Let us go to the cliffs which overlook the sea this afternoon," she suggested. "There is bound to be a breeze off the water, don't you think?"

"More than likely, but you did promise Cynefred you'd show him how to mix the herbs for that stew my lord liked so much a week past," returned the older woman uncompromisingly.

Judith frowned. "So I did." She grimaced. "There's never enough time to do the things that give me pleasure."

Arnhilda's scraggly eyebrows climbed. "Are you a heedless child who'd put pleasure before duty?"

"No," answered the girl. "No, of course not." She moved to the window and looked out over the field behind the hall. The squires were hard at work there, one by one charging a dummy hung from a tree. The mannequin was made of straw, tightly bound, and some fool had topped it with a battered Viking helmet dug up Heaven knew where. Judith's chores seemed to stretch in a never-ending line before her, and no other could do them quite so well as she. The thought of standing at the cliff top with the wind in her hair was alluring but unrealistic. There was Cynefred to instruct, spices to be doled out for the next meal, the sewing of the maidservants to check, and this evening she must sit with Brother Plegmund for a review of a Latin scroll he'd loaned her.

"Tell you what we might do," said Arnhilda from behind her. "After you've spent an hour with the cook, we could work for a while on those bedcurtains of yours. And while we work, you could tell me again of that story about the dragon and the priest, the one you made up when you were just a little bit of a thing. It's always been my favorite."

Dear Heaven! Judith thought in some surprise and guilt, *how she works to keep me from melancholy*! She smiled at the woman. "Yes, I'd like that," she said. "But only for a while. I've yet to visit Eric, the carpenter. I'm sure the cut foot is mending properly, but he's yet to walk on it, and I'd best see that he doesn't strain it overmuch."

Arnhilda smiled approval. Her little girl was growing up. "Aye, 'tis a goodly thought. Men being what they are, it's never wise to leave too much to their clumsy hands. 'Tis a good thing they've us to look after 'em."

‡

At last it was time for the harvest, which came early this year. On a mid-September evening, Judith approached Raoul as he sat watching the jongleur perform his antics. Aubrey was attempting, with limited success, to balance a distaff on the tip of his nose. Wagers were placed on his chances of failure, and Judith felt it a suitable moment to broach a private matter with the lord while attention was focused elsewhere.

"My lord," she began diffidently, as Conan placed her stool near the Hawk's chair.

"No," he said quickly.

"But you haven't even heard . . ."

"If it is about the serfs again, I don't *want* to hear!"

Judith giggled at his expression of mock alarm. Indeed, she had often interceded for the folk, much to their lord's exasperation. Sitting at his gesture, she arranged her skirts about her. "Nay, 'tis of myself I would speak," she assured him.

"Oho!" he said lightly, returning her smile. "Some weighty matter, I trust?"

"'Tis of some import," she agreed. "You will recall that when I last spoke of bridals, you bade me wait upon the harvest. Well, my lord the grain is in the threshing barns and . . ."

"Aye, so it is," he cut in hurriedly. "Quite a relief it is, too! I'd been afraid some of the new fields might do badly, being planted later than the others, but they did right well. And once or twice I'd feared an unseasonable rain might dampen more than moods!"

Judith smiled reluctantly. "You change the subject, my lord."

"Alas, Lady Judith, I only attempted what is clearly an impossible feat. Very well, since you are determined to do so, let us discuss bridals. You had, of course, your own in mind?"

She nodded. "I am of age, Lord Hawk."

"So," he said. "I see. And have you determined upon a choice for this honor? One of my knights, perhaps?"

His eyes were on her face, staring with intensity. Judith knew that this was a question of considerable importance since her future lay in the balance. The idea of a husband was quite natural, but she'd considered it in the abstract only. While there were some men she clearly did not want to wed, she had no real favorite. He was waiting for an answer. "Well, no, my lord, I'd not thought. . ."

"Obviously," he murmured. He seemed to be more relaxed, and the corner of his mouth twitched, telling the knowledgeable that he was amused. "Have you no preference, then? Is there not one among so many knights who takes a maiden's fancy?" He cast a sparkling glance about the hall. "I'd not thought them such a poor lot that there is nothing to choose from amongst them."

"You mean. . . you mean I am allowed to *choose*?" she asked disbelieving.

"Why not?" responded Hawk gaily. "We shall leave out Sir Tancred and Sir Robert, since both are already wed and have no wish to anger their ladies, to say nothing of the Church, but I believe there is still a likely field." His eyes brimmed with merriment at her confusion. "Come, *demoiselle*, have you no partiality for one over the others?"

She cleared her throat. "Well." She fell silent. It had never occurred to her that she would be the one to make the choice of a husband. Always, in her experience, fathers, older brothers, or uncles determined their women's fate. Now, faced with a decision of this magnitude, she did not know what to say.

Suddenly she stiffened. "Not Sir Eustace!" Judith begged in an agitated whisper. "Please, my lord, I crave pardon if I have offended. . ." she broke off, distressed. Hopefully, he would not be angered. It was, after all, the rest of her life they were deciding.

But Hawk smiled. Oddly, he seemed to be even more relieved than before. "You have not angered me, *demoiselle*. Were I a maid, I too would hesitate at such a match. But what is to be done? Here you are, hot to be wed, and not one name occurs to you! Since you are so reluctant to settle upon a knight as a prospective bridegroom, will you agree to abide by my choice?"

Judith regarded his laughing eyes with suspicion. "Not Sir Eustace?"

"No," he agreed. "We will leave my unfortunate brother out of the reckoning."

"Very well, my lord. You have my parole."

Raoul chuckled. "I wonder if you will reproach me for this later, *demoiselle*?" he murmured as he rose to his feet. A gesture brought a servant running. Hawk whispered instructions and the man raced from the hall.

The Lord of Oakwood stared after the servant for a long moment, then glanced at Judith. He extended his right hand, and after a moment she placed her hand on his. The strong fingers closed hard over her own, and he pulled her to her feet. The stool fell over backwards, but she scarcely noticed. Her heart began to thump painfully against her ribs. Her throat was dry. Somehow, until this moment, she had not considered how serious a decision was to be made or how final it would be. Feverishly her eyes searched out the faces of the knights. Armand had a big nose, Bertram had sad eyes, and Andre had red hair and freckles. Which would Hawk choose? Surely not Maurice, who drank too much, nor Henri, who was growing alarmingly plump despite daily exercise! Then, because she was afraid and hated giving in to fear, she raised her chin, squared her shoulders, and smiled.

The Norman lord signaled to Conan, who nodded to one of the men-at-arms on guard near the door. This worthy thumped the butt of his spear loudly on the floor. Folk turned, surprised and curious when they saw that Hawk's posture indicated an announcement of some import. After a few moments, the hall grew silent, except for the cracking of the fire and the dogs scrabbling in the rushes.

"My friends," began Raoul gravely. "I am about to become profound and I crave your indulgence. We have had a good harvest and may look forward to a comfortable winter, a great relief to us all." He glanced about and motioned to several wenches who had appeared, on cue from Conan, from the kitchen, with trays of tankards and drinking horns. "A cup for everyone," he instructed. There was some bustle while this was provided, then expectant silence once more.

Raoul raised his own goblet. "Traditionally, here in England as well as in our native Normandy, the harvest has been at time for feasting and rejoicing. Let us all, then, feast and rejoice. To the harvest!"

He drank and they all drank with him. He grinned. "Into each life comes change in one form or another. For me this is especially true. In Normandy, I was a younger son of no importance, until change came in the form of the good Duke William, who knighted me and took me into his own household. Then there were battles and new friends, and at last, the voyage and the great battle at Hastings, where it pleased God to grant us victory. William became our King, and I became Baron of Oakwood. And now, it seems God's will to make yet another change in my life. I make known to you all the Lady Judith of Oakwood . . . to whom I am this day betrothed."

There was a moment of breathless silence, followed by cheers and cries of congratulations. Under the cover of the noise, Raoul grinned boyishly and squeezed Judith's hand. "Feel like putting a knife between my ribs, *demoiselle*?"

"I don't know how I feel!" she whispered back, a trifle dazed. "Did I just imagine that?"

He laughed. "I am astonished you never suspected my intentions, considering the trouble I went to in hinting at the matter!"

"You mean, when you said that about the bedcurtains I embroidered?" she asked hesitantly, not wanting to seem too forward by mentioning the kiss.

"That and my setting Conan over you as guard. I thought surely you must know from the first." He tugged at a long, golden braid. "Arnhilda knew."

"Arnhilda knows everything," replied Judith.

‡

Later, when there were fewer listeners, Judith had a moment with Raoul by the fire. "I don't understand," she murmured. "Why me instead of Lady Agnes?"

"Did you honestly think I'd take a whore like Lady Agnes to my bed?" he countered, taking her hand.

"How did you know?" she demanded, surprised. "Is it true, then, that a man may know if a maid be virtuous merely by the look of her?"

"Nay," he replied, laughing and shaking his head at her innocence. "Oh, little girl, I wonder if you are ready for the marriage bed after all!"

Judith blushed hotly. She was amazed at his attitude. Now that she was his betrothed, all reserve vanished. Why, he behaved as if they were friends of long standing! It was a heady thought. Could there *be* friendship in marriage?

"I had heard of you all from Aubrey," he informed her. "And that was long before I left Normandy. It was in my mind even then to ask Duke William for lordship over these lands could I but distinguish myself in combat. And it was also in my mind to have you to wife."

"What? Merely because a jongleur warranted me virtuous? That could have been untrue."

He noticed that although he had given her the opportunity, she had not removed her hand from his. Good. "Ah, lady," he said softly. "I think I know the truth when I hear it. The jongleur spoke of a tiny, golden girl with enormous blue eyes and the courage of a lioness. I knew then I meant to have you, virtuous or not. Besides, you are Cerdic's only living blood relative. This makes everything simpler; I am sure you will agree. No one could dispute the right of our children to the land."

She digested this while folk moved around them, still exclaiming and bestowing slaps on the back or touches on the back of the hand. The mention of children brought a deeper flush to her cheek, and then she did remove her hand from his. But he only smiled knowingly at her.

From across the room, Judith felt the fury of Lady Bertha, who came forward with one of the other women to offer congratulations. A smile as treacherous as a raptor's heart lifted Lady Bertha's lips in a parody of happiness. "So, you have won this round," she murmured as she touched her cheek to Judith's. "Enjoy it while you can." She moved away and moments later climbed the stair for the chamber she shared with Agnes. Judith stared after her soberly but was forced to give her attention to others, all anxious to share in the excitement of the moment and to impress the lord's intended bride.

At one point during the merriment, Judith looked up and found the jongleur staring fiercely into her eyes. To her surprise, he gave a bitter laugh, raised his tankard to her in a silent, private toast, and drained it to the dregs. He looked away, pulled a flute from his belt, and gave the folk a merry air for dancing.

Dimly she heard Raoul set the date for the wedding, but later she could not remember it. Father Hubert said something about reading the banns. She felt only shock. Never in her wildest imaginings had she thought to match with the Hawk! She stole a glance at him. He stood beside her, virile and confident, chatting easily with the knights and ladies. She wondered how it would be as his lady wife. Then she recalled that kiss in the fallow, and how she had felt while his lips touched hers and their bodies had come close together, and she began to smile.

‡

Lady Edith, their late difficulty forgotten, accompanied Lady Judith to her chamber that night. It would not do for the lord's promised bride to wander about unattended.

"I am so happy for you, Lady Judith," she said shyly. "It is no small thing to be wife to the Hawk. His name is well known in Normandy and France as a fearless fighter."

She lowered her voice deliberately as they climbed the stair, glancing about to be sure none could overhear. "They say he had a mistress once from some pagan tribe in the Holy Land. A heathen! And that he killed her when he found her with another man!" She shivered deliciously.

"Who says so?" inquired Judith, wide-eyed. They stopped at her chamber, where Arnhilda opened the door and brought stools for them to sit upon. She offered refreshment, but Lady Edith declined.

"Well, Sir Eustace, who is his own brother, and my lord, Sir Tancred, have both spoken of it in my hearing," she said, as if that were proof enough. She ignored Arnhilda's presence; servants were of no account.

"Hmmm." Judith was all too aware of the importance of the moment, which would likely set the tone of her relationship with this woman for life. She could not call Sir Tancred or even Sir Eustace a liar. Nor could she show even the tiniest doubt of her betrothed's character. This must be handled delicately. "Did they say they'd actually seen this act with their own eyes?" she asked a moment later.

"Well, no, lady, they did not," Lady Edith replied. It came to her suddenly, too late, that she might have said something to upset the girl. Ah, well. T'was too late now for anything but the truth. "They repeated a tale they'd heard from others, they said."

"Then I don't believe it," remarked Judith, unmoved. "Oh, I'll allow 'tis possible that he had such a woman but not that he killed her. Sir Tancred must have heard it from one who did not know all the facts and made up what he guessed from rumors. Sir Tancred would not know the difference. You know how men are when they're in their cups."

"Yes, that's truth," Lady Edith agreed. "But whyfore do you doubt that the Hawk would have killed her?"

"He's not that sort of man. He might," Judith admitted, "give her to another if he tire of her or toss her to his men if she took a lover, but he would not care enough to kill. Now, if she'd stolen from him . . ."

"I know what you mean!" agreed Lady Edith with a pleasant shudder at imaginary violence. "He can be so cold and stern! Are you not afraid of him? I vow, I am!"

Arnhilda, bored but discreet, handed her mistress a horn of warm chamomile and rosemary tea with honey, then excused herself from the chamber with an amused smile for Lady Edith's foolishness.

"Afraid?" Judith giggled suddenly. "Yes. Perhaps a little. Mostly not, though. He is stern because his responsibilities are so very great, you see. But cold?" She laughed merrily. "Oh, how can you say so, lady? How could he be cold when his eyes are so full of laughter?"

"Eyes? Laughter?" echoed Lady Edith blankly.

Judith stared at her. "But surely you must have remarked it, since you have known him longer! Why, it is always so when he is amused!"

Lady Edith stared back, brown eyes round with wonder. "I have never seen him so. Nor," she added with the air of an expert, "have any of the other women."

"But he does it all the time!"

"Well, never mind," said Lady Edith hastily. "I am sure you must be correct, and 'tis just I've never noticed. I only hope he is kind to you, my dear."

"He already is, *very* kind! He might have given me to anyone in marriage, you know. He need not have wed me himself, and I am truly grateful. I do not *think* he will beat me," she added hopefully.

"Perhaps not," Lady Edith agreed, doubt patent in her voice. Clearly, she stood in considerable awe of Lord Raoul. There was a small pause, then she asked, "You are not bothered greatly by marriage with a Norman, Lady Judith? You do not hate us for the death of your father and the conquest of your land?"

Judith smiled and touched Lady Edith's hand briefly. "In regard to my father's death, grateful, more like," she answered ruefully. "He wanted sons, you see, and despised me for being female. There was only hatred between us. Oh dear! Now I've shocked you!" Judith raised an eyebrow at Lady Edith's gasp. "Would you have preferred me to say his death caused me grief?"

It was Lady Edith's turn to laugh. "God's Faith, lady. I am indeed surprised, for 'tis seldom one hears the truth in such matters. I am more relieved than shocked, however, for honesty is refreshing. My own father was worse than any demon from Hell, although I was never allowed to say so, and have not, even to Sir Tancred. My father used to beat me, sometimes 'til I was nigh senseless, and he broke my arm once. He locked my mother in the donjon for a year for open disobedience to his will in the matter of saving the life of a serf's child," she gasped out in a rush. "Merciful Mother! I never thought to tell that to another living soul!"

Judith nodded. "I know exactly how you feel. "Tis almost as if we feared to complain of undeserved harsh treatment because we thought t'was our own fault."

"Yes, that is it exactly!" cried Lady Edith. "But I swear to you, lady, I tried and *tried* to behave as my father wished, only it seemed to me that the harder I tried, the more I was punished!"

"You know," commented Judith thoughtfully, "I think t'was worse for us because we were girlchildren, and folk think we are not as human, being female and of little import. If we are abused and in misery, why, it is our lot, and who cares? But I do not believe my lord will be like that," she added, almost sure of her words. "After all, before I gave the matter into his hands, he was willing to let me choose a husband for *myself*!"

Lady Edith gasped. "No! You cannot be serious! I've never heard of such a thing!"

"I swear by the Trinity!" Judith declared, crossing herself against harm. "Can you imagine? T'was only when I could not think of anyone with whom I'd wish to be wed that he said he'd have me himself. He is the kindest man I've ever known."

"Well!" Lady Edith mulled that over for a few moments. "I don't know I've ever heard the like." She smiled shyly. "You know, Sir Tancred is most gentle with me, too, and kind always. I was so happy when his father and mine decided we should be wed, even though he was a younger son and had no prospects at all. T'was like this: all the other men I'd known were rough and harsh, with loud voices and careless ways. But Sir Tancred had ever a smile and a soft word for me, even though I am not at all pretty and had only a small dowry."

"Lady, you *are* pretty!" exclaimed Judith indignantly. She though Lady Edith had the sweetest face she had ever set eyes upon. "You are most fair. When first I saw you, my thought was that I wished I looked like you, so dark, lovely and merry."

"Why, Lady Judith!" she said softly, much touched. "How sweet of you!"

"Nay, 'tis only the truth, my dear. I always feel. . . well, *pale* when you are by," Judith confessed, hanging her head a little.

Lady Edith laughed. "And to think I've always envied you your golden locks and those ravishing blue eyes!"

They smiled at one another in perfect harmony.

"Have you been long wed, Lady Edith?"

The other girl flushed becomingly. "Nay, 'tis only since just before he sailed to England. We had so little time together, I suppose, that I still feel strange when I realize I am a woman grown and married. It was lonely, when he was gone, and I in his father's tower. I had no place there," she explained, at Judith's questioning look. "There was nothing to do and no one who cared. I might as well have been a spirit, rather than a lady of that household. And I was afraid, always, that Sir Tancred might be slain. Then what would have become of me?

"I have only been in this country since the start of the year, but already it is better than back in Normandy." She sighed.

"Well, now we are at peace," Judith comforted. "Sir Tancred will be so often under foot there are bound to be babies soon, and then, no doubt, you'll wish him off somewhere just to give you a few moments of quiet!"

They laughed and chattered, as girls will, of men and babies, and which of the new gowns Judith should choose for her marriage day. T'was only when Arnhilda came to ready Judith for bed that they realized how long they'd sat together.

‡

Lady Edith raced for her own chamber, afraid of Sir Tancred's displeasure at her long absence. "Husband!" she gasped as she pulled back the curtain and entered their room. "Forgive me! I have just this instant left Lady Judith."

The bailiff looked into his wife's wide eyes and smiled. "Calm yourself, my lady. All is well."

"You are not angry with me?" she asked as she knelt to help him detach his gaiters.

"Not at all, my lady. Ah, that feels so much better!" He stood and removed his clothing, motioning for her to do the same. "In fact, I must admit that your good sense is a pleasant surprise. I am pleased, *most* pleased."

Lady Edith set her girdle of silver upon the clothing chest and pulled off her clothes, folding them carefully. "What pleases you so, my lord?" She turned to fold his clothing as well.

"Ah, you needn't try to fool me, my lady; not after I've caught you out! Playing the innocent!" he chuckled as he climbed into bed and pulled the coverlet up to his chin. "Do not pretend you've no idea how important it is to be upon intimate terms with the lady of the hall! Hah! And to think I once nearly agreed to wed my cousin Maria instead of you! Why, the day I took you to wife was clearly the most fortunate day of my life! 'Why am I pleased?' indeed!"

Lady Edith joined him in bed, snuggling down comfortably into his arms, and wisely chose not to contradict her husband. She thanked the Holy Virgin for her good fortune at his mistake, for although she had known etiquette dictated she accompany Lady Judith from the hall, she had not thought at all of the political benefits to her husband! She would not, she vowed, forget in the future.

‡

The marriage of the most ranking lord in the district was an important affair. Sir Eustace rode in from Danesford. If he were angry, which he was, it didn't show. And Sir Robert and Lady Blanche rode in from Deerfield. Lord Edward, who had the keep at Northwatch, some miles to the north of Danesford, came with both his lady and his mistress, which made sleeping arrangements a bit awkward until it proved the girl was willing to condescend to a straw pallet with the sewing-maids. Tents were everywhere.

Long tables were set up in the meadow near the graveyard, so that all the folk might fill their bellies at the lord's expense, and the crowd converged upon the food like ravening wolves. Aubrey juggled, tumbled, played upon flute and gittern, and told fantastic tales to amuse the people, while small children darted hither and yon, aping the jongleur or playing at tag among the trees close by. Everyone wore their best clothing, adding color and sparkle to the scene. Judith had many compliments upon her gown of rich blue velvet trimmed with miniver.

Music and chattering voices made a pleasant background as Judith and Raoul walked apart from the others some hours after the celebration had begun. She nibbled at a honeycake, and he the leg of a fowl as they strolled casually along the stream, their soft leather shoes causing the leaves to rustle as they passed. She watched him from the corner of her eye, liking the way the sunlight glinted in his brown hair. "Why did you choose to wed me?" she asked in a calm, curious voice.

He looked over at her in surprise, and his lips twitched. "So, you do not like pretty lies or reassurances about the importance of your lineage?"

"Only the truth, my lord. You already held the land, and my father was dead, with no sons left behind to challenge lordship. You did not need me to secure your grasp. In truth, you are lord of Oakwood, beyond any doubt or denying. And there are pretty maidens would be only too glad of the position as your lady, some of them rich. So, since it was not needful, why did you choose *me* for your bride?"

Raoul tossed the drumstick over his shoulder and took her hand. His eyes were dark with emotion. "If it is the truth you want, my lady, then that is what you shall have. I am a strong man and a good warrior, little girl. I would be more. It is my ambition to be one of the most powerful men in England. And one of the richest.

"All of my life I've been poor, until now. I'd even less than you did under your father's rule." He grimaced, letting go of her hand, and shrugged. Raoul held his hands out from his sides, as if his arms could encompass all of his new lands. "My father's barony is so small it could sit in a corner of the Oakwood lands and go unnoticed. I will not live so again, nor will any son or daughter of mine. Our younger sons will have an inheritance! None of them will be made to feel resented, like an encumbrance the family can ill afford." He dropped his hands.

"I knew, once I'd determined upon my course, that I'd need a strong woman at my side, one folk would respect and obey when I am away on knight's service to the King. I could have wed the daughter of a count when it was known I'd be lord here. She would have brought me Norman lands and a measure of wealth, but by then I'd set my mind on you. I knew if you'd the courage and strength to fight for your survival against your father and that heartless harlot he'd wed; you'd be strong enough to give me what I want." He looked into her eyes. "Also, Arnhilda says you're likely to be a good breeder." He added with an impudent grin, "Wide hips."

The twinkle in her eyes matched with his own, but she nodded solemnly. "You want sons, then?"

"Many," he answered. "And daughters. Wise marriages make strong allies." He sobered and said straightly, "I expect loyalty and chastity from my wife, Lady Judith."

Her chin went up. "And I, my lord, expect loyalty and kindness from you. Will you beat me?"

Raoul saw, then, that her hands were clenched in fear. She was serious, not teasing. Sweet Christ! How bad had it been for her that the jongleur had not told him? He reached out and touched her hand lightly. "Shall we make a bargain, my lady? I vow never to beat you, and you swear always to be my true and faithful wife. Agreed?"

"And. . . and will you also swear that you will take no other woman to your bed?" she asked in a low voice, greatly daring.

The Hawk raised his eyebrows.

She said nothing, only looked up seriously into his eyes.

Finally, he sighed. "This is of some import to you, then?"

Judith nodded unhappily. "My father was one who had other women, almost all the time. I have given this much thought. Just as my honor is yours, I believe that your honor is mine. Is this not so? How could I serve you with loyalty an I knew you held my honor cheap?"

"You ask a great deal, my lady!" declared Raoul angrily, letting go her hand again. "It is a woman's place to do as her lord bids her and to accept graciously what he cares to give!"

"So I have often heard," Judith acknowledged in a musing tone. "'Tis strange that always when I heard it, t'was a man's voice rang in my ears."

His innate sense of justice forced a rueful smile to his lips in spite of himself. "There's some truth in that, I suppose. Yet all nobles have their little loves. It is an accepted thing. No one thinks that there's aught to wonder at in it. In fact, it might cause talk if there were not a flock of bastards attached to the house of a great lord."

"Perhaps," Judith said thoughtfully, undeterred. "Yet I've heard it said that King William has none other than his lady wife and cares not what men may say. I have never seen the King, of course," she added diffidently. "And yet, from the tales folk tell, I believe that you are as great a man as he."

Raoul tweaked one of her braids. It was his favorite gesture. "You are entirely too clever, little girl. You speak of honor and minister to my vanity, and your eyes are as innocent as those of a newborn babe! Very well, then. Since it means that much to you, we are agreed." He gave an unaccustomed shout of laughter. "Hell's Fires! Folk will think I've take a vow of abstinence!"

"Oh, surely not, my lord," returned Judith demurely, placing her hand on his proffered arm as he led her back toward the crowd. "Not when I appear year after year with my belly swollen with all those sons and daughters you mentioned!"

He laughed so loudly that folk turned to stare. "I vow, my lady," he said more quietly, "if you prove as lively in lovemaking as in conversation, those sons and daughters will be an even greater pleasure to get than I'd planned on!" He laughed even harder at her flushed cheeks.

‡

The festivities lasted through the night, with people snoring on the grass, overpowered by too much ale, or equally overcome by amorousness. Peasant couples moved, with a modicum of discretion, to spots under tables or bushes to meet needs less simple. (Brother Plegmund tsked and shook his head; Father Hubert ignored these activities with magnificent unconcern.)

With the coming of darkness, however, the women of the hall led Judith indoors to the lord's chamber. There were flowers strewn amongst the rushes, and the new bedcurtains she'd embroidered so diligently had been hung about the great bed of carved oak but pulled back so that the red velvet coverlet might be admired.

She was bathed in an oaken tub by the married ladies and Arnhilda, embarrassed at so many hands scrubbing at her skin. And their voices too, caused her already blushing cheeks to burn.

"Raise up to meet him in the first stroke, dear," stated lady Blanche of Deerfield loudly. "Best to have it over with quickly the first time."

Lewd laughter greeted this sally, and more advice of the same nature followed. Wine goblets were passed, jokes told, and jovial arguments entered into with gusto.

"Oh, no!" exclaimed Lady Maria of Northwatch, amazed. "Is it truly possible to do it standing up on a log in midstream?!" Shrieks of laughter followed.

"For three hours without stopping? Fah, 'tis not possible unless he was under five and twenty years of age at the time."

"Now, you cup them gently, Lady Judith. . ."

". . .and now they have eleven children and no inclination to be alone together, even in the same hall with witnesses!"

Lady Bertha, flushed with wine, ran her hand lightly over her stepdaughter's soapy breasts, enjoying Judith's shudder of revulsion. "Well, Hawk will have a soft place to rest his head," she remarked, bringing giggles from the others.

"If he *gets* any rest!" added Lady Blanche. "If I were a man, I'd keep her at it until she fainted dead away! See how soft her skin is!"

Two of the women touched her skin tentatively at shoulder and breast, and Arnhilda chuckled as she assisted the girl from her bath. "Aye, that's the way of it! Wear him out, my lady, so he knows who rules the bedchamber! Give no quarter."

The women howled with laughter, wiping at watering eyes and holding their sides. They called out ribald suggestions that would have shocked the men below stairs.

Judith said nothing. Most of her was frightened of the ordeal to come, but a part of her, deep inside, trembled with a fierce excitement, controlled but reinforced by the talk of the women and their deliberate, teasing touches. She let them dry her, shivering when Lady Maria intentionally brushed her hand down across the girl's soft belly and on to the apex of her thighs in a lingering caress. Everyone laughed as Blanche advised, "Don't be so skittish, Lady Judith! You'll be used to such before dawn!"

"Even there her hair is gold!" exclaimed Lady Edith boldly. "What a pretty nest for a little bird!"

"'Tis no 'little bird,' child," corrected Lady Blanche, rolling her eyes. "I assisted with his bath once in Normandy. God's Blood, if he were any bigger, one might well mistake him for a bull!"

"It's not how big they are that counts," Lady Bertha put in with a lascivious grin. "It's how well they move determines if you'll be smiling come the morn!"

Edwina aided Arnhilda to dry her body with a large, soft piece of linen. The women pressed her to drink from a goblet of spiced wine laced with herbs known for centuries to be aphrodisiacs, the goblet held by a third goggle-eyed serving wench.

She lay naked upon the sheet as they bade her, not protesting when they refused to allow her to pull the coverlet higher than her waist, for the Norman customs had been explained to her days before by Lady Edith. She felt as if every separate hair on her body stood on end. Her mouth was dry.

The door to the lord's chamber burst open, and suddenly the room was filled with drunken knights and squires, openly ogling Judith's lightly covered hips and bare breasts. There were more crude jokes and laughter, but at last, at Lord Raoul's order and with Conan's strong shoulder, all quitted the chamber, including the man-at-arms.

Raoul barred the door. He smiled at her. With slow deliberation and an air of the commonplace, he removed his clothing.

It was no new thing for Judith, the sight of a man's body. As all well brought up maidens, she had often assisted at the bath to welcome guests to Oakwood Hall. But this was no polite ceremony, over with only a few bawdy jokes and a wink or two. She raised her chin and smiled.

Unconscious of the effect of his nudity, Raoul folded his garments and placed them atop his chest at the foot of the bed. Then he turned and saw her eyes. He'd forgotten how inexperienced she was. She was so brave, lying there without a sound and forcing herself to be calm.

"Afraid?" he asked casually.

"No, my lord," she lied.

He sat beside her, lightly caressing her cheek. "There is no shame in fear," he told her, touched. "It is a powerful emotion which smites equally the strongest knight and most timid of field mice. I have been afraid many times, little girl. Do you think I am weakened because of it?"

She shook her head, her unbound hair lying in glorious golden waves spread upon the bedclothes.

"'Tis not fear that is important," Raoul informed her, hands sliding to her shoulders, massaging gently the rigid muscles. "Sweet Savior, you're tense! Here, roll over," he instructed briskly. His fingers moved firmly, skillfully, over her back and neck and shoulders, coaxing muscles to relax.

"As I was saying," he continued, "fear is a little thing. It is what you do with your fear that is important. We've both of us seen those fools who, when fear grips them, lose their wits and run about squawking like hens. Others stand firm in the face of danger. The ones who stand firm are no less afraid. 'Tis only control separates the brave man from the coward."

Raoul went on talking. Judith listened, losing herself in the deep sound of his voice and the ease his fingers produced along her spine. She knew, of course, when his hands moved to the round cheeks of her buttocks, soothing and massaging, but his voice continued unchanged, and she did not feel vulnerable or threatened.

He moved to the bottom of the bed to rub the muscles of her calves, still talking. She was only vaguely aware that he parted her legs until she felt a warm hand between them. A shock of pure pleasure shot through her belly and she gasped. His hand stilled. Shamelessly, Judith opened her legs wider. Her eyes closed.

He chuckled. "You like this?"

"Yes," She whispered.

"Then, you want me to go on?"

"Yes."

"Say 'please'," he told her.

Judith swallowed and closed her eyes tighter. "Please."

His hand moved again, slowly, insistently, until her breath came quick and hot from between her parted lips and she began to move restlessly.

"Roll over," he ordered, taking away his hand.

"No, please don't stop!" she pleaded.

"To get pleasure, you must give pleasure, little girl," said Raoul gently. "Roll over."

She did. She would do anything he said if he would touch her like that again.

He knelt between her parted thighs and leaned forward to kiss her, probing the inside of her mouth, and caressing her belly with one big hand. He leaned back to see her flushed face.

Her breath caught. Never had she imagined a kiss could produce chills and fever and that delicious ache in her belly. "Please, Raoul," she whispered, her need overriding protocol, which demanded she always use her lord's title. He did not seem to mind.

Raoul grinned, moving his hands to her breasts. "Soon. Don't be so greedy; we have all night." With infinite care he pinched her nipples. She moaned in pleasure.

"Touch me," he told her.

Judith put her hand around him. Soft on the outside, hard within, she thought. Like iron wrapped in velvet. She moved the foreskin back and slid her thumb in a delicate circle over the smooth tip of him, as she heard one of the women whisper to her to do. She smiled slyly at his gasp.

"You like this?" she whispered, echoing his earlier questions and moving her thumb again.

"Yes."

"Then, you want me to go on?"

He laughed at her attempt to take control, but it was a kindly amusement. "Another time, little one." He slid his hand between her thighs, smiling at her gasp. "Ah, yes, you do like that, do you not?" Gently he teased her, nibbling at her breasts, his hand giving her unbearable ecstasy. "Who is master here, Judith?" he demanded.

She writhed and moaned, gripping the linen sheet with desperate fingers as he brought her to the brink of some unknown place. Dimly his words penetrated. Then his hand stilled. She understood he would not give her what she needed so badly unless he had the answer he wanted. She resisted, not wanting to surrender. His hand moved again, in a different way, and chills chased one another over her skin. He stopped again.

"Say it, Judith!" his voice insisted. "Who is master here?"

Her body was arched like a bow, begging for him. Did it matter so much if she gave in? No, she thought. "You are!" she cried. "You are master, Raoul!"

"Now we both know it," he said as he moved into her deeply. And for her the pain was less than the pleasure at their joining.

CHAPTER 6

t was strange to Judith, and wonderful, the secret relationship she had with her husband when they were alone together. In public, formality was expected, demanded even, by the code of society. Anything else would have caused a scandal impossible to live down. But at night, in the privacy of their shared chamber, he insisted she call him by his given name, as she had that first night, and did the same by her. It was as if they were peasant lovers, who could be intimate without the constraints of the nobility. It was, said Raoul, the only time he could be completely himself, with no role to fill except that of friend and lover. They told one another their innermost thoughts, laughed, made love, and played like children, for all that Hawk was a warrior and several years her senior.

‡

On a night in late November, they sat alone in their chamber, she sewing a new shirt for her lord and Raoul busy with a polishing cloth and his shield. A fire burned cheerily on the hearth, and from the hall below came the sound of men's voices, sleepily discussing the hunt they'd enjoyed that day.

"Arnhilda says I am with child," Judith announced quietly.

Raoul's head snapped up from his work. "So soon! Are you sure?"

She nodded, pleased and proud. "It has been one month, and I can keep nothing down but a little bread, and not much of that. You've not been paying attention at table."

"Ah, you are correct, little girl. I've been too busy making plans. How long will this sickness last, think you?"

"It varies from woman to woman. It should pass in a few months, though. I'll probably eat like a pig once the queasiness is gone."

"Are we to begin on all those sons and daughters, then?" he teased. "God's Blood, you take your duty seriously!"

She threw a skein of wool from her workbasket at his head. "'Tis a fine time to tell me an you wanted to wait!" she declared, laughing.

"Oho!" cried the Hawk, dropping his cloth and flinging himself on the bed beside her. "So, you want to fight, do you?" He wrapped his arms about her and wrestled her to the mattress, pulling her underneath him and forcing himself, but gently, between her thighs. "Will you yield, you willful wench?" he demanded.

Judith shook her head, grinning and wriggling in an attempt to escape the imprisoning weight of him. "This is not an equal contest," she complained, when she found she could not.

He grasped both of her wrists in one hand and caressed her breasts with the other. "Why should I want that?" Raoul grinned. "If you will not yield freely, perhaps I can persuade you," he murmured. His lips traced a burning trail down the side of her neck.

She liked the scrape of his day's growth of beard, as the flick of his tongue against her throat took her thoughts from the contest. Her breath came faster as she felt him harden and press himself against her. She sighed. Her bones began to melt; she became steeped in languor. "I yield me captive, my lord," she whispered. The chamber spun around her as he entered her ready body and they came together.

Much later, Raoul lay looking up at the shadowed ceiling beams, one arm beneath his head. "Judith?"

"Mmmmmm?" She shifted on the bed, straw rustling beneath her.

"Are you afraid?"

She yawned. "Of bearing a child? Aye. 'Tis no light thing, after all."

"Is it the pain disturbs you?" he asked, curious. It was the most distressing part of the thing to him, the thought of being in pain like that for hours on end.

"Well, I'd as lief do without," she returned, smiling a little.

"You're young and strong, little girl, and Arnhilda will do all that is possible to ease your labor," said Raoul gently, smoothing his hand over her thigh in comfort.

Judith smiled. "Men!" She sat up, chuckled, and shook her head at him. "There's not much can be done to make the pain easier. But that, I can endure. It is not the pain that bothers me most." Her face grew pensive.

"What then?"

She turned away from him, staring out into the dying light of the fire. "Death. Many women die in childbed; my own mother did so with a stillborn son. God give her soul ease. And I am not ready."

"How do you mean, 'not ready'?"

"I've many things to do," she told him impatiently, hugging her knees to her chest. "There are so many tasks I've set myself will go undone unless I see to them, for none other would do what must be accomplished."

He touched her hair. "Would it ease your mind if I vowed to do these things which mean so much to you?"

Her lips curved in tender amusement. He would promise faithfully, she knew, to do whatever she asked. He would mean to fulfill his word. Then, at some future date, in the arms of a second wife, forget he'd ever uttered the promise. "No, Raoul. They are women's things of which I speak."

He shrugged. Women were known to be fanciful when they were breeding. Still, he was strangely frightened for her. Somehow, she had come to be more than a means to an end. She was not only a woman in his bed, a mother for his children, or his chatelaine. She was essential to his comfort in a way he did not understand—like an amulet, a symbol of what could be. Nothing must be allowed to harm her. "I will have Father Hubert and Brother Plegmund pray for your safe delivery," he promised.

She was touched by his kindness, and kissed him in a way that took his mind off troublesome things. They slept after a while, but Judith was restless and woke long before dawn. She rose silently and poked up the fire. The chamber was cold. She took an old cloak from her chest and wrapped herself against the chill. Its folds were scratchy but warm as she stooped to put wood on the fire.

Later, the crackling of the flames woke Raoul, and he propped himself up in bed on one elbow.

"What do you there?" he demanded irritably.

"Nothing."

He snorted. "Then come back to bed, woman!"

"Nay, 'tis almost time to be up and about. I heard a cock crow not long since."

"Ah, well." Raoul groaned and stretched, yawning prodigiously. He rose, scratching himself and blinking in the dim light. The basin of water had a thin film of ice, which had to be broken before he could wash away the sleep. Raoul shivered, drying himself upon a rough towel of linen. "T'will snow soon, I expect." He cleaned his teeth with a twig that was broken to fibers at one end.

"Aye."

He eyed her thoughtfully. "Lady Bertha asked again yesterday if Agnes might be allowed to rejoin us in the hall," Raoul told her.

"What did you say?"

"No."

Judith looked up at him curiously. "Why did you refuse? Surely, she has suffered enough, alone in her chamber all these months and more. T'was only to be a few months, you said in the beginning."

His lips thinned. "The bitch could have endangered our children's inheritance. You expect me to forgive that?"

"It was only spite because you favored me above her," said Judith coaxingly. "She had no thought beyond my discomfiture, not really. 'Tis unChristian to keep her imprisoned so long for a few stupid lies." She came to him across the chamber. "Help me to remove this cloak, please," she said, pouting her lips and flirting from beneath her lashes.

His eyes darkened and he grinned. "Do you try to seduce me, little girl?"

"Let us say, rather, that I try to *persuade* you. It sounds much better, don't you think?" She ran a hand over his chest and down the center of his body and cupped him in her hand. "Ah! You are ready for me so soon!"

"Ready for the chamber pot, more like!" he retorted, but he did not move away.

"Well, if that is what you'd prefer . . ."

"Little witch!" He tugged at the cloak and gazed hungrily at her body, revealed as the wool tumbled to the floor. His hands moved of their own volition to her breasts, then lower. He marveled at the heat of her. "Sweet Christ, but you turn my blood to fire!" he growled.

"You have equal skill," she gasped, as his caresses grew bolder. Then, as a draught from the shuttered window swirled about the floor, "'Tis cold in here!"

Raoul tugged at her hips, turning her until she felt him pressed firmly against her buttocks, hard and warm. His hands rose to her breasts again, caressing her nipples until she groaned and ground back against him in need. "Feeling warmer, little girl?" He asked with a chuckle.

She pulled him to the bed, falling with him in a tangle of limbs. "I'd feel warmer with you inside me."

He smiled down at her, passion warring with tenderness in his eyes. "You look too young to be carrying my babe," he whispered. "You're a babe yourself!"

Judith touched him in a way she knew he liked. She was ready now, and suddenly he wanted to talk! "Do it!" she urged, fondling him again, almost beside herself with need.

He moved into her gently, feeling afraid now that he thought of the babe, concerned that he might harm it. But Judith moaned and pressed him with her hands, and he forgot everything else in his passion but the need for fulfillment. He kissed her roughly and she gloried in it, pressing her fingers hard against his back and pushing her tongue into his mouth to taste him. She had never felt so wanton or so free. It was glorious.

‡

In the hall later that morning, Agnes hastened to her place at table and sat eating barley bread and boiled bacon, with the folk all about pretending that nothing had happened. Raoul watched her suspiciously, but Judith beamed. Now surely, she thought, all would be well.

When the tables had been stacked away and the women gathered in a group near the hearth for Judith's instructions, she gave Lady Agnes a needle and thread. She bade her assist in the embroidering of a tapestry which was designed for hanging in the great hall of the new castle, the walls of which were rising ever higher on its hill. The section she assigned to Lady Agnes was filled with horseman and archers, her stepsister's favorite subjects for needlework. Without a doubt it must please her, Judith thought, hope in her heart. Certainly, Agnes smiled with friendly gratitude.

‡

As Judith came to dwell more upon her pregnancy, Lady Edith, too, found she was with child. They spent many hours together, making plans for the babes over their needlework and spinning.

Raoul, bored with the enforced confinement of winter, began to carve a wooden knight for the unborn babe, and Judith made tiny shirts, tunics, and hemmed swaddling bands and cloths. The folk of the hall were delighted with both the peace in the land and the possibility of an heir.

Often, alone in their chamber, Raoul would lay his hands on her still flat belly, wondering at the miracle of life within. He could not understand how his son or daughter was actually alive and growing in there, so close but just beyond his reach and hidden from his eyes. It touched him in a way he could not express, but Judith saw his expression in his eyes and was moved by it.

Snow fell day after day with monotonous regularity, depressing the knights and men-at-arms, and enchanting Judith with its glistening beauty. Serfs kept the courtyard clear of snow so that the horses might be exercised, but since the great beasts floundered in shoulder-deep drifts whenever they ventured further afield, the men were forced to remain within the confines of the hall for endless hours. Luckily, Judith remembered the teachings of Brother Plegmund, and life was far easier than it might have been without the diversions she arranged.

In those cold, short days of that first winter, it seemed to Judith that life was nearly perfect. If complete happiness was not possible for those in the hall, at least the self-effacement of Lady Bertha and the new, friendly attitude of Agnes made for harmony of sorts, and Judith cherished that peace and quiet, too.

On one clear afternoon, Judith sat alone, her stool drawn close to the hearth, sewing a shirt for Lady Edith's babe. It was to be a surprise gift, and Judith imagined Lady Edith's pleasure as she embroidered tiny flowers about the neck of the garment.

"That is beautiful work, sister," said Agnes, coming to place her stool beside her. She seated herself a bit tentatively.

Judith looked up, startled and not a little pleased. "Why, I give you thanks."

Agnes looked uncomfortable. "I owe it to you that I am not in my chamber yet, I have heard," she mumbled, eyes on the floor. Her toe stirred the rushes. "I have said nothing 'ere now, for I could not find the words. I don't have them yet but could not wait the longer to express my gratitude without grave discourtesy to you."

"Please!" cried Judith, embarrassed and touched. "Let it be forgotten. Are we not sisters, after all? I do wish we might be closer, though, as true sisters should be."

Agnes smiled. She had learned of her mother the trick of doing so without showing her bad teeth. "I would like that. It has not been easy to show that sometimes I wished to be your friend. You know how my lady mother is," she added by way of explanation.

Judith nodded sympathetically. "My father was no spring flower, either."

"Well," Agnes declared firmly. "All those unhappy times must be put behind us, to lie in the past where they belong. I shall not refer to it again. But, if I may, I would like to speak to you now as one who has your welfare at heart."

Judith raised her eyebrows inquiringly.

"I am a little worried that you do not eat more. It is not good for the babe; the women said at the table this morn. If I brought you a little spiced wine and a piece of bread, think you that it might tempt you? For me?" she added, her voice pleading.

The mere thought of food made Judith's stomach lurch distressingly. "I don't know. . ."

"Won't you please try?" begged Agnes. "It would make me feel I am truly forgiven for my sins, sister."

Judith laughed. "Oh, very well. For you I will try."

Agnes begged the key to the spice chest and hurried away importantly. She returned shortly with a goblet of wine and a slice of bread still warm from the oven. Giggling a bit, she returned the key. "Cynefred was ready to plunge his sharpest carving knife into my heart 'til I told him t'was for you, Lady Judith," she reported breathlessly. "You must eat this now, for I vow I risked my life to procure it!" Her eyes brimmed with mischief.

Judith laughed. She decided to please Agnes, no matter how badly her stomach pitched at the smell of food. She bit into the bread with strong, white teeth and choked it down. "Do you know, Lady Agnes, this is delicious! But it makes me very thirsty."

Smiling, Agnes handed her the wine. "I've a heavy hand with spices, I fear. Too much cinnamon."

Judith lied, protesting that it was just as she liked it, and to prove her lie truth, drank it down. Her new friendship with Agnes, she felt, was too fragile to stand the strain of even a small criticism. She saw that Arnhilda watched from a corner, disapproval writ plain across her face, but Judith knew she could bring Arnhilda around to her way of thinking. As Brother Plegmund often said, there was in every one of God's creatures a spark of good, needing only a small breeze of encouragement to fan it into a blaze of love.

‡

In the middle of the night, Judith awoke with a gripping pain in her belly. "Raoul!" she gasped. "Holy Mother, I think the babe comes! Dear God, fetch Arnhilda. Quickly!" She moaned piteously as the pain came again, and doubled over. She began to pray, but already she felt the blood spilling warmly over her thighs. It was too late.

‡

Arnhilda knelt wearily beside Judith's bed, her eyes never faltering from the pale, young face. She had been watching so long that when the younger woman's eyelids flickered, she thought at first she'd imagined it. Then she was staring into cool, blue eyes. She felt tears of relief fill her own. "How feel you, loveling?" She whispered hoarsely.

"Floating," replied Judith dreamily. "No more sleeping draughts, Arnhilda. I will not get strong that way."

"No more," agreed the maidservant. She glanced at the corner where Lord Raoul sat dozing on a stool, then decided to take no chances. She spoke in Saxon. "You know what happened, do you not?"

"I lost my babe," said Judith flatly, her eyes like stones.

"And do you know why?"

A tear trickled down Judith's cheek, and she caught it on the tip of her tongue. "God's will?"

The older woman clenched her teeth. "Lady Agnes' will, more like!" she hissed.

Judith's eyes blazed as comprehension came to her. "The wine! She drugged the wine! Are you certain of this? What proof have you?" In her agitation, she struggled to sit.

Arnhilda pressed her flat, a hurried glance at the sleeping Norman lord. "Gently, sweeting. Do not tire yourself. Aubrey saw Lady Agnes in the courtyard emptying the contents of a vial into the goblet she gave you yesterday. She hid it under a bush in the hedge, where he showed it to me earlier this day. T'was blackspurred rye, and how you survived this I know not! Aubrey says at the time he thought it a love potion for one of the knights. Men are so stupid!"

"Well, I was stupid, too. I trusted her. What are we going to do?" demanded Judith.

Arnhilda smiled bitterly. "You are the lady of this hall and a woman grown. What would you have done? T'was not her alone planned this mischief. Lady Agnes contrived it, but she knows naught of simples except that little you taught her at Lord Hawk's insistence, which was not enough for this. T'was our gracious Lady Bertha mixed the brew killed your babe." She bared her straggly teeth. "What fate for a murderess Lady Judith? What penalty for the death of an innocent?"

"Bring me the herbs," whispered Judith, her tortured face white in the fire's glow. "You know which ones."

The maidservant did as she was told. She rummaged in a small chest under the table. Returning to the bedside, she stood waiting, holding in her hands several small leather pouches. Judith lifted her hand, and after a moment's hesitation, placed it on a pouch with a small red symbol painted on it. "This is for Lady Bertha. Your hand becomes mine; what you do, I do. You are only the instrument. Justice must be done." Her hand dropped wearily to the bed. "Only Lady Bertha," she insisted in a shaky voice. "She whose hand held the cup will find another fate."

"How do you mean, dearling?"

"She betrayed me and ruined my happiness. She *knew* my babe would die and killed my hope for the future with it. A reward should be suited to the deed; do you not agree?"

"Aye, my lady." Arnhilda left, and Judith stared up at the darkness.

She placed a hand on her childless belly and tears spilled from the corners of her eyes unchecked. She did not doubt God's existence, nor did she blame Him for the tragedy of the babe's death. T'was done and the infant gone. Nothing she could do, say, or feel would change that. Nor, in her agony, did her thoughts dwell upon Agnes' role in this. Merely, she mourned the loss of her son. She had imagined that child growing up straight, tall, and proud. The little boy who would look like Raoul, who would laugh and question at her knee, that angel she had loved already, would now never be. His loss was devastating.

The hot tears streamed from her eyes and she held back sobs until she nearly choked. Her very soul screamed out in agony at her loss, but no sound escaped her lips. For more than an hour she lay thus, shrieking silently, until at last the faint glow of dawn filtered into the chamber, and she slept from exhaustion.

‡

Edwina and Gytha knelt side by side on the stone floor of the village church, far behind the nobles, knights, and the like. The floor was cold enough to make their bones ache.

"I'd not grudge time for a funeral in the normal way of things," whispered Gytha, her breath rising in a stream on the air. "But to have to bide here, pretending I care for the rest of Lady Bertha is too much! She was a vicious mistress to all who served her! Aye, and a whore."

Edwina stifled a giggle. "'Tis not as if our prayers will help *that* one much, anyway! We all know where she's bound!"

"There's truth." Gytha sniffled and wiped her nose on her sleeve. "I heard as she died of a fit. Is that the way of it?"

"No. Arnhilda said as how it was a seizure of the heart, come on all sudden-like." She shook her head in admiration. "My, but you should have heard her scream! It was so loud it woke us all in the dead of night. No one knew what was toward. So, we all flung on our clothes and ran to see." Edwina tossed her head a little in pardonable pride. "I was one of the first to discover the source of the trouble. Arnhilda and my lord were the only ones before me."

"What happened?" gasped Gytha eagerly.

"Well, there was Lady Bertha, as still as could be and sort of blue-looking, with her eyes staring big as cart wheels! Lady Agnes was sitting on the bed, wrapped in the coverlet and weeping buckets."

"It must be awful for her, being orphaned and all, right before her eyes. Will she go back to Normandy?"

"No, she is Lord Raoul's ward, now. He'll marry her off to some knight or other." She shuddered. "You'd not have believed the expression on Lady Bertha's face! They say a stoppage of the heart is fast, but she must have suffered horribly; you could see it. And the smell! Ugh! They had to make up a new pallet for the bed."

"Ah, well," Gytha murmured. "Death does loosen the bowels."

She considered the matter. "'Tis more likely that Satan himself came to collect Lady Bertha's soul, wicked creature that she was!" snorted Gytha. "Which brings me back to what I've already said. There's no point to pretending I cared for her or that prayers for her soul will do any good!"

"I feel the same, for all I traveled with her to England. She had a heavy hand and never any gratitude for a service done." Edwina grimaced.

"Hush!" hissed someone behind her. "We're in the church, you know. You should have more respect!"

"Humph!" she muttered, hitching her shawl more closely about her. "Respect to them as have earned it, is what I say!"

‡

Judith mended quickly. She ate whatever Arnhilda put before her. She prayed for strength, and within two days of the death of her stepmother, she was allowed to take a few hesitant steps about her bedchamber. At the end of three weeks, she was up and about her usual tasks as if nothing had occurred. Her first courses came normally when they were due, and Arnhilda crossed herself in gratitude at this evidence of Lady Judith's health.

‡

When first they made love after the death of the babe, Raoul was tender, fearful of causing her pain. Judith felt only joy at their union, and he was relieved, for he knew that the loss of a babe sometimes caused deeper problems. Afterwards, Raoul lay upon his back, and Judith, on her side and facing him, moved her hand slowly over his chest.

"Lady Edith told me once that you had killed a woman."

His body tensed all over. "When did she say that?"

"Oh, t'was on the night you announced our betrothal, I think. Does it matter when?"

"No."

She leaned forward to kiss his neck. "Did you?"

"Did I what?"

"Did you kill a woman?"

"No," he said tightly. "I did no such thing."

"I thought not," she remarked calmly, smiling as his body began to relax.

"Eustace did it," he told her, relaxing more and sighing as her hand moved in an intricate pattern across his belly. "You really believed me innocent without question?"

"Of course," she murmured, surprised that he needed to ask. "And in any case, I knew you would not lie to me if I asked."

"You," said Raoul with conviction, "are a most remarkable woman."

"Mmmm." She licked delicately at the front of his throat. "Lady Edith said that the one who died was *your* woman, a pagan from the Holy Land. Was she?"

He understood her then and smiled. "And you want to know of what she was like?"

"Well, yes, I do," returned Judith, bashful at being found out. "Was she pretty?"

"Beautiful," he said. Her hand ceased its caress, and his smiled deepened. "No, don't stop, Judith. That feels good."

She touched him, teasingly. "Was she prettier than I?"

"How can one compare? She had black hair, black eyes, and skin the color of honey," he told her. "Her people lived in tents made of goat hides, in a land that is all sand, traveling from one water well to another."

Her hand paused a moment, then moved again. "Where did you find her?"

Raoul groaned at a particularly delicious touch. She had to repeat the question.

"When she was a child, her parents sold her to a slave merchant.

She came to France after many years with a ship's captain, and since her master at the time had wearied of her, I bought her for a couple of silver pennies."

"And she was your woman," said Judith, moving her hand slowly toward the place she knew he wanted it. "So why did Eustace kill her?"

"He has some fever of the brain, I've often thought. He likes to hurt people and animals, helpless things." He closed his eyes and reached down to still her hand for a moment.

"It took me a long time to understand how dangerous he is. When William knighted me, I had no room for a woman. I could not take her with me or leave her in some small village to die, so I gave her to Eustace. He vowed he'd not harm her, but he drank too much one night, I've been told, and beat her until she died. I've never trusted him since. Oh, I trust him in battle but not with women or those too young to defend themselves." He let her hand resume its travels.

"I'm not surprised," she murmured. She traced the place where his thigh joined his torso with her fingertip, and he shivered. Then she took him in hand, firmly, the way he liked it best. After a few moments, she quickened the movement of her hand along his rigid member.

Raoul caught his breath and groaned. "Sweet Savior, do it faster!"

"Did you care for your pagan woman?"

He cried out as Judith leaned forward suddenly and put her mouth over his stiffness. "God's Blood, but that's good!"

She lifted her head. "Did you care for her?"

"Yes! Don't talk, Judith, just do that again!" he gasped. "Ah, yes, yes!" He held her head in his hands, moving it in time with his thrusting hips, and when it happened for him, he gasped her name.

‡

"'Tis cold," she murmured, pulling the coverlet over their bodies.

Raoul looked at her in wonder. "Why did you do that?"

"Because I thought it would feel good. Why? Did you not like it? Are you angry with me?" she asked anxiously.

His teeth gleamed in the darkness. "Oh, I liked if very well, little girl, but the priests say it is a sin."

"Surely not!" she cried in astonishment. "God would not forbid a thing which can bring only pleasure!"

He laughed. "What a woman you are, Judith of Oakwood! No one ever did such a thing to me before. Shall I do it for you? Would you like that?"

"Not tonight," she told him, smilingly sleepily. "But I wish you would hold me. I like the feel of your arms."

There was a deep, contented silence. Then he felt her stir against him.

"Raoul?"

"What is it?"

"I was jealous tonight. Of that pagan woman you had."

He chuckled. "I know. But you need not have been. I gave her willingly enough to my brother. Now, with you, I'd kill my brother before I'd let him come nigh. Go to sleep."

And she did.

‡

The following morning, Raoul had conversation with Aubrey, who sought him out on the pretext of purchasing one of the village children to train as a jongleur. After their conference, however, Raoul paced the hall looking for his lady. He found Arnhilda instead and half-dragged the aged maidservant to his chamber.

"Now," he snarled as he barred the door. "What is this I hear about Lady Agnes being responsible for the death of the babe?"

After one scared glance at his face, Arnhilda told all. He listened silently to the tale. He betrayed no emotion when she told him of Lady Bertha's execution. Only when she relayed to him Lady Judith's order concerning Lady Agnes did he frown. "Does she expect me to do *nothing*?" he demanded angrily.

"I think she has some scheme in mind, although she won't confide it yet. The longer it takes to achieve it, the better for her, though," stated Arnhilda positively. "Her hatred has made her heal and given her strength. In all truth, my lord, I thought we'd lost her that night, it was so close a thing. If I hadn't been able to stop the bleeding. . ."

"Have done, Arnhilda," Raoul said, patting her shoulder gently. "You did stop it. It was enough, and she lived. But she still pretends this friendship with Lady Agnes, which is beyond my comprehension! All I need do is try her and have her hanged. My justice is law."

Arnhilda smiled. "I think, my lord, that Lady Judith will find a punishment suitable to the crime. Women are more subtle than men, and far more ruthless. Let it be for now. Leave it to my lady, and you won't be disappointed, I promise you."

And later that month, when Judith proposed a match between her stepsister and the lord's brother, Sir Eustace, Raoul smiled grimly and understood.

CHAPTER 7

n the early spring of 1068, before Lord Raoul could decide the pressing questions of which fields to plant with which seeds, or supervise the lots drawn by the serfs for their personal plots of the planting season, a rider came to summon him to knight's service. Judith was apprehensive. She sat in their chamber, watching him sift through his equipment with his new body servant, Humphrey. Bits of leather creaked or flapped; metal chimed and clanked. What would she do while he was gone? How could she manage everything? Oakwood was so much larger and more complex since the Normans came.

Raoul glanced up at her, keen eyes taking in the sadness and bewilderment. "So, my lady. I trust you are prepared to rule in my absence?"

She blinked. "I? Do you mean the defense as well?"

"Of course. Who else? Now, Sir Tancred will see to the patrols about our borders, but I would wish you'd check with him daily. He'll explain what he has planned, and if you see ought needs correcting, have him see to it at once.

"You'll have to move into the castle without me, but we've been over the plans together, and I reckon things'll run smoothly enough with your guidance. I'd recommend starving the hall cats for two or three days and sending 'em into the castle cellars ahead of you to clear away whatever vermin have found refuge there."

"Aye." T'was common knowledge that rat bites turned septic, so it was best not to risk them. "And the harvest?" she asked, mind ranging ahead.

"You will have to see to the planting first, little girl." He grinned at her. "But you were here when I made the assignments last season. I doubt you'll make any errors. The field that was put to rye last season, and barley, you said, the season previous, will do for fallow in which the men may practice until the fall."

She clasped her hands together tightly. "Surely, my lord, you will have returned by then."

"Never can tell," he replied cheerfully, shaking his head at the hauberk Humphrey held up for his approval. "The *other* one! This one's too fine, and the rings do not overlap as smoothly as I'd like. Put it in with the rest of the baggage, though. Doubtless I'll find an armorer with King William who can mend it properly."

Raoul was most casual about this business of going off to parts unknown, Judith realized. He looked forward to the adventure, mayhap. Could his lady behave with less dignity? Many eyes would soon be upon her, judging of her ability to lead in his absence. It was, after all, not only her Oakwood folk who dwelt here now. She squared her shoulders.

"Think you that you may return before the birth of the babe?" she inquired. She had few worries about this second pregnancy but wanted him there for the birth.

"Now that's something you can rely upon, lady wife," he said with a grin. He turned away again at a question from Humphrey. "Yes, and best take that belt, too. Oh, and one pair of soft shoes, in case King William intends to hold court."

Judith sighed, seeing that his mind was more upon the journey ahead than his responsibilities at Oakwood. Well, that was like all the men she'd ever known, so while it was a disappointment, it was not a devastating one. "Will you at least tell me *why* King William has summoned you?" she asked her husband with a touch of impatience.

He looked over. "What? Oh, that!" Raoul moved closer, one eye upon Humphrey's packing. "Well, it seems that in December King William returned to England from a trip to Normandy to discover that Harold Godwineson's mother, the Lady Gytha, was still holding out against our men in Wessex. I am thankful I was not there to catch the tongue-lashing they must have received! All those battle-hardened veterans fought to a standstill by one elderly female!" He shook his head and chuckled. "She must have more stomach than any of 'em, and some of those men I've fought beside more than once!" He chuckled. "The man who brought me the news says it was a marvel to hear them chastened.

"In the event, King William called out most of the fyrd and led them into Wessex to see the task completed. T'was only eighteen days after his arrival upon the scene that the men of Devon and Cornwall came to terms, and Lady Gytha is now withdrawn to the Isle of Flatholme. As I understand it, King William next returned to London to prepare for the arrival of his lady wife, Lady Matilda, who was due shortly for her coronation.

"Then, around Whitsuntide, mayhap a bit earlier, Lords Edwin and Morcar of Mercia declared themselves in revolt against King William's rule. That," he added with a grin, "is where I come in. We're off to Yorkshire to settle things. Should be fun."

Fun? Judith shook her head in wonder that men could call risking their lives an amusement of apparently the highest order. Did they *never* grow out of their boyhood?

Indeed, Raoul was not the only man of the hall excited and anxious to be on the road. Only Sir Tancred, who made no bones about his dislike of life in a military camp, seemed immune from the thrill of action. Young men hurried back and forth, shouting to one another, laughing, or sitting out of the way sharpening weapons and bragging of their skill. The older men with more experience, were less loud and rushed, and disinclined to boast. Yet even their eyes flashed, and there was an understated urgency about them that spoke of eagerness to be gone. Since she could not puzzle how this could be, Judith shrugged and accepted it. She conducted herself with calm dignity, waving at the cavalcade, which left before first light the following morning, relieved that Raoul had made love with her one last time before his departure. She felt lonely already, and even more so when Sir Tancred approached her for his orders. Soon her head was filled with numbers of soldiers on hand, routes of patrol, hours of duty, times of practice, and so on.

Later in the day, Judith sat among her ladies, all of them diligently working upon the tapestry for the castle. She relaxed as she plied her needle, her mind returning to the past week.

Raoul had arranged his brother's marriage to Lady Agnes the winter past, and Sir Eustace had been eager for the match. The Danesford kitchen wenches were a paltry lot, and Lady Agnes, as stepdaughter to the happily deceased Cerdic, gave him a rather nebulous claim upon Oakwood, in the event his brother died without an heir. Her blackened teeth ruined what claim to beauty she might have had, but he told Raoul and Judith, laughing, that at least she was well-born, and he planned to cover her face with a cloth and make good use of her other attractions. When Raoul regretfully informed him that the girl was no virgin, Sir Eustace had frowned, then grinned unpleasantly. Had all her lovers been Saxons? Yes? Well, then! Those Englishmen were known for their lack of imagination, were they not? When the first maidenhead was gone, there was a second available if a man were not put off by Holy Writ. And he, Eustace, was not a superstitious man! The dowry, jewels belonging to Lady Bertha from her first husband's mother's dowry, plus a team of oxen and four strong serfs, Eustace considered adequate, so agreement had been made.

Judith had a pang or two of regret once agreement had been reached. Still, she told herself, Agnes had murdered her child. For that reason alone, she deserved punishment. Doubtless, God might be angry with her for the severity of it, but Judith had no choice when the future of Oakwood was thrown into the balance. Her stepsister must be controlled and away from Oakwood. She agreed with Raoul and Sir Eustace that there was no need to wait for the banns to be read.

As for Lady Agnes, she trembled with excitement when she heard of the proposed wedding. A year's enforced abstinence, the shock of her mother's death, and the constant fear that Lady Judith would somehow discover her guilt in the murder of the unborn babe all had her nerves stretched taut. She welcomed escape from the tension of life at the hall and looked forward to bedding with the lord's brother. Sir Eustace was a well-made man, and the serving wenches warranted him lusty. She longed for the opportunity to be mistress of her own keep, out from the governance of her prudish stepsister. And until Lord Raoul had an heir of an age to hold the land, who knew what might happen? So Lady Agnes smiled (carefully, with her lips closed to hide her teeth) and ogled her betrothed, waiting with bated breath for their wedding eve, when her restriction would be at an end.

From Deerfield, Sir Robert and Lady Blanche traveled through the mud for half a day to attend Sir Eustace's marriage, bringing Hywel's widow in their train. Quarters were cramped in the hall, but the excitement and gaiety of the festivities more than made up for any lack of comfort.

Judith had laughed, joked, and teased with the other married women as Agnes sat in her bath. It was *her* turn to smile with the superiority of a wedded woman while a bride sat at their mercy. Not, it must be admitted, that knowledge of such intimacies was unknown to Agnes. Judith was in a position of superiority, and she enjoyed it to the full. Once, feeling Arnhilda's gaze upon her, Judith looked up and their eyes met. Both women smiled.

‡

After the bedding ceremony, Lady Margaret of Deerfield detained her outside the nuptial chamber. "If I might have a word with you, Lady Judith," she whispered nervously, glancing at the folk about them.

Judith's brows rose. "How may I serve you?" she asked warily.

Lady Margaret licked her lips, her hands clasped tightly enough to whiten her knuckles. "If it would not be too much trouble, my lady, is there no place more private?"

A burst of laughter drowned out her reply. The knights had retreated into the corridor upon leaving the bedding chamber, but as there was no door to ensure privacy, they stood jostling one another at the portal, peering around the heavy, leather curtain. They commented freely upon Sir Eustace's performance, which was prodigious if Agnes' cries and the wet, slapping sound of flesh upon flesh were aught to measure by. A few men, drunker than others, slipped back into the chamber for a clearer view. Agnes shrieked at their presence, and Judith heard the smack of an open-handed blow and Sir Eustace's harsh voice commanding Agnes to be silent and keep moving. The other men grinned at that and crowded back through the portal, Lord Raoul and Sir Robert not last among the spectators.

Shaking her head, Judith took Lady Margaret's arm and said, "Come, lady. Let us go to my chamber where we may refresh ourselves away from the noise and speak without interruption."

They walked quickly to the lord's chamber and Judith closed the door firmly behind them, appreciating its existence as never before. She turned to the troubled woman and, smiling still, drew up two stools near the fire. "Sit with me a space, Lady Margaret," she invited, sinking down and carefully arranging her skirts about her against the draughts.

Lady Margaret sat. "It has been a long time since I heard that title addressed to me," she remarked, gripping her thin hands together in her lap. "I . . . I know not how to tell you, Lady Judith, what it is troubles me. It is difficult."

Judith nodded with real sympathy. "Is it that Lady Blanche has been unkind?" she asked.

"Oh, *that*!" sighed Lady Margaret. "Well, it is a hard thing to be a servant in mine own hall, but that I can bear, for I am in authority over others still and not disregarded in daily concerns. 'Tis Sir Robert makes all a nightmare." She took a deep breath. "I know not whether you deal well or ill with Lord Raoul. Think you he would grant your request an you asked to have me stay here for a small space?"

"He might," replied Judith cautiously. "What does Sir Robert which is of such distress to you, lady?"

Lady Margaret rose and began pacing the floor, the wooden boards beneath the rushes creaking in places under her feet. The tension in her sang through the chamber. "I was a true wife to Lord Hywel," she said after a moment. "We were wed when I was twelve. I warmed his bed and bore his sons and tended his folk and manor as I was taught to do. But Lord Hywel is long dead and our sons with him. I had thought that in time I might be wife to one of the lord's men, but I think now Sir Robert would prevent it. He . . . he wants me for his own bed."

"You are certain that this is not what you want as well?" inquired Judith mildly.

"I am no whore!" Lady Margaret snapped. "Nay, forgive me, Lady Judith. 'Tis that I'm so bedeviled I know not what I say. Were there no Lady Blanche, I'd bed him right enough. He's no beauty, but he's a man, and I've been without someone to lean on a long time."

Lady Margaret put a hand to her forehead, then dropped it to her side. "Yes, I know that adultery is a mortal sin, and I am a good Christian woman. He says he'll take the sin on himself, and I shall escape God's just punishment. But I know it's not so."

Judith bit her lip. Now here was a problem! "And Lady Blanche?"

"She's no fool. I speak only enough of their tongue to get by, but when a man pushes you against the wall and puts his hand under your skirt, you know well enough what it is he wants. When his lady is standing by, she knows, as well."

"Jesu!" gasped Judith incredulously. "Lady Blanche was there?"

"Was your own father any different, lady?" inquired Lady Margaret with a bitter smile.

"He . . . he never took any but serving wenches to his bed and then decently out of sight of Lady Bertha," Judith defended hotly.

Lady Margaret cocked her head to one side. "Does that make it any better? Is not a serving wench a woman like any other?"

Judith thought then of what she would likely feel did she one day come across Lord Raoul in the bushes with a serf's daughter. She nodded. "Has he made advances since that time?"

"Every day, my lady. He gives me no rest."

"Of course, you resist." Judith suggested.

"Mostly, when he tries to put it in," she admitted ruefully. "Mother of God, my lady, I'm woman grown! I tremble these days when even a scullion looks my way and wonder what t'would be like! One night soon, I will yield and commit a grievous sin, and what comes to me then?"

"Hmmm," murmured Judith, deep in thought. "Will not Lady Blanche assist you? She must know what Sir Robert is. If you go to her, will she withhold her protection?"

Lady Margaret seated herself again, shoulders sagging. "You do not understand, my lady. What protection could she give? He is like Sir Eustace in yon chamber, making a wanton strumpet of his own lady. Sir Robert cares not if any see, least of all his lady wife! Certainly, he favors her wishes not, even in the smallest things. Mayhap it is to punish her for being barren; I know not. But there is no hope for me in that household."

Lady Margaret buried her face in her hands. "Ah, who would have thought life would take so strange a turn? But two years past I had Lord Hywel, who honored me and was a kind and faithful husband; and my sons growing strong and brave before my eyes. Now I am little more than a slave in my own hall, bereft of my lord and the sons of my heart, with no kin left to aid me. Oh, dear Lady Judith, can you not succor me?"

Silence reigned as Judith considered. It was as Arnhilda said, absence made the heart fond. Lord Hywel had been a less-than-perfect lord, but now that he was gone, his widow remembered only his virtues. The current situation was a delicate one. Care must be taken not to offend Sir Robert, whose service Raoul valued. At the same time, as lady of Oakwood, Judith's duty was clearly to give aid when requested, particularly when a woman's soul was in the balance. "I lost a babe not long since, and my lord takes the greatest care of my comfort," she said slowly. "We could tell folk that talk of the old days might bring me cheer. Lady Agnes' chamber will be vacant on the morrow and could be given over to your use. What say you, lady?"

The older woman wept in gratitude, which much discomposed her hostess. Judith sent her off with relief and a determination to come to her aid.

Thus it was that when Raoul entered the chamber later that night, she broached the matter straightaway.

"Well?" she asked when she had related the whole. "Does it meet with your approval?"

Raoul removed his garments with difficulty. "Aye, do what you will with her," he answered, his voice muffled by the tunic he dragged over his head. He dropped it in the general direction of his clothing chest. "I'll speak with Sir Robert myself. If I explain 'tis but a whim of my wife's, he'll not dare to cross me for fear I disapprove of his intentions toward a woman gently born, even if she is Saxon." His gait was unsteady as he crossed the floor.

"God's Beard!" he exclaimed as he stumbled. "The chamber's moving!"

She laughed, never having seen him so. "You're full to overflowing with wine, you fool! Come to bed 'ere you fall!"

He drew himself up with dignity. "No one calls the Hawk a fool," he told her sternly. Then he laughed. "At least, no one does so to my face!"

"You're pickled, my lord. Come to bed," she repeated.

"I'd come to bed an I could find it!" he retorted, tripping over an inconveniently placed stool. Slowly he groped his way to the bed, collapsing at her side and laughing. "God's Blood, what a night! You should have stayed before," he told her.

"Lady Agnes was full of fury that he'd let us watch, and he had to tie her to the bed. Even then, she liked it well enough in the end, moaning and groaning 'til her voice was so weak we could scarce hear her. She's not so happy now, though. Eustace did just what he said he would. You remember. *That* brought her voice back quick enough. She made so great a fuss I feared the rafters would cave in!"

Judith felt the burden of belated guilt. She had, in fact, heard the shrieking. "Mayhap I shouldn't have been so quick to arrange . . ."

"Best thing you could have done," he assured her. "Eustace'll keep her under this thumb or kill her. Either way, we're rid of the problem." He rolled over and tugged her until she lay against his chest. "What I've seen this night has given me an appetite t'will be hard to deny, Judith. Will you fuck a drunken sot such as I am?"

She giggled. "I've half a mind to say you nay, so soused as you are."

"Ah, no," he murmured, running his hands over her back and buttocks. "You'd not do that surely!"

"And what if I did?" she teased.

"Would you have me resort to my hand?" he nibbled at her throat. "Ah, how soft you are!" He pulled her kirtle over her head. One hand cupped a round breast, and he chuckled as the nipple sprang erect against his palm. "Yes, that pleases you, doesn't it?" His tongue made lazy circles on her skin, then moved to the nipple begging for attention. "Remember what you did for me that one time?" he whispered. "I want to do it for you. Will you let me?"

"You mean . . ." She rolled over onto her back when he pushed.

"Mmmmm. Will you?" His hands explored her feverishly, parting her thighs and holding her open to him. His fingers touched her gently, exciting her so that she arched up against his hand. "Well? Will you?"

Judith nodded, eyes glittering. "Since you insist so, Raoul, how can I say nay?" She giggled again. Then his mouth found her, and she gasped. She shivered, and moaned, and writhed, begging him to stop, pleading with him to continue. Judith knew not what she said, and Raoul didn't listen. He did what he wanted until she was half mad with excitement. Then he moved and lay on his back.

"Come here, little girl."

She crawled over the bed, trembling.

"This night, you play stallion," he whispered hoarsely.

Awkwardly, she positioned herself over him, then sank down, taking him deep inside her. "Ah, Raoul!" She began to move, uttering little cries and shivering with delight.

The wine had made him wild, and he was not long content to remain passive. He pushed her aside and moved over her, grasping her hips so that the marks remained for days. It shocked her later to realize that she had reveled in it. Twice she had shuddered with blessed relief 'ere he called her name and was still.

‡

While Raoul was away in Yorkshire, Judith commanded Oakwood with a garrison of four knights and thirty men-at-arms. Raiders had been reported across the Welsh border not far away to the south, but Judith increased the patrols, and the Oakwood lands were not touched. Deerfield lost some cattle and a few serfs; Danesford Tower reported no trouble.

‡

In July, the Lady Edith was delivered of a daughter, a grave disappointment to Sir Tancred but one that he bore with fortitude. Judith assisted Arnhilda at the child's birth and trembled with the knowledge that this pain and suffering would one day be hers. Nightly thereafter she prayed she bore a son in her belly, that she might not see in Raoul's eyes the same defeated look she had glimpsed in the eyes of his bailiff.

‡

The castle was completed in August, and Judith supervised the move carefully. She sat at the high table in the great hall of the stone structure, which had been set up as if for a meal, with Sir Tancred at her side. Together they pored over the plans drawn up months before.

"See?" she said, pointing at the masons' drawing. "The unwed knights are placed here, on the ground floor between the armory and the donjon. The men-at-arms are in the upper rooms above the knights' quarters, and beside the donjon tower, which contains the guardroom.

"Ummmm," said Sir Tancred. "You realize there will be complaints."

"Oh, naturally. The knights will not like sleeping on the ground floor. They will like even less the fact that they are quartered away from the women," she responded with asperity. "However, as you pointed out months ago, we need them on this level in case, God and all the Holy Saints forbid, we are attacked. As for being away from the women, this is a lord's demesne, not a place of employment for strumpets! Should any of the men desire to wed, there are chambers in plenty can be made habitable for their use."

He cleared his throat, smoothing a hand down the front of his blue tunic. "As you say, my lady."

"I am determined that mine shall be a seemly household," she continued more calmly. "Thus, I have arranged separate sleeping halls for the scullions and the serving maids. T'will not bring me popularity, perhaps, but I will not countenance the laxity that was used to reign under my stepmother's rule. I have put Oslac, who is the eldest of them, in charge over the men. He is as strict a disciplinarian as one could wish. Arnhilda will watch over the women. T'would be a clever wench could escape her eye!"

"Too true," murmured Sir Tancred. He applauded the lady's determination to run a respectable establishment but could sympathize with the difficulties this would pose in the future for unmarried men. "Still, the knights and men-at-arms will be less than happy with the arrangement."

She shrugged. "Should any man feel so moved, he may visit the folk of Oakwood Village or ride to the fishing vill. I've no objection to that. But these so-called innocent visits to the stables which turn into lover's trysts with the women of the hall will no longer be tolerated."

When the lady set her chin in just that fashion, Sir Tancred had learned not to argue. "Yes, Lord Raoul did mention something of this to me before he left, and while I am not insensitive to the needs of unmarried men, I must say I am in agreement with your policy. I, too, appreciate an ordered household," he declared, puffing out his chest a little. "I have already told the men how cleverly they are to be placed, so that they can draw their weapons from the armory quickly in time of trouble."

It occurred to Judith suddenly that Sir Tancred might have been expecting, as bailiff, to be given command of Oakwood upon Raoul's departure. It must rankle that the command he cherished had been placed upon the shoulders of a young woman. She smiled at him and made her eyes admiring. "Indeed, how clever of you, Sir Tancred! The way you explained it should cut down on complaints, since the plan has military merit. That was well done! I am so glad you are here to help me, for you think of everything!"

"Oh, well," he muttered, flushing. "I've had a deal of experience, I suppose."

"Indeed, it shows," she assured him. "I don't know how I should go on if you were not by."

His gratified flush deepened, but he controlled himself and returned to the drawings. His long finger poked at one. "This long room here is the one you've selected as the ladies' dormer?"

"Yes. Although Lady Margaret is the only unmarried lady in residence at the moment, one can never tell when there will be more. And this one over here," she pointed. "It faces north, which means good light for sewing. It will be the solar. It does not have import for a man, but it is such a comfort to know there will be a place for the women to sit and sew without dogs tangling the threads or men trampling the work because they are in a rush to be elsewhere and do not take care where they set their feet." Also, Judith reckoned, in daylight at least, the solar would keep the women of her bower from the advances of Raoul's soldiery. The kitchen wenches would be harder to regulate during waking hours, but they were usually harlots in any case, and perhaps, she thought hopefully, the sleeping arrangements might force them to become more circumspect. Castle servants would have little time to care for their offspring, and there were only so many infants could be fostered in the vill. With luck, the new arrangements would cut down on the wenches' birth rate.

"I suppose men do tend to ignore needlework beneath their feet," remarked Sir Tancred with an amused twinkle. "At least, that's what my wife says. She has complained more than once about her embroidery stepped upon or hidden beneath accounts."

"Irritating," Judith agreed. "Now, you are the expert here. Where should the weapons be stored in the armory? I do not know whether they should be placed next to the entrance, in racks along the walls, or best put at the far end to be away from prying eyes. Perhaps you will see to that for me until my lord returns to order things as he likes?"

"But of course, my lady. I shall see to it at once. And you will order the storerooms in the cellars?"

"Certainly. Now, I'd thought to put the flour and the unmilled grains here, in the stone bins my lord ordered. The barrels of salt meat will be placed beyond, just over there. Onions, garlic, apples and pears will be strung from the rafters, as is usual, and the butter and cheeses on wooden shelves above the grains. Honey and vinegar, now . . ."

The planning session took several hours, and all the while a long line of oxcarts trundled to and fro, from the old hall to the castle, carrying heavy furniture, clothing, arms, and supplies. The move occupied the better part of two weeks; the settling-in process much longer, for Lady Judith and Sir Tancred were determined upon the exactness of every detail. The carpenter and his apprentice slaved from first light to dusk, constructing beds, shelves, chests, chairs, and tables. Judith and her women labored from dawn to sunset arranging them to their satisfaction.

The castle was far larger than the old Saxon hall, bigger, in fact, than any building of Judith's imagination. Brother Plegmund's descriptions of French fortifications had not prepared her for the reality. The towers . . . well, towered, and the hardpacked courtyard was enormous. It was intimidating, but then, that was the purpose.

She loved the pretty cloistered walks about what would be the back gardens, though. She liked the huge, round Great Hall, too. It had a raised stone dais for the lord's chair, a curving corridor-like covered stair on its inner wall, and an overlooking gallery above. Gray stone walls stared out over the countryside from atop the castle hill and were visible for miles, dominating the scenery.

Judith feared it would be far colder in winter than the cozy wooden hall. Still, she saw the defensive advantages every bit as well as Raoul and agreed that these far outweighed any emotional attachment to the Saxon building. In addition to all else, a castle added enormously to Raoul's status and power. Permission to build one had been denied to all but a handful of King William's barons. So, despite the labor, Judith made no complaint, but took Brother Plegmund aside to assure herself that she knew the proper running of a Norman keep.

Fourth in size only to the great hall, the chapel, and the dormitory for the men-at-arms of the castle, the lord's chamber delighted Judith. It stood opposite the nursery and near enough to the chapel for her to slip down the corridor at night to pray from the tiny carved stone gallery, which looked out over the nave. There were two high, narrow windows in the chamber, which overlooked the as-yet-unplanted gardens, and best of all, a stout oaken door, which could be barred from within.

Raoul had told her privately that the chamber contained a secret stair, which explained the delay in completion of the castle. It was why, he told her, the presence of four of the masons and several apprentices had been required for some time after the others had gone. The stair led to a narrow passageway, running under the moat and the land beyond, ending in the wood near the ancient Roman road.

"God forbid the need ever arise!" Judith had cried when Raoul explained how to open the hidden door.

But the Hawk had shrugged. "Nevertheless, little girl, if it does, 'tis an escape for you and the children we'll have. There are places would be safe enough to hide in 'til our sons are of an age to reclaim that which is theirs." He had gone on to outline a plan he had formulated for her survival in such a circumstance. Judith, neither complaining nor protesting further, had listened intently and nodded her agreement.

T'was a grim discussion but necessary. "Eustace can be treacherous as a serpent," Raoul told her. "He fears me enough that he treads carefully, but I have known for years he's not be trusted when my back is turned. Never let him cozen you into believing him of honorable intent. As for Sir Robert, he means well, which is the worst can be said of any man. He bends with every changing breeze. They've both been well rewarded for past services, but I'd trust neither with the care of my heirs. Remember that."

"They'd harm innocent children?" she demanded, incensed.

"Innocent children grow up to avenge fathers murdered by traitors," he had replied matter-of-factly. "Although most of my family has a love of children in their blood, you know of what Eustace is made. If our babes were all that stood between him and power, he'd not hesitate for an instant, and Sir Robert would go along with whatever he said, even though it'd keep him awake nights afterward."

"And Eustace has Agnes now, who has no scruples in such matters," Judith had murmured thoughtfully. "I'll remember." It was a frightening conversation, the more so because it forced her to imagine life without Raoul. She did not want to contemplate that.

Lord Raoul's return was heralded with much bustle and fanfare. He was a bit leaner and with a new scratch or two to show for his efforts. The campaign, he insisted, was too boring to discuss. Mainly, King William marched them into Yorkshire with little resistance and built castles at Warwick, Nottingham, and York. Lords Edwin and Morcar were repentant and had renewed their allegiance to the King. It had all been very tame.

‡

That evening Raoul sat beside his wife at the high table and surveyed the great hall. "I like the tapestry above the door, my lady. Your design?"

"Yes. I thought you'd like a battle scene. I am glad it pleases you. Do you also find the carving to your liking?"

He craned his neck to stare up at the wall behind him. Judith had badgered the castle carpenter until he'd completed the piece, a gigantic oaken shield carved with the device of a hawk in flight, talons extended. The background was Oakwood castle. "It pleases me very much, particularly the colors. Where had you the pigments?"

"Different types of stones and earths. Brother Plegmund is very knowledgeable in such matters."

"He is to be commended." Raoul sank his teeth appreciatively into a choice morsel of venison, while Judith stretched and rubbed her back, for it was near time for her child to be delivered. The babe kicked strongly, and she grunted, so used by now to the movement of the life within her that she ceased months ago to smile in wonderment. Raoul, however, was not so casual. He saw and reached over to place his hand on her belly, eyes dancing with delight. Folk up and down the tables nudged one another and grinned, taking in this demonstration of the lord's pleasure in his lady and his coming offspring.

"I do hope she bears him a son," muttered Sir Tancred, seated beside his lady at the head of one of the lower tables.

"Yes," agreed Lady Edith shortly, all too aware of her own shortcomings in that department.

"I dare say it won't matter," Father Hubert put in from Lady Edith's left. "He's obviously fond of Lady Judith. A daughter would be none so bad."

Lady Edith motioned to a serving maid to refill the goblet she shared with her husband, and Sir Tancred patted her hand by way of thanks. "Should she bear a girl," he murmured, "well, she's young, as is my own dear lady, and there is plenty of time in future to breed sons."

"True, true," the priest nodded, sending his chins ajiggle. "We must pray to the Blessed Virgin for the child's safe delivery." His eyes strayed to Lady Edith's trencher. "Ah, boiled turnips in wine! I must have missed that when they brought the platters around!" He shook his head at the oversight. "Do you mind if I help myself to a taste?"

"Why, no," she murmured, but his fingers were already plucking vegetables from the soggy bread which held them.

Caught between two men concerned first with their own satisfaction, Lady Edith sighed and set herself to endure the meal with as good a grace as she could.

CHAPTER 8

Before cockcrow on the first day of October, Edwina, the sewing maid slipped around the screen at the side entrance of the great hall. The wooden door behind it opened quietly onto a side area of the courtyard between the hall and several outbuildings. The aroma of bread was heavy in the air, along with wood smoke from both kitchen and smith, and dung from the stables. She wrapped a gray wool cloak tightly about her against the early morning chill and walked swiftly toward the dairy barn. This was earlier than she was usually about, but she wanted to be the first with the news.

A single horn lantern at each end of the dairy barn gave light enough for work, and Gytha was already busy. She looked up in some surprise as her friend entered. "My, but you gave me a start! Is aught amiss?"

"No, no, all's well. I just thought you'd like to be first to hear the news, that's all."

Milk hissed steaming into the bucket as Gytha continued with her task. "Well, then! Something's happened, has it, in the hall?"

"Lady Judith was delivered a few hours past of a son!" announced Edwina importantly.

"A son! Now, that's grand! I'd wager the Hawk was pleased," she commented comfortably.

"Made a big to-do of it, he did," she muttered, almost to herself.

"You'd think t'was a miracle.

Knowing that her friend was more partial to Lord Raoul than was seemly, Gytha ignored the tone. Her own loyalty was to Lady Judith, but Edwina was no threat to her lady's happiness, so she saw no harm in a few wistful glances. "Is he healthy?" she asked.

"Oh, aye. Sucked at once, so Lady Margaret told Lady Edith, and of a goodly size, too."

"Well, that's fine news!" declared Gytha, pleased and relieved. "Who's the babe take after?"

Edwina shrugged. Her news was all secondhand, since only Arnhilda and Lady Margaret had attended the birthing, but she wasn't about to admit that. "It has dark hair, so it's likely it'll look like my lord. It's too early to tell about the eyes," she added.

A stirring by the door heralded the entry of Osric, one of the stable hands. "Come and hear Edwina's news!" Gytha called out. "Lady Judith has borne a son!"

Osric exclaimed and ran off to fetch others. In minutes, Edwina was surrounded by an eager audience. A bucket was overturned for a stool and a piggin of warm milk pressed into her hands. Questions came from all sides. A tide of contentment stole over the redheaded woman as she passed on real and imagined details of the babe's birth. There were times when life was very good.

‡

Raoul had spent the night pacing the great hall and harassing the servants with his constant demands to be informed of Lady Judith's condition. In the past, he had laughed at fathers-to-be and their anxieties. That was before he understood. The excitement of the coming child, the nerve-wracking wondering whether it would be a son, and the terror when he thought of how many women died in childbed combined to make him nearly frantic. Wine was a waste of time and seemed to upset his stomach, besides. The pacing helped but only a little. When a servant finally brought him the tidings that the child had been born, he did not stay even to hear its sex but plunged up the stair and down the corridor. He threw open the chamber door. All was quiet within, no panic, no screams, no weeping. He closed the door behind him carefully, striving for calm.

Judith lay pale and still upon their bed. Her hair was loose but carefully brushed, her eyes closed. Raoul thought she slept and was loath to wake her, but she opened her eyes and smiled wearily. "We have a fine son, Raoul," she told him proudly. "Come and look."

The babe slept, cleaned and wrapped in fine linen, and nestled in the crook of her arm.

"He's very red," observed the Hawk. "And so small!"

Arnhilda looked up from her place by the hearth, her few remaining teeth prominently displayed by her grin. "They're all small in the beginning, my lord. He'll grow. 'Tis lucky he wasn't much bigger; my lady's only torn in two places. She'll mend easy."

Raoul winced. "Jesu!" He thought with horror of his own flesh being torn in so tender a region, and shuddered. "I heard you scream once, Judith. Was it very bad?"

"T'was nothing," she lied. "Do not fret yourself, my lord. It is over now, in any case, and the next time will go easier, they say. The first's always the hardest."

He touched the babe's cheek with a finger, marveling at the softness. Its head turned toward him, mouth instinctively groping.

"Just like a man!" declared Arnhilda with a humorous snort. "Looking for a wench already!"

The child whimpered and Judith smiled. She thumbed up her nipple as Arnhilda had told her to do and put the baby to her breast. The little mouth tugged fiercely, and she gasped. "He's hungry!" Then waves of sweet sensation lapped at her, far different from sexual excitement. She bent down to kiss the downy head.

With infinite care, Raoul reached out to examine a little hand. The tiny fingers held him hard. "Sweet Savior, what a grip! They'll call him Strongarm!" He grinned his pride and delight.

"What name for our first son?" asked Judith, her blue eyes warm with love for him and their child.

"Richard," he replied promptly. "Think you it sounds well?"

"Richard," she murmured. "Richard. Richard, Hawk's son. Aye, it has a pleasant ring." She glanced at Arnhilda. "Has anyone thought to wake Brother Plegmund? He must mark the hour of Richard's birth and cast his horoscope."

Arnhilda grunted as she rose. "I'll go and see if he's awake, but I imagine he's already busy doing just that, my lady." She opened the door, then looked back over her shoulder. "Will you want a wetnurse?"

Judith held the babe more tightly. "No! He's mine!" she said sharply. Then a sheepish smile crept across her lips. "Well, one of the village girls to nursemaid when he's older. But I'll see to his nourishing myself."

Arnhilda left, satisfied.

"Jesu, but you're fierce," remarked Raoul, chuckling delightedly as he sat on the side of the bed. "For a moment there you put me in mind of a she-wolf defending her young!"

Judith smiled back at him. "Aye, well, so he will be, fierce like me and strong, brave, and wise like you." Suddenly she yawned as weariness engulfed her. The babe, she noted, had already gone back to sleep. It had been a hard night's work for both of them. "I am so tired, Raoul. Will you pull up the coverlet? The babe must not be chilled."

He leaned forward to do so and kissed her gently on the cheek, but Judith was already fast asleep. He smiled wryly, reckoning that there would be many a night from now until Judith recovered from childbed when he would look at her while she slept. Hawk sighed, tucked the blanket about them both, and returned to the great hall for breakfast.

‡

Sir Eustace and Lady Agnes were invited to sponsor the heir to Oakwood. "Not that I'd leave him for an instant in their charge," Raoul explained to his lady, "But they'll expect to be asked. 'Tis better so. I'd not give my brother cause for complaint against me without need."

‡

Judith lay abed fretting, while downstairs in the new chapel Father Hubert blessed the three-day-old infant and charged its godparents with their duty to the child. She remembered Agnes' villainy with their first babe and shuddered at the thought of Richard lying helpless in the arms of that faithless bitch. He was Raoul's hope for the future and already held her own heart in his tiny hands. She relaxed only when Arnhilda returned the babe to the safety of her own arms. After his soaked clothing had been exchanged for fresh, however, the maidservant held out her arms once more.

Judith surrendered Richard reluctantly. "Where do you take him now?"

"Lord Hawk has demanded that his knights and men swear allegiance to the child this very eve!" she snorted. "Foolishness!"

But Judith shook her head. "No, 'tis a wise policy to do it so. Remind my lord that Father Hubert has a reliquary with a hair from the head of John the Baptist, and be sure he remembers to mention the folk."

"The folk?" asked Arnhilda with knit brows.

"Never mind," returned Judith, smiling. "He won't forget."

So Richard of Oakwood was returned to the chapel once more, where his father's knights and men-at-arms were gathered. There they stood, one at a time, one hand upon the sacred relic and the other upon the babe's small chest, swearing by all the saints their feudal oath to Lord Raoul of Oakwood and to his son, Richard. Then, since the babe was not of age to speak for himself, Lord Raoul pledged Richard's loyalty to King William and his heirs, and declared his duty to defend and protect the people of Oakwood, and to protect its lands from all enemies.

‡

While the men attended the second ceremony, Lady Agnes, excluded from this male-oriented rite with the other women, climbed the stair to the master's chamber. At Judith's smiling gesture, Agnes seated herself in a newly fashioned chair. It had been drawn up to the side of the bed where Oakwood's lady held court.

"You have become very grand," commented Agnes snidely. "Carved chairs instead of stools! I wonder what your mother would have made of all this."

"My mother, God rest her soul, would have checked for dust to ensure that my housekeeping was up to her standard," replied Judith with an impish grin. "However, she would have approved the particular chair upon which you sit. The design is copied from an old Saxon scroll and was probably in fashion even before Christianity came to England."

Agnes tried to smile politely. She was pale, and there were dark circles under her eyes. When, inadvertently, she leaned back against the chair, she winced. Judith guessed she'd been beaten recently. She recalled several beatings she'd received as a result of Agnes' lies when they were girls and regarded her stepsister without pity.

"Your Richard is a beautiful babe," Agnes said. "Truly. All that curly hair! He has a great look of his father, too. Especially about the mouth and nose. I suppose he'll have brown eyes?"

"It's probable, although my lord did say his grandsire had blue eyes." She shrugged. "It is too early to be sure."

Lady Agnes nodded. "I vow you look well enough, sister. I'd half-expected to find you lying upon your bed and moaning in high fever. They say a first delivery is usually hard."

"I'm stronger than I look," returned Judith evenly. "And this is my *second* time in childbed, though to be sure the first babe was born too young to survive."

"To be sure," Agnes said hurriedly. "Well, it is a great relief that you have had no complications with this one."

"God has been good to us."

"Yes, as you say," murmured the other woman, her eyes taking a comprehensive look about the chamber. There were new clothes chests, a small but exquisite tapestry upon the wall, and on the table a jewel casket she had never seen before. Agnes got up to investigate. "Did you do this work?" she asked, eyes on the needlework.

"No, it was done by my lady mother. My father had it put away in a chest at her death. I found it again when we moved from the hall."

Agnes nodded and moved away to the table. "Why, what is this, sister?" She opened the box and gave an involuntary gasp. With a wondering sigh, she lifted out a gold chain decked with a single large pearl. Her finger caressed the cream-colored bauble, investigating its uneven bumps. "Merciful God! This must be worth's a king's ransom!"

"A gift from Lord Raoul," said Judith softly. "He takes great pleasure in the birth of his son."

Agnes dropped the necklet and closed the box with a snap. "How lovely for you." She returned to her chair. "I've been hoping for a child myself."

Judith's brows rose. "Then, you think . . ."

"No, not yet," sighed Agnes. "Although t'will not be for any lack of trying an I find I am not! Sweet Mary, when Sir Eustace was told the news his brother again expected an heir, he swore he'd get one on me or kill me in the attempt!" She laughed as she spoke, but there was a tightness about her mouth and eyes. "I vow, sister, he mounts me thrice a day at least to see his goal accomplished!"

Judith cocked her head to one side. "You are less than a year wed. Do you tell me you tire of lovemaking so soon?"

"Lovemaking!" retorted Agnes, "Is that what you call it? The man rides me like a bull with a cow and cares not whether he pleasures me with his rough handling!"

"Did you not tell me once that such caresses were not distasteful to you?" Judith responded. Agnes' very manner, sulky and jealous, made it difficult for one to feel even the beginning of sympathy. Indeed, t'was clear that she felt sorry enough for herself that she needed no one else's pity.

"Once I liked it well enough, but of late I find it is a chore like any other which must be got over before I go on to the next." She glanced at Judith from under her lashes. "That is a woman's lot, my dear. Doubtless it is the same for you, would you not say?"

"Well, not really," answered Judith, cursing her blush. "With my lord Hawk it is a joy."

"He's not rough with you, then?" persisted Agnes avidly.

"Only when I like him to be," Judith stretched a bit and grimaced. "Though t'will be long 'ere I can test his manhood, now I've given birth. The price of giving him an heir is higher than I'd counted on!" she added with a rueful laugh.

Agnes stared at her, torn by jealousy and hatred. "Must be your Saxon blood makes you as hot as any kitchen slattern for the bedding!"

So! Judith lowered her lashes, unwilling to show that she understood her sister's envy. "I reckon it must be," she agreed. "Whatever it is, I'll swear my lord likes it well enough! He's as eager as I and will find the waiting just as hard, I'll warrant."

"*If* he waits," remarked Agnes slyly. "There are wenches in plenty would be only too glad of a place in his bed."

"Yes, I suppose there are," she murmured, glancing about humorously. "But if they tried to fill it, things might become a trifle crowded!"

Agnes tossed her head, unamused.

Bored with the ensuing silence, Judith unplaited her braids and reached for a wooden comb that lay, with other of her things, upon the coverlet. She slid it though the shining waves and smiled. "Tell me, sister, how like you Danesford Tower?"

"It suits me," said Agnes shortly, nettled at her lack of success.

She had thought surely Judith would be upset by a suggestion of her lord's infidelity.

"It pleases me to hear you are content." Judith continued to comb her hair.

"Of course," Agnes waved a hand at the magnificence about her, "it cannot compare with all of *this*. Do you know, often I have thought of you, lost in this great castle, and been moved to the heart. How difficult it must be for you to cope with things for which you are unsuited, not having been reared to deal with them! The old hall . . . well, you must forgive me, dear sister, was . . . more hovel than castle. It was certainly unlike the gracious home I had in Normandy! How puzzling it must be for you now, to live in so great a place and not know how to go on!"

Judith smiled sardonically beneath the curtain of her hair. "Have no fears for me, Lady Agnes, I manage to bumble along somehow."

"Yes, but the Norman customs are so different from your Saxon ones," the other woman persisted doggedly. "You must have had a great many difficulties."

Judith seemed to consider. "Difficulties? No, I cannot think of any have taxed me unduly. We're certainly less cramped here, which is a blessing, but now I've the space, I have ordered the household as I've always thought it should be. I keep the scullions and men-at-arms away from my housemaids, and these days only the dogs sleep in the rushes. 'Tis a thousand pities you cannot be similarly situated at Danesford, sister. You can have no idea what a relief it is to preside over a seemly establishment."

Agnes choked back a hot reply. "Sir Eustace told me how you encouraged him before you were wed to Lord Raoul," she remarked nastily. But even that hopeful comment, a shot taken at venture, drew no more than amusement.

"Now, really!" Judith laughed. "How inflated a value men set upon their charms! I had speech exactly once with my lord's brother, and upon that occasion, as witnesses will bear me out, the only encouragement he received was the point of my knife."

Agnes shrugged. "Doubtless, then, I misunderstood what he said." She thought for a moment. "I have heard that Lady Margaret bides with you still. Surely with the birth of the new babe you are well over the loss of your first."

Judith's eyes flashed dangerously for a second before she hid them beneath lowered lids. "As you say."

"Then, does Lady Margaret not mean to return to Deerfield? After all, it is her rightful place, is it not?" asked Agnes nervously. She had seen violence in Judith's gaze, if only for a moment. Shocked, she wondered yet again if her stepsister might have knowledge of her guilt. Surely not, she told herself for the thousandth time. No one had seen her slip the potion into the goblet; she was sure of it.

"Why should Lady Margaret return to Deerfield?" countered Judith, her eyebrows delicately raised. "I believe she is content to be here with us, and since Lady Blanche is mistress of Deerfield, I imagine *she* is able to run her household without undue strain."

"Ummmm," said Agnes.

"In point of fact," Judith continued, "Lady Margaret is such a help overseeing the women of the bower that I should be loath to give her up. Does Lady Blanche wish for her return so badly that she must send you as emissary? Should I speak to her regarding the matter?"

"No! No!" exclaimed Agnes hastily. "It is nothing of the sort, sister; t'was merely my feminine curiosity. I dare say Lady Blanche was glad to see her go, what with Sir Robert so hot for her he could not show his own lady the barest civil courtesy."

Judith opened her eyes to their widest. "Indeed? Is this so? Why, how very well informed you are, sister! One might also conclude you had a spy in their service."

"Oh!" gasped Agnes, now thoroughly alarmed. "I . . . I am sure t'was only gossip I heard somewhere. There is probably naught in it. A spy in their household! How very droll you are, my dear, to think up such nonsense. As if I would ever consider such an action!"

"If you say so." Privately, Judith was more than a little disgusted. Sir Eustace and Sir Robert had chosen a poor tool to ferret out information.

The door swung open and Arnhilda entered, carrying the babe. Close on her heels was the jongleur, Aubrey.

Arnhilda cast a sharp glance at the young woman in the chair. "Greetings, Lady Agnes," she said grudgingly.

Lady Agnes nodded but made no reply. Her attention was riveted on the handsome young man in multicolored clothing. The well-formed Aubrey had always interested her, and now that her mother was no more, she considered her options. He had always seemed like one who might not be rough or hasty with a lady's person in bedsport.

The jongleur was aware of interested feminine eyes and, as was his habit, puffed out his chest a bit. His own eyes, however, were drawn irresistibly to Lady Judith. He had known many ladies far more beautiful than she but none with her gentleness or her spirit. Like to like, the old saying went, and he had known always that she was destined to marry a noble of some sort or other. Still, he did not consider the matter hopeless. When the opportunity arose, he had directed Hawk's attention toward Oakwood and Lady Judith, for Aubrey had his own plans for the future. As a young and inexperienced bride, Lady Judith of Oakwood was far beyond his touch. As a bored wife of long standing, however, she might well respond to a rascal like himself in the years to come. In fact, he was counting on it. She would not be the first.

Aubrey bowed. "Lady Judith, I come to take my leave of you. I have already spoken with Lord Hawk, and he bade me see you in farewell."

"Do you leave us so soon?" she asked politely, reaching out hungry arms for the babe.

"To my regret, I do. I go to France, if it pleases you, Lady Judith, to learn the newest songs and tales. I shall stop in London, too, to learn all the gossip of King William's court." He went down on one knee. "'Tis in my mind to return with a troupe of my own to entertain Oakwood."

"Then, this is not a permanent separation?" she inquired, loosening her gown. Beneath the curtain of her hair, she put the infant to her breast.

Aubrey looked up at her, swallowing hard at the sight of her long, golden hair half hiding her breast as the babe suckled. Strangely, the tableau aroused tenderness in him, rather than an urge for sex. "I . . . I should like to return after the next harvest, should it please you," he said.

Aubrey wanted to lift her chin with his hand, as he would do with any peasant woman he fancied, and kiss those smiling lips. Suddenly, he hardened for the core of her and was astonished that it should be so. Christ on the Cross, but she tempted him! T'was as well he was leaving.

Judith's eyes were on Richard. She stroked his soft baby head with a loving hand. "Why, your return will be a day to which all of Oakwood will look forward," she remarked with easy courtesy. "Godspeed upon your journey, Aubrey."

There came a burst of raucous laughter from the great hall below, and Judith looked up inquiringly at the jongleur.

"Lord Raoul has found two cocks for the entertainment of the folk," he explained. "I've seen them myself, my lady, and I think t'will be a fight worth watching."

She nodded, uninterested. Lady Agnes, however, stood suddenly, an eager expression on her face. "Do you give me your escort, Aubrey. I have been dull of late and would dearly love to witness the contest." She turned to Judith. "With your permission, sister?"

"Of course. Enjoy the fight."

"Why, t'would be my great pleasure to accompany you, Lady Agnes," said the jongleur. He knew what she truly wanted and was pleased that it should be so. God knew it would ease the ache he felt at present! He took hold of Lady Judith's sleeve and pressed his lips to the hem of it. "God keep you safe, my lady," he murmured. Then he rose, and with some grace bowed to Lady Agnes, extending his arm.

Agnes nearly devoured him with her eyes as she bid Lady Judith a hurried farewell and practically dragged the jongleur from the chamber.

Judith was hard-pressed not to laugh. She waited until the door was firmly closed. "Find you Lady Margaret and Lady Edith," she said to Arnhilda. "'Tis no *fight* my dear sister has on her mind! It may be that we'll need a strong club should the time come she threatens our peace."

Arnhilda departed looking pleased, and Judith bent her head once more to her son.

‡

Her bedside candle was considerably shortened, but Raoul was yet occupied with the guests in the great hall. Richard, fed and sleepy, was tucked on his side in his cradle. Judith took up a tunic of golden velvet and resumed her needlework, filling in a bunch of grapes along the garment's hem. Earlier in the evening, she had felt some resentment that she was confined to her chamber whilst the guests made merry. Now, considering the probability of Agnes' adultery, she was content to lean back against her pile of wolf pelts and consider the situation.

For the first time, she was aware of information as a possible weapon. As a girl she had known, as did all of Oakwood, of Lady Bertha's many infidelities, but it had never occurred to her to use that knowledge in any way. In those days, her object had been to keep such facts from her father. When enraged, Cerdic had turned on all about him, exhausting his wrath upon his people regardless of guilt or innocence. To have told him of his lady's wantonness would have been unthinkable. But now Cerdic was no more, and in this new situation, there were many possibilities.

Of course, Agnes was a danger, and Judith determined that she would take the greatest care not to betray the hold she had over her. However, Raoul must certainly be told. Lady Edith was a mouse, who spoke to none of the women of Judith's bower except when necessary because she suspected, quite without basis in fact, that one or more of them were bent upon seducing her husband. Since that one disastrous mistake in believing Lady Agnes' lies, she gossiped with no one. She never spoke of women's affairs to her husband, and Judith knew she would not relate even so juicy a morsel as this for fear of piquing Sir Tancred's interest. Lady Margaret, on the other hand, would hold her tongue out of deference to Judith's wishes.

Arnhilda returned. Her eyes glittered with suppressed excitement. She shut the door tightly before she spoke. "You were right," she declared with a rich chuckle. "However much Lady Agnes may dislike spreading herself for Sir Eustace, she was willing and more for yon Aubrey! Like mother like daughter, they say, and for the same man, too! I'm surprised at the jongleur, though. Thought he was bigger than that. I reckon t'was only padding in his hose."

Judith tried to look reproving and failed. A giggle escaped her. "Truly? I'd not thought men so vain as that!" Her giggling grew worse.

"Oh, I dare say 'tis like the kerchiefs a maid will stuff down her bodice, my lady. A lure for the fools to ogle. Small though he is, what there was of that fool jongleur was eager for the contest," returned the maidservant, grinning broadly. "Clever with it, too. The position he chose, his partner could see naught. Lady Agnes likely thinks him hung like a Flemish stallion!"

"Well," Judith uttered, controlling the giggles at last. "What leafy glade did our lovers choose for their tryst?"

"You'll not believe me! I'd thought surely a vacant chamber or the knights' quarters since they're all below stairs, but no! They picked the ladies' dormer, where Lady Margaret could walk in at any moment!" She shook her head at such fecklessness. "You'd think that at least Lady Agnes would have had more sense, being married and all, but I don't believe there's a working brain between 'em."

"So, it's my Saxon blood makes me yearn for bedsport, is it?" Judith murmured with a smug grin. She glanced at the older woman. "You had witnesses?"

Arnhilda nodded vigorously. "Aye, my lady, as you bade me. Ladies Edith and Margaret were close to hand, walking in the gallery. I had to let Lady Blanche of Deerfield come as well, since she stood near and heard. Don't you worry over her," she added, seeing Judith's frown. "Lady Blanche'll keep her tongue between her teeth. 'Tis right grateful she is you took Margaret from her manor, for she feared Sir Robert might put her aside, seeing she's barren as a thrice-used field. She had it in mind he meant to set Lady Margaret in her place. I'm bound to say it seems likely, what with Lady Margaret having proved her fertility many times over." She frowned. "Now I think of it, though, she had four as died while they were yet in swaddling bands." She shrugged bony shoulders. "In any case, t'was a close thing for Lady Blanche, and she's not like to forget what she owes you."

Judith met Arnhilda's limpid gaze with a quizzical look of her own. "Strange how no hint of this undying gratitude has displayed itself in her previous dealings with me."

The maid busied herself with folding Lady Judith's embroidery and replacing the colored silks and wools in the rush workbasket. "'Tis only this night she's had the thought fixed in her head that Lady Margaret might yet return to Deerfield."

"Now, I wonder how she might have come by that notion?" mused Judith. She looked suspiciously at her companion.

"You know how people talk, my lady."

"Hmmmm. She'll keep silent then?" she asked, tacitly approving these somewhat ruthless methods.

"Oh, aye, so long as Lady Margaret remains here unwed."

"Poor Lady Margaret," Judith sighed. She looked thoughtful. "I don't suppose we've any proof that Lady Blanche has been similarly tempted?"

"What, like Lady Agnes, that worthless strumpet? Very careful is Lady Blanche," Arnhilda said regretfully. "And feared of her lord. I don't think there's aught to be found against her."

Judith shrugged. "Ah, well, that's life! Always a worm in the apple! Still, we've naught to fear until Lady Margaret weds, and I won't hurry the event can I help it." She cocked an eyebrow. "Since we speak of Lady Margaret, do you know if she has a fancy for any of the knights?"

Arnhilda grimaced. "Aye. She is often to be found walking with Sir Basil of an evening."

"I think it will not do," remarked Judith after a considerable pause. "Too ambitious by far is Sir Basil. I recall well the look in his eye when my lord spoke of building a keep to the north of Danesford. Has he a woman among the kitchen wenches?"

"No, my lady. He prefers to go to the vill. More variety and less fuss," she explained.

"Yes, well, pass that along to Lady Margaret at an appropriate time. T'will cool her interest somewhat if he beds another while courting her. And I think I will speak to my lord regarding this. He should be warned of Sir Eustace's interest in matters dealing with Lady Margaret."

"It does give one pause," agreed Arnhilda.

"I think it probable that Sir Robert has been visiting Danesford and asked him to find out our intentions in regard to her future. Sir Robert and Sir Eustace may have grown closer than I'd guessed," she mused. "Arnhilda, see can you find out how often they've seen one another, will you?"

"Aye, my lady."

‡

But as it turned out, it was several weeks before she mentioned the matter to Raoul, for it was not pressing, and she was too wrapped up in Richard to give it much heed. Also, Raoul had set her a problem that occupied a great deal of her attention. He had said that it was necessary to obtain the favor of the Church did he wish to become prosperous and powerful, so naturally Judith applied her mind to the task. After much consideration, she believed she had found an answer. She waited until a winter's eve when the dinner had been especially good and they were closed privately in their chamber for the night.

"If you gifted the Church with enough land for an abbey, Raoul," she ventured, "would not the Church be inclined to look upon you with favor?"

He stared, aghast. "What?! Gift the Church with my hard-won land? I'd die, rather! God's Teeth, woman, have you taken leave of your senses?" Raoul snorted derisively and went to put more wood on the fire.

Judith took careful stitches in the last grape of her embroidery and suppressed a smile. "I suppose t'was a foolish notion. But you must admit t'would have made you look well in the Archbishop's eyes, my lord."

"Oh, beyond all doubt," he agreed sardonically. "And beggared me in the process."

"Not necessarily. Besides, the King is a man of great piety, as I have heard. He, too, would have been impressed," Judith pointed out. She bit off her thread and held the finished work before her, considering whether it was fine enough for Raoul to wear to the Christmas feasting.

Her husband poked at the burning logs. "Tell, me, are not Father Hubert and Brother Plegmund enough? Would you *surround* us with holy men?"

"No, I'd thought of women," she replied absently, as if the matter were done and of no consequence. "My lord, would you reach into the chest beside you and bring me that red tunic I began before Richard's birth? Yes, that's it. This one is well enough, but you'd look grander in the red with the golden hawk, can I finish it in time." She accepted the garment from his hand and threaded her needle with brown silk.

"I've heard it said that nuns are less greedy than monks and apt to keep to their vows of chastity," she continued. "T'would have made things easier in the village if you'd favored the plan. They are most of them skilled with herbs and healing, too, which would have benefited us all."

Raoul scowled, tossing the iron poker atop the woodbin. "You'd have given them my best lands for their bellies' lining! Part of the lord's demesne, doubtless!"

The embroidery had been more than half-finished when she'd set it aside, Judith noted with satisfaction. "No, why should I have wanted to do that? I never gave it much thought, though perhaps that bit along the edge of the sea cliffs would have been appropriate. Not by the waterfall, but further south, where the meadow was blasted by lightening the summer before last. Of course, it's so rocky there you can't walk two paces in any direction without stubbing a toe, and the soil is poor. We'll never farm it though, and t'would have been no great loss since it has no direct access to the sea.

"Would you light another candle, my lord?" she requested. "This one gutters so I cannot see to set my stitches."

He did so in silence, his thoughts otherwhere, and Judith did not interrupt him. She worked quietly, edging the tip of a feather with brown silk before filling in the gold. It was coming along very nicely, she thought, one of her better efforts.

"Would you have given them the woodlands as well?" asked Raoul suddenly.

Judith looked up from her work. "Hmmmm? Oh. Why should I give them the woodlands? The serfs would have sold them deadfall for firewood, and the nuns are not great hunters, after all. No, I thought the cliff land plenty generous."

"*More* than generous," he stressed, but absently. "Can the land be worked, think you?"

Judith shrugged. "Certainly, if anyone cared to have the rocks hauled off and the weeds cleared. Then all would have to be manured. T'would be a prodigious undertaking, though."

"Had you intended gifting them with folk to clear the land and work it?"

"Not even at spearpoint!" declared Judith with comic surprise. "We need every serf and villein we have. I reckon the land would have been enough. I wanted you to impress the Archbishop, not declare yourself a candidate for sainthood!"

He laughed, crossing the floor again to stand beside the bed upon which she sat. "You're near to finished with this one. It looks very well. Why did you put it aside?"

"Oh, I'd tired of it, I suppose, and wanted something new to look upon for a space. Now, with Richard safely born and the gold tunic out of the way, I am eager to see this one done as well."

He peeped longingly at her breasts, barely concealed beneath the clinging kirtle she wore, her only covering since she'd removed her gown for the night. Normally she slept naked, as he did himself, but not since the babe's coming. He stifled a sigh and turned his thoughts in another direction, knowing t'would be weeks yet before she recovered completely from Richard's birthing. "I've no objection to holy nuns living at the cliffs' edge," he told her. "In fact, 'tis a goodly thought. In the spring we'll have to send Brother Plegmund to make the arrangements. Do you have him write out the paper for your approval and I'll deed the cliff land to the Church."

Judith kept her eyes upon her needle. "As you wish, my lord."

CHAPTER 9

By the New Year, Judith was healed from the effects of the babe's birth, and more than anxious to resume those aspects of wedded life which childbed had interrupted. Yet each time Raoul took her in his arms, no sooner did she begin to respond to his ardent wooing, than the child would wake, crying fretfully. Every time, she would have to leave their bed and go to him. After four such nights, Raoul was in a foul humor, venting his frustration upon all in range of his sarcasm, and Judith's own temper was frayed about the edges. Upon the fifth night, the Hawk entered their bedchamber with a grim expression.

Judith stood warming herself at the fire, naked but for a woolen cloak she had donned against the draughts that whistled past the wooden shutters. Her belly was flat again, although that could not be seen under the heavy folds of fabric; her breasts, grown large and full since the birth of their son, peeped at him from the cloak's opening. She looked up expectantly at his entrance and smiled. "I wondered when you'd come," she remarked. "Tis late."

Raoul grunted and removed his belt. "I thought I'd wait 'til Richard slept soundly," he told her, unlacing his soft leather shoes and tossing them into a corner. "Not," he added bitterly, "that it will make much difference. I have no doubt he'll soon wake with his usual enthusiasm."

"He's not here," she told him, playing with the edges of the cloak. "I put him in the nursery."

"What?!"

"I had Arnhilda fetch Dorothea from the village to be nursemaid to Richard," she explained patiently. "He's a strong, healthy babe, and she's a good girl who has had charge of younger brothers and sisters. I can still suckle him, but I'd an odd desire to sleep without an ear cocked for his crying."

He whipped the tunic over his head and stripped off his hose, dropping them to the floor. "What you're saying is, we'll be alone together of a night?" he demanded eagerly. "Merciful Savior, woman! Don't waste time talking! Get out of that cloak!"

But Judith wanted to play. "Make me," she said.

He stood still. "What did you say?"

"An you want me, my lord, you'll have to take me," she challenged.

"Would you play at rape, my lady?" He threw back his head and laughed.

She allowed the gap at the front of the cloak to widen a little. "Why not?"

Raoul's dark eyes mocked her. "Very well, little girl. What would you have me do first?"

"How should I know?" She ran her hands slowly over her breasts. "I have never had such a thing happen to me."

He watched her, breathing unsteadily as she touched herself. "You'd not find it amusing an it happened in reality," he muttered. Jesu, how he wanted her!

"That's truth," she said softly, smiling and daring him with her eyes. "Yet in play it might be a thing we'd both enjoy. Unless, of course, you don't think you can do it?"

"Take off that cloak!" he commanded hoarsely.

She did so, letting it slide to the floor. Her hands returned to her breasts and she teased him with her body.

Raoul watched her until the heat within him could no longer be denied. "So, lady!" he snarled crossing the floor and dragging her hard against him. "If 'tis rape you want, I can see your need well met!" He threw her to the rushes and mounted her, but Judith was ready. She strained to meet him again and again. Then, when her goal was almost reached and she shivered with anticipation, Raoul pulled away.

He looked down at her with glittering eyes. She reached out for him, but he pushed her hands aside. "Beg me!" he ordered.

Judith stared up at him. The stone floor was cold against her back and prickly with rushes. She longed for the comfort of their bed, but she had challenged him and must now play the game on his terms or suffer a breach between them. She held out her arms once more. "Please, Raoul," she whispered. She hoped he did not hear the irritation behind the tone.

He sensed that the excitement was not as fierce for her now, so he smiled in his victory and trailed his hand down her body, his lips following slowly, teasing her until she began to twist and turn on the rushes. Then he covered her again.

They sweated and strained, clutching each other, the sounds of their gasping breaths loud in the chamber, the scent of their love filling the air. Firelight played over them, casting fantastic shadows on the walls. Judith clutched his hips with her legs. "Please, Raoul," she begged. "Please! Now!" And then he arched into her, crying out, and she followed him into wonder, muffling her scream of joy against his shoulder.

‡

On a bright morning, Brother Plegmund, full of importance, entered their chamber and handed to Lady Judith the parchment upon which he had writ Richard's horoscope. The words were in Latin, and plain enough to Judith, who could read them, but the borders and various places in the text were decorated with arcane symbols and drawings. For Lord Raoul's benefit, the cleric informed them of what was writ upon that vital document.

"The child was born under the sign of Libra, the Scales. The stars have indicated a long life and many sons. He will rule at Oakwood after you are gone, although this event will not take place for many years. You may note some resistance to total obedience as he grows older and a love of a good fight, but he will be a sweet-natured child, and a peacemaker."

Raoul nodded gravely. "Thank you, Brother Plegmund. My lady and I are grateful." When the monk had withdrawn from the chamber, however, Raoul grinned and flicked the end of the parchment with a careless finger. "It is all nonsense."

Judith glared at him, offended, and flounced down upon their bed. "How can you say so, Raoul?" she demanded. "Brother Plegmund knew from the stars that King William would invade England and that he would take the crown for his own. He told me so soon after we were wed, although I'd suspected it from his remarks long before. He also knew that I would be wife to the new lord of this place, even without knowing who you were!"

Raoul laughed at her, stretching out full length upon the coverlet. He propped himself upon one elbow and gave her a sardonic glance. "Innocent! Anyone who has spent even a small space of time in Normandy, which your monk did, knows enough of King William to realize he'd fight for the crown. And since he'd the right on his side, to say nothing of the Pope, he was bound to win."

He shook his head at her. "Tell me, little one, do you rate your beauty so low that you'd believe even for an instant any knight amongst us hot-blooded Normans would refuse to take you to his bed? Once you'd been seen, *especially* alongside these poor excuses for women with whom Oakwood abounds, your future would have been assured. Nay, my lady, none will make me believe in the power of the stars to predict the course of a man's life. It's common sense and guesswork, that's all, mixed up with mumbled Latin and little pictures to fool the credulous. But rest you content. If it gives you comfort to believe your monk has the gift of Sight he claims; I'll not dispute it within his hearing." They did not discuss the matter further.

‡

In early March the castle warder brought word to Lady Judith that a messenger waited at the gate with word for the Hawk.

"Have him brought to the great hall and treated with all honor," she instructed, and watched his back somberly as he strode off. Then she looked about her. Pale spring sunlight brightened the solar, where her women were gathered, busily occupied with spinning and sewing. All had stopped working at the news, for such a visitor could only mean that Lord Raoul was summoned by the King for knight's service, and that most likely meant war. Lady Edith bit her lip, and Judith smiled to reassure her before turning to a squire, who stood by awaiting orders.

"Holy Saints, one cannot doubt the coming of spring now!" she commented with a rueful smile. "Well, you'd best fetch my lord. He's in the armory, I think, or in the chapel. Sir Tancred will know. I will see to this messenger's comfort until my lord comes." She signaled the women to continue their tasks and followed the squire down the stone stair.

Yawning delicately, Judith mentally cursed the King for his continuing springtime campaigns. She was again with child and always sleepy. Already her milk had dried up and she had been forced to resort to a wetnurse for Richard, a necessity she resented. So great was her aversion to what she considered the usurping of her rights as the child's mother, that she kept the woman away from the babe except at mealtimes. She had ordered Dorothea to see the child was weaned to a cup as soon as possible, and since Dorothea feared the influence of the wetnurse might undermine her own, she complied scrupulously.

The messenger was an older man, which surprised Judith, used to pages and young boys sent for this purpose. He was obviously known to Raoul, who laughed and greeted him my name.

"Roger! Good to see you, man! How goes it? Speared any fish lately?"

The older man laughed heartily, grasping the Hawk by his forearms and shaking him vigorously. "To think you remember that after all these years!" He smiled at Judith, looking for all the world like a misplaced Viking, with his bright blue eyes and reddish-gold curls. "Once, in France, I was so intent upon teaching young Raoul here to spear fish in a pond that I clean forgot to watch what I was about and put a lance through my own foot!"

Judith smiled in sympathy with their enjoyment of what was, apparently, a moment treasured by both, and sent a wench for wine and cheese.

Sir Roger de Rouen clapped the Hawk across the back. "Nice little place you've got for yourself here, my lord. And I see," he added, glancing humorously at Judith's rounded belly, "that congratulations are in order!"

"Our second," Raoul responded, his chest expanded a bit with pride. "The first's a boy; I've named him Richard." He took his lady's hand. "May I present my old fishing instructor, my lady? Sir Roger de Rouen, one of the best of King William's knights. Roger, my wife, Lady Judith of Oakwood."

"Enchanted, my lady," he bowed. Then he grinned. "The first a boy, *hein*? Well, you always did know how to manage things properly, Hawk. Well done!" he declared heartily. "Well done, indeed!"

A table was hastily set up on Judith's orders, and the men seated themselves. When Judith joined them, de Rouen raised his brows inquiringly, but Raoul merely smiled. "My lady commands in my absence," he said, and the other man's face assumed an expression of greater respect.

"King William summons you to meet him on the road to Durham, Hawk," Sir Roger reported, his eyes now serious. "You'll remember that King William chose Robert of Comines to replace Gospatric as Earl in Northumbria?"

"A good choice," remarked Raoul, reaching out to take the tankard extended him by a serving wench. "Sir Robert saved my life more than once in France, and yours too, if I remember aright. Your health," he added, gesturing with his wine.

Sir Roger drained his tankard and held it out to be refilled. "He'll not do so again, my friend. The Northumbrians attacked him from ambush and killed him, along with his entire force."

Raoul put down his tankard with a snap. "God's Blood! When was this?"

"January. It took a while for the word to reach us."

"How many men had be with him?"

"Five hundred good ones. All lost."

"Five hundred! Sweet Savior!" Raoul wiped his face with one hand. "Do you journey with me to Durham, or have you others to visit on your way?" he asked, his eyes distant. Already his thoughts were focused on the road to war.

"Oh, I'd planned to ride with you, Hawk, an you'll have me. T'will be like old times," added Sir Roger, with a reminiscent grin. "Do you remember that ride to Val-es-Dunes?"

"I'm not like to forget it! That was by far the sweetest . . ." A flush rose to stain Hawk's cheekbones. He glanced at his wife. "I will give you my instructions while I pack," he told her in a tone that was clearly dismissive.

Judith nodded and rose. *Men were such fools*, she thought crossly, as she made her way to the kitchen. Did he think she hadn't known there was more than one woman before their marriage? And that Sir Roger de Rouen referred to some encounter with a woman was plain from the satisfied smirk on his lips. Then she shrugged. There were more important things to claim her attention.

She consulted with Cynefred about rations for the march, informed Raoul's servant, Humphrey, that he'd best sort through his lord's gear for packing. Then she told Sir Tancred of the situation and suggested he see Lord Raoul at once for orders concerning the number of men required for the new venture. After that, she took herself off to her chamber. With a sigh for the inevitable joint coming of spring and war, Judith began sorting the clothing her husband would need on the road.

Well did she know, that for men like Raoul winter was a difficult time, for he was all warrior. Although he knew farming and supervised it well, his real inclination was to rush off down the road with his sword and shield at the ready, and his men at his back. Somehow that knowledge saddened her. She felt lonely but shrugged it off. Remembering his last campaign, Judith sent Arnhilda to fetch Brother Plegmund. Raoul would not want to be burdened with the monk on the march to Durham, but in deference to Judith's pregnancy, he would raise no objection. And this time, Judith vowed, she'd have news of his doings within three weeks instead of a carefully edited version months later.

She hoped Raoul would put off his departure until the morrow; she badly wanted to lay with him once more before he left. And then Judith wondered just exactly what it was had happened that Raoul found so unforgettable on the road to Val-es-Dunes.

CHAPTER 10

he mill stood solid and heavy at the water's edge, along the stream that flowed past the village graveyard. The church, a stone building of great age, played the part of sentinel in the background. The building stones for the mill had been quarried locally, but Raoul had, the previous fall, sent all the way to Normandy for the huge millstones.

"My lady," said Jack the Miller. "Would you care to step inside and watch the first bag of wheat being ground?" He was a plump young fellow, grateful for the chance to be independent of his father and anxious to please his new lord. "Please," he urged, "this way. T'will only take a moment."

Judith nodded and followed, Conan at her heals and Arnhilda jealously pacing beside him.

"Careful where you step, my lady," cautioned Arnhilda. "It is a bit dark in here."

"But so cool!" marveled Judith, looking about at the shafts of sunlight pouring in the windows.

"It's the water turning the wheel keeps down the heat," shouted the miller over the tremendous grinding sound produced by the stones. "And the movement stirs the air."

Judith was amazed by the modern machine. In moments the smell of the flour was overwhelming, and bits of dust floated in the air to produce sneezing and coughs. She smiled her satisfaction and thanked

Jack the Miller. Then she retreated to the road, her two companions following. They walked toward the vill, Judith rubbing her back, which hurt. Her time was near; she knew it. Her body felt just as it had shortly before Richard's birth.

"Well, Arnhilda," said Judith. "What do you think?"

"Interesting," was the reply. "But the folk don't like it."

Judith sighed. "I know. First, they had to provide the labor for the building of it, and now they must give up a portion of their grain as payment for its use. But Sweet Christ, do they realize the burden this lifts from their women?!"

"What makes you think they care about their woman, my lady?" was the sardonic response.

She frowned, but Judith knew that the maidservant was correct. The men of the village did not care how many hours their women slaved over their querns, painfully grinding grains into flour, so long as they paid nothing for the service. Judith was determined nevertheless to make life better, even if her innovations were unpopular at first. The folk would grow accustomed, she told herself. Also, she'd an eye to the future. Lord Edward, Sir Eustace, and Sir Robert, however reluctantly, would all be compelled by their own needs to use the mill and would pay in coin for the service. Judith intended to put the profits to good use, with Hawk's approval, of course, she reminded herself.

"Conan, do you think there will be trouble over this?"

The man-at-arms shook his head, his dark eyes direct, his usual impassive expression intact. "No, I think not, my lady." He hopped over a hole in the track the size of a pot, and the rings on his mail glinted in the sunlight. "As you saw, Sir Tancred has stationed a man-at-arms at the mill to oversee things. The scales have been balanced by Wighere, from the vill, which will silence all complaints of unfairness in that regard, for he complained most loudly of all. The people may not like it, but they've no ground for argument and they know it. All I expect is a bit of grumbling."

"Good." Judith sighed again, noticing as she walked that the hem of her pale blue gown was hopelessly frayed. She would have to give it to Dorothea, she supposed. Pity. "Did you note, Arnhilda, that the flour is finer than that produced by hand?"

"Aye," muttered the older woman sourly. "You'd think t'would be the other way around." She shrugged, then glanced at her mistress from the corner of her eye, catching a grimace of discomfort as Judith stepped over a rut in the track.

"You should not be walking so far, my lady. Why did you not take the oxcart as I advised?"

"It would have taken us forever. Walking's much faster." Judith did not want to admit it, but as uncomfortable as she was, it would have been pleasant to sit now and relax on a ride back to the castle, no matter how long it took. She was not looking forward toward to climbing that hill! Ah, well, what could not be mended must endured.

"You keep on pushing yourself the way you have been," warned Arnhilda, "and that babe will be born sooner than it should." She clomped as she walked, a venting of frustration. Her wooden shoes sent small puffs of dust billowing about her much-mended red skirt.

"Nonsense!" snapped Judith, but she slowed her walk.

A few moments later an oxcart creaked up from a side road, drawing to a halt beside them. "My lady," called out the castle cooper. "I delivered them barrels to the brewhouse like you said. Was you wishful of a ride back to the castle?"

Judith glared with suspicion at Arnhilda, who held out her palms to display her innocence. "Yes, we could use the ride, thank you," she admitted grudgingly. She did not note the conspiratorial grin exchanged between the cooper and the man-at-arms, as the latter helped her up into the bed of the cart. Arnhilda caught it from the corner of her eye and blinked in surprise. She did not sniff in disdain when Conan offered her a hand up into the cart, but for the first time, nodded to him in regal acceptance.

‡

After the fall slaughter, the first of Brother Plegmund's messengers arrived at Oakwood with a thick roll of parchment for Lady Judith's perusal. He had written in Latin, as was his custom, so after the evening meal, Judith sat alone at the head table and translated the gist of his words into French, that the knights and others at table might know the happenings of the past months. "As you know," she began, "the Northumbrians revolted against King William in the spring. Edgar Aetheling, of the line of the Saxon King Ethelred the Ill-Advised, led this particular revolution. He entered England from Scotland, where he had sought refuge from King Malcolm. He was aided by Lord Waltheof when he laid siege to King William's forces in York."

There were murmurings and nodding up and down the lower tables, and someone said "Ethelred the Senseless," which she ignored, however true it might have been.

"Then, in early September, came a Danish fleet of more than two hundred ships, which attacked Kent and East Anglia. They did not make full landing but sailed on to join Edgar in the Humber," she told her rapt listeners. "The Vikings were commanded by Osbern, brother to King Svein of Denmark. Brother Plegmund says they attacked Dover and Sandwich without success."

"I wish I'd been there!" declared one man.

"Well, I don't," another commented, shaking his head. "The Danes must be getting soft! Why, in the old days, so I've heard, they'd not have given up 'til the whole countryside was laid waste!"

"Aye!" called out still another. "And all the women of the district marched off as slaves." He waggled his eyebrows and grinned.

There were salacious chuckles at this and more comments of the same sort. Lady Judith frowned, however, and they grew silent, as children will at the displeasure of their nurse.

"The scroll goes on to say that the Danes were joined by Earl Gospatric, Edgar Aetheling, and Waltheof of Huntingdon. The local people seem to be for the rebels and have welcomed the Danish force."

Now, the men were silent. Their comrades had ridden into a more dangerous situation than they had previously supposed, if the whole of the countryside was against them.

"Despite a valiant fight by the Norman defenders, the rebels have taken King William's castles and sacked York. Risings are reported everywhere." She raised her eyes to the audience. "Brother Plegmund warns us that Eadric the Wild has crossed over the border from Wales and is reported in Shrewsbury, which means he may come at us from the south. Also, there are bands of rebels organized in Devon, Staffordshire, Cornwall, Dorset, and Summerset."

One of the men-at-arms leaned forward and coughed. "Looks as though we'll be doubling the guard, friends!"

Sir Tancred glared at him for interrupting. "Lady Judith so ordered earlier this afternoon!"

The man to whom he spoke gazed at the Lady Judith with new respect and said no more. Plainly, she knew what she was about where the defense of Oakwood was concerned. He settled back on his bench, satisfied.

Judith continued. "Part of the King's forces were left to hold the Danes, but Lord Raoul and the Oakwood men traveled with King William to Staffordshire. The rebels there were defeated, of course, and the King returned to meet the Danish force." She did not related to them that portion of the missive about Raoul being wounded on the thigh, a scratch really, the monk had insisted, nor did she think the men would be interested in his account of their journey, since it dealt largely with descriptions of the land and the indigestibility of march rations.

"They were in Nottingham when King William learned that the Danes had re-entered York. And the King has instructed his forces to lay waste to the areas round about York so that the enemy will be denied substance." She smiled, trying not to show how shaken she was by this. "Brother Plegmund says he will send word when he has more to tell us." She handed the scroll to Father Hubert in case he might have interest in reading descriptions of the lands near York, but he returned it after only a token perusal. Despite his calling, the priest's literary skills were largely undeveloped.

Sir Tancred nodded wisely as Judith finished her narration. "'Tis a good policy to lay waste to the area. Since they've already sacked the town once, we should be able to starve them out that much faster. I must say," he added approvingly, "it is pleasant to hear of what has occurred so soon after the event. Makes me feel less left out of things."

Several men muttered agreement. Judith shivered at the thought of the women and children of York, who would suffer for the folly of their menfolk. As a Saxon, she could understand how many of her fellow countrymen could be moved to rebel against the rule of an alien race. Her problem was that she and the people of Oakwood were better treated by the Normans now than by their own kind in times past. The man who had fathered her child and who treated her with honour and tenderness was one of the folk most Saxons called enemies. While she agreed with the rebels in theory, she was compelled by her common sense to support the Normans in fact. It was all very confusing.

Father Hubert pursed his lips. "I am greatly concerned over this campaign," he said, folding his hands over his paunch. "King William will triumph if God wills it so, but I had speech with Brother Plegmund 'ere he left, and he told me he'd read it in the stars that there would be much death and destruction, and not all of it destined for the enemy."

One of the knights scowled and spat on the floor. "The stars! God's Beard, does that sniveling fool truly expect the stars to tell him what the future holds in store?!"

There were violent protests, with more than half the men protesting that such prophesies were invariably correct and had been proven to save lives. The others claimed with equal vigor that only superstitious fools believed in the maunderings of so-called magicians and astrologers and the like.

The knight who had started the quarrel grinned at the furor. He made a gesture of contempt and insisted loudly, "It's all a pack of lies, I tell you! I don't believe any of it! Why, I'd as soon consult the witch who lives in the southern wood as trust in what folk believe they read in the stars!"

Father Hubert lifted his lids and looked about him with a widened gaze. "There is a *witch* here?! Who is she? Has nothing been done about it?" he demanded. "Why, we could be in the gravest danger even as I speak!" His voice rose in alarm.

"Nay, good Father, 'tis only an old woman sells love potions to silly maids," soothed Judith, mentally cursing the knight's loose tongue. "There's no harm in her and less wit. And she's a good enough Christian, I pledge my word."

"But she's a witch; he said so! She probably makes charms and potions!"

Judith smiled. "What, a few sprigs of watercress tied with a ribbon? It might look pretty, but I was assured by a bishop who visited a few years back that t'would have no effect at all. The only potions she makes are spring water dyed with burnt onion leaves! Come, Father Hubert! There's no harm in what she does, truly!"

The priest grunted and sucked noisily at his teeth. "A bishop, you say," he murmured, considering. If a bishop had already looked into the matter and found nothing wrong, perhaps all might be resolved peacefully. "Tell me, has she been in the village church? Would I have seen her?"

Judith shook her head and prayed silently. "No, she's bedfast. It's her daughter gathers the herbs, and the old woman ties the ribbons."

"Well, then," he pronounced pontifically, more than satisfied, "if she stays out of my chapel and bothers no one, I'll not see fit to punish where a bishop has seen no wrong. Since, as you say, she is not truly a witch, t'would be a waste of time hunting her down and informing the Archbishop. And then there'd be an inquiry, a trial, and a burning if she were found to be guilty." He sighed at the mere thought of so much effort. "Are you absolutely certain she's not communing with demons and the like?"

"I am positive," Judith said firmly.

He smiled relief. "Then that's that! Could we send someone out to the kitchen to see if there's any of that pigeon pasty left?" he asked plaintively. "I haven't been feeling myself lately, and one must keep up one's strength."

"Of course." Judith sent a serving woman scurrying and a swift prayer of thanks to God for the priest's good humor and indolence. In all truth, the old woman in the wood could have harmed no one. She was exactly as Judith described her physically and little more than a wise old woman. She did know her simples, though, and frequently offered herbal remedies to folk who could not take time to visit the castle for their medical needs.

The very next morning, Judith bade Arnhilda visit the old woman, warning her that her activities must henceforth be more discreet. Also, deeming it wise to take no chance of offending the crone, she sent along a bundle containing a loaf of rye and barley bread, a bit of salt, a tub of butter, and a woolen cloak to keep the crone warm through the winter. It was, Arnhilda assured her later, most appreciated.

Judith was relieved. Despite her assurances to Father Hubert, no one knew what powers the witch truly had. At least now all was peaceful, and Oakwood stood in well with both the witch and the Church.

‡

Within three days of Brother Plegmund's message, Lady Judith was brought to bed with twins. Castle and village buzzed with the news, for the birth of twins was considered a good omen and sufficiently rare to occasion comment. A boy and a girl, both strong enough to suckle, reinforced the villeins' opinion that Lord Hawk was a mighty man indeed and their mistress a lady as knew her duty to her wedded lord. And Judith, who had just weeks previously dispensed with the services of a wetnurse, was obliged to find another. In the face of Raoul's absence, she named the babes herself, calling the second son Giles and her first daughter Elizabeth. Both were good Norman names, and the Normans smiled approvingly. The Saxons shrugged. Best to nod to the conquerors and say nothing. Lady Judith's children carried Saxon blood in their veins, and that was satisfaction enough.

Richard toddled about on his sturdy legs and stared with supreme indifference at his new brother and sister. He played with the carved knight his father had made and a crude drum fashioned by one of the men-at-arms. Conan gave him a leather ball, too, filled with straw. Arnhilda had made him a rattle. But his erratic interest was equally divided between his lady mother, whom he adored, and the smithy, where Dorothea sometimes took him to alleviate his boredom and because the smith was a likely-looking man with no wife.

Sir Tancred and Lady Edith were asked to be godparents to the twins, which made them beam at the honor and ensured their loyalty. Agnes sent word from Danesford that she was ill and could not attend the ceremony of christening, which excuse made Judith suspicious. She immediately sent Conan to spy on her stepsister.

A few days later he returned, meeting with Lady Judith in her chamber. The information included the fact that Sir Eustace, who had not accompanied the Hawk in the current military venture with the King's forces, was angered by the mill charges.

Judith nodded at the news. "Well, we did not exactly expect him to rejoice. Still, it would be more proper for him to complain directly to me, I think. Is this to insult us, this refusal to attend the christening?"

"More a way of expressing anger, my lady," said Conan. Although his face showed no emotion, his voice conveyed his displeasure at Sir Eustace's actions. "But it is in poor taste to so use his liege lady when her lord is not by. Never mind that 'tis his own brother, to whom he owes fealty. Sir Eustace might be expected to uphold his brother's decisions before strangers."

He sighed, frustrated. "I've heard nothing I could grasp hold of, but I know he's made no secret of his feelings. Were I a betting man, I'd lay odds he means to do my lord a mischief, to avenge what he claims is an injury."

"What injury?" demanded Judith indignantly. "The mill charges are fair!"

"So I think," replied the soldier. "Yet, even the peasants are unhappy about it. The Danesford men say Lord Raoul should have allowed Sir Eustace free use of the mill, seeing as he's the lord's own brother and has been his loyal man all these years."

Judith snorted at so specious an argument. "He's been loyal only because he could never have won lands for himself! Did you glean any knowledge of how he means to take his revenge?"

Conan shook his head regretfully, his hands folded behind his back as he towered over her. "Not a peep, my lady. I think he knows not how himself yet. T'was all loud talk and angry looks. Mind you, he and Sir Robert are wondrous great friends these days, which is not in my lord's interest. And I did hear that Lord Edward has twice been to visit Danesford this past winter, despite the snow and ice. I'll keep watch, but I doubt me there'll be trouble yet awhile."

"Yet you do think there will be a reckoning one day?" she asked with a worried frown.

"Aye," he replied stolidly. "I've been with my lord since before Val-es-Dune, my lady, and know Sir Eustace of old. He's one as holds a grudge, even for an imagined slight. He'll wait to claim what he considers his due, but he'll not forget it."

"You confirm my suspicions," sighed Judith. "He's far more trouble than he's worth. 'Tis a thousand pities my lord did not think to take him along on this campaign." She glanced at Conan from the corner of her eye, and her smile was sly. "Did you follow my other instructions?"

An embarrassed grin folded his lips, and a flush mounted to his cheekbones. "One of the kitchen women, my lady, and not too ugly. She'll meet me in three days' time at the edge of Danesford Bog."

"Ah!" Judith's eyes twinkled merrily. "I know t'was a deal to ask of you, Conan, but the information she can supply may be important if Sir Eustace makes problems for us. See you're careful, though. Sir Eustace may discover your liaison and think to use you for his own ends."

"I know how to keep my tongue with a wench in hearing," responded the man easily, unmoved by the fear of capture. "The hard part'll be keeping the truth from my comrades, my lady. They'd never let me live it down!"

"I have faith in you," she returned with a smile so eloquent of gratitude that the man blushed more deeply. "There are few enough men I can trust so completely with my lord not by. Your loyalty is beyond price. Remember that should aught befall you. I'd pay a king's ransom to have you returned safely to Oakwood and never count the cost."

Conan bowed deeply. That his lady placed so great a value upon him moved him more than mere words could express. He vowed in his heart to serve her with all of his strength, all the days of his life.

‡

A short message from Brother Plegmund arrived at Christmastide. He said only that Raoul was in fine condition, and all his men, as well. There were no serious wounds or illness. The army, he informed her, was still laying waste to the land about York. From that Judith concluded that she would not see her lord before spring, if then.

She missed him, his laughter and his ridiculous teasing. The responsibility for the welfare of all the people rested heavily upon her shoulders, and she longed to be able to discuss some of the daily problems with him as she had been used to do. Also, alone in their bed at night, with the curtains pulled closed to shut out the droughts, she longed for the comfort of his body. It had been so long!

The winter seemed to stretch out of sight before her, but the children kept her busy enough. Richard began to speak a word here and there, which delighted her. Often she retired from the hall early, knowing that Sir Tancred would keep order there, and repaired to the nursery. It soothed her worry about Raoul, who was so far away and perhaps in danger, to sit with the babes beside the hearth and to hear Richard prattling contentedly at her knee.

Conan kept company with his kitchen wench, meeting her once or twice in the week at the boundary of the bog, and reported no hint of trouble from Danesford. Agnes was at last with child, however, which news had not been officially transmitted to Oakwood. It was also reported that Sir Eustace boasted openly that his son would be heir to more than a simple wooden tower at the river's edge.

The cold gradually loosed its grip upon Oakwood. New leaves appeared, and flowers began to show their timid faces to the sun. A cool day in May found Lady Judith abroad with her women. Dark clouds threatened away to the west, but Oakwood's stock of medicines was perilously low. So Judith braved the wind that whipped at her skirts and led maidservants and ladies through woodland and meadow in search of herbs. Those herbs, with the precious spices brought at great expense from the Levant and Cathay, were the only medicines for healing which existed.

It was time for the gathering of strawberry leaves, which treated kidney pains, dysentery, or jaundice. Chamomile was ready for gathering, a great regulator of the menstrual cycle, and which expelled worms and eased dropsy. In addition, it sometimes prevented gangrene in wounds and acted as a sedative. Horsetail was needed, as well, an astringent for running sores and wounds, a diuretic, and an excellent addition to furniture polish.

Late afternoon found them in the rock-strewn lea along the cliffs where dandelion grew in wild profusion. Judith stood resting a moment, a wary eye cocked at the ever-darkening clouds sweeping in from the sea. A little while longer, she decided, and they must return to the castle. The storm would surely be upon them by nightfall. She glanced behind her to where Conan and three other men-at-arms under his control rested against one of the oxcarts, which had transported the castle women. Three of them played at dice, bored with women's pursuits, and Judith could not find it in her heart to begrudge them their distraction. Yet ever since she had heard of Agnes' pregnancy, she had been bothered by nagging fears. Raoul was far away on the King's business, and only the lives of two tiny boys kept Sir Eustace from the lord's chair at Oakwood Castle. Therefore, she kept her guards about her and the babes, even though Arnhilda scolded her for such foolishness.

Her gaze shifted to Conan, who left the cart and moved to the edge of the meadow, standing straight and tall, apart from the other men. His watchful eyes searched constantly in the nearby wood for hidden menace, and Judith felt herself relax. His very presence was soothing, so competent as he was. It was odd, she mused, that of all her folk, only Conan, a Norman, should agree with her as to the danger Sir Eustace represented.

About her in the meadow, the women bent to pick the yellow flowers. Here and there one stood erect for a moment to stretch muscles, which protested vigorously at strenuous activity after a sedentary winter. Then, feeling Lady Judith's eyes upon her, the woman would return to her task, for Judith was a stern mistress, though to be sure she worked harder than any to see a task accomplished.

Tiny insects flitted from flower to flower or scuttled in alarm before encroaching feet. Occasionally, a small animal bolted from the cover of a bush or rock for the safety of its den. Birds fluttered down to gobble up succulent insects flushed from hiding by the women's hands. And from the limb of a solitary tree, a querulous squirrel insulted them, the movement of its tail punctuating its chittering utterances.

Excepted by age and Lady Judith's strict order from more arduous labors, Arnhilda wandered idly along the cliff edge, stooping here and there to pluck flowers. Judith watched her with affection. The woman's hair was almost white and her joints afflicted with rheumatic pains, yet she kept a careful eye on the women in her charge. Order and cleanliness Lady Judith had commanded, and seemly behavior amongst the woman of her bower. Arnhilda saw that those orders were obeyed. This winter past, not one woman in her charge had reported a pregnancy, an impressive testament to her rigor. She oversaw Dorothea's rearing of the babes in her care, much to that one's resentment. But Dorothea knew the power that Arnhilda wielded and bowed her head meekly to the older woman's strictures.

Another glance at the sky prompted Judith to signal her women that they were to return to the carts with their baskets. She was moving in that direction herself when a cry from Arnhilda caught her ear. The woman's words were carried off by the gusting wind, but she gestured wildly. Judith picked up her skirts and ran.

"What is it?" she demanded breathlessly.

Arnhilda turned away and pointed to the sea. "Down there!"

Far below on the churning water, a ship tossed wildly among the rocks. "Merciful God!" gasped Judith in horror. "They'll never survive that!"

Even as she spoke, the roiling waters dashed the craft against an upright stone. Men were flung from her decks into the hungry sea, and a gaping hole was opened in the vessel's side. Again the waters took hold of the ship. She was smashed against another boulder, then flung fiercely between two rocks like serpent's teeth. The ship stuck there, tilted at a crazy angle, and the waves beat ceaselessly against the fragile hull. The cries of the men echoed faintly among the cliffs.

"They'll drown!" Arnhilda had to scream against the rapidly growing wind to be heard.

Judith bit her lip. "Get the men-at-arms and the women and follow me!" She did not wait for a reply but flung herself down the steep path to the beach, braids flying as she pelted along the narrow track. This was a favorite place of hers from childhood, and she was sure-footed as a goat, giving no thought to the possibility of a fall.

The wounded vessel lay on its side as she reached the sand, stirring restlessly as waves worried split timbers. In the water, men, animals, bales, and barrels bobbed about like corks. The wind whistled through the caves and cliffs, sounding like the moans of lost souls in hell. It swirled sand about Judith's knees and stung her eyes with salt spray. Thunder rumbled dully overhead. Judith had never learned to swim, nor had any of her people excepting the fisherfolk, who were too far away to arrive in time. She prayed, helpless to assist the seamen until they reached shore.

Goats and sheep reached the land before men. Judith instructed her women to catch the exhausted animals. The men-at-arms came to stand behind her, all of them willing the swimmers to safety. One by one, the seamen gained land, and Judith's men rushed forward to aid them.

Judith moved among the sailors, checking for gashes and broken bones. Luckily, the soaked, dispirited men were unhurt but for minor cuts and scrapes, and those were already washed clean by the salt water.

One of the newcomers, obviously the ship's captain, limped to her side. "All my men are safe, praise be to the Blessed Virgin. 'Tis a nasty channel you have here, girl," he remarked in strongly accented English. He winced as she inspected a nasty scratch on his shoulder.

"Aye, that it is, yet it keeps all but the most determined Norseman from our door," she returned with a grin.

The man nodded with a strained laugh. "That it would do," he agreed. He began to squeeze the water from his beard. "I am Guy of Flanders, at your service." He nodded to where the women struggled comically with the terrified animals. "I've to thank you for your assistance."

"'Tis naught," Judith disclaimed, thinking rapidly. "Is this your first time in our waters?"

"And my last," he said grimly, "I've lost both ship and cargo this day."

"There is an inlet further to the north would have accommodated your vessel," she returned. "As to your cargo, 'tis safe enough, I think. Look yonder." She pointed to a flotilla of small boats, which appeared suddenly from among the rocks and moved determinedly toward the wreck.

"Christ's Wounds," the sailor cried furiously. "Are you daft, girl? Those are scavengers. They'll pick her clean!"

Conan lunged forward at the insult to his lady, but Judith motioned him back. "They are *my* folk, Master Guy. Your goods shall be returned to you." She beckoned to one of her men.

"Tell Olaf of the fisherfolk that whatever is salvaged will be delivered this day to the castle, or if the storm worsens, by morning. There will be beef, bread, and ale for all when they are done and lengths of woolen cloth, as well."

"Aye, my lady." The man was off and running.

Master Guy stared. "God's Bones! Are you lady here? I took you for a serf!"

Arnhilda gasped at such impudence, but Judith chose to ignore it. She smiled charmingly. "I am the Lady Judith of Oakwood, wife to Lord Raoul," she told him. "Please to accept our hospitality for yourself and your men until you are fit to travel." She glanced at Conan. "One of my men will remain with you while my women and I go ahead to make ready for your comfort. I will send horses and folk to help with the animals."

The seaman was clearly distressed. "I thank you, lady. If I have said aught to give you cause to . . ."

"Why, you have suffered a tragic loss!" returned Judith gracefully. "Think no more of aught but the welfare of your men." She turned and moved off toward the cliff path, Conan looming protectively at her back.

Leaving Arnhilda to shepherd the women and herbs, Judith appropriated the horse of one of her men and rode with Conan back to the castle. Lack of a sidesaddle did not hamper her; she had ridden astride all her life. Her brain whirled.

The possibilities of this chance encounter were endless! Situated in so remote an area, the only merchants to visit Oakwood were itinerate peddlers, and precious few of those. If Master Guy's ship were not too badly damaged, and if she could somehow persuade him to return later in the year with goods to trade for her own wool and hides, Oakwood need not depend upon supplies from town merchants in distant places, who charged outrageous prices for inferior goods. She wished that Raoul were not away, for he would have known exactly how to manage such a transaction. But he *was* away; the entire matter rested with her. She clasped the horse tightly with her thighs and prayed she would not fail in her purpose.

In the castle bailey, Judith surrendered the horse to one of the grooms who came racing from the stable at the first sound of hooves. She sent another racing to fetch Sir Tancred. The bailiff met her in the kitchen. He had to step over a woodpile and was not best pleased. While Judith doled out the spices and conferred with Cynefred, she somehow explained the situation.

It would have been easier, she admitted to herself later, to have handled all the arrangements herself, but Sir Tancred's feelings were easily hurt. And she needed his loyalty. So she appealed to his sense of responsibility and left the details of the rescue's completion to him, whilst she diverted a few serving wenches from their usual duties to prepare a chamber for Master Guy and sleeping space for his men among the soldiers of the donjon. As she crossed the courtyard on her way from the kitchen to the castle proper, the first heavy drops of rain spattered in the dirt.

Judith bade Dorothea leave the children in the care of her assistant and aid her in bathing and combing her hair.

The nursemaid struggled with the much-mended gown, "My lady, what persuaded you to wear a gown fits you so ill?"

"Well, it seems folly to don a beautiful silk or velvet only to stain and rend it whilst working in the meadow," she responded, pulling the heavy wool up over her head at last.

"And that kirtle!" exclaimed Dorothea, scandalized at the state of the undergarment revealed when the gown was removed. "No truly, my lady! You must give it to me and I shall make a gown for one of the babes with what material I can salvage."

"It is a bit ragged," admitted Judith, surveying the offending garment. "I've had it since I was a girl."

Dorothea sniffed as she slid it off over Lady Judith's head. "I am not surprised, my lady."

"Yes, well, t'was one thing to dress in my oldest raiment for harvesting nature's bounty. 'Tis another to impress a sea captain and do honor to my lord's position," Judith sighed.

"As you say, my lady."

She rushed over to a clothes chest and removed a fresh linen kirtle and the blue velvet of her wedding. "I think this is grand enough."

"Oh, yes, my lady! And perhaps a veil to cover your hair?" Dorothea hinted.

Brought from Normandy, it was becoming a fashion in England, this modest covering of a woman's so-called "crowning glory." Judith, while she found it attractive for grand occasions, was uncomfortable with headcloths flapping about her while she attended to her various daily chores. "Yes, I suppose t'would be best," she conceded. Oakwood was far from the urban centers where such things were important, but she did not want Master Guy to think they were uncivilized. She sighed again as she slid into the hot water.

Before she donned more than her kirtle, the twins were brought to her for suckling, though she had little enough milk for them and soon surrendered them to the wet nurse. Richard ran in for a tender embrace and a quick story before bedtime. Then she drew on the blue velvet and went to examine her appearance in the looking glass Raoul had purchased for her on his last journey. She arranged the gossamer veil to her satisfaction, clasped the pearl pendant round her neck, and descended the stair to greet her guests.

Bathed, shaven, and garbed in borrowed clothing, Master Guy was far more presentable than the sodden, angry man on the beach. Judith seated him at her right hand at the high table, with his own goblet and trencher, which honor gratified him deeply. She conversed with him in Flemish.

"A grievous pity the storm caught you in our channel," she said during the first course. "I trust all of your men are none the worse for their experience?"

He inspected a platter offered by one of the wenches and speared a plump pigeon on the point of his eating knife. "Nothing worse than a scratch or two, which your women tended most skillfully, I thank you. You have my everlasting gratitude, Lady Judith. Your people saved most of my cargo," he added, flushing a little at the admission.

"Was much damage done?"

He shrugged. "T'was better than I expected. A few bales of wool lost and my ships records, but the spices were unharmed, and no damage done to the wine."

"And your ship?" She sipped delicately from the silver goblet, which had once belonged to her father.

"Alas, she broke apart on the rocks as I watched," sighed Master Guy, shaking his head sadly.

Judith dipped her fingers into a proffered bowl and withdrew a few small boiled onions, which she placed beside the portion of roast hare on her trencher. "You have my deep sympathy at your loss, Master Guy. I will naturally provide you with transport upon your journey. Where are you bound?"

"London now, I suppose, my lady. "Tis the best place to find a ship bound for home."

She nodded. "As I said, it will be no great matter to see you safely there."

He thanked her graciously and attacked his meal, consuming great quantities of meat and surprising little wine. Judith noted that the man wished to keep a clear head about him, and he rose considerably in her estimation. "Tell me, Master Guy, where were you bound originally?"

"I'd contracted to deliver a ram and three ewes to one of King Malcolm's nobles, along with the wine and spices," he told her. That's impossible now, but I beg you will accept them as mark of my gratitude." The gesture obviously pained him, costing as it did an impressive tally of silver marks worth of livestock and trade goods.

"That is most kind in you," she accepted graciously.

The seaman cleared his throat. "Er, one of your men said . . . that is, I am under the impression that your lord is Lord Raoul the Hawk, late of Normandy. Is this indeed the case?"

"Why, yes," replied Judith, surprised at his intensity.

"Then I am doubly honored, my lady, for his name is not unknown in Flanders. He has ridden with King William to avenge the murder of Robert of Comines?" he inquired eagerly.

Judith eyed him blandly, and her answer was caution. "Yes, he is with the King. I expect his return at any time now." She smiled and nodded to the scullions to bring forward ewers and basins.

"That is a pity," Master Guy remarked. "I'd hoped to meet him. I'd a cousin rode out as man-at-arms to Robert, and is now counted among the dead when they were all cruelly slain."

"May God rest him," murmured Judith, crossing herself. She washed her hands carefully and dried them on a rough linen towel held by a lad clothed in the shapeless trull common to scullions and serving-maids. "Have you any news of the campaign, Master Guy?"

He sighed his regret. "None, barring that King William has laid waste to the land about York. Your man informed me that you'd heard already about the Danish force which took the place." He winced. "T'was that information which earlier convinced me to venture to the western shore of England, not wishing to fall prey to the marauding Norsemen. I'd have done better to stick to my usual route and braved the danger."

Conversation was of a desultory nature while meat pasties, pigs' feet, and stewed radishes were served, and they spoke now in French, for the benefit of the other diners. When the platters of fresh oysters were presented, however, Master Guy praised the last of those succulent shellfish of the season, remarking that they were late but most tasty. Then he said casually that he feared t'would be long 'ere he found another vessel. Judith saw her opportunity. She clasped her hands tightly in her lap and smiled.

"It costs a great deal, the building of a ship?"

He nodded, sliding an oyster neatly from the shell to mouth. "I'll be forced to go to the moneylenders, I reckon, if I wish to put out to sea again. And since that is my calling, I have no other choice."

Judith gazed at him, the picture of innocence. "I have heard that they charge dearly for their services."

"Oh, aye," he replied, tossing several empty shells to the rushes. "'Tis little profit I'll see for many years to come, I fear me."

"Need it be so?" she asked. "My lord has silver enough to build you a good ship, and we have need of trade goods here at Oakwood."

The seaman stared at her. "Your lord is away."

She raised her brows politely. "I command in his absence, Master Guy. He will not dispute the decisions I make and will honor my word as his own." She saw Sir Tancred frantically signaling to her from a few feet away but ignored him. "What say you? An association with us would be to your benefit as well as our own. Also, I would charge you no interest."

"No interest?" Guy responded instantly. His eyes blazed.

Judith smiled ruefully. "Now, that would not be to my advantage. Why should you deal with me an I offered you no more than the moneylenders? Nay, rather I offer an alliance would bring profit to you sooner than you might otherwise expect, and will further accept the goods you have offered as a gift in part payment of your debt. In return, you make at least one stop at Oakwood in the year, and keep an open mind to other ventures in the future. Does that meet with your approval?"

"I think you need not ask, my lady," he commented, amused and relieved.

"I suppose not," she agreed. "Also, I have linen, wool, and hides would bring a fair price in any port. There is not much market hereabouts in which to trade them."

Guy eyed her shrewdly. "Might you then be agreeable to taking, say, only a portion of my cargo in payment on each voyage?"

"Certainly. There could be no gain for you in this venture did you not make a profit of some sort upon every voyage."

"Hmmmm." Master guy gazed thoughtfully at the great doors at the far end of the hall. "Of course, there's no safe harbor here," he said at length.

"But there is!" exclaimed Judith, heart pounding with anxiety. "At the mouth of the river but a little space to the north of the rocks where you came ashore. My fishermen can show it to you on the morrow. They live there, you see, and can tell you the safest passage to the north and south, as well."

He pressed the tips of his fingers together. "Have you any notion of the price of a worthy vessel, my lady?"

"No. Tell me."

He did, and Judith smiled calmly. "T'will be no problem, then, Master Guy. It is a stake in our joint future, is it not? May I assume we are agreed?"

The man chuckled and put out his hand. They shook hands solemnly, then grinned. "By God's Holy Face, lady, you'd make a fine merchant, and that's a compliment, though there are some would not think so."

"I thank you," she said. "And to return the compliment, I have more faith in your word than I would with one or two knights with whom I am acquainted."

"Why?" he asked, head tilted to one side. "You hardly know me."

"Your men are well-fed but not fat or lazy. Thus, I conclude that you believe in hard work but reward your people in proportion. That indicates fairness. None of your men fear you unduly, so you are not petty or cruel. Finally, you were on your way to do business with King Malcolm's court. They are Scots, and whatever I think of those folk when they come over the border, they know how to choose those with whom they do business." She tilted her own head. "Besides, you have steady hands, and I trust what I read in your eyes, Master Guy."

He laughed and drank to her health, and so the pact was made.

‡

Three days later, Master Guy and his men set off for London, accompanied by five men-at-arms to guard the sailors, silver, and the trade goods from Oakwood. Father Hubert rode in the van, journeying to the Archbishop with the deed to the abbey lands. Judith listened meekly to Sir Tancred's strictures but smiled with satisfaction as she waved them farewell from the warder's tower above the portcullis. The silver traveled inconspicuously, which should keep it safe. It was a gamester's gesture, this spending of Oakwood's treasure. Nothing was certain in this world, but if sufficient trade could be generated through Oakwood Village, the future was as assured as she could make it.

CHAPTER 11

s she had confidently predicted to Master Guy, Raoul was not in the least disturbed by her expenditure of coin . . . although she had been less certain of this than she had admitted, even to herself. He returned in June of that year, thin and weary from the long campaign, and glad to be home. Judith stood before the door to the great hall as he rode into the courtyard; she watched him dismount, and cross the dusty bailey. She held out the great welcoming cup (a wedding gift from Lord Edward of Northwatch), then shoved it into the retainer's arms when Raoul wanted an embrace instead. While Sir Tancred coughed into his fist to protest so public a display of affection, the watching folk cheered and whistled their approval. She held him close, noting with alarm that she could feel every one of his ribs through his tunic.

"I've missed you," she whispered against his shoulder.

"And I you." He held her back and smiled wearily into her eyes. "You've lost a belly since last I held you, wife."

Judith beckoned to Dorothea, who led Richard forward and carried Giles in her arms. Her assistant followed with Elizabeth. Raoul stared and then laughed. He grabbed Richard under the arms, swinging him up in the air. Then he caught him close, kissing his baby cheeks and chuckling with delight.

The little boy gazed at him with suspicion. "Are you *really* my papa?"

"Of a certainty, little man. Did you doubt it?" He kissed Richard again.

"Why did you go away?" the child demanded angrily.

Raoul took in his wife's expression of dismay. It pleased him a bit to know she was not so in command of the situation as she wished. He looked at his son seriously. "I am a knight, Richard, and one of King William's barons. 'Tis my duty and my privilege to go to war for my liege. When he calls me to service, I must obey, even if I don't always want to. You are old enough to understand that, aren't you? It is very important that a man knows his duty, my son." He smiled at the boy's hesitant nod. "I've brought you a gift, little man. It is in my baggage."

Richard's brown eyes sparked with excitement. "A gift? For me? What is it? May I see it now?"

"Soon," replied his father with a rich chuckle. He turned to Dorothea. "Whom have we here?"

"Your son, Giles," Judith told him, signaling to the other woman. "And here is your daughter, Elizabeth."

Raoul started, his eyes going from one infant to the other. "Why, they're exactly alike!"

Judith giggled at his astonishment. "Not quite, my lord. One of them is a girl."

He bent and kissed their tiny heads. "Your daughter's hair is the color of your own," he told Judith, pleased. He poked a long finger at Giles, who clasped it and tried to carry it to his mouth. "What a handsome son! I hope," he told the baby, "that you will grow up to be as brave and strong as your big brother." Richard, still in his father's arms, flushed with pride, and stared at the knight in open adoration. Even Conan was of a greater height than his father, but from that moment forward, the Hawk eclipsed everyone in Richard's eyes.

"Come," urged Judith gently as she took Richard and returned him to Dorothea's charge. "Your father will want his bath and a change of clothing. Afterward, you may sit with him and see your gift."

Richard went off, reluctant to be separated from the wonderful knight with the laughing eyes, but obedient to his mother's will.

"You've done wonders with that one, my lady. And twins! You have been busier than I'd any right to expect!" He took her hand on his in a formal gesture and led her inside.

"Serving you is my greatest pleasure," Judith replied, eyes twinkling. "Will you eat first, or is a bath more to your liking?"

They were moving toward the curved stair, Raoul's hand pulling her forward. He pushed her ahead of him on the steps. "The bath comes first, little girl, and the food third."

She smiled coyly back over her shoulder. "And the second thing you would do?"

"I think you know well enough," he replied mockingly. Judith was silenced.

‡

They lay on the wide bed with the curtains drawn around them. Raoul traced imaginary lines along Judith's hip and sighed. "It was not good for you?"

"It was good," she lied, snuggling her head against his shoulder and breathing deeply of the scent of him. How she had longed for this man!

"But not as good as other times," he persisted.

"It was too fast," she answered with a sigh, not wanting to hurt him with unkind words, but knowing he wanted the truth.

"It has been more than a year, little girl. Next time, I will do better by you."

"I know," said Judith, pushing the hair from his eyes. "I remember your skill of old. Did I mention that I've missed you?"

"'Tis good to hear," he murmured, kissing her forehead. "Now tell me what has taken place since I left. Had you trouble? I heard there were rebels everywhere."

"No, no trouble of that sort. We were fortunate." She paused, reluctant to give him cause for concern. "Eustace has complained of the mill charges."

Raoul grunted. "He'll survive."

"He has a son," she added.

He tensed, then shrugged, but his manner had changed. "Were we asked to sponsor the child?"

"No. In fact, I only learned of his birth indirectly. They've named him Rudolf, I'm told."

"I see." He frowned. "I must pay a surprise visit to my brother at Danesford, I think."

"A . . . friendly one, Raoul?"

He smiled grimly. "Now, what other kind would there be between brothers?"

"Um, I think I should tell you that I set Conan to spy on him," she said hesitantly. It had seemed to be the correct thing to do at the time, but now she was afraid Raoul would be angry.

"Did you? What did he discover?"

She let out a relieved breath. "Naught but that Eustace is bitter over your lordship and the mill. He's boasted that his son will be more than keeper of Danesford Tower one day. Conan thinks he plans some revenge but has not yet decided how to go about it."

Raoul yawned. "That comes as no surprise. Eustace was a spiteful child always. Our father beat him more than once for a vengeful act. What else is there to tell?"

"Well," ventured Judith, "I paid out a goodly amount of silver to purchase a ship."

"Did you so? What sort of a ship?"

"A merchant ship. We are now by way of being partners with a Flemish sea captain named Master Guy."

"I trust you left us enough coin for our needs," he commented.

She sat up and stared at him. "Are you not angry that I did such a thing without consulting you?"

"Why? Are you doubtful t'was the right thing to do?" he asked lazily.

"No, of course not! T'will be a profitable venture and do much good for us and our people. If it provides profit enough, you might want to buy another ship later and hire a seaman to sail it for you. I wasn't sure, though, whether you'd approve."

"Don't let it worry you, my dear. To be sure, I expect to make decisions when I am here, but when I am away, you command, as I have told you." Raoul smiled teasingly and tugged at a long, golden braid. "What made you doubt your judgment? Did I not give you my parole I'd never beat you?"

She smiled trustingly into his brown eyes. "Truth to tell, t'was Sir Tancred put the thought in my mind."

"Hah!" Raoul snorted. "Tancred was a poor knight but loyal. He makes an excellent bailiff, for he pays attention to the smallest detail. 'Tis his nature to fuss over every expenditure. Heed him in matters of the land and castle only. In all else, trust in your own knowledge. I do.

I'd not have wed you if I'd thought you lacking in brains. Now, tell me of this ship you've beggared us to purchase."

He approved of all that she had done in his absence, expressing his satisfaction with the previous year's harvest, and the new land under cultivation. So pleased was he, that she ventured to discuss a plan she had conceived for the manufacture of linen by some of the Oakwood peasants.

When she told him that Father Hubert had taken the deed to the Archbishop, Raoul sighed and nodded acceptance of the necessity. It went against the grain to give away his land. Still, it needed to be done. The Hawk sighed again.

‡

At table that evening, he spoke with them all of the ravaging of the land and the submissions to the King of Lords Waltheof and Gaspatric. Both had been restored to their earldoms, and King William promised to give his niece to Waltheof as wife. He spoke as he always had, easily and with humor. But alone in their chamber in the nights that followed, Raoul tossed and fretted in his sleep, crying out so that Judith wakened and was troubled.

‡

"Raoul," she whispered. She hated to wake him, but it was the fifth night of such dreams. "Raoul, wake up!"

"Ah? What?" He sat up and rubbed at his eyes. "Is it morning already?"

"No. You had a bad dream." She touched his arm. "You cried out."

"Oh." Hawk shivered, reached for her and held her tight. "Lie back down, Judith. Go to sleep. I'll be alright now."

"How could I sleep when you are so troubled in your mind?" she protested gently, caressing his cheek with one hand. "Tell me what gives you such unease, Raoul."

So he told her, haltingly, of the bloody slaughter the King had ordered, so violent and relentless that even Raoul, a battle-hardened knight of many years' experience, was sickened by the awful destruction.

"All were slain," he told her, his eyes narrowed in remembrance.

"The women, the children, and the aged, all butchered alongside the cattle, poultry, dogs, and cats. Nothing lives there now. I have seen the like before, but this time there were so many children. So many children." He sighed but said no more. And Judith snuggled close, giving what comfort she could.

Sometimes in the weeks after, Judith awoke in the night to Raoul's cries as the dreams of horror played in his mind to torment him. Judith held him then, soothing and murmuring, as she did to comfort Richard when he wept in fear of imaginary dangers. They never spoke of those times, and after a while Raoul was bothered by them no longer, sleeping though the night uninterrupted.

‡

In July, Raoul agreed to the wedding of the Lady Margaret and Sir Artaud, the most trusted of his knights. It was, Judith decided, time to allow her friend to live her life as she wished. Also, Sir Artaud was a different man entirely than Sir Basil.

Sir Eustace, seemingly reconciled to the mill charges by his brother's visit to Danesford earlier in the season, attended the festivities accompanied by Lady Agnes and their son, Rudolf. Judith made much over the babe but privately thought him a disappointment. His whimpering was irritating when compared to the healthy good humor of her own babes.

Sometime before the ceremony of marriage, Judith had assigned to Sir Artaud a new chamber, removed from the bachelor knights' quarters, since a wedded couple might rightfully demand their privacy. As a wedding gift, she had the castle carpenter fashion a stout door and frame and had it set in the portal. It was fastened only be a simple leather loop, but Margaret was overwhelmingly grateful.

CHAPTER 12

aoul raced down the corridor of the knights' quarters with Richard at his heels. The little boy squealed with laughter. "Run fast, Papa. I'll get you!" he shouted.

Armed guards made way for their lord as he dashed up the steps of the dungeon tower and smiled tolerantly as his son rushed by in hot pursuit. Raoul allowed himself to be caught upon the battlements. He grabbed at Richard as his son 'wrestled' him to the stone flooring and laughed at the boy's mock ferocity.

"Christ's Wounds, but you'll make a valiant knight!" he told Richard.

"I want to be like you, Papa!"

"Aye, well, it may be that you'll be even better! Look you. When you've got an opponent running the way I did, can you hook your foot around his ankle like *so*, he'll fall like new-cut timber, and then you've got him. Come on, let's practice."

"I don't want to hurt you," Richard protested.

His father grinned and tousled the boy's hair. "There's a special way to fall saves you from pain an you know the way of it. I'll teach you that, too. Just remember, though, you cannot practice this with anyone younger than you," He cautioned, imagining Richard toppling ranks of peasant urchins for the sport of it.

"I promise," the boy said solemnly.

"Good. Now then . . ."

‡

In the solar Lady Judith received the Abbess Sexburga. Newly arrived from London, she was a stately woman, well into her thirties and of stocky build. Already the masons she'd brought were hard at work building the new abbey on the promontory. Mother Sexburga confidently predicted that the nuns' living quarters and the chapel would be completed before winter. The other buildings naturally, would take longer, but her folk could not be expected to remain under the somewhat precarious shelter of the old Saxon Hall throughout the cold months.

"Really, the entire structure should be put to the torch," complained the Abbess fretfully. "The north wall is rotten, and there are holes in the roof, all of which my carpenters will have to repair. New floors are needed, as well, to say nothing of the rats and other vermin we've had to chase out!"

"It has been abandoned a long time," murmured Judith for excuse, although she resented having to make explanations. It was at Oakwood's bounty that these folk had any shelter at all, aside from tents, and she had already provided wood for the repairs. "I've often thought of having it taken down completely, but there were always more pressing tasks. And now that you are come, I'm glad it still stands. You would not want your holy nuns forced to live among the castle folk and be tempted by worldly things," she added pointedly.

"To be sure, to be sure." Abbess Sexburga sniffed, her sensibilities offended that more comfortable quarters had not been immediately provided. "Still, you are cozy enough here. The drafts in that old hall are not to be believed!" She eyed the stout, tapestry-lined walls with resentment.

"Yes, I am aware of its shortcomings. I lived there for many years, and in colder weather than this," Lady Judith reminded the older woman. "But with all its faults, 'tis better than making an encampment in the open, is it not?"

"Frankly," returned the Abbess, "I'd hoped that some of the older women amongst my people might be put up here in the castle." There, it was out! She awaited the expected offer, for herself at least, to move into the keep.

Judith said nothing. She felt that Raoul had been exceedingly generous to gift the Church with the abbey lands and gracious in permitting the holy nuns to reside in the empty hall until their own building was completed. She had no intention of putting herself or her servants to the trouble of catering to the nuns and their dependents. Besides, when the carpenters repaired the north wall, the old hall would actually be warmer than when Judith had occupied it last.

Disappointed and ruffled that Lady Judith made no move to invite even a part of the religious community to share the castle, the Abbess stared at this wisp of a girl. The child dared hold herself in such esteem that she ignored a hint from a representative of the Church! After a moment, she reconsidered. It was plain that Lady Judith of Oakwood had a careful eye to the demands placed upon Oakwood's resources. Abbess Sexburga sighed and realized anew that this child was the lady of these lands and held more direct power than was usual. It nettled her that this should be so. An older woman might have been more amenable, but this younger generation seemed to delight in rebelling against the established order, for all they paid it lip service.

"Doubtless 'tis better that we live apart," conceded the Abbess in a superior tone. "Your women would surely be a . . . shall we say 'disruptive' influence in our midst."

Lady Judith smiled condescendingly. "Only if the sisters attempted to consort with the kitchen wenches, Reverend Mother. The women of my bower are above reproach." This wasn't completely untrue. Since the move to the castle and the rigorous supervision of Arnhilda, the bower women *were* a seemly lot. Now.

Abbess Sexburga recollected that until the abbey lands were productive, she and her folk would be depended upon the bounty of Oakwood for their sustenance. This thought closed her lips on whatever angry retort she might have made. She smiled instead and said, "You are full young to have charge of so large an establishment, Lady Judith. I am bound to say, however, that all here is ordered properly. Most commendable."

"Why, thank you," returned Judith, somewhat taken aback. She did not understand how the Abbess could think her so young, for she was the mother of three children and had been wed near three years, which put her age at somewhere near seventeen, by her own guess. Perhaps women married older in London, she mused, then brushed the matter aside. Now she had time to think, it occurred to her that she might make a friend of this woman, who would be a power in the community and had acquaintances in the capital. This gave her access to information that might prove useful. It would be best, Judith decided, to take her mind off the disagreeable topic of quarters.

"Tell me, Reverend Mother, were you in London for the coronation of Queen Matilda?"

"Oh, aye." Upon this topic, at least, Abbess Sexberga knew herself to be superior. She condescended to let fall a bit of gossip, which favor might, in future, be returned. "The Queen! A tiny thing, she is, even smaller than you, with red hair and the most beautiful green eyes! A lovelier lady you could not imagine. And her clothes are everything one would expect from the wife of King William. The colors of her gowns are gorgeous and so unusual! I cannot imagine where she came by the dyes!" she declared.

"How do you mean, 'unusual'?" asked Judith.

"Well, no simple reds or greens or blues for the Queen, I can tell you that. She has a gown in the bright blue of a peacock's tail-feather, and one that's not quite pink and not quite russet, but somewhere in between; I forget what it's called. There is one fabric in so dark a green 'tis almost black! It is most striking, I assure you."

"It sounds lovely," sighed Lady Judith, trying hard to imagine the hues.

"You've heard the tale, no doubt," rumored the Abbess, unable to hold back the latest story making the rounds, "that the King's courtship of the Queen was somewhat stormy?"

Judith shook her head. "Not a word." She omitted any title, not wanting to remind the other woman of her vocation when the dignity of her office might preclude further confidences.

The Abbess settled herself more comfortably on the stool. "Well! Duke William (as he was then) first sent a proposal of marriage to the father of Matilda of Flanders, and received, as I understand, an impertinent reply back from the daughter. 'Tis shocking, of course, and most improper for a lady to reply directly in her father's place, as if she had any say-so in the decision. Then, too, I believe she referred to him as 'William the Bastard' or something similar. Not very tactful. A man may be forgiven for losing his temper under such a circumstance. Anyway, 'tis said he got ahorse and rode all the night . . . or mayhap for several nights, I know not how far away is Flanders from Normandy, but it cannot have been easy for the horse. He came upon the Lady Matilda with her maidservant in the streets of the town." She smiled seraphically. "As I mentioned, he was in the Devil's own temper, and no wonder. (That long ride could not have made his anger any easier to bear.) When he spied her in the street, he dismounted and approached her. Without saying one word, he picked her up bodily and rolled her in a puddle of mud, right there in the street before all the people of the town. Then, still without a word, mind you, he mounted his horse and rode back to Normandy!"

"No!" exclaimed Judith in amazement. "It is incredible that she still consented to marry him after such behavior!"

"My dear!" protested the laughing Abbess. "I think t'was the act which turned her mind in his *favor*!"

Judith thought upon that for a few moments, then laughed. "I think I can see her point."

The women chatted comfortably for an hour longer, Abbess Sexburga confiding further that the Queen was a lady much admired for her bearing, and who took great interest in religious matters. For her part, Lady Judith pledged the Abbess her continued patronage and agreed to supply the nuns with meats, fish, dairy products, and fresh vegetables whenever possible until they could provide their own in the following autumn. The meeting ended upon a note of mutual respect, both ladies tolerably satisfied with their interview.

‡

In the nursery, Raoul tickled and laughed with the twins under the pleased eyes of their nurses, while Judith spoke to a small gathering of village women. All were of middle age and widows, with no men to provide for them, and all had some skill in the art of weaving.

"'Tis a simple idea," Lady Judith explained carefully. "The flax fields are small and yield but poor quality. However, if we increased the number of fields to say, three, and planted closer than for seed flax, the yield would be sufficient to enable us to make more cloth and sell it to others at a profit."

The women eyed one anther askance. Lady Judith suppressed a smile for their suspicion. "You, Gunhilde," she addressed the eldest. "You are the best weaver; I've seen your work. We have young girls aplenty in the vill, who would fling themselves under a cart for the chance to be placed in tutelage under you, to live in the old hall and avoid marriage."

"Live in the old hall?" echoed Gunhilde. "The holy nuns are there!"

"And will be gone soon enough, as I have told you," Judith went on patiently. "Mayhap by the harvest. By then all our plans will be made, and you may move in with your children. The hall itself will do well enough for looms; I'll have the castle carpenter make up new ones. You'll have warm chambers for sleeping, and you'll keep for yourselves a fourth of the profit from the cloth you weave. What say you?"

"Well, it *sounds* good," Gunhilde admitted, pushing back behind her ear a lock of gray hair.

One of the other women cleared her throat and coughed apologetically. "It'll look peculiar, us living in the hall. Folk won't like it. They'll say things." There were murmurs of agreement.

"What do you care?" asked Lady Judith with a sympathetic look. "Surely, you've had your bellyful of forever being grateful to your neighbors for your living, for having to beg for scraps left over from their meals. Think how t'will be to earn your own bread and never again having to be beholden to any for the food on your table. I think it possible that there might be beef and pork provided."

"*Meat* on the table," sighed one woman. "Even Jack Miller doesn't eat that good!"

"That's truth," responded another. "I don't know how long it's been since I'd bacon to feed my young ones. Eggs I can get once in a while, and a little fat from here and there, even if it has turned a bit. But real meat! My lady it is like a miracle just to think on it."

Lady Judith nodded encouragement, realizing that a decision was close. "All food will be held in common. Three cows will I give you from the lord's herd, two piglets, five hens, and a cock. Also, free service for your cows by my lord's red bull for two years. That'll do you for a start, and the price of the livestock paid back a little at a time from your profits. A side of beef, one fat ham, a side of bacon, grain, lentils, and onions I'll supply free of charge, and one barrel of ale per month. All that until you can produce your own."

Gunhilde eyed her speculatively. "What does the lord get from all this, my lady, if I may be so bold in inquiring?" It was asked politely, but everyone knew the nobility did nothing without reason or profit.

"'Tis simple, Gunhilde. You remember the days of my father's rule, when we all starved if the harvest was a poor one. Well, Lord Raoul has said there is a way we can all fill our bellies even after a meager reaping. If we can sell cloth to traders and merchants in far places for good silver, come a bad harvest we'll send men to a place with a good harvest and buy enough to feed our folk."

"Why should Lord Hawk care whether or not we starve? Lord Cerdic didn't, and *he* was a *Saxon*."

"My father was a bad thane, as all know who suffered under his rule. Lord Raoul is a better one. 'Tis only common sense that if the folk are weak with starvation, there is no way they can find the strength to work their own fields or the lord's demesne. The lord would go hungry as well. Besides, he has me to plead the case of my people," she added. She knew they'd never believed their lord concerned himself with their welfare. Not yet, at any rate.

"I recall the famine of '44," Gunhilde admitted. "Lost two little ones to the hunger, and my third has never been right in the head since. I'd not wish to live through that again."

The other women nodded. It had been an awful year, although most of them had been children at the time. Still, this new scheme might not work. They considered it, drawing a little away to whisper amongst themselves. Finally, one of the women approached their mistress.

"We'll need new cards, Lady Judith," she said.

"Aye," said Gunhilde, coming up to join her, approval written on her strong features. "The carpenter knows just how to set the teeth on 'em. The stream's near enough for the retting, I reckon, and the breaking can be done on the floor of the hall."

"How many looms?" asked someone else as the others crowded around.

Lady Judith thought. "Six to start, I think. One for each of you, and one for whichever of the village girls you think most able and willing. The flax harvest will be small this year in any case. We'll put in four new fields in the spring instead of three, if you think you can handle the load, and by next fall we'll add another three or four looms."

"Instead of an extra girl from the vill, how about letting my Wiglaf try his hand at a loom," asked Gunhilde. "He's not smart, poor lad, but he's helped me often enough, and the others will give witness he's near as good as I am at the task."

There was a chorus of nods, and Judith agreed. "So, then, have we a pact?"

Gunhilde nodded. "Who takes charge of the weaver's hall, my lady?"

"You do," answered Lady Judith promptly. "You're the eldest and have had the most experience. Any troubles beset you that you cannot decide, you come to me. I'll settle things with the rest of the vill so that no one causes you grief. Have we a bargain?"

One by one the women nodded, and all began to smile. It was a daring enterprise and completely outside their experience, but it would, if it worked, benefit them all. The village women began to think in terms of wooden floors instead of packed earth, and winters without wind whistling though the wattle to freeze their bones. Judith walked back to the castle envisioning looms busily turning out ell after ell of fine quality linen to trade for spices and all the other things in short supply at Oakwood.

‡

To ensure easy commerce with Master Guy, Lord Raoul ordered a wharf constructed beside the fishing village. As usual, the folk objected strenuously, but when Hawk spoke, few cared to disobey, and the dock was built. Happily, the erection of the wharf softened the feeling of the folk toward the mill. The lord let it be known he charged no extra tithes for the use of the dock, since it had been built from trees in areas designated for planting the following spring and with iron nails bought with profits realized by the mill.

‡

Upon Master Guy's return, Lady Judith was introduced to a new and utterly delightful experience. The trader had brought with him, as part payment for his new ship, a heavy barrel filled with sugar. Judith had never tasted the sweet stuff nor heard of it. She spent several happy days in the kitchen grating the hard lumps, sifting, and experimenting. Lady Edith explained what she had heard of sweet jams and jellies, and Cynefred was ecstatic. Like the spices, sugar was very expensive. It was kept under lock and key in the storage space beneath the great hall.

‡

A long sunbeam from a chink in the wall illuminated the dairymaid as she sat at her labors. Her yellow hair was bound with an old linen cloth of indiscriminate color, and her feet, in their worn wooden clogs, were planted firmly on either side of the churn. Her dress might have been blue at some time in the past, and the hem was ragged. The other woman wore a finer gown, a cast-off of Lady Edith's, in fine green wool with only a few patches on the skirt. She, too, wore clogs.

"It don't sound right, that's all I'm saying," insisted Gytha, arms pumping as she churned butter from cream. "Wasn't it her as saved the man's life?"

Edwina shrugged one thin shoulder and kicked the hay. "You know how men are," she said excusingly. "They've important affairs to discuss, no doubt, and don't wish for a woman's nonsense at such a time."

"'Woman's nonsense' indeed!" snorted the dairymaid. "T'was Lady Judith managed all whilst my lord Hawk was off on whatever silly errand the King had him on, and I say she should ought to be included in matters now. If she was clever enough to rule over Oakwood then, she's clever enough to take part in matters now he's back."

Edwina was torn. Hawk was her hero, but she had watched with the rest of the castle folk as their mistress was relegated to the background upon their lord's return, and even more since Master Guy's arrival. This state of affairs had not met with unqualified approval.

"I don't know Gytha," she sighed. "It does seem strange, though, how men expect their women to take charge when it is necessary, then to give up all authority in matters when they return. You'd not see a man allowing that to be done to *him*!"

"Not without strong protest, at any rate," agreed the dairymaid. She could not imagine her own man permitting such a state of affairs. "Lord Raoul is not unkind to my lady, though? 'Tis not as if he no longer valued her?" she questioned suddenly, a worried crease between her brows.

"No, no, nothing like that!" Edwina rushed to assure her. "'Tis merely that he rules now, and she is expected to return to her sewing and her babes, and show no interest in more important pursuits. Of course, Lord Raoul is better at making decisions than his lady, more decisive, if you know what I mean."

"If it is decisive you want," snapped Arnhilda from the doorway, "I'd be only too happy to show it to you! Get yourself back to the bower where you belong and be about your work! Sitting out here half the morning gossiping about your betters! The idea! Go on, move!" Arnhilda pointed across the bailey to the rounded bulk of the great hall. She watched with her hands upon her hips as the Norman servant scurried past her and out into the sunlight. "Humph! Silly clunk-head!"

"Not so silly she don't see the truth in some things," commented Gytha, whose churning had not missed a beat. "I think she's changed some since she came with Lady Bertha all those years ago. She's gotten to be more civilized. And she meant no disrespect to my lady. I'd not have put up with that."

"No, I know you wouldn't." Arnhilda smiled. She turned to go, then looked back over her shoulder. "There's naught wrong between my lord and my lady, child. Don't fret yourself over anything that fool had to say."

"I won't, but all she said was, 'tis not right that men don't value their women as much as themselves."

"There's no novelty in that notion," returned Arnhilda as she left.

‡

Lady Judith would have agreed with her servants. She was pleased that Raoul liked Master Guy. But it rankled that she had been of intelligence enough to discuss important topics while alone with either of them. Yet, once the men were together, she was only a female and should concern herself with the running of domestic matters only. She was happy to have Raoul home once more and reveled in his lovemaking. Yet sometimes she caught herself wishing he'd go off on a short journey that she might take charge of her folk again. Such feelings shamed and confused her; she pushed them from her mind. She wished she would find herself again with child and began to watch for signs.

CHAPTER 13

t was on a sunny afternoon that Judith sat on a flat rock on the bank of the stream, with Elizabeth asleep in her arms. A few feet away, Giles drowsily plucked at the sweet grass with his plump fist. Beyond him, Raoul wrestled with Richard, not allowing him to win so easily as he had in weeks past.

She was expecting another child and sighed happily, though her breasts were so sore she could scarce keep her arms at her sides. She had almost dozed off in the warm sunlight when a shrill cry from Richard brought her to full awareness. The boy was standing nearby, facing the wood on the far side of the water, a stubby finger pointing. She followed his gaze and gasped as she saw the creatures come staggering forward at the edge of the trees. They seemed barely human, dressed in tatters, their hair matted with filth. So thin were they that they resembled the stick-men folk put up in the fields to ward off thieving crows. As she watched, they were joined by others, until more than a score of men and women moved unsteadily across the meadow toward the spot where she sat with her babes.

Grabbing Richard by the hand, Raoul stooped to pull Giles into his free arm. He hustled Judith and Elizabeth up the hill, back over the drawbridge, and into the bailey. The Hawk's face was pale and grim as he handed Giles to Arnhilda. Richard pressed himself to Arnhilda's side as his father moved away.

"Who are they, my lord?" demanded Judith breathlessly.

He ordered the portcullis lowered and extra guards mounted on the castle walls. "Refugees," he said. "From York, most probably."

"Sweet Savior! How thin they are!" she exclaimed. "How did they come so far? They must be near starvation!"

Men-at-arms boiled in ordered fashion out of the hall behind them and raced for their posts atop the ramparts. Dogs raced out of the hall and began to bark. Castle servants and other folk, roused from their duties by the bustle, gathered in the bailey to find the cause of the commotion.

The strangers had reached the drawbridge and everyone could hear their pitiful cries. "Help us!" They pleaded. "Bread! Food! In God's name, give us food!"

A woman pressed against the iron bars of the portcullis. In her emaciated arms, she held a dead child, its body bloated and beginning to rot. Judith retched as bile came up bitter in her throat.

"Take ten men," snapped Lord Raoul at a soldier. "Use the postern gate. Rouse the villagers to be prepared to defend the fields if need be!" The man ran off at once.

Lady Judith shuddered uncontrollably. She gave Elizabeth into Dorothea's care and hugged herself. The wretched pleas of the starving cut at her like sharp knives. "Do something!" she begged of her husband. "I cannot bear the sounds of their cries any longer!"

"Archers! Stand ready!" shouted Lord Raoul. His face was white and drawn.

Judith gasped. "Holy Mother of God, my lord! You cannot!"

His expression was savage in the harsh sunlight. "Do not think you can order my action, lady!" he snarled.

"No," whispered Lady Judith shakily, aware of the people about her. It would never do to be seen at odds with their lord. "But do not do this thing, I beg of you! Indeed, they mean us no harm!"

Lord Raoul shook his head violently. "Little fool!" he hissed from behind clenched teeth. "See you not the sores they bear? God's Blood, will you infect us all with plague to succor these few? They are better dead alone than to take us all with them!"

"It is not the plague, my lord, I pledge you my oath! Think you I do not know, who have tended the ills of our people all my life? 'Tis but the hunger which shows in the skin, nothing more. An I thought it plague,

I'd say not a word, my lord, for do I not love our babes even as you do? These folk suffer only from their bellies' need and the long march. Spare them, my lord, I beseech you," she pleaded softly. There was the merest flicker of indecision in his eyes, and she grasped a handful of cloth at the front of his tunic. "Think, my lord, think!" she urged quietly so the others could not hear. "These are God's creatures, even as we are! Have they escaped the sword and desperate hunger only to die at our feet while we have but to put out a hand to ease their suffering? Our cellars are yet half-full with last year's harvest, and there is salt beef in plenty. What can it hurt to show a little charity?"

He thrust his fingers through his hair and drew a deep breath. Already the rage and fear had subsided in him, although the residue touched him yet with icy talons. He glared at Judith. Then, as if goaded beyond measure, he shoved her aside and signaled to his archers to lower their weapons.

The people outside the gate had fallen to their knees, arms outstretched, weeping and begging for mercy. Lord Raoul glanced at them with contempt. "Regard the vermin," he spat. "You would save *these*?"

"For pity's sake, aye," she replied gently, troubled by this unexpected hardness in him. A warrior must be hard, she knew, but this . . .

"Then mayhap the holy nuns will be moved to do the same," he suggested. "Send them to the old hall and be done with the matter."

Lady Judith gazed searchingly into his eyes. "Why do you hate them so, my lord? What great wrong have they done to you, that you would condemn them to death?"

"You speak in riddles, woman!" he retorted. His brown eyes slid uneasily away from hers.

"My lord, you did not think t'was plague they carry," she said slowly, her eyes fixed on his face. "You have sat out sieges and know the signs of hunger even better than I. What mean these poor folk to you, that you are so filled with hatred for them?"

"You're mad!" he ground out, his fists clenched. "These pathetic swine are strangers to me!"

"Mayhap, my lord. But some demon rides you because of them. Tell me, Raoul," she whispered softly, letting go his tunic to place a comforting hand on his arm. "Bare your heart and purge yourself of this anger."

His mouth was taut with the force of his feelings, and his frame trembled. Judith had never seen him so enraged, and almost she quailed in the face of his barely controlled violence. She felt God's commandments strong upon her, however, and would not yield. He turned away from her and of a sudden leaned heavily upon the cold stone wall.

"In the winter," he said, "t'was at the King's order, so I could not refuse. I longed to turn away from my duty, but I could not."

She moved closer until she leaned against him, comfort radiating. "Tell me."

"Know you what it means to lay waste to villages and towns?" He shuddered. "The army rides in, and sometimes the folk know you come, and 'tis none so bad. But when they are unprepared, it is a butchering awful to behold, for none bear arms to defend the place. Folk run screaming into the fields or into their homes. And some, like those at our gate, fall to their knees and plead for mercy. 'Save me,' they say, or 'Save my child.' Only, the King commanded that no quarter might be given: not to men, nor to old women and children, nor yet even to the beasts in the fields, or the fowls upon the dungheaps. So I did what I had to do, as duty bade me, and the cries of the dead and dying yet fill my sleep!"

Lady Judith knew, then, the full measure of the horror that lived in him and tormented his soul. She longed to take his head against her breast and give him peace from the memories, but the folk watched, and the starving outside the gate screamed for aid. She squeezed his arm lightly instead. "Oh, my lord, a heavy burden it is indeed that you bear! And yet you have said yourself that you acted upon the King's command. What you did is over now and was done at King William's behest, not of your own will. Think you that God, so merciful and just, would judge you harshly that you fulfilled your pledged service to the King?"

"I know not," he mumbled, eyes closed so that he might not see her face, lest he read condemnation there. "I know only the images which fill my nights and give me no peace."

"Then, my lord, if you would have ease of your pain, you must do penance for the sins you have committed. Does not our Blessed Savior command us to feed the hungry and to clothe the naked? Did He not do so Himself? Save those people, my lord. T'will bring forgiveness in Heaven, surely, and peace of mind on earth. Besides all else," she added, with a swift glance to where Richard stood staring at the gate, his lower lip trembling, "your son should learn that a great man must have pity upon the weak and defenseless."

Raoul was silent a moment, then slowly opened his eyes. She had not rejected him! Judith did not condemn him; she understood! Tension left his body in a rush. It was more of a miracle than he had dared hope for from one as concerned with her Saxons as his lady inexplicably was. All else was easy beside this, he thought. "Do you believe that God will grant me absolution for this penance?" he asked her.

"Ask Father Hubert," she urged. "He will know."

Lord Raoul smiled rather wryly and shook his head. "No, I'll not go to him for the answer to this question. I think me you are close enough to God's Heart to give me all the answer I need, little girl. 'Tis justice that I, who have taken so many lives, will now save them." He nodded toward the portcullis. "Do what you will with them," he bade her in a tired voice.

She sagged in relief. Cynefred stood nearby, and Lady Judith gestured at the cook. "Take the barley bread meant for the next meal, and give it to the people through the gate. Tell them there will be more later and that I will see to their hurts do they but leave the drawbridge and rest themselves along the moat."

Hawk looked drained. Judith squeezed his arm again and smiled. "I thank you, my lord. 'Tis a great kindness you have done. Will you explain to Richard that these folk have come to us for aid? I hate to ask it of you, but he is frightened by the noise and the strangeness, and young yet to be brave in the face of danger. You are easier with him than I, and he loves you best. He might not believe what I say; I have noticed that tendency in him lately," she added ruefully.

"You are not firm enough with the boy," declared Raoul, straightening his shoulders. "Will you send these folk to the nuns when they have been fed?"

"Well, if you truly wish it, my lord," Judith replied hesitantly.

He looked a little amused now and resigned. "But what?"

"I do not see that it is wise policy to throw away perfectly good serfs," she admitted, with a grimace for his insight. "When they are fed and tended, perhaps rested for a fortnight, they will be ready for work in the fields. Why should we provide the Abbey with more than they need and deprive ourselves of more laborers at the same time?"

"First they were my penance; now you turn them into a gift from God," remarked Raoul with something approaching his old humor. "Do you think these poor folk consider themselves in that light?"

"One never knows," she answered with a smile. "Whatever they are, you cannot deny that we could use them here at Oakwood as well as the nuns could."

Under the eyes of the watching castle folk, Lord Raoul bent and kissed her full on the mouth. "Did I not say you might do with them as you will? See you to their needs, wife. I must comfort Richard." He moved away to his son.

Cynefred and an assistant made their way toward the gate with huge baskets of bread carried upon their shoulders. Nervously, they began handing the loaves to the starving through the grate of the portcullis.

The refugees tore at the bread, grunting like animals. Some vomited as their shrunken bellies rejected the food due to the unaccustomed stretching. The madwoman held a piece of bread to the purple lips of her dead son, urging him repeatedly to eat. Lady Judith turned away, sickened. She sent Arnhilda for her medicines, then sought out the clerics.

"Brother Plegmund, will you accompany me to see to these unhappy folk?" she asked.

"Of course, my lady. I am ready to go at once."

Father Hubert, however, forestalled any question of his participation. "So grievous a situation, Lady Judith, calls for the direct intervention of the Blessed Virgin," he declared, his face pale and beaded with perspiration. "I must go at once to my chapel and pray for Her assistance." He raised a trembling hand in benediction and practically ran from their presence.

Lady Judith glanced at the monk out of the corner of her eye. "If you repeat this, I'll swear you lie, but I believe we will do a great deal better without Father Hubert's help. Of all the craven buffoons!"

"I heard not a word you said," returned the monk with a grin. "If I *had* heard you, I would be forced to agree. Still, who is to say that the Blessed Virgin would not listen, even to such a one as our priest?"

With a nod, Lady Judith put out her chin and forced herself to walk toward the pitiful creatures on the other side of the castle walls.

‡

Often, she had seen, smelled, and tended festering wounds, and a fortunate circumstance that was. For the sickly odor of the starving enveloped her like a malignant cloud. She dressed running sores calmly with her salves, the pot held by one of her servingwomen. She took extra care to cause no alarm among the suffering folk.

She was filled with compassion for their plight, weeping with them as they clutched at her hands or kissed the hem of her gown in their gratitude. Arnhilda had bullied the women under her charge to attend upon their mistress, and Lady Judith knew a great relief when two of them approached the madwoman in company with Brother Plegmund and gently led her away. Certainly, she would have taken the grim task upon herself, but convincing a broken mind that the dead must be buried was a chore for which she'd little enthusiasm. She listened to the piteous voices, her eyes sad and gentle, as the people told her tales so hideous her soul flinched at the hearing.

King William, they said, had enacted a terrible punishment upon rebellious Yorkshire, smiting the innocent and guilty alike in his rage. They spoke of tiny babes spitted on spears and young girls brutally raped before their mothers' eyes, then hacked to pieces. Whole families had been forced inside their burning homes to perish in the flames, old women disemboweled as they fell to their knees in supplication, and young boys pinned to trees by the thirsty arrows of King William's men-at-arms. All the countryside was piled with the stinking corpses of men and animals, and with heaps of ashes, which had been grain and other foodstuffs. Those few who had escaped the carnage had been wounded and left for dead, or had been away from home or fled, and returned to solitary horror. They found themselves in a barren land with death ever before them. What game there had been in winter had been driven off by the knights of the Norman King. Edible fruits and nuts of the wood had been hacked down and trampled by their horses' hooves. The survivors were forced to eat the very bark from the trees to still their bellies' rumblings. In some places illness and plague ravaged them, so that the few folk who had escaped the army's butchering fell in the snow, victims to disease.

Wrapped in rags plucked from corpses to keep them from the cold, two brothers from a small village met a man in a wood. A few days later, they were joined by two women and an orphaned child. All were from different places, all fleeing the King's wrath. They traveled together, joined from time to time by others, hoping to find a village or small manor where death had not visited. But every known place of habitation was like the last, burned to the ground, the ashes strewn with the charred bodies of the slain. They were too weak to catch even the carrion crows. Desperate in their agony, many ate of the newly dead. Those who would not, died of starvation and were consumed in their turn by the others. Some fell to the wolves who stalked their meager numbers. Some, maddened by suffering, horror, and grief, despaired of rescue from their doom, simply sat on the frozen ground in numb acceptance as they waited for death.

Appalled, Lady Judith sent Cynefred back to the kitchen for meat and stayed to give the people what comfort she could. Raoul the Hawk was a fair lord, she assured them, and they might remain safely at Oakwood. Behind Judith, the castle gate creaked open, and scullions bore wooden bowls of boiled beef and onions reluctantly along the drawbridge. They inched their way closer, plainly terrified, and Judith glared at her cowardly servants.

"Mary Mother!" she snapped. "Dolts! Move along! Think you these good folk will eat you?" She clamped a hand over her mouth, shocked at her stupidity. How *could* she have said such a thing?

There was a moment of stunned silence, and then the folk about her began to grin. A few of the men chuckled wearily. One, obviously the leader of the refugee band, grinned with grim humor at the approaching scullions. "Fear not, lads!" he called out. "We'll not eat manmeat when there's good beef to be had!"

A few others twitted the castle servants until Lady Judith called them to order, after which they applied themselves to eating, and napping, and eating again.

‡

On Lord Raoul's orders, a tent had been pitched to shelter the new serfs outside the castle walls, until new wattle huts in the village were completed for their use. Buckets of water were brought so they might bathe. They were given clean clothes in place of their vermin-infested rags, and the refugees were led into the great hall to express their thanks to Lord Raoul for his charity. One of the men volunteered the information that he could read and write in Latin and do sums, whereupon Raoul named him clerk and sent him off to assist Sir Tancred in record-keeping. Those with special skills were assigned to carpenter's shop, stable, smithy, or bower, and the rest were to tend the fields.

Lady Judith translated these orders from her lord's Norman French into English so that the Saxons might understand. Afterward, the new serfs filed dutifully out of the hall. They were relieved to escape the presence of the stern Norman baron and silently gave thanks for the gentle Saxon lady who had taken them to her heart. It occurred only to the new clerk, who had been their leader on the march, that while the lady might indeed have saved them, t'was only the lord's authority that gave her intentions force. Their new master might be a better lord than first thought.

‡

In their chamber that night, Raoul tried to take his lady to him and could not. He turned away from her in shame.

"Raoul?"

He made no answer.

Judith snuggled against his back, slipping her arm around his waist to caress his belly with her fingertips. "Raoul, do not shut yourself off from me, I pray you. 'Tis no great thing that you are too tired to be hard for me this night."

"I am not tired," he answered, his words like stones.

She kissed his shoulder. "Then your mind is heavy with worry, and that stops you pleasuring us both. Arnhilda says 'tis a common occurrence. Once your mind is at ease, your body will bend to your will. Not," she added, chuckling, "that you wish it to *bend*, precisely."

He turned to her, grinning reluctantly. "And Arnhilda knows all?"

"Well, she does," returned Judith. "She is right about this, for Lady Edith says that though they were newly wed, Sir Tancred was like this before he left Normandy for the conquest of England, and . . ."

Raoul was moved to sit up in bed. "Do you mean to tell me that you discuss with your women my conduct in *bed*?!" he demanded incredulously.

"No, Raoul, how can you think so? 'Tis merely that they will talk, and t'would be impolite an I did not listen."

"Humph!" he snorted, laying himself back once more by her side. He sighed as she began to caress him again. "Well?" he asked, as she remained silent. "What happened to poor Tancred?"

"Oh. Well, Lady Edith says that when she joined him in London some months later, all was well. She felt t'was the worry over the campaign bedeviled him so he could not . . . well, you know," she finished lamely.

"He's had no trouble since?"

"Once or twice after she knew she was with child, for fear of harming the babe. Otherwise, no." She nestled her head on his shoulder, her soft hand moving in lazy circles over his broad chest and stomach. "What is it frets you, Raoul? Do you think still of the folk from York?"

"Aye. They are on my mind." He snuggled her close and rested his chin atop her head. "I thought I knew one of them."

"Truly?"

"I am not certain."

Judith chucked. "Well, my lord, how could you tell? You've said often enough that all of us Saxons look alike to you!"

"Shrew!" He grinned in spite of himself, then grew thoughtful again. "Nay, I do not know, Judith. There were so many villages on that campaign, and I noticed no one man particularly at the time. 'Tis that the face is familiar, no more." He stirred slightly, his attention more half claimed by the tempting things she did with her hand. "T'was a village near the Tees, I think me, but I cannot remember. There were so many!"

Judith moved slowly and nibbled his ear. "A chance likeness, that is all. Life is filled with such."

She felt a slight stiffening and went to kneel between his knees. "Forget it, my lord," she whispered. "Close your eyes and forget all else but me." She put her mouth over him and he groaned his appreciation, the easing of his spirit allowing his body to find relief in her sweetness.

Sir Eustace rode into the bailey a few weeks after, smiling in good humor. Three men-at-arms rode at his back. He drew reign and spotted his brother's wife walking in the middle of the courtyard. He eyed Lady Judith's breasts with a lascivious grin. "God's greetings to you, sister!"

he called, as she paused in her errand and crossed the courtyard to greet him.

As always, his gaze made her feel in urgent need of bathing. "Welcome," she said with civility. "How left you Lady Agnes and your son?"

"They're well," replied the knight, swinging down from the saddle. He tossed his reins to a waiting groom, then gaped as his eyes fell to her gently rounded belly. "Christ's Beard! You're with child again!"

Judith flushed, but managed a smile. "By God's Grace, aye."

"By Raoul's rutting ways, more like!" he retorted, not best pleased. He had only the one child by his wife, although there were more than half a dozen by servants. Eustace wanted legitimate sons, and lots of them. So far as his plans for the future were concerned, bastards didn't count. "If you keep on in this way," he told Judith sourly, "you'll overrun us all with Raoul's brats, so that no man may move without fear of stepping on one!" His smile had a suggestion of gritted teeth. "Where is my brother, lady? I'd like a few words with him, if he'll deign to receive me."

"You speak foolishness," she reproved gently as she led him toward the hall. His escort remained lounging in the bailey. "Why should my lord refuse to see you?"

Sir Eustace hunched a shoulder. "Oh, now he lives in his fine castle, with his grand title, he eclipses even our elder brother, who was our father's heir. I suppose he is grown so great in his own esteem that he thinks he is better than any other of his blood."

"Not at all," Lady Judith returned, striving to hide her dislike to this petty, jealous man. "Come, Raoul is within."

"What?!" he exclaimed in shock. "You give your wedded lord his *name*?! Were you mine, I should certainly beat you for your disrespect!"

She gave him a sharp glance. "Then we may both give thanks that I am your elder brother's lady instead, may we not?"

His nostrils flared. "Indeed! You may be sure, however, that he will hear of this from me!"

"As you will," Lady Judith replied indifferently. She led him across the bailey and through the great hall to the narrow corridor, which opened on the armory. Raoul was within, testing the balance of a new sword. He came forward at their entrance, slipping the weapon back into its scabbard and setting it aside upon a bench. Lady Judith misliked the appraising eye Sir Eustace cast upon the stacked arms which lined the chamber.

"Eustace!" said Raoul, smiling and extending a hand. "'Tis good to see you, brother. What brings you south? I trust all's well at Danesford?" They took each other's forearm in a strong grip.

"No, nothing's amiss at home," Sir Eustace affirmed. "I see your lady wife is to present you soon with yet another son. My felicitations."

"Why, I thank you." Hawk took in Eustace's tight lips and the hectic flush on Judith's cheeks. His eyes narrowed.

"She's an insolent wench," declared Eustace, jerking his head in Lady Judith's direction, "but she seems to have her uses. Tell me, brother, has she your permission to use your name? She did so with me only a moment ago."

The Hawk's face went very still. He did not move; Judith was sure of it. Yet a menacing air surrounded him of a sudden, and she feared violence.

"My lady wife has my permission to do anything she pleases," said Lord Raoul quietly. "Even to the use of my name. She has my complete trust, brother; t'would be wise of you to remember that in the future. Also, I pray you, use all proper courtesy to my lady." There could be no doubt of the seriousness of his intent.

"No offense meant," relied Sir Eustace promptly, sweat breaking out on his upper lip. He had been away from his brother for a long while. He'd quite forgotten how dangerous Raoul could be when he felt his honor smirched. His smile showed more teeth than normal, and his eyes promised Lady Judith a reckoning for this humiliation, even as he made placatory gestures.

"Indeed," Sir Eustace told his brother, "your lady wife has my profound admiration."

"So." Lord Raoul's mood lightened slightly. "What brings you to Oakwood, brother?"

"Why, 'tis that I wished to see you, Raoul," declared Sir Eustace in a tone of sweet conciliation. "Is it necessary these days that I have more reason to visit my kin than family affection?" His eyes challenged mockingly.

"Of course not. I'd be pleased to think t'was for that reason you came," Lord Raoul said. His tone said otherwise as he gave his brother look for look. He gestured toward the door, and the three of them walked back to the great hall. A man-at-arms locked the armory as they left.

Lady Judith ordered wine and moved as if to leave the men alone, but the Hawk took her hand and pulled her gently into the curve of his arm. He was heedless of the handful of servants, who peeped up from their labors to waggle their eyebrows at one another over so public a display. Lord Raoul kept his eyes steady on his brother's face as they walked up to the high table, hastily set up to serve them.

Wanting Lady Judith as he did, as he had so fiercely from the first time he'd seen her, Sir Eustace was discomfited by the sight of their affection. He averted his eyes pointedly. One side of Lord Raoul's mouth tilted up in a smile.

A servant poured wine into the goblets he set upon the table, then withdrew. Lord Raoul handed Sir Eustace a goblet and took a sip from his own. He leaned against the table, forgetting, apparently, to offer his guest a seat.

"It is a great pity, Eustace, you did not think to bring Lady Agnes and Rudolf along on your visit. I feel sure our children would have been pleased to renew their acquaintance with their cousin."

"When he's older," said Sir Eustace. His eyes kept sliding against his will to Lady Judith's breasts, which were full and sweetly rounded. No *wonder* Raoul couldn't keep his hands from her! If only *he'd* been the elder, Lady Judith and all this land would have been his, he told himself resentfully. He was as good a knight as Raoul! T'was only that King William had never seen it because Raoul was always overshadowing him with showy deeds designed to take attention away from others more worthy!

"I regret that I was not able to be present for Rudolf's christening," continued Raoul casually over the top of his goblet. "As I mentioned briefly on my visit to Danesford, it was in every way unfortunate I could not be here for the event. My lady would have attended, but the messenger you sent must have met with foul play, for he never arrived. So, you took the babe north to Lord Edward's for the rite?"

Sir Eustace's face flushed. There could be no excuse for excluding his brother, who was also his liege, from so important an occasion. The fault was made the much worse by the fact that he had been asked to sponsor his brother's first son. "T'was a whim of my wife's," he muttered, eyes lowered to the floor. "She's grown wondrous great with Lord Edward's lady. If you'd not been on campaign, I would naturally have asked you to sponsor the lad, but as we knew not when you'd return . . ."

"Oh, I understand completely," Lord Raoul informed him in his driest tone. He took another sip of his wine, watching his brother all the while. "By the bye, since you speak of him, you'd best be careful if you seek to make a close friend of Edward of Northwatch. King William has banished him from court for the seduction of a baron's wife. Rumor has it t'was more rape than seduction, and that the King is angry enough that there's talk of stripping him of his lands. It seems the lady was so ill-used as to suffer a stroke after his wooing."

"I'll take good care where I make my friends," said Sir Eustace. He took his first sip of wine.

The air was thick with tension. Lady Judith sought to ease it. "Tell me, brother, would it be possible for Lady Agnes to come for a visit later in the summer? She always enjoyed the seaside when we were girls, and I've not seen her for an age."

He ignored her. "You know, brother," he said, staring at Lord Raoul, "I've heard a rumor of my own. 'Tis said you've come into a windfall."

"Oh?" The Hawk lifted Lady Judith's hand absently and kissed her fingers. "To what do you refer?"

Sir Eustace's smile had a suggestion of gritted teeth, and he took another small sip of wine to cover it. "Why, your new serfs, of course. Refugees from York, they say. I saw a few of them in the vill on my way in, but I can't say I'm much impressed. A weak-looking lot, if you do not mind my saying so."

"Now, why should I mind?" asked Lord Raoul pleasantly.

"How polite you are!" Sir Eustace mocked. "So, you think to work them in so sorry a condition? They'll never survive."

"Oh, they'll mend, never fear. 'Tis only hunger ails them and the hardships they've suffered." Lord Raoul placed his goblet on a nearby chest. Almost magically a servant appeared and all but snatched it up. She wiped the wood with a rag, knowing she'd have no peace if her lady discovered one of those white rings on its carved surface. Carefully, she wiped the bottom of the goblet, then put it on the table and withdrew.

The Hawk, meanwhile, wrapped both arms loosely about his lady from behind and rested his chin atop her head. "I expect the new serfs will do very well here."

"I hope you may be correct!" snapped Sir Eustace, jealously watching how Lady Judith, although uncomfortably aware of her audience, nevertheless leaned back to enjoy her closeness with her lord. Even obviously pregnant as she was, Sir Eustace felt his body react to the fantasies in his head. He'd returned to them again and again over the years, his mind playing with this image or that. Her nearness was almost painful. It was not fair that Raoul should have both her and the land! He had to remind himself forcefully of his purpose in coming to Oakwood.

"Er, just how many refugees have you?" he asked.

Lord Raoul lifted an eyebrow. "Seven and thirty, I think. Was that the figure, my lady?"

"Aye," she said. "Exactly that, my lord."

Hawk cocked his head. "Why do you ask?"

"It is a goodly number," said Sir Eustace. "With so many new hands to work your fields, you can surely spare me another serf or two for the Danesford demesne."

The Hawk released his wife, but began to play idly with one of her braids. "Now, I thought me," he mused, "that I'd already given you men enough to tend your land."

Sir Eustace shrugged, showing a mended place on his leather surcoat. "T'was a hard winter, brother, and I lost three serfs with no way to replace them."

Lord Raoul was not appeased. "The winter was no harder at Danesford than here, and we lost none except an old woman nigh on sixty summers and a newborn babe too weak to suck. How came your folk to die?"

Again Sir Eustace shrugged, but now his smile was gone. "One was insolent, and I had him whipped. Oh, do not show me that look, brother! He must have had some malady of the heart, for he died under the lash after only twelve strokes! The other two were plotting against me." He flushed under his brother's contemptuous regard. "They were conspiring against me, I tell you! I *had* to hang them as a lesson to the others!"

Lord Raoul grunted and let his lady's braid fall from his hand. "Then let it be a lesson to you, as well. Not one of my folk will I give you, until I am certain you'll value their worth and use them accordingly."

"You cannot mean what you say!" gasped Sir Eustace, shocked to the heart. "You'd set a serf's life above your own brother's comfort? What madness!"

"Not such madness as the wasting of three good peasants for your bloodsport!" declared Lord Raoul angrily. "Since childhood you've indulged yourself in bloody games with others' lives, Eustace. At first t'was animals, then people. It is more than time you learned such things have their price. My new folk tell me some of their number went in the direction of Deerfield when last seen. I advise you to approach Lord Robert in this matter. Perhaps he'll sell you a few of his folk, and mayhap you'll appreciate your serfs more if you're forced to pay for their purchase."

"I've not enough silver for that, and you know it!" Sir Eustace muttered bitterly. "You've grown mean, brother! Why, you never even shared the prize silver William gave you for that last campaign in France!"

"You were not even *on* that campaign, Eustace," said Lord Raoul with great patience. "And if you will but cast your mind back a few years, I gave you seventy silver marks but one month after we landed in England. Surely you must have some of that left. God knows t'was a princely sum, and more than I've given to any other."

"Flemish and Rhenish wines are not cheap, as you well know," Sir Eustace protested angrily. "I'd other expenses, too; what with one thing and another, I've none of that coin left."

"What about Lady Agnes' dowry?" Lord Raoul asked. "Surely you may sell some of the jewels."

"I've told you, there were other expenses!"

"Well, did you not make arrangements through my lady to sell your wool clip when Master Guy returns? I believe he paid you an advance on that, did he not?"

"I owed a few gaming debts." Sir Eustace looked into his cup to avoid his brother's eyes. "They came to more than I'd thought."

"Then," murmured Lord Raoul, "I fear you will have to make do with the peasants you now have."

Sir Eustace dashed his cup to the floor in a fury. His eyes blazed as the wine spilled in a circle of dark red, like blood. "I'll not forget this great kindness, brother dear!" he grated, pulling his gloves from his belt. He slapped the gauntlets across the palm of his hand, gave Lady

Judith a look of hatred, and left, striding stiff-legged out of the hall. His voice could be heard in the bailey as he called angrily for his horse.

"No," said Raoul thoughtfully, looking after him. "No, I don't expect you will." He looked at Judith. "From now on, my lady, we go nowhere without an armed escort."

Judith nodded soberly.

CHAPTER 14

hat is it bothers you?" Edwina asked, pulling her shawl tight about her. The sun did little to warm either of them, but the exertion of the walk put pink in her cheeks.

"I don't like the look of my lady," muttered Gytha, brows drawn together in worry. "See how she walks, always with a hand on her belly?"

Edwina scratched her own swollen belly and shrugged. "Don't we all?"

"Nay, not like that. Here, move over. There's a cart coming up behind us." Both women moved to the side of the road as the miller's wagon rumbled past on its way to the castle, sacks of flour piled to the top.

"How's your youngest?" asked Edwina. She tucked a curl of red hair back under the headcover it had escaped.

Gytha smiled. "T'was only a new tooth. He's fine." She noted her friend's unease as they walked from the village back to the castle after a day spent in the comfort of Gytha's mother's cottage. "Are you well? Should I run after the miller and see if he'll take you up?"

"Oh, no. I'm well enough," replied the redhead with a grimace. "Tis only that the babe keeps pushing its foot against my side." She was silent a moment. "What meant you about Lady Judith? She looks to be healthy."

Gytha shook her head and wiped her nose on the sleeve of her brown wool gown. "She usually makes nothing of a birthing, but not this time. I mislike the look of her skin, and she walks as if t'was her last month instead of her eighth. The babe could be too big, I'm thinking.

That's trouble."

Edwina crossed herself and spat to ward off ill luck. Six months along herself, she was nervous at the veriest hint of trouble in childbed. "Does my skin look alright?"

"You're fine," Gytha assured her with a quick pat on the shoulder. "No cause for alarm. It's my lady concerns me." She caught the distress remaining in Edwina's eyes. "Now, behave yourself, do! Haven't I told you and told you you'll be well? You're small in body, and your man's small, too. Unless you've been seeing someone on the sly, the babe'll be small, as well."

"Gytha!" her friend gasped. "As if I'd dare!"

The Saxon woman laughed. "Your own fault for picking a solider!"

"I'm not scared of him, really," Edwina said. "He's a good man, and not rough or mean as you might expect from a man-at-arms."

"I know. He's alright, for a Norman," sighed Gytha.

"There's some say he looks a bit like the Hawk," suggested Edwina hopefully.

Gytha held out her arm to help her friend up the castle hill, no easy climb in Edwin's condition. "Yes, dear. So he does." It took more than brown hair and eyes to make a man look like Lord Raoul, but Gytha kept that observation to herself. Ahead she could see that the miller had taken Lady Judith up in his wagon. A good thing, too. She would never have made it to the top without assistance. Gytha shook her head and decided to have a word with Arnhilda on the subject.

‡

Weak sunshine lightened the gloom of the nursery, where Judith sat bundled in furs against the chill. Richard stood before her, wrapped in layers of clothing, sucking his thumb and entranced at her undivided attention.

"One day, when you are grown," she said, "you will be Lord Richard. You will be a strong, brave knight just like Papa. And when God calls Papa to heaven, my strong, brave Richard will be Lord of Oakwood. You will watch over our people just as Papa does, and you will protect them and keep them safe."

Richard blinked. "I'll be just like Papa," he said around the thumb.

Judith smiled tenderly. "That's my brave knight! You will be wise and just and kind to our folk, and no one at Oakwood will go hungry. All will have work to keep them from mischief, and their cottages will have stout walls and good thatching to keep out the cold and damp. And then God will love you, and mama, who loves you, too, will be very, very proud."

The boy glanced across the chamber to where Giles napped peacefully. "Will my brother be Lord of Oakwood, too?"

"No, only you may be that," Judith replied gravely. "You are the firstborn. When Giles is a man, he'll be lord on lands of his own."

"And 'Lizabeth? Will she go away to be a lord, too?" he asked.

Judith chuckled and gently pulled his thumb from between his lips. "No, your sister cannot be a lord, sweeting. She's a maiden. But she'll have a fine dowry, and papa will give her to a husband who is kind and just."

"I don't want 'Lizabeth to go away," he protested. "She's too little." He slipped the thumb back into his mouth with a worried frown.

"Elizabeth will be here for years yet, foolish one. Maids don't wed until they're all grown up," reassured Judith with a fond caress, removing the thumb again. "Your sister will be fifteen before she goes to her husband's demesne."

"Good." Richard abandoned interest in the future. "I know how many one pig and one pig are!" he announced importantly. "It's two pigs!"

"How clever you are!" exclaimed his mother. "Know you how many there are an you have yet another pig?"

Richard frowned and stared at his stubby fingers. "One pig and one pig and one pig?" he wriggled and muttered to himself. "Three pigs?"

"Aye, three pigs," agreed Judith, laughing.

"I'll tell Papa. He will be surprised I know." Richard giggled. "I'm a big boy now!"

"So you are. Soon Brother Plegmund will show you how to put on parchment the marks to say you've three pigs. That way, if someone comes and says you only have two pigs, you will be able to get the paper and prove him wrong." She motioned for Dorothea to come help her to rise, for Judith was very near her time and could not seem to make her body move as it should. "You are a good boy, Richard, and Mama is very proud you learn so well. There are many men full grown who do not know the things you do. See whether by the morrow you can tell me how many there are if you add two arrows and two arrows." She kissed his brow and rose awkwardly, leaning on the maidservant's arm.

Dorothea clucked reproof. "You should rest, my lady."

"Who then would see done the tasks I've set?" She shrugged. "No, t'was a kind thought, and I thank you, but I'll be off to the solar now, should any come in search of me." She cast a last fond look at Richard. "He resembles his father more with each day that passes."

"Acts like him, too, my lady" returned the woman dryly. "He's forever ordering the younger ones about as if he were lord already."

"'Tis best they learn to obey him now," Judith decided after a moment's thought. "Still, too much power is a dangerous thing for one so young. I recall how Eric the tanner's son misused his brothers and sisters for pride at being the eldest. Should there be the slightest sign he bullies them needlessly, bring the matter to my ears at once. A good leader must know how to follow orders before he understands how to give commands of his own."

Dorothea chucked. "Aye, my lady. But he'll soon be of age to question our right to turn him over a knee, however well-deserved the punishment."

"By then he'll be in his father's keeping more than ours. My lord will have no trouble putting him in his proper place."

"True enough, my lady."

‡

Judith's entrance into the solar halted the cozy gossip of her women. As one they bent over their stitchery or plied spindles or shuttlecocks at the loom with great industry. She smiled wryly. *They worked hard and were deserving of a reward,* she thought. She glanced at the chest containing the lengths of cloth Raoul had brought from somewhere as spoils of war. "It seems to me that it is more than time, now that the servants' garments are finished, to turn our attention to ourselves." She searched though the keys at her girdle for the one that opened the bower chest. "Here, let us see what we may contrive in the way of new gowns."

Mending, spinning, and half-woven fabrics were alike forgotten. The chest revealed a treasure trove of materials, some of which had been woven at Oakwood. Most, however, came from far away Flanders, or France, or even fabled Cathay, where the folk had methods, doubtless arcane, for producing woolens of an unbelievable lightness and smoothness. The women cooed and sighed over the stuffs.

"Oooooh!" breathed Lady Edith over a pale blue. "How lovely!"

Lady Margaret's eyes met Judith's. "Yes, it is pretty," Lady Margaret agreed. "Yet see how much nicer is the red."

Lady Edith's eyes narrowed slightly. She looked from Lady Judith to Lady Margaret. "What is it?" she demanded suspiciously. "Had you arranged earlier for the blue to go to Lady Margaret?!"

"No, how could you imagine we would do such a thing?" soothed Lady Judith. "'Tis only as Lady Blanche often says, that pale colors are for pale faces, bright ones for dark hair. Hold the blue next to your cheek, lady. Edwina, come and look. Does the shade look well with Lady Edith's face?"

"It is a pleasant hue," said the sewingmaid diplomatically.

"Now exchange that for the red," Judith instructed Lady Edith.

"Why, there is a difference!" explained Edwina surprised. "Who'd have thought it?"

"Lady Judith did, obviously!" Lady Edith retorted, her disappointment giving her a waspish tone. She had only just recovered from childbed, and the women made allowances for her grief at a second stillborn son. She cast a resentful glance at her mistress. "The red is truly more becoming?"

"I give you my word. The rust might also be attractive. Shall we try that?" asked Judith. She understood the other woman; there was a shade of red that *she* adored that made her look like one on the verge of death.

Edith shook her head. "No, I can see that Lady Margaret agrees. Three of you can't be wrong." She sighed heavily. "I suppose the red will do." The blue wool was replaced in the chest, the red spread over her lap. "Which one for Lady Margaret?" she asked with forced cheer.

Judith frowned. "I'm not sure. Perhaps the darker blue. What think you, lady?" she asked of her friend.

"I have seen enough blue gowns to last a lifetime!" declared the tawny blond Lady Margaret, rolling her eyes in a droll manner that brought giggles form the others. "What would be the effect, I wonder, of the dark green there? Would it go well, think you?"

"Let us see," Lady Judith replied, passing the fabric to the lady nearest, who passed it on.

When it was finally held next to Lady Margaret's skin, everyone agreed that it was very pretty indeed, so the decision was made. Slightly coarser wools were chosen for the sewingmaids, who were not, after all, noble, and the work began. Measurements were taken with knotted string, and sheers snicked through material. Thread was chosen to match as closely as possible. Soon the women were basting seams, excited and happy. At her lady's request, Lady Edith sang a lively air from Normandy while the women worked. The bower became a scene of perfect domestic tranquility.

Of a sudden, Judith bent double as the first pang of labor stabbed at her belly. It was coming early but not dangerously so. "Jesu!" she muttered. "Could this not have waited until nightfall?!" It was so annoying to have her sewing interrupted.

Ladies Margaret and Edith assisted her to her bed and someone raced off to tell Arnhilda to fetch clean linen, and hot water.

‡

T'was a hard birthing, for the new babe was larger than her others had been. Lady Judith was badly torn and feverish. For seven days, Arnhilda ignored her own rheumatic joints to hover anxiously over her lady's bed, dosing her with wolfsbane, bishopswort, and cinnamon. Father Hubert and Brother Plegmund spent hours on their knees in the chapel; all the household feared the worst. Servants huddled in corners, whispering, until Lady Margaret routed them out and shooed them about their business. Even Sir Tancred, normally unmoved by domestic crises, considered whether he should send a messenger to Lord Raoul, who was with the King's forces in the fens. He had seen death in childbed before, and did the lady not die on a rush of blood, t'was usually of a fever. This looked uncomfortably like the latter.

Judith clung stubbornly to life. Leg swollen with the milk fever, sinking sometimes from delirium into stupor, she yet refused to succumb to the weakness that assailed her. On the eighth day after her delivery, she opened her eyes. The shutters over the arrow slits had been closed against a late snowstorm, but pale light filtered through the cracks. She tried to move, but was prevented by a number of fur pelts piled atop the coverlet.

"It is hot," she complained. Her voice, a mere reedy whisper of itself, shocked her.

Arnhilda scurried across the chamber. She peered down, wisps of white hair framing her wrinkled face. "By the Holy Virgin!" She laid a gnarled hand long Judith's cheek. "God be praised, the fever's broke!" She smiled. "How feel you, my lady?"

"Weak. And I thirst."

"Aye, aye, 'tis always the way after a fever! Never fear, I'm prepared." The aged maidservant sighed her relief. "You had me in a worry, my lady. I'd faith in my skill, but even I'll not deny you gave us some worrisome moments." She took a goblet from the floor beside the bed and pressed it to Judith's lips. "Drink this. 'Tis barley-water to ease that parched feeling. Later, I'll give you a little eel broth that Cynefred's been saving, and if you feel up to it, a nice bit of frumenty."

Judith sipped, then turned her head from the cup. "How fares the babe?"

"Ho! A fine, strapping boy, my lady! He was lodged backwards in the channel, as I told you, and came feet first. They're usually a bit weak when they pop out like that, if they live at all, but I called on the Holy Virgin and all the Saints, and the little lad slipped out screaming the battlements down around our ears!" Arnhilda removed a few pelts from the coverlet to the floor. She presented the goblet once more, pleased that Judith drank greedily now she was assured of the child's health. She used a soft cloth to blot the sweat from Judith's face and neck. "Just you rest now, my lady; you need to save your strength."

"No," returned Judith fretfully. "I'll see Father Hubert. The babe must be christened." She lifted a hand to brush the hair from her neck. "'Tis a good thing I thought to send that clerk with my lord when he refused to take Brother Plegmund with him again. Has there been word?"

"No, my lady, I doubt me there's been time." She cast her mind about for something to calm her patient. "The monk has the babe's horoscope done. You may read it when you've more strength." Arnhilda tossed a few leaves of coltsfoot into a pan of steaming water set on a brazier beside her. She intended on taking no chance on her lady's being taken with a chill on top of everything else! "In any case, you've no need to worry over the babe. Hung like a bull-calf, he is! He'll take to the sword like his father before him, and like as not, sire a score of brats in the village 'ere he's wed decent!" She shook her silvery head in admiration. "They didn't make 'em like that when *I* was a maid!"

"Fetch the priest," insisted Judith, smiling in spite of herself. "Healthy he may be, but he still needs the protection of the Holy Church."

"Now, now," soothed Arnhilda as she removed more pelts and fussed with the coverlet. "T'was all done days ago while you were still out of your head with the sickness. Lady Margaret and Sir Artaud stood up for the babe. All as you had planned, my lady, and messages sent to Lord Raoul, as well as Danesford, Deerfield, and Northwatch. Did you think folk would forget your commands?"

Judith sighed her relief. "All's well, then?"

"Haven't I just said so?" reproved Arnhilda gently. She held the goblet out once more. "Just you take a bit more of this, dearling, while I tell you the latest gossip. You'll not credit it, but we've had word from Deerfield that the Lady Blanche is with child at last! She was too ill to travel, but she's sent a fine dagger with a carved silver sheath as a birthing gift for your little Charles," she reported with satisfaction. "I never thought to see her quicken, especially at her age. I reckon Sir Robert'll have a seizure of the heart when he learns of his good fortune!"

"I hope it is in truth a child in her, and not some growth of the belly like the one killed Edith of the fisherfolk last season," murmured Judith wearily. Still, weak as she was, duty came before rest. "We'd best send her a small cask of cider to hearten her, and a pot of the blackberry conserves to sweeten the babe's disposition. Ask Lady Margaret to see to it."

"As you will," Arnhilda replied.

Judith waited until it was plain that the older woman would not speak. "Well? What word from Danesford?"

The maidservant shrugged. "Naught. 'Tis likely jealously for a full nursery. Lady Agnes has but the one son and no sign of another on the way, if Danesford kitchen wenches are to be trusted."

"How was our messenger received?" she pressed, sensing some unease in her woman's manner. "Whom did you send?"

"Rollo Red-Hair," answered Arnhilda reluctantly. "Oh, you'll hear it soon enough from others an I keep it from you, so I'll tell you the whole. Rollo said as Sir Eustace flung a horn of ale at his head and wished him to the Devil! Then he had his guards throw Red-Hair bodily from the keep and sent his horse off at a run. Took the poor fellow half a day to catch the silly beast. You know what my lord's brother is like, my lady," she added in a vain hope of soothing Judith's worry. "Doubtless he was in his cups again. He's too much like Lord Cerdic, that one."

Judith nodded. "He'll bear watching. A lucky thing for him my lord is busy elsewhere. An it were not for Hereward the Wake, Sir Eustace would have had a sharp lesson in courtesy." She closed her eyes. "Ah, well. I'm tired, Arnhilda. Have Rollo come to me after supper; a man who is handled so roughly when on his lord's business deserves to hear our gratitude with his own ears. Tell Dorothea to bring Charles to me when I wake, and say that Richard may sit by my bed for his evening meal. And for Heaven's sake, do not let him be affrighted by tales of my illness."

"Yes, my lady. Although why you must needs give your babes heathen names, I know not!" grumbled the maidservant as she poked at the fire. "'Tis not as if we hadn't plenty of good Saxon names! If it'd been *my* choice, I'd have called him 'Wolfnoth.' Now, there's a name for a lad, one as he can grow into. Not like that silly Norman 'Charles.'"

Judith smiled at the woman's muttering as she fell asleep.

‡

Her recovery was swift. Within a fortnight, Judith was on her feet and relieved to be so, for she was convinced that her household was ill-run when she was not by to oversee it in person. It was as well that her healing was quick, for there was trouble brewing.

A chilly April morning found Judith in the buttery. Gytha, her regular dairymaid, was infected with kinepox and sat isolated in the infirmary, with her plastered hands wrapped in poultices. The infected cattle had been destroyed, the straw burnt. Grumbling grooms had washed down the walls with lye, and even the soil was replaced on the barn floor to foil whatever evil humors might be lurking about. A girl had been brought in from the vill to replace the dairymaid until her hoped-for recovery.

"Now, remember," instructed Lady Judith sternly. As Arnhilda had taught her in childhood, so she taught another now. "In cold weather like this, the milk must be warm as blood before straining. The cream will rise to the top. See?" she skimmed a hand across the top of the milk pail and showed a handful of the thick cream. "You put it into the crock so, and stir the whole each time before you add more cream."

"The way I always do it, my lady, is . . ."

Judith cut her off with a shake of her head. "Never mind what it is you always do at home. Anything produced in the dairy is a wet thing, having an affinity with water, which is an element that may attract evil humours. We must take every precaution to avoid this! Do everything exactly the way I've instructed you. Is that clear?"

"Aye, my lady, I'll remember," said the girl nervously, her hands twisting in the skirts of her dress of faded green wool.

"Good. After churning, you'll add a pinch of salt for every handful of butter. And be careful not to work the butter overmuch, eh? Pack it in these stone jars, but only to here," she added, holding out a filled jar for the maid's inspection. Her scarf of white gauze fluttered behind her in an errant breeze. "Then pour in the brine almost to the rim." She did so, making certain the girl watched. "Be sure to set the lids on firmly."

"Now, what else?" mused Judith, setting the butter aside. The hem of her sky blue gown had already picked up dust from the bailey. She shook her skirts absently as she thought. "You know how much to set aside for Cynefred's precious cheeses, and . . . Oh, of *course*! The soured milk you'll feed to the piglets, which are in your charge. There'll be other things, rinds and the like, from the kitchen when they're older. We take good care of our pigs here. Cynefred will know and send a scullion with a bucket of scraps for you at the appropriate time.

"I know not how long Gytha will be kept from her chores by this malady, so you'd best send word to your man that you'll be keeping to the castle for the present. An he wishes to visit you, I've no objection once the cattle are penned up for the night," Judith concluded, wiping her hands on a linen rag and handing it to the girl. Wages and meals had been discussed earlier. "Have you any questions?"

The girl shook her head mutely, totally cowed by Oakwood's lady.

"Very well, then. I'll leave you to it. Should you think of aught for which you need an answer, send one of the grooms to fetch Arnhilda from the bower."

"Lady Judith?" Sir Tancred appeared in the doorway. "If I might have a word with you?"

"Of course." Lady Judith took her cloak from a bench and slipped it over her shoulders. "See you wash your hands and dry them before you even *look* at a milk pail," she admonished the girl. "No telling what sort of humours abide in earth, you know, and we'd not want to have *that* dripping into the milk!" Then, with a final nod of dismissal, she turned and followed Sir Tancred out into the bailey. Behind her, the new dairymaid raised a hand to wipe away the sweat from her brow and let out a sigh of relief. Even her own grandmother was not so strict, and all in the village acknowledged Old Ardith as a shrew.

Things seemed to be much as usual on the castle grounds. Smoke and steam gusted from the forge while the smith's hammer clanged in a steady rhythm. A whiff of lye and thin clouds of steam drifted out from the laundry. Grooms cursed as they mucked out the stable; the head falconer berated an apprentice for the mishandling of a prime hawk. A troop of men-at-arms rounded the guard tower, headed toward the drawbridge. Ducks and hens scattered squawking out of the path of the soldiers' boots. Servants of both sexes moved to and fro on errands, exchanging greetings or avoiding one another as their paths crossed.

Judith slanted a glance at her bailiff. "There's trouble," she stated flatly.

"Yes, my lady." Sir Tancred stood close, his hands clasped behind this back. Beneath his brown velvet robe he wore boots, for he took his position seriously and often accompanied the patrols. The chilly wind ruffled the fox fur, which trimmed his robe, and flattened its skirts against his torso. "Two of the village men were missing from their fires last night," he told her. "The morn patrol found them at the far end of the village fields with their throats cut."

"Jesu!" Judith crossed herself. *Sir Eustace*, she thought suddenly. *This had something to do with Eustace.*

Sir Tancred rubbed the back of his neck. "There were signs of mounted men, my lady. Four of them, I'd say, though the tracks are confused. No sense in sending a troop to rout them out, though. The peasants have been dead all night, and their murderers are long gone."

"Yes, if they'd any sense at all they'd be away well before daylight," she agreed. "The patrol followed their tracks?"

"Aye." Sir Tancred looked at the scuffed toe of one boot, clearly reluctant to continue.

Lady Judith resisted the temptation to put her fists on her hips and crossed her arms over her breasts instead. "Well, where did the tracks lead?"

"To the north," he replied, lifting his glance to watch her from the corner of his eye.

"Hmmmm. And you think?" she prodded, exasperated at his reluctance.

"I don't know. It could have been Eadric the Wild over the border again with his Welsh cutthroats." He grimaced. "Or outlaws, mayhap, escaped the King's justice in York. Chances are that they're headed for other parts and won't trouble us again," he finished hopefully.

"Rubbish!" snapped Lady Judith, out of patience. "We'd have had an attack on the vill had it been Eadric, and traveling raiders would've taken supplies, foodstuffs, and the like." She frowned. "Anyway, why bother to kill two serfs and leave them to be found? There's no sense in that. No raider would want to alert the demesne to a possible threat. No, in that case the bodies would have been well hidden. It is almost as if someone *wanted* the bodies found."

Sir Tancred scratched his newly grown beard, which his lady assured him gave him an appearance of great dignity, and squinted brown eyes in puzzlement. "Why would anyone want to leave dead bodies lying about?"

"As a warning?" wondered Judith aloud. "No, the message is unclear. 'Tis more of a threat, to show what can be done with my lord gone." She drew a breath and hugged her cloak about her against the cold air. "Be honest, man. 'Tis my lord's brother makes this mischief, and you know it!"

The bailiff swallowed nervously. "My lady, we have no proof!"

"Oh, have done with cautious words! We both know the truth! Merciful God, Sir Eustace's envy of my lord must have driven him mad to have committed such folly!"

"But, my lady!" he protested, shocked and not wanting to believe. "My lord's own brother! No, 'tis not possible!"

She snorted. "Cain was Abel's brother, Sir Tancred, and little good poor Abel got from their blood tie! Nay, I'd wager the nose off my face I've the right of this! May God damn him to hellfire eternal for harming my folk!"

Sir Tancred dug the toe of his boot into the dirt. "The tracks came originally from the north and returned there, as I said. They could have come from Danesford," he admitted. "Still, lady, we've no proof."

"Then we'll have to get proof!" returned Judith impatiently.

"And when we know beyond doubt that Sir Eustace is guilty?" he asked.

Lady Judith's brows rose in surprise. "Why, then we take Danesford Tower, of course."

The bailiff gasped. "Take Danesford Tower? Christ's Nails, my lady, think what you do!"

"I am thinking, Sir Tancred! You know Sir Eustace of old. He's been envious always of my lord's good fortune, refusing to believe it's been earned. Think you he'd stop at this paltry revenge when he knows my lord is from home with most of his men? Must we wait until all our folk are butchered corpses 'ere we act?" she demanded angrily. "Pah! An my lord were here, he'd have been hard on Eustace's heels by now!"

"But it could be raiders from Wales or from someplace else," he insisted stubbornly. "If we took Danesford and were proved wrong, how could we face our judgment in Heaven with such an act to argue against us? T'would be best to wait for proof and not act unadvisedly in so great a matter."

Judith bit her lip, vexed. "Tell me this, then. If we had the proof we seek, have we men enough to take Danesford?"

"I know not, lady. Oh, if he's only the men bound to him, t'would be easy enough, although we'd more likely have to sit out a siege unless we fired the tower. However, he's been lately, as you know, to visit Sir Edward at Northwatch. I'd hazard a guess that he's some of Edward's men with him. In that case, t'would be impossible, for we've only a token force ourselves." Sir Tancred smiled, knowing he'd won.

Lady Judith folded her arms under the cloak and tapped a foot. The soft leather shoe was eloquent with annoyance. "Holy Mother! Well, it galls me to wait and mayhap put ourselves in greater jeopardy thereby, but what you say has merit. I must think this through. Send Conan to me in the garden, if you would be so good, and have someone see to the burial of my folk. Brother Plegmund will be pleased to assist you." She shook her head. "What were the names of those slain?"

Sir Tancred blinked, surprised. "Why, they were peasants, my lady.

I've no idea of their names."

"Sweet Savior, you should!" she snapped. "All of our folk should be known to you, Sir Bailiff, if for no other reason than the collection of the tax! Now that two of our men are dead, heriot is due from their sons according to Norman law." She frowned for a moment, thinking of the hardship this death duty might cause. "If there's a family with young children, take not the best milk cow. My lord's herd is in good heart, despite the kinepox. A young goat would do just as well."

"As you will, Lady Judith," murmured Sir Tancred, embarrassed to have been found wanting in knowledge which should have been his. Any resentment in his clerkly soul at her attitude was drowned out, for indeed, the tax required him to know all the names of the serfs, and now he came to think of it, it might be best if he knew everyone by sight. A tedious task, he thought with a sigh, but one that clearly needed doing. He bowed to Lady Judith and left, determined to prove his worth.

‡

Conan rode out after dark. The following afternoon, a barn was set afire in the vill, and from another part of the village, a young girl carried off. Things were looking very grave. Judith ordered patrols increased yet again and prayed Conan would return safely.

He did, but only just. As Judith had commanded, he had visited the Danesford wench whose favor he'd obtained. He'd had to go to the tower kitchen to find her, but they were discovered by two of Sir Eustace's men. They dragged him away from the tower and beat him without mercy. Then they tied him to his horse and sent it back on the road to Oakwood. The woman was dead, a sword through her heart.

"I've failed you, my lady," he muttered through battered lips. "The wench knew nothing of Sir Eustace's plans." He winced as Judith spread salve on his cuts. "She said he's been in good spirits lately, and that there are extra mouths to feed these days, men from farther north. They came upon us 'ere I could learn aught else. They killed her, poor thing." He added in sorrow. "I couldn't stop them."

"T'was through no fault of yours, Conan," Lady Judith assured him. "You did what you could. But the arrogance of him! To use you so and return you to me! He's cried challenge; that's certain. You've no notion how many men he had from Lord Edward?"

"No, my lady. All the wench said was that the kitchen's overworked. I'd say ten, at the very least." He winced and ducked his head away from her hand.

Judith was sure that he'd shown less reaction to the beating than to her healing. Men! Finished with her tending of cuts in any case, Judith wiped off her hands while Arnhilda covered jars and cleared away the mess.

"Ten at least," mused Judith, pacing the floor. "And Lord Edward, while he's not precisely an enemy, is not much of a friend. He's jealous of the size of Oakwood and might be playing his own game. T'would make sense to encourage the quarrel, then steal land from the winner, unnoticed. Like as not, he sent more than ten if he knew that Sir Eustace meant to move against Oakwood. If my lord were here, he could take the tower no matter what the odds, but I've not his experience. So." She stopped pacing and came to sit by the table. "I fear we've no choice but to wait upon my lord's return. Until then, we must be vigilant. Bring me word of any activity that seems unusual, no matter how slight. And warn the villagers that we've raiders in these parts. Tell them to go always accompanied into the fields and otherwise to stay close to the vill. I will give orders that men-at-arms will guard them on their way to and from the fields."

"Yes, my lady."

She saw his chagrin. "Never mind, Conan. You've done me a great service. My thanks." Then she smiled. "Get you to the kitchen and have Cynefred prepare you something to eat. If ever a man deserved to be well fed, you do!"

"I could do with a little something to line my belly," he admitted. He bowed and left the chamber. Arnhilda closed the door.

"It's that slut, Lady Agnes, is behind this!" burst out the maidservant. "Just like her mother; may the Devil take her soul!"

"I think not," Judith replied wearily. "Oh, she's eager to be lady of the castle, I've no doubt of that." She shrugged. "But Sir Eustace has always craved to stand in his brother's shoes, and the sooner the better. It is he began this venture."

Arnhilda watched the firelight play over Judith's face, noting how tired she looked, and in this moment, older by far than her years. "Is there any chance they'll try to take the castle?" she asked.

"Aye, there's always that possibility." She smoothed the dark blue wool of her skirt.

"So." the older woman nodded grimly. "Well, if they think to take the place without a bit of blood spilt, they'll find themselves in error. I may be old, but I'm not dead yet! I reckon I can still give a fair accounting of myself, should it come to that."

"No!" Judith shook her head emphatically. "Heed me in this. Our men are loyal and will fight well, but if there is at any time danger of our losing the castle, Arnhilda, and this is for your ears alone: at the first warning of trouble, take the babes and their nurses and bring them to the lord's bedchamber at once. At once, do you hear?"

"Aye, but . . ."

"Ask me no questions. Only do as I say. And should we come to such a pass, see to it that they are clothed warmly. And yourself," she added.

"As you command, my lady," murmured Arnhilda. But there was hope in her eyes as she assisted Judith in undressing. She felt certain that Sir Eustace would attack, but for the first time, she was not entirely certain that the event would mean their deaths.

CHAPTER 15

A lowering sky lent extra chill to the morning as the Norman sewingmaid slipped from the hall, across the court, and into the sturdy dairy barn. The odor of animals enveloped her as she entered, and the heat of their bodies made the temperature of the building noticeably warmer than the courtyard had been. She answered her friend's welcoming smile with one of her own and handed her a sweet biscuit, a successful experiment of Lady Judith's in her latest foray into the kitchen. The Saxon woman munched contentedly, then wiped her hands upon her apron, and returned to her chores.

"So, what's happening?" she demanded as she spilled another bucket of scraps in the trough. Young pigs came squealing and tumbling over one another at the sound.

"There's to be guards posted over the fields every day," Edwina returned, raising her voice to be heard over the snorting. She was grateful when her friend motioned to the far end of the barn. She had never liked the acrid smell of the pigs.

"Is it raiders, then?" inquired Gytha eagerly. She liked a bit of excitement, provided there was little risk to herself. The castle would keep her safe enough, she reckoned.

"So they say," returned her friend. "The guard patrols are tripled to avoid any more killings on the way to and from the fields. It is good," she added gruffly, "your man works in the smithy now. You've settled into your room in the castle?"

"Aye, it's small, but there's space enough for us, an' the babes, and my old mother. Strange not to have the livestock in with us at night, though."

"Did you sell them?"

"My brother minds 'em, but that's a long tale. The best part is that I've my young ones under my own eye."

"True," murmured Edwina, thinking of her own son. Luckily a kitchen wench, whose own child had died at three weeks of age, had volunteered to wetnurse Edwina's own Robert in exchange for a knitted shawl and a weekly pitcher of ale. Had it not been for this, her little one would have had to be fostered out in the village. "With raiders about, it must ease your mind to know them safe in the castle. It gives me the shivers to think of being murdered on the way to the fields."

"I wonder if 'tis Hereward the Wake?" murmured Gytha, adjusting her linen headcloth. She'd dressed in a hurry this morn, and now the covering showed an exasperating tendency to slide to the left. "I mean, I know 'tis Saxons have been killed, but he might be angered at their being bound to a Norman lord, mightn't he?"

Edwina shot her a goaded look. "By all the saints, how could it be so? You've know he's being chased even now by my lord far to the east!"

"So 'tis said," agreed Gytha, liking the mystic. "But still . . ."

"Doubtless it is some poor Saxon noble tired of living off nuts and berries in the forest," Edwina remarked spitefully. Hereward the Wake, that's what they had, a Saxon. Why were there no Norman heroes? "The soldiers will catch him."

"Mayhap." Gytha shrugged and tugged at her headgear. "How is my Lady Judith holding up?"

"She's fine, as always. A bit tired, of course, as is to be expected after the milk fever, but she'll do. You always ask about her. Why the concern?"

"Did you never notice that I've no scars from the kinepox?" replied Gytha with raised eyebrows.

"What?!"

"I said, 'I've no scars!'" Gytha said impatiently, wiping her hands on her skirt of faded red.

"But . . . but that's not possible! Everyone gets scars from the kinepox!"

"Look at my hands," Gytha insisted, placing them before her friend's eyes. "Took care of me, she did, as if I'd been her own daughter. Changed the bandages three times a day, and gently, too. Made sure I'd enough to eat and even checked the pallet to be certain there were no extra guests living there to annoy me." She nodded emphatically. "Someone goes that far out the way to help you, it gives you the right to worry about them, too, a bit."

Edwina dropped her eyes to the barn floor, embarrassed. Her best friend in the world had recovered from the kinepox with a miraculous lack of scarring, and she had not even noticed. Also, Lady Judith had been kind to Gytha, more kind than any noblewoman of Edwina's acquaintance. (Not that she knew many, but still . . .) She was deserving of more respect than she had been shown. Edwina fussed with her skirt; then her hands stilled as she recalled how Lady Judith had insisted the pale green would be just the touch to add luster to the sewingmaid's red hair. It had been the first new gown she could remember ever having owned, the others being cast-offs of the nobility. Her man, Edouard, had been very appreciative of the honor done them both. "All the work she does, my lady pushes herself too hard," she said slowly.

"Always has," Gytha returned, eyeing her friend with concern. "Are you alright?"

Edwina brushed that off. "Fine. She really should rest more and worry less. Mayhap there are chores I could do would take some of the burden from her. I'd best ask Arnhilda, I suppose." The sewingmaid sighed; Arnhilda was intimidating. Ah, well. What must be done was better not put off. She looked up with apology. "I'd best get back before I'm missed. I'll see you at supper then." She squeezed Gytha's shoulder in a quick hug and rushed off.

Gytha looked after her, grinning slowly. "I knew you'd come round once you got to know my lady like I do!" She chuckled and returned to her work.

‡

Despite occasional minor raids upon Oakwood lands, the spring planting was accomplished. It took longer than usual, what with the guards searching for dangers before folk were allowed to disperse for the day's work, but the caution was well-founded. Judith reckoned that

Sir Eustace would avoid an open conflict with Raoul's soldiery, and so it proved. Young girls were warned to keep within the confines of the village, and peasant lads colorfully admonished by their elders to maintain a sharp watch over the livestock. By summer's end, only two peasant's huts had been destroyed. One of the village women had been raped and throttled, but all agreed that by wandering off beyond the stream at sunset she'd asked for trouble.

‡

Abbess Sexburga, mounted upon a gentle palfrey, rode into the bailey, her nuns forming two neat lines as they walked behind her. The big courtyard was lined with folk come to watch her take leave of Lady Judith. She was pleased that the Lady of Oakwood had seen fit to make a ceremonial occasion of this formality. It was truly with pleasure that she accepted Oakwood's parting gifts of a cask of brandy and a bundle of wax candles.

Back at the Saxon hold, the weavers were moving their belongings into the old hall before the holy folk were out of sight down the track. Looms were put together and arranged along the walls of the large downstairs room, which had once been the Saxon great hall. Sleeping pallets found their way into upstairs bedrooms. The separate kitchen, repaired by the holy sisters, would do for storage, the women decided. All preferred the peasant custom of cooking in the main building, however much grander it was than their abandoned huts. Thus, cooking utensils were arranged along the huge hearth. Foodstuffs from the castle were delivered and stacked in the cellar. By common consent, a modest yet filling feast of celebration was prepared.

‡

Many months passed before Judith received a brief message from the clerk with Raoul. He indicated that all was well at Ely, Raoul having no hurt other than a graze from a spent arrow. He wrote further that word of Charles' birth had been greeted with joy and many tankards of ale. Also, he reported, Earl Edwine had been killed by his own men as he attempted flight across the border to seek refuge at Malcolm's court. A fitting end for a traitor, even if he was a Saxon, the clerk had added on his own. The rebels had been most embarrassed.

Judith re-read the message, then sighed. Raoul might have sent a personal message through the scribe. Ah, well. She glanced up at Arnhilda. "Do you feel up to a trip to the weavers' hall?"

"Oh, as you wish," sighed the maidservant, making much of the matter. Knowing Judith, she thought, there would be no oxcart to ease their way. "I know not what draws your eye in that direction, though. You've been over there every other day for weeks!"

"Hardly that often," Judith commented, amused. She adjusted the brass pins holding the pink scarf over her hair, then settled the silver girdle firmly about her hips. "I'd say I visit the weavers' hall more like once a fortnight, what with all my other duties." The rose-colored velvet gown fit well, she thought, now that her waist was back down to the proper size after childbed.

"You don't get enough rest," muttered Arnhilda. She pulled a green woolen shawl about her bony shoulders and picked at the stuff of her yellow skirts. Her white hair poked out of its thin braids in several directions.

"I'll have time for rest when I'm in my grave," Judith answered. "Besides, you liked sitting in the sun with nothing to do while the threshing was going on."

Arnhilda grunted, but in fact she *had* rather enjoyed that. "Mayhap. I recollect as how Master Guy said t'was high quality flax. Will it bring us much profit?"

"All depends upon the market, upon how many folk want good linen." In her mind she saw again how the Flemish sea captain had grinned at the waist-high flax plants, the thin branches supporting slender leaves, but few flowers.

"You should never've pulled the flax at the harvest last year," grumbled Arnhilda. "Made you look like a peasant, slopping about in the muck and dirt! 'Tis not the sort of behavior expected of Hawk's lady."

"Nonsense!" returned Judith. "Besides, there wasn't much muck left by then. It was dry."

"The point remains," sniffed Arnhilda. "Then you insisted upon counting the seeds and seeing them packed away in sacks like some greedy merchant guarding his silver! Humph!"

"The seeds were pretty, I thought; I like that glossy kind of brown."

"You'll not lure me from the track so easily, my lady," Arnhilda asserted belligerently. "It is not dignified in a lady to be so involved with the work of lesser hands. A lady," she added in a morally instructive way, "does not soil her hands with the labor meant for her serfs, except to teach."

Judith smiled and took the maidservant's arm, helping her down the stair and across the great hall. "I think you will be pleased with the progress the weavers have made," she said, ignoring the reprimand. "I will allow that the soaking was a fairly boring business, and I had to skip the hackling altogether. You've no reason for complaint."

"'Hackling?' What in the Apostles' Names is that?" demanded the older woman. She stopped on the bottom step before the hall and cracked a snaggle-toothed grin at the cart that waited there. "This is more like it!"

Judith simply shook her head, smiling.

Conan helped the women to climb into the conveyance, then mounted his horse. The small cavalcade of oxcart with driver, two women, and six men-at-arms moved out of the bailey.

Arnhilda poked Judith with a sharp elbow. "You said you'd tell me about the heckling."

"Hackling," Judith corrected automatically. "You know it; 'tis only the combing of the flax fibers."

"Well, why did you not *say* so?"

"I did. The proper term is 'hackling,'" said Judith, trying hard not to roll her eyes like some impatient child.

Household duties and hearing reports from her patrols had kept her from watching as the fibers were placed on a wooden card set with iron teeth. Another card would have been drawn gently across at right angles to loosen and straighten the flax fibers. "I was forced by the press of obligations to forego the hackling. I will not, however, miss the first lengths of fine linen being woven," she told the maidservant firmly.

"No one said as you had to miss it," Arnhilda mumbled. "We all know as how you think naught goes well out from under your all-seeing eye."

"What?"

"Naught."

"Hmmmm." Judith eyed her narrowly. While it was commonly thought wrong to allow too much license to body servants, even those of long standing, she had not the heart to reprimand Arnhilda. Not that it would do much good if she did reprimand her, she thought wryly.

"So, the short fibers have already been made into cloth?" asked Arnhilda, peering across the cart. Her eyes were growing dimmer these days, and she had trouble focusing even in good light. She would not admit it, however. T'was no one's affair but her own.

"Aye. The tow was made into rough fabric. T'will do for drying cloths and to make the New Year's gift of clothing to the servants. The weavers were done with that days ago. Today should see the finish of the first lengths of fine stuffs. I admit I am eager to see how well we've done."

"If it is as good as you think, why not bring the bower women down for a look later?" suggested the maidservant.

"Why, 'tis a goodly notion!" Judith exclaimed. "T'would be a break from routine, and please the weavers at the same time, to see how their labors are appreciated."

"Aye." Arnhilda nodded and crackled. "I'll stay behind at the castle. T'will be a novelty to have peace and quiet in the bower for a few hours instead of all that gossip and bickering."

"Arnhilda!" Judith reproved gently.

"Don't 'Arnhilda' me," retorted the maidservant. "Lady Edith is sour enough to turn wine to vinegar!"

Judith sighed sadly. "Well, she's cause for her unhappiness. Out of all the babe's she conceived, only the first has survived."

"None of *mine* survived to their tenth birthday, yet you don't see me complaining and stabbing about with my tongue the way she does!"

"It seems you complain a lot to me," muttered Judith.

"What?"

"Naught."

"Hmmmm."

‡

Master Guy was thrilled with the quality of the linen when he returned late in the season to pick up Oakwood's trade goods. He promised it would fetch a good price in the markets. Judith was busy for weeks after with plans for the forthcoming capital.

That fall Lady Margaret was delivered of a daughter. Sir Artaud, who had a son by a previous marriage now living with his brother in Normandy, was frankly enchanted. Judith was sponsor to the little Catherine. She gifted Lady Margaret with a silver chain and the babe an embroidered gown fashioned from Oakwood's finest linen. Lady Margaret was teary-eyed with happiness.

‡

During the harvest, when the raiders might have been expected to attack while all were busy in the fields, there had been no sign of trouble. But as the winter approached and Judith relaxed her guard, a peasant was reported missing from the village. He was found beaten to death, his body mutilated. This incident was followed by redoubling the guard. No more murders took place, but twice livestock were slain, and one cottage roof set ablaze.

‡

Gytha slipped out to the bailey for a bit of fresh air and to meet with Edwina. The two women paced back and forth, arms linked.

"So," said Edwina with a grin, "you'll never guess the latest."

"What?" the dairymaid demanded eagerly.

"You know Conan, the tall man-at-arms?"

"Who doesn't?"

"Well, the other guards are teasing him something awful. Seems he's got his eye on Eddeva, Arnhilda's assistant."

Gytha gasped, delighted. "No!"

"Oh, aye. They've been eyeing one another for a month or so, and someone saw them smiling and looking into each other's eyes. A little touch of the hands, and the word has spread. I expect the banns will be read on the Sabbath." Edwina grinned. "No one knew as Conan even *had* feelings!"

"Everyone has feelings," said Gytha.

"To be sure. But no one believed Conan would ever marry. Looks like we were all wrong."

Gytha smiled. "I like weddings," she said.

‡

A few weeks later, just after cockcrow on a misty morning, the castle warder sent word that Lady Agnes of Danesford and her son were before the drawbridge, requesting admittance.

As badly as Judith wished she could deny them refuge, she had no choice but to admit them. Raoul was lord of this land, and to refuse succor to a dependent was to discredit his rule. With a feeling of deep foreboding, she gave the necessary orders and made her way to the great hall to receive her stepsister.

A crowd was gathering hurriedly, Judith saw as she crossed the floor. Her gown of dull gold wool swept the rushes behind her. People rubbed the sleep from their eyes, tugged garments into place, and gazed about with some curiosity. The headscarves of the women fluttered as they turned to gossip with neighbors. Judith took her seat and sighed. Doubtless they wondered what was toward, for it was very unlike Agnes to make a visit to Oakwood. At this time of day, and totally unexpected, the visit could only be the result of an emergency . . . or, Judith reminded herself, a trap.

There was a small bustle at the door, and the guard called out, "Lady Agnes of Danesford and her son, Rudolf!"

Lady Agnes came forward, slowly, an uncertain look on her face. She wore a stained and worn red velvet gown, and good hide boots. A cap of white linen covered the top of her head, while the rest of her hair was tangled and hung down her back. The child in her arms was awake and staring about him with lively wonder. His clothes were likewise stained, but of better quality. Doubtless he was of more importance in his father's house than was his mother. Not that it mattered. Her loyalty, such as it was, would be to her husband, for therein lay her security.

Lady Judith rose courteously and motioned to a servant. When he brought a stool for the guest, she resumed her seat. "Give you good day, sister," she said. "I trust I see you well?"

"Only by God's grace," replied the other woman, plopping herself wearily on the seat and settling the child in her lap. "I come to beg shelter for myself and my son here at Oakwood until the raiders that plagued Danesford are gone. Will you aid me?"

A lie! thought Judith. She was certain that the only raiders plaguing Danesford were men of Danesford Tower, but she had no proof. Without it, she could only watch and wait. She smiled graciously and inclined her head. "Of course. We will be pleased to assist you, as Oakwood helps all those in need. Tell us, I beg you, of these raiders. Know you who they are?"

"No, but my lord believes them to be Welshmen. Doubtless he knows better than I, who have no aptitude for such things."

It was meant for a subtle cut at Judith, who ruled the fief in her lord's absence and engaged in many "unfeminine" activities, so-called by ladies too weak, untrained, or simply too lazy to attempt them. The Lady of Oakwood raised a tawny eyebrow. "Indeed. A pity. Yet I dare swear you know best your own limitations and are wise to keep within them."

She gestured gracefully toward a servant who had come forward with bread, cheese, and wine. "May I offer you refreshment?" she asked. A large ruby gleamed from the gold ring she wore on the forefinger of her right hand, a gift Raoul had brought her from York.

"You are most generous," Agnes murmured, reaching for the wine. She drank it unwatered, which produced knowing looks amongst the spectators. Only those who drank deeply and often took their wine without water to temper its fire. The castle servants were scandalized, even those having known her of old. Judith beckoned to Lady Edith. "Have the green guesting chamber prepared for Lady Agnes, please," she murmured, referring to the chamber by the color of the bedcurtains.

"At once, my lady." Lady Edith moved away, waving two servants before her up the stair. She liked to set things into a bustle of activity and viewed her position at Oakwood as the feminine counterpart to that of her husband. By the look of Lady Agnes' garments, she would be needing the loan of a few things until her own were cleaned. Her child would need a change of clothes, at the very least, as well. With a feeling of satisfaction, Lady Edith set about making arrangements for the stay of Oakwood's guests.

"Does Danesford need a party of soldiers to aid them in defense of the tower?" asked Lady Judith politely.

Lady Agnes almost choked on a mouthful of cheese. "No, I thank you!"

"Are you certain? It would be no burden," Lady Judith insisted. She would like an excuse to send in her own men-at-arms, Judith admitted to herself. If things came to a fight, she'd prefer it to take place at Danesford.

"I am positive," returned Lady Agnes firmly. "My lord is equal to the task of maintaining his demesne."

"If you are certain, we will await word from Danesford," Lady Judith acquiesced. "So. My folk are preparing your chamber as we speak. Your son will be well tended in the nursery with my own babes, of course."

"I . . . I would prefer to have him with me in my own chamber," Agnes said quickly. "We . . . that is, he is not well. I will sleep better with him by my side." She licked her lips nervously.

Little Rudolf was thin and pale, and too quiet for Judith's liking, but seemed perfectly healthy. However, she did not dispute the lie. Were their situations reversed, Judith would never have permitted her children to rest unprotected in Danesford's nursery. She could understand Agnes' reluctance to do the same.

"It shall be as you wish, sister. You brought no woman with you to see to your needs?"

Agnes looked at the floor. "There was no time to make adequate arrangements."

"Then I will assign one of my women to look after you and see to your requirements." It was not a good idea to leave Agnes unobserved and with free run of the castle. Judith's eye caught that of Edwina, the sewingmaid. The lady's eyebrow rose inquiringly; the redheaded servant nodded her acceptance of the charge. "Edwina will be pleased to care for you," said Judith softly. "She came to Oakwood at the same time as you, if you remember."

Agnes looked agitated. "This is not necessary."

"But I insist," Judith said, with a touch more firmness in her tone. "Indeed, t'would be an insult to my lord husband to treat his brother's lady with less than the honor due to her. Edwina is well versed in the requirements of a Norman lady and knows how to keep one's chambers in order."

"I fear I had no time to gather my belongings 'ere I fled Danesford," Agnes sighed, and gave a rueful smile. "She will have little to keep in order."

"As to that, I could hardly expect you to wear a stained and torn gown day upon day! My gowns might be a shade too small for a good fit, but I am certain Lady Margaret and Lady Edith can find something in their coffers would look well enough. Please, consider the matter closed."

Lady Agnes could do nothing other than accept with as good a grace as possible. She allowed herself to be shown up to her chamber by Edwina, Rudolf clutched in her arms.

‡

"She's up to something!" hissed Arnhilda in her lady's ear as the spectators milled about and servants began to set up trestle tables for the morning meal.

"I agree," Judith murmured, "but what is it?"

"Whatever it is, Edwina's presence'll slow her down a bit."

"Will it?"

"You doubt Edwina's loyalty?" asked Arnhilda, surprised.

"Oh, no, not that. 'Tis only that I'd be astonished if *anything* would slow Lady Agnes once she's set on a goal."

"I wish the Hawk would come back," the maidservant said on a sigh.

"So do I," muttered her lady. "So do I."

‡

For most of the day, Lady Agnes kept to her chamber. She wore a blue gown that Lady Margaret had provided. She seemed pleased with it and her surroundings. She ordered servants to provide her with bread, fruit conserves, and wine, *lots* of wine, Edwina reported. Judith assigned two men-at-arms to make themselves conspicuous in Lady Agnes' presence during the day, though she could not see what Lady Agnes could accomplish by herself. She was not a danger, Judith decided. T'was *Sir Eustace* she must be worried about. He would arrive in a day or two with a mounted troop and seek to visit his wife, no doubt, counting upon Judith's lack of experience to admit him and his armed men into the bailey. Well, she thought grimly, her brother-in-law would learn a thing or two if *that* was his game!

Unfortunately, Sir Eustace had another, better plan in mind. During the night, when the guards dozed at their posts and all was still, Lady Agnes slipped from her bed and made her way out to the porter's tower. Jean Porter woke with a knife under his ear.

"Wha'. . ."

"Be silent!" hissed Lady Agnes, her eyes glittering in the light of a candle she'd set on the floor. "If you would live, get up quietly and come with me into the other room. Should there be a sound or a move from you I like not, I shall kill you and your wife. Nod if you understand me."

The porter nodded. Sweat formed on this forehead and upper lip, and there was a cold, sick feeling in his stomach. He wondered that his wife, a warm, softly snoring presence at his side, did not wake.

"Get up now," Lady Agnes hissed. "And do it slowly!"

Jean did so, afraid of the knife in the hand of this madwoman and embarrassed by his nudity before her. A small part of his mind was shocked that she should insist upon his not taking time to cover himself. She was of the nobility, after all.

They moved slowly and silently across the floor, into the next room. "This knife is very sharp." She told him, but he already knew that. Just after she'd roused him with a hand over his mouth, the other hand, the one holding the knife, had slipped only a little, but he'd felt the trickle of blood run along the side of his neck and down to the bed.

"What do you want?" he whispered fearfully.

Lady Agnes felt her hand tremble and pressed the blade more firmly against him. She was terrified. All he need do was strike her arm away from the proper angle and overpower her, and all would be lost. It must not happen. "Keep silent!" she ordered. "Do not make me say it again! Walk to the stair." She kept herself pressed to his side. "Go down the stair. Carefully," she cautioned. "We wouldn't want this knife to slip too much, now would we?"

He shivered and obeyed, not knowing what else to do. Jean had been a silversmith's apprentice in Normandy. He'd run off to join Duke William's army in search of excitement, but having no talent for soldiering, he'd ended up caring for Lord Raoul's horses instead. The promotion to castle porter had been a piece of good luck, yet he felt anything but lucky now. The stone steps were cold under his bare feet, the hard-packed earth of the courtyard scarcely warmer.

"To the wheel!" Lady Agnes instructed. "I want that portcullis raised."

"Lady. . ." His voice cut off as he felt the knifepoint move. Horror raged in his head. She was going to let in the raiders; he knew it.

"Do it or die!"

His hands shook as he obeyed. *I don't want to die*, he thought, tears trickling down his stubbled cheeks. *Blessed Christ, I don't want to die!* The chain rattled and the wood creaked as the gate began to creep up from the ground. *I don't want to die!* It was a litany in his head. And then, *Can't anyone hear this? I don't want to die!*

Inch by inch the heavy iron rose. Horseman waited on the other side. As soon as the portcullis was high enough, they bent in their saddles and urged their mounts underneath. Lady Agnes reached her free hand around the porter and locked the wheel in position to keep the gate from falling. Suddenly, she shoved the knife deep into the man's neck and sliced outward. Blood hissed and sprayed in the air. She turned away and ran to find her husband.

Jean Porter fell to his knees, his hands raised to his ruined throat. His body toppled sideways to the cold earth. *But. . .* he thought. The night enfolded him.

‡

Not for nothing was Conan his lord's most trusted man. Several times each night he rose from his bed to prowl the castle, assuring himself that all was well during the Hawk's absence. Thus, while making one of these rounds, he discovered the great hall door ajar. A closer investigation revealed armed men moving around the bailey. "Jesu!" He jumped back to bar the door and shouted the alarm.

Men-at-arms, half dressed and cursing, poured out of the guard tower. Scullions rushed into the hall brandishing meat hooks and knives. Kitchen wenches shrieked frightened questions to which none paid heed. Conan raced up the stair, nearly colliding with Judith on her way down.

"Sir Eustace . . . in the bailey!" he panted. "Someone opened the gate to him whilst we slept!"

"Agnes!" Judith spat out the name like a piece of rotten meat. "She's not in her chamber!"

A violent crash sounded below, and Conan grunted. "Battering ram. They'll have the door down soon."

"The knights?" she asked.

Conan put a hand on her arm. "On patrol in the vill, all but Sir Basil, and he's bedfast with a broken leg. They'll take the castle, my lady."

"I know it." Her body felt icy with fear, but she willed herself to remain in control. She turned at Arnhilda's approach. "Wrap the children warmly and get them to my chamber," she ordered. Arnhilda retreated without a word. Judith turned back to Conan. "Fetch two men you can trust." He left at a run.

Ladies Edith and Margaret sped past on their way to the nursery, their babes in their arms. Like Judith, they'd dressed hastily and warmly. The ram crashed against the door below as Judith raced to the green chamber. Her eyes glinted as she moved to the bed, for Rudolf sat crying upon the coverlet. Heart pounding, Judith scooped him into her arms and ran to the nursery.

Already the nurses had their charges bundled in wool and furs. Dorothea threw together a large pile of changing cloths as she shooed everyone toward the corridor. Judith tied a cap on Rudolf and wrapped a warm fur about him.

Richard stared, clutching at her skirts. "What's wrong, Mama?"

"We're in danger, lambkin. You must be very quiet and brave, and do exactly as I tell you. Can you do that for me?"

"Yes, Mama. Are you scared?" he asked, on the verge of tears himself.

"Of course. We all are, sweeting," she replied, her heart going out to him. In God's Holy Name, *why* must children suffer?! "It is alright to be afraid, Richard. But we must not let it stop us doing what we know to be our duty."

He took a deep breath and wiped his nose on his sleeve. "Yes, I understand. I will protect you," he said gravely. His hands shook, but like his mother, he ignored that. He broke away from his nurse to retrieve his small dagger from his coffer. "I'm ready, Mama," his four-year-old voice firm.

Judith did not smile. Young as he was, the boy knew how to use the knife to good effect; his father had made certain of that. "That's my brave knight," she praised softly. "You must go with your nurse and guard the smaller children."

"Why are you carrying *him*?" Richard asked, indicating Rudolf with a jealous tilt of his chin.

"We could not leave your cousin to be hurt by the bad men, could we?" she countered.

"No!"

She turned to Arnhilda. "Ready?"

The older woman plucked two wooden pails from a corner and nodded. "Aye, my lady."

They crowded into the lord's chamber, frightened and desperate. By the noises below, the invaders had not yet gained the hall. Hopefully, the men gathered there would buy time for their escape. Conan barred the chamber door and Judith, holding her nephew in one arm, shoved the bed away from the wall. Later she would marvel that she had the strength to manage with one arm what she normally needed both to move, but at the time she gave it no thought. With an angry gesture, she silenced the other women as Conan pushed on a stone in the wall behind the hangings. As if by sorcerer's work, a small section of stones swung aside to reveal an iron bound wooden door. Conan opened the door and took three torches from a rush basket in the passage beyond. He lit them from the hearth and handed them to his men.

Judith made a gesture with her head. Arnhilda turned silently and followed one of the men through the door and down the wooden stair beyond. Just as quietly, the other women followed her, one or two covering a child's mouth with a cautionary hand.

The second man-at-arms picked up Judith's jewel casket and, at her whispered order, her workbasket as well. Conan shoved her after the other women and went to remove the bar from the chamber door. He joined Judith in the passage and with a mighty heave on a rope she had not noticed before, pulled the bed back into position, then cut the rope. Conan used a long-handled rake to move the rushes near the bed so they did not look disturbed.

He tossed the rake to one side of the passage. The stone section of the wall slid back into place. The other man beside her grinned as Conan shut the wooden door at the end of the passage and slammed home heavy iron bolts. They descended the stair.

"Best stand back, my lady," grunted Conan, as he reached the bottom stair, behind her. She did so just in time. He tugged what appeared to be a loose board, then jumped out of the way as the whole stair came crashing down. Dust billowed up in a choking cloud. There were muffled shrieks behind them, quickly stifled. They backed away to see more clearly. Where the wooden step had been was now a sheer drop more than thrice the height of a man.

Conan chuckled, wiping dust from his eyes with a sleeve. "That'll hold 'em for a while, my lady."

Judith touched his arm in gratitude as they moved off after the others, Sir Eustace's son held firmly against her heart.

‡

Edwina trudged along the passage with the others, her arms filled with a combination of what looked like bedding and children's clothes. She was stunned by the suddenness of the attack, relieved to have escaped, if escape they had, and frightened of recapture. It had all been so fast that only those women of the bower, quick enough to follow Arnhilda, had met in the lord's chamber before the door was barred. Her own son was safely tied to her back with a shawl, but she worried about her friend Gytha and *her* babes.

Before her, and behind, a line of women and children shuffled down the passage in single file. Light from the torches threw eerie shadows on the walls and did little to alleviate the surrounding gloom. The stone was damp and slimy to the touch. There had been a faint sound of rushing water as they passed under the moat, but since then, nothing.

Two men led the column of women; one brought up in the rear. No one spoke, but more than once there was a short, muffled cry of alarm as one woman or another felt some small night creature, a mouse or a rat, perhaps, dashing past her feet into the safety of the darkness beyond. The stone and earth kept from them any sound of the battle raging in the castle. Edwina had no idea whether they were headed for some place of safety; she'd thought the castle the safest place in the world until tonight. She was too tired to puzzle it all out, too tired to wonder about tomorrow. She just kept putting one foot in front of the other, the small weight of her son warm and comforting against her back. She hoped her man was unharmed. He was good to the child and treated her well.

Judith thought the silence of the passage unnerving. She could only guess when Sir Eustace must have won past the guards in the great hall to reach the upper rooms. He would have checked the nursery first, then the lord's chamber, then sent his men to search out every nook of the castle for his prey. She wondered what he thought when there was no trace of any of them. Conan had whispered that some of the rushes had been glued to the undersides of the legs of the bed. Combined with the raking he'd done, the camouflage would be perfect. This would seem to Sir Eustace a mystery indeed.

Rudolf whimpered as he slept in her arms, and she hugged him closer. What, she wondered, would befall Lady Agnes when the child's absence was discovered? A bitter smile touched her lips as she bent her head and soothed the babe's cheek with her own. She pitied the poor little thing, having such treacherous, uncaring parents.

Conan ordered the torches put out on the ground as they neared the end of the passage. He went alone into the darkness ahead and returned a few moments later. "I'd say it's near to dawn, my lady. We'd best go quickly."

"The women need a rest," she objected, with a jerk of her head for the tired folk behind her.

He shook his head. "There'll be search parties out at first light. They'll find us sure unless we leave now."

Judith sighed, nodded, and followed his lead with no further protest.

The tunnel ended abruptly in a grove of trees well into the woods and out of sight of the castle. The opening was so small, most had to bend nearly double to exit the passage. It was dark yet, and the walking rough, as the ground was both hilly and rocky. Large stones loomed among the ancient trees like sentinels. Judith could barely distinguish one shape from another, but Conan led them unerringly around obstacles, up and down slopes. Far in the rear of their little column there were soft sounds as the younger of Conan's men covered the marks of their passing with leaves and branches. The walk seemed to take forever. The sky lightened as they entered the rock hills of that section of the forest where Judith used to wander as a little girl. She had not been here in some time, for a local brook had dried up the spring before the Normans had come, and the herbs which had once grown on its banks, dwindled.

There was no sign yet that they were followed, and the thought that it was more than lucky nagged at Judith. As dawn increased visibility, a heavy rain began to fall, obliterating whatever signs the men-at-arms might have missed. Judith thanked the Holy Virgin for such mercy.

Wet, cold, and miserable, the women halted beside the rock wall along which they had traveled for a considerable time. The rock was a little taller than Judith and formed the side of a long hill.

Conan moved a clump of brambles, which screened the opening of a cave. One by one they entered, stooping through the entrance and walking along the downward incline inside. The man bringing up the rear of the line of folk spread wet leaves to hide their footprints. When finished, he pulled the brambles back into position. Everyone shed sopping cloaks and wet shoes. Judith looked about her with interest.

Raoul had chosen wisely. The small, narrow entrance opened into a cavern roughly the size of the Oakwood chapel, a large room and high-ceilinged. There were three shallow caverns which opened off of the main one, rather like chambers. Small, narrow chinks here and there in the rock wall allowed a pale light to filter through to lighten the cave enough so that one could walk around, rather than into, others. Along one wall of the main chamber was firewood, a pile of weapons, three wooden barrels and two chests. Conan sent one of the men to dig a pit in the eastern floor of their smallest cavern room, and Judith, eager to inspect their supplies, handed Rudolf to a nurse.

"A moment, my lady," murmured Conan. "The Hawk was prepared for this emergency, but we are yet in grave peril. He bade me give you his instructions should we find ourselves in so grave a circumstance."

She motioned to the women to seat themselves, as she sank down upon the rock floor. It was dry and thick with the dust of seasons. She looked at Conan steadily. "What must we do?"

The man removed his helm and crouched before her. "First of all, none must speak above a whisper," he told her softly. "Once Sir Eustace discovers you gone, he'll search again and again. He cannot afford to have you free, so his men will not rest. Sound does carry in such places as this, and even a small noise at an unwary movement might give us away. Do as little talking as possible, and then, only in whispers."

"But the children . . .!" protested Lady Edith on a rising wail.

"Softly!" Judith admonished.

"If one cries, either suckle it or put a hand over its mouth," Conan said, uncompromising. "Our lives are at stake. And remember this, lady, these men have already proved they do not scruple to kill the innocent."

Lady Edith was silenced.

"There'll be no fire in daylight," the man-at-arms continued. "T'will be cold, I know, but there's bedding in one of the chests, and the clothes on your backs are warm. Even the fires at night will be small ones, to cook food, but no more. We've grain and legumes among other foods, but we'll have to hunt our meat. That adds to the danger, but Jean-Paul and Rollo are careful hunters.

"The closest thing to a garderobe we'll have is the hole Rollo's making in yon cave. Unlike the castle, there'll be no wooden seats, so you'll have to hang your back ends over the hole carefully." He grinned. "Remember, if you fall in, we've no tub for bathing!"

There were a few tired giggles, quickly hushed, and Conan smiled approval. "Keep a careful guard over the children," he instructed. "Until Hawk returns, not one of you may leave this cave. The instant one of you is seen, all are lost. Beginning on the morrow my men and I will keep watch against Lord Raoul's coming. With God's help we will not be here long, but we must be careful."

Judith nodded. "We will do as you say, and indeed, we are grateful for your care of us all."

All the women nodded and murmured agreement. Those with children in their arms hugged them tighter.

"Will it be safe to set out our buckets to catch the rain?" asked Judith after a moment. "We'll need water for drinking and cooking, and to wash changing cloths for the babes."

"It is a heavy rain," mused Conan. "And Sir Eustace'll search the village before sending his men farther afield. It should be safe enough." He gestured to Jean-Paul, who took the buckets from Arnhilda and set them outside the cave. "We've a small cask of wine in one of the other caves, but not enough, I fear, to quench the thirst of all. There is a larger cask of ale, but it's been here a long time."

Jean-Paul disappeared, then returned. "It's alright for drinking, but that won't last long either. There are some empty wine skins we should fill with rain water for drinking."

"Do it," murmured Judith.

"Aye, my lady." He went off to fetch them.

"There are some wooden piggins and a few bowls in the chests yonder and a cooking pot. There's not enough for everyone, so we'll have to share," Conan added apologetically to Judith.

"Sweet Savior, you and my lord seem to have thought of everything!" she exclaimed softly. "Well, 'tis morn, and we all need our sleep. Come, let us see what may be found in these chests."

Rough bedding was found in one chest to augment what the women had brought. They spread pelts in the largest of the side caverns. The two straw pallets were given to the men, one of whom would be on guard while the others slept or hunted. There were cooking utensils of various sizes, querns, dried vegetables and fruits, and grain. One filled water pail was placed against the far wall. The other already contained a few soiled cloths, and was placed in the area with the garderobe pit. Soon everyone was preparing for sleep, except Conan, who had chosen the first watch.

Judith lay on her back, Charles nestled in one arm, and Richard snuggling warm on the other side. Now that the need for action had passed, she felt fear's icy touch along her nerves. She raised her head and saw the twins curled up in the arms of their nurses. Rudolf dozed between Arnhilda and Dorothea; Ladies Edith and Margaret, and the other women and children, slept already with their babes beside them. Judith hugged her sons closer and wondered how long it would be until Raoul's return. She refused to let her mind linger on the possibility that he might never come back.

CHAPTER 16

want to go outside and play," Richard pouted, his brown eyes angry, small arms folded across his chest. It was full dark, and the flames of the small cookfire gave barely enough light to see his smudged, discontented face.

Judith sighed and pulled him into her arms. "Ah, sweet, you know why you may not."

"There aren't any of the bad men out there now," he protested softly. "We heard them ride away a long time ago."

"But what if they only pretended to leave?" suggested his mother. "'Tis a common ambush tactic, Richard, as Conan has already told you. They might be lying in wait, hoping that we'll show ourselves, so they can attack."

"Mayhap they're not smart enough to think of that," he returned hopefully.

"Never count on your enemy to be stupid, and he'll never give you an unpleasant surprise," Judith countered.

The little boy sagged against her in disappointment, his head hitting her collarbone hard enough to leave a bruise. "I hate it here! I want to go home!" he whispered fiercely.

"I know." She brushed a consoling hand across his back.

Edwina made her way across the cavern and knelt beside her. "I could take him for a while, my lady," she murmured. "My little one is asleep, and I know some French children's rhymes might make him smile."

"What's a 'rhyme'?" demanded Richard. "Is it a trick? Is it hard to do?"

The woman held out her hand, grinning when he put his own into her grasp. "It's more like a trick with words, Lord Richard, and some of them have funny sounds."

They moved away, and Lady Judith looked in gratitude after them. She stretched, then went off to take her turn at the quern making flour. There was no oven for baking bread, but the women made flat grain cakes, which they cooked on a hot flat rock wrapped about bits of meat and vegetables. They didn't taste much like bread, but they were filling. Until their sojourn in the cave, Judith had forgotten just how much she had hated grinding by hand.

Edwina kept Richard and some of the other children occupied, but just before dawn he wandered back to his mother's side. He was sleepy and demanded her attention. She sat behind his sleeping fur and smoothed the hair back from his forehead. "You must rest now, my son. You need your sleep so you may grow strong and healthy and be a good leader of our people."

"I know." He plucked at the ragged coverlet with his fingers. "When will Papa come home?"

"I don't know. Soon, I hope."

"I want Papa. I miss him."

"So do I."

"If Papa were here, he'd kill all those wicked men, and we could go back to the castle where it's warm," he murmured wistfully. "And I could play with my toys and ride my pony." A terrible thought occurred to him. "Do you think the bad men will play with my toys?" he demanded, outraged at the notion.

Judith forced herself not to smile. "I don't know, lambkin. 'Tis not likely."

"If those bad men even *touch* my toys, I'll kill them with my knife!" he announced fiercely, eyes glittered in anger.

"I'd like to stick a knife in a few of them myself," commented his mother sympathetically, kissing his forehead.

He was comforted. "When Papa comes home, he's going to give me a hawk of my very own," Richard told her. "He promised."

"I know. He told me so himself. You'll have to be very careful with your hawk and take good care of it." She patted his cheek. "Now, go to sleep." She snuggled down at his side.

‡

They'd been in the cavern for nearly a month. The children had adapted well enough to the restrictions; it was the adults who chafed at the restrictions most. None of the women were used to such enforced inactivity. Ladies Edith and Margaret knew not whether their men had survived the invasions. It seemed unlikely. They said nothing, but their haunted eyes proclaimed their fears. Lady Judith could do little to ease their worry. She found a bit of plain linen in her basket, long and narrow, so she set them to embroidering a scene of the escape from the castle, a long line of women and babes in a dark passage. The design had a Norman man-at-arms bearing a torch at their head and the suggestion of mice here and there near their feet. At least sewing kept their hands busy.

Confined as they were, there were yet daily tasks to be accomplished. Lady Judith set the nurses to work in the twilight and dawn hours, grinding their dwindling supply of grain. They laundered changing cloths by night in tepid water, spreading the damp articles on rocks to dry. They did the same with menstrual rags. Since they had no table or trenchers, they ate from a communal pot, as the villeins were wont to do. The children had no complaint to make, but Judith worried that proper etiquette would have to be retaught. It was one more concern in a growing mountain of them. By far more important, was the lack of any herbs and medicines. They all had stuffed noses and mildly congested lungs, but she had nothing with which to treat them. Fortunately, no one was so ill that she needed fear a death. . . not yet, at any rate.

Of them all, Arnhilda suffered most. The damp chill of their cavern aggravated her rheumatic joints until she could only lay crippled upon her bed of furs, yet she made no complaint. Judith had not even a pinch of cocklebur to ease the pain. Arnhilda insisted they prop her against the wall in the hours near morning, and sleepy children gathered round her to hear the stories she told of the old days. Saxon kings ruled then, she told them, and dragons and monsters, heroes and sorcerers roamed the land. She knew that she was dying, admitting the fact with calm acceptance. Judith hid her grief in the face of such fortitude.

Conan taught the boys something of archery in the far long chamber, and the use of the knife. To Richard, he gave lessons in tactics, as well. Lady Judith instructed the better born among them in writing and mathematics, drawing with a stick in the dirt. It wasn't enough, and she wished that Brother Plegmund had managed to come with them. If nothing else, he could have led them in prayer. Lady Judith, herself, had performed this function since their escape from the castle, but feared she did not do it well enough. She missed the sacraments, as did the others. She worried constantly about the small things as well as the large; it was her duty to do so. The folk were in her charge.

Conan ranged deep into the woods in his search for meat. There was some danger of meeting a hunting party from the castle, but the greater peril came from wolves, which roamed the forests, even in these modern times. Still, not once did he return empty-handed. They ate acorns and chestnuts, hares, doves, venison, and squirrels. A wild pig with a broken leg had miraculously appeared near the cave only a few days before and kept them fed well enough, but meat rotted quickly with no salt brine to preserve it and the inability to light a large enough fire to dry it. Lady Judith worried about this, too, for soon the snows would be upon them and game scarce. Meanwhile, there were hides, which the women scraped and rubbed with the animal's brain to soften it. Once cured, the leather was useful for clothing or bedding.

Conan woke her early. In the dying afternoon light, Lady Judith cleaned and plucked six pheasants, the fruits of his wanderings. True dark came, and Conan built up the fire. By the time Lady Judith had the birds ready for the crude spit, the others were rising. In addition to the pheasants, she tied on the pig's stomach, which had been washed and stuffed with barley meal, acorns, and chopped wild onion. There was also soup, composed of meat scrapes and whatever else could be found. The children, having slept all day, came to sit before the blaze to warm their hands. Richard, the eldest boy, gravely turned the spit as his mother basted the fowls with pig's grease. The others sniffed and licked their lips hungrily. It smelled wonderful.

An owl hooted thrice as they prepared to eat. All stopped to listen. It hooted thrice more, Rollo's signal. Conan grinned and went to nudge Jean-Paul awake. The children returned to their meal; the women kept an eye on the entrance, just in case.

The bramble was pulled aside, yet the man who slipped into the cave was no man-at-arms but a mailed knight. The women started, and one or two gasped or cried out in surprise. Lady Judith scrambled to her feet and ran to his waiting arms.

"Raoul!" she sobbed, burying her face in the cold metal rings, which covered his chest. "Raoul!"

He held her close, his big hands gentle, his arms strong. "Judith! Little angel! Shhhhh. All's well, little girl. Nay, don't weep." Lord Raoul held her a little way back from him and lifted her chin in one hand. He kissed her slowly, tenderly. Then he smiled. "Dry your eyes, lady, lest you rust my armor."

She gave a watery chuckle. "How did you know the castle was taken?" she asked.

"Gunhilde Weaver set her son to watch for us. When he saw my outriders, he ran to the road to stop them and told them what was toward. I rode straight here in hope that you had escaped." His hand cupped her cheek for brief moment. "I thank God I was right."

"Papa! Papa!" cried Richard, tugging at his father's mail shirt to get his attention. "Bad men came and made us leave the castle! We have to sleep in here, and I don't like it!"

"I don't like it either," stated the Hawk, smiling a bit at the boy's anger.

"I can't go outside to practice archery or *anything*," the boy continued. "And I had to leave all my toys and my pony! I *did* remember to bring my knife, though."

"That's very good," Lord Raoul told him seriously. "A true warrior never forgets his weapons."

"I . . . I was scared, Papa," Richard admitted, eyes downcast.

"But you did your duty to your people by taking along a knife to protect them," Lord Raoul pointed out.

"Then you aren't angry with me?"

"I am very proud of you, my son."

Richard thought about that for a moment, then puffed out his chest. "Mama said when you came back, we could go home. Can we? Did you kill all of the bad men?"

Lord Raoul laughed and heaved the boy to sit on his mailed shoulder. "Not yet, but I will."

"Me!" demanded Giles imperatively. "Papa, carry me, too!"

So the Hawk carried them both around the cave. Then he carried Elizabeth, who stared up adoringly out of eyes like her mother's. He held Charles and kissed his cheek, and he had a kiss even for the timid Rudolf, who blinked and stared as if unused to such caresses. The women pressed him to eat. Only when he had his fill of food did he speak of serious matters.

"You've done well," he told Conan. "It's a service can never be repaid. Know you how they fair at Oakwood?"

Conan shook his head. "No, my lord. I've not gone nigh the village for fear of a trap," he said apologetically. "Also, there was some danger they'd track me back here. I'd not risk my lady and the little ones."

"One of Sir Eustace's patrols passed the spot where I hid yesterday," volunteered Jean-Paul from his post by the cave's entrance. "I caught a few words only, my lord, but they spoke of prisoners in the donjon, so I think a few of our men live."

"Then we've yet men we can trust within the castle walls," remarked Lord Raoul with satisfaction.

"But shackled to the walls," Jean-Paul reminded.

"Not," said the Hawk, "for long."

Conan regarded him with suppressed excitement. "You've a plan, my lord?"

"Has my cur of a brother discovered the location of the passage?"

"Not yet. I went back to set traps along that passage and not one of 'em's been sprung. Nor did I find tracks in the area."

Hawk's eye's gleamed. "Excellent! He'll know it exists somewhere, but not being able to locate it will keep him on edge. I doubt me he's had a good night's sleep since the place was taken. By the bye," he added, turning to Lady Judith. "T'was a goodly notion to take a hostage. My brother little realized what a she-wolf you are when he chose to challenge you in my absence!"

Judith glanced at Rudolf, a shy and nervous child who seemed ever to be surprised by kindness. She looked back at Raoul. "My lord, surely we need not . . ."

"I mislike bargaining with rebels," he answered promptly, avoiding the issue and her eyes. "I doubt there'll be the need."

Conan added a chunk of wood to the fire. He squatted hunter-fashion beside the blaze. "When do we take the castle, my lord?"

Raoul grinned. "Tonight, of course. My son does not like this place."

Richard beamed. Lady Judith sighed. Forever after this night, Richard would believe that his father had retaken Oakwood Castle to ensure his son's comfort. This was not entirely untrue, but Richard would be impossible to live with! Her eyes sought out her husband's.

"Aside from all else," added Raoul, shrugging, "I've a fancy to sleep in my own bed after so long away." He wasn't sure what he'd said that was wrong, although if Judith's gaze was anything to judge by, he was on heavy ground. Well, they'd talk about it on the morrow. He stood and picked up the helm he'd shed when he entered the cave. "And it seems I've eaten most of your supper," he added, watching Lady Margaret divide the remaining food into portions. "'Tis the least I can do to provide a meal from our own kitchen, is it not?"

Everyone stared.

"But it's dark," said Lady Judith in concern. "The portcullis will surely be closed, and you know that Eustace must have taken the lord's chamber. The bed will block the entrance in the passage!"

"True." Raoul tugged the end of one of her braids. "But I know more than one way to trap a jackal, little girl." He looked at Conan.

"Aye," said the man-at-arms. "That door swings either way. There'll be no trouble getting in." He smiled grimly. "What would you have me do, my lord?"

"There's a tunnel leads to the donjon. You'll take the men-at-arms and release our men. Arm those who can fight and make for the great hall. I'll take the knights through the other passage and surprise my brother in my bed."

Conan nodded. "I pulled down the stair in the passage, but the ladder's still on the floor about halfway back. The torches are there at the entrance."

"Good, good," Raoul approved, pulling his gauntlets from his belt. He smiled down at the children, winking at them. His eye returned to Conan. "My army's hid behind the old Saxon hall. Sir Balderic knows where to find the door to the donjon tower." He yawned suddenly. "Christ's Bleeding Wounds! That I've to retake my own hall after such a ride as I've had adds one more grievance to swell Eustace's list! You'd think he'd have more sense, wouldn't you? Ah, well. Best get the task done so we can all rest comfortably."

Judith walked with him to the cave opening. She took his hand and whispered. The sound traveled so that all the women heard. Raoul grinned, knowing this full well. "Have no fear, my lady. I'll go afoot into Oakwood, and no knight should die anywhere but in the saddle." His eyes gleamed wickedly. "Although not necessarily on a horse!"

"My lord!" Judith's cheeks flamed, and she shook her head at him while the women giggled. However, she made no further objection, which, she reflected wryly, had probably been his intention.

Richard had to be firmly ordered to remain with his mother. "'Tis not that I doubt your courage or your skill, little man," explained his father gravely. "It is that Conan, Rollo, and Jean-Paul must go with me. If you come too, there will be no one left to defend your lady mother, and your brothers and sister."

He smiled as the boy blinked back tears of disappointment. "Tell you what, wolf cub, when you're of an age to be squire, I'll take you with me to serve the King. Will that satisfy your lust for fighting? What say you?"

Richard nodded and sniffled. "Alright, Papa." The firelight flickered as brown eyes met brown. Heartbreak was easy to read.

"Hmmm," said Raoul. He looked about him. "Giles, come here."

The younger boy scurried forward, thrilled to be noticed.

"Now, I know," said his father, "that you are too little to do as much as Richard, but it's more than time your training began. I don't know anyone better than your big brother to show you, so you watch him and listen to everything he tells you."

"Yes, Papa," Giles returned in his baby lisp.

Raoul took Richard by the shoulder. "I will leave his training in your hands for the moment," he said. "Remember that he is smaller than you and easily hurt, so you must be gentle. Think you that it would be well to begin with the catch-me game since he is so little?"

Richard considered. "Aye, it is a good idea, Papa. I think he could learn that."

"You must bear in mind that when you let him catch you, he can be hurt if you fall wrong. You must be as careful as . . . as . . ."

"Like when I hold a baby bird?" asked Richard eagerly.

"Aye, like that." His father grinned. "And for the sake of all the

Heavenly Host, don't get under your mother's feet or she'll have my ears for encouraging you!"

"Very well, Papa." Richard turned to his brother. "Come with me, Giles. I'll show you how to be a brave knight. Knights are supposed to protect folk, you know." They went together to one of the smaller caves.

Lord Raoul turned to his lady. "Bide you safely here, my lady. I'll send you word and transport when it is safe to return to the castle."

And with this, he left. Shrieks of laughter could be heard from the boys in the other rock chamber. Judith gritted her teeth in frustration. Men!

‡

At mid-morning came a horse-cart driven by the squire, Louis. "The castle's ours, my lady!" he called from outside the cave. "Are you and your women ready to return?"

"We've been nothing else since we left!" she replied tartly, shoving the bramble aside.

It was a beautiful day, the sky a cloudless, arching blue overhead. Women and children straggled out of the cavern, blinking and shading their eyes from the strong daylight. They clambered up onto the wagon as best they could. Louis descended to carry Arnhilda. Bodies were crushed together in the back of the cart. The squire handed Lady Judith onto the seat beside his place, as the others hauled themselves into the rear.

"How fares my lord?" Lady Judith demanded as she settled herself. The faded blue of her skirt picked up a splinter almost at once, but that hardly mattered. Filthy as it was, she intended to toss it on the rubbish heap that very day.

"Hawk has not a scratch," replied the squire promptly. He shook his head in admiration. "All went smooth as a greased piglet and not a man of our own injured. Hawk found Sir Eustace dead drunk and abed with two kitchen wenches. Couldn't have moved if Saint Peter himself commanded! The guards were all drunk or asleep. Conan and the rest had no trouble in the donjon." Louis pulled Richard up to sit between himself and Lady Judith. He ruffled the boy's dark hair and grinned. "You did well caring for your mother, lad. My lord said to be sure to tell you how proud he is that he could place his faith in one so worthy of praise."

Richard glowed. "Did my father kill all the bad men, Louis?"

"Not all of 'em, bantam." Louis clucked to the horse, and it moved down the trail at a walk. It wasn't much of a trail, having been made by the horse itself only moments before on its way to the cavern, so the going was exceedingly slow. "Sir Eustace is in the donjon with his men to await my lord's justice," he said with a shrug. "He was so befuddled with wine I doubt he's even now realized what's occurred. Hawk says he'll hear the case after the midday meal."

Lady Judith glanced back at her women, "And Sir Tancred and Sir Artaud? What of them?"

"Both are well, my lady, barring a few scrapes. They stood in urgent need of a bath, however, when last I set eyes on them," he added with a chuckle. "I haven't smelled anything like that since I was shoved into a dungheap as a lad."

"Were any of our men killed?" asked Lady Judith, conscious that the servants had families, too.

"Only a few of the villagers, my lady. And several of the men-at-arms, but those had no kin this side of the Channel," Louis assured her merrily.

The women smiled and crossed themselves for this unexpected mercy. Judith knew widows of dependent knights lived on charity unless they remarried. It would not have been a pleasant fate, no matter how kind the chatelaine was. Judith reached back to touch their hands briefly, smiling at Lady Edith's grateful tears. She turned once more to the squire. "And the Lady Agnes?" she inquired in a hard voice. "What of her?"

Louis chuckled again to the horse and said nothing. Hawk's lady hoped with violent rage that the bitch was already dead or dying. The Earth, she felt with some justification, had harbored the evil strumpet entirely too long.

‡

Castle folk and peasants from the vill crowded the bailey, cheering as the horse-cart pulled to a stop and Lady Judith alighted. She acknowledged their presence with a smile and a wave, but was more concerned with helping Arnhilda from the conveyance. The others had by that time adjusted to full daylight, but the ageing maidservant was weak and her vision impaired. Lady Judith signaled to Louis, who gallantly took Arnhilda in his arms and carried her into the infirmary. The older woman was tenderly laid upon a straw pallet, and Lady Judith gave minute instructions to the girl in charge as she bathed Arnhilda's twisted hands and feet in a healing solution. Lady Judith, herself, mixed the portion to ease pain and held it to Arnhilda's lips. She left the infirmary only when she was assured that the attendant understood her duties and that Arnhilda slept.

Even though Oakwood and its castle were once more in Lord Raoul's capable hands, Lady Judith could not be easy. She ordered extra guards to stand watch over the nursery occupants, who, in their turn, were too filled with excitement and relief to fear for their own safety. They were home, after all, excepting Rudolf, and even he was flushed with adventure and the wonder of playmates to share it. She made a trip to the kitchen, where she conferred with Cynefred about the midday menu, the viands for supper, and the names of any who had been harmed by the traitors. Then, at last, convinced that all was secure and all preparations made, Lady Judith was free to enter her own chamber, where she found her lord ensconced in a steaming tub.

Well!" she exclaimed, irritated beyond measure. How *dared* he relax and enjoy himself when she had worried for hours over his survival?! "You seem to be no worse for the wear, my lord!"

Raoul understood and grinned at her. "You'd be the better for a good soaking yourself, little girl. Might improve your temper, too."

Judith threw down her tattered cloak and strode to the side of the tub. "I waited in the mouldering cave for *weeks*, listening to babes whimper and women whine, wondering when you'd come or *if* you'd come, and when at last you did come, you were gone within the hour! Your mongrel cur of a brother takes my home and imperils the lives of my babes, I hide in terror and live in want, and all you can think of to say is that I'd be well advised to bathe away my *dirt*?"

"Did no one ever tell you how comely you are when you're in a temper?" he inquired mildly.

Infuriated, Judith lifted a hand to box his ears. Raoul laughed. He grabbed her wrist and pulled her, clothes and all, into the tub. Pinning her arms to her sides, he laughed into her flashing eyes. "There's only one way to placate an angry wench," he remarked. He lowered his head and kissed her.

Judith fought him, beside herself with fury. She bucked and struggled vainly against his superior strength. Water splashed everywhere. She could have bitten him, but somehow, she did not want to do that.

His kisses drugged her with their sweetness. The scent of him filled her nostrils, making her thoughts chaotic. It had been too long, she thought vaguely as she weakened. Far too long. She sighed, finally, returning his embrace, drinking the taste and feel of him.

"Raoul, you shouldn't," she murmured as his lips traced the line of her throat.

"Why not?" He found a particularly soft spot and lingered.

She freed an arm so that she could scratch at her scalp. "I'm lousy, of course. All those weeks in a cave without washing! What else did you expect?"

His lips continued to nibble at her tender skin. "The bath will amend that minor problem, lady."

"Yes, but my clothes . . ."

"I'll help you take 'em off," he answered, kneading her breast.

Judith surrendered unconditionally.

‡

For a few hours, Oakwood Castle was the scene of many happy reunions as friends and loved ones assured one another that no harm had been done them. The laundry was busy with bathers demanding to rid themselves of dirt and vermin. New clothes were found for those who had been in the cave. The first part of the midday meal was a festive and light-hearted affair with much toasting and laughing. After the last course the mood was more sober, however, with thoughts turning toward the trial to take place.

‡

When Raoul held court, it was always a solemn occasion, with precedence and formality rigidly observed. Lady Judith had often attended to hear complaints of peasants and see justice done; for among Saxons even more than Normans, the law was the very heartbeat of their way of life. There were usually a fair number of spectators at these times, for entertainment of any kind was rare in the villages. Also, Lord Raoul believed that the more folk who saw the stern merit of his decisions, the fewer transgressors there would be in the future. It didn't always work out that way, but the folk enjoyed the show nonetheless. Lady Judith sometimes found she had to cover a laugh as the villeins showed their agreement with baronial decisions with wise wags of the head and lifted brows that proclaimed they'd known all along how it would be.

Lord Raoul sat in his great, carved chair on the dais, Lady Judith in a smaller one to his right. The hall was full to overflowing with knights, men-at-arms, and the common folk, come to see how their lord dealt with a murdering, rebellious vassal. That the vassal in question was the lord's own brother added spice. The gray of the castle servants, the brown and gold of the squires, and the scarlet of the pages was this day obscured by the faded reds, greens, browns, and blues of the villagers. Among the crowd Lady Judith espied many of the fisherfolk, conspicuous in their scale-speckled clothing. The miller and his wife attended, as well, with both of their children, all clothed in fine wool with new leather shoes. This was a far cry from the garb of the fisherfolk and villagers. She made a mental note to check into the mill accounts.

Folk stared at the stone walls and bright-colored tapestries, and the even more brightly-colored clothing of the nobility. The few pieces of furniture were ogled. One of the village women held a babe to her breast and stared up at the gallery in awe. In the forefront of the crowd stood Dorothea, holding Richard by the hand. Folk nearby reached out to touch him, Hawk's heir. These were faces he knew, and Richard smiled back at them, waving at his special friends, like the beekeeper and the blacksmith, winning hearts without being aware he did so. Lady Judith smiled to see it.

But even the weeks in the cavern had not prepared her for the odor of more than a hundred unwashed bodies packed into a relatively small space. She held a scented handkerchief to her nose, preferring the strong, headache-producing attar of roses to the grease and grime of years.

Folk nudged, whispered, and jostled one another, pointing to this person or that, or at some article of furniture unfamiliar to those who had not visited the castle before. They stilled when Conan rapped the butt of his spear sharply on the floor. The sound of heavy, deliberate footsteps echoed loudly as a troop of armed men led the captives into the hall to stand before the baron. The prisoners were a bit the worse for wear, the crowd noted gleefully, with their hands bound behind them and their heads bowed in defeat. Those of the village folk who had lost loved ones pushed to the fore, more eager than the rest for punishment to be meted out. No one blamed them.

Lord Raoul eyed the captives impassively. His scarlet tunic with its golden hawk embroidered across the front, matched the banners hung from the gallery drawing the eyes of all who watched. One by one he looked at the prisoners, his gaze resting longest upon his brother's face.

Sir Eustace returned look for look, the only one of the captives who kept his shoulders straight and his head up. There was, the crowd could tell, no shame in him.

"My lady, if you would translate," murmured Lord Raoul.

"Bailiff," said the Hawk loudly so that all might hear. "What are the charges against these men?"

Lady Judith's voice was a firm but softer counterpoint, heard when someone had finished speaking.

Sir Tancred drew himself up. "My lord, Sir Eustace here present did willfully and in certain knowledge of his guilt, break his feudal oath to Lord Raoul, Baron of Oakwood." He paused for Lady Judith to explain to the crowd, then continued.

"He and his men damaged crops and houses in the village of Oakwood, and also in the village of the fisherfolk, likewise bound to the Oakwood demesne. He and his followers misused the people of Oakwood and its villages, committing rape, murder, theft, and arson. They attacked in unlawful fashion the castle of Oakwood and took possession of the same in the absence of its rightful lord. Their avowed purpose was the murder of the sons of Lord Raoul of Oakwood by his wife, the Lady Judith. This act of rebellion against the Baron of Oakwood goes against every principle of knightly vassalage, which Sir Eustace owes his lord in payment for the keep known as Danesford Tower."

"Who stands witness to these acts said to have been committed by Sir Eustace and his men?" asked Lord Raoul sternly.

Conan stepped forward with all the scullions, Cynefred, the smith, and the warder's eldest son. The villeins whose families had been misused joined them.

The Hawk leaned forward in his chair and stared at each of them in turn. "This is a charge of great severity," he said in the rough Saxon he'd learned for such occasions. "You all swear of your own knowledge that the charges against these men are true?"

The Englishmen replied, "Yes, my lord," in a ragged unison.

He repeated the question in French for Conan and the warder's son, and so the prisoners could understand. The answer was the same, affirmation.

"Very well," said the Hawk. "I will hear your testimony one at a time, and my lady will translate your words so that all might hear and understand." He pointed at Conan, who began his recital. One by one the others followed in their turn. It took a long time, and the accounts of horrors, particularly the rapes, murders, and house burnings, moved some to tears, Lord Raoul among them. It was no bad thing that their lord felt pity for their losses, the folk whispered among themselves.

Hawk looked over the crowd, unashamedly wiping away a tear shed for the rape and murder of an eight-year-old girl. "Is there any person here will dispute the evidence just given?"

The crowd was silent.

"Is there one here wishes to speak on behalf of Sir Eustace or one of his men?"

Again silence, broken only by the thin wail of a babe, quickly shushed to quiet.

"Well," remarked Lord Raoul in a more casual voice. "It appears that all here have agreed upon the guilt of the prisoners." He gazed dispassionately upon his brother. "Have you aught to say in your own defense, brother?"

Sir Eustace glared defiance. "What has that bitch done with my son?" he demanded loudly.

A guard slammed the butt of a spear into Sir Eustace's belly. He sagged, gasping, and retching.

"You will use courtesy to my lady, as I have told you more than once," said Lord Raoul in a mild tone. His eyes, however, were hard as granite.

This time Edwina, standing near the other women of the bower, whispered the translation to Gytha. It spread quickly through the crowd and brought angry murmurs. Those who had not suffered at Sir Eustace's hand were affronted for Lady Judith's sake. She grudged no effort when her medicinal skills were needed by the folk, and spoke for them to the lord. They honored her for that.

Sir Eustace fought for breath and straightened painfully. "Where is my son?"

"My nephew is lodged safely in the nursery with my own sons," Lord Raoul answered. "I do not make war on children."

"Your mistake, brother!" spat Sir Eustace venomously. "My son will live to avenge me!"

Hawk shrugged. "Time will show which of us is the wiser. For now, I have given you the opportunity to speak on behalf of yourself and your men. What would you say in your defense?"

"What is there to say?" Sir Eustace laughed bitterly. "I wanted the castle, and I took it. I am not shamed of that. You'd have done the same in my shoes."

"No, brother. If you will recall, our brother had our father's lands in Normandy, as was his right as eldest. I never disputed that. Instead, I served Duke William, that I might win lands of my own, in all honor. Of my bounty, I gave you Danesford Tower to be your demesne, in return for loyal service to me, and you repaid me with treachery. There is no honor in you."

Lady Judith's voice was a muted softness repeating the words of both men.

"I regret only that I failed," snarled Sir Eustace, lunging at the dais. The guards hauled him back in line with the other prisoners. "I'd do it again, and gladly!" he spat.

The Hawk clenched his hands on the arms of his chair. "Your own words condemn you." He stood. "Hear then, good people of Oakwood, my ruling in this matter. For grievous crimes against your sworn lord, you Eustace of Danesford, are this day stripped of your possessions. Your property reverts to the demesne of Oakwood, and your wife and son are made wards of my estate. For the sake for your son, who is blameless and dear to me, I will be merciful. Instead of the death you fully deserve, I command you imprisoned in a cell in the Oakwood donjon for the remainder of your life."

He glanced at the crowd, reading disappointment. He understood, but he was unwilling to take the life of blood kin in defiance of Holy Scripture, even for their hurts.

"For your men, who served you so ill and murdered innocent folk, who wantonly destroyed property, raped, and pillaged, there is no mercy; they will be hanged. These punishments will be carried out at dawn tomorrow, by which time Father Hubert will have had ample time to hear the confessions of any who care to make them."

Lady Judith touched the hem of his sleeve and Raoul bent to hear her whisper. "Ah, yes," he murmured, straightening. "My dear lady has requested reparation be made to those families who have suffered at the hands of these men. I refuse her nothing. Those who are eligible will consult with my bailiff on the morrow. There are geldings and coins amongst the prisoners' possessions and articles of personal worth which may, in part, recompense you for your losses. Sir Tancred will see to the details."

"Lord Edward will have your head for this!" cried Sir Eustace in fury. "Several of these men are his!"

Hawk smiled coldly. "I think not, brother. Whatever faults may be attributed to the Baron of Northwatch, he is not a fool. No noble owing fealty to William will openly foster rebellion against another for fear of the King's wrath. Lord Edward will swear these knaves deserted his demesne and acted without his consent, and you are aware of this." He glanced at the leader of his men-at-arms and nodded.

Three times Conan rapped the butt of his spear on the floor. The men-at-arms led the dazed captives away and the buzz of conversation commenced throughout the hall.

Lord Raoul stood, turned, and offered his arm to his lady. Lady Judith rose, placing her hand upon his arm. Decorously they quitted the dais, heading for a side corridor.

"They wanted you to order his death," she murmured.

"I probably should have done so," replied the Hawk with a shrug.

She crossed herself. "T'would have been fratricide!"

"Aye, that's what stopped me." His lips quirked. "I don't feel so sure of God's Grace that I can afford a sin of that magnitude."

Judith gave him a level look. "Also, you've no desire to have Rudolf bred up in our household thinking you're the man killed his father."

"Another good point," Raoul agreed smoothly. His eyes lingered appreciatively on the contrast of the white linen underdress and the crimson gauze, which fluttered attractively to enhance the beauty of her hair rather than hide it. A thousand pities, he mused vaguely, that no one thought to make gowns of gauze. No, better not, he decided. He'd never get anything done with such distractions.

As they approached the door to the garden, which was recessed into the stone wall, an embracing couple who had hidden there sprang apart. The scullion shrank back as if to merge with the stones at his back, but the wench took to her heels, seeking the relative safety of the kitchen, Judith's eyes burning holes in her back with every hurried step.

Raoul motioned with his chin and sent the scullion back to his chores as he opened the garden door. His lips twitched at his wife's mood. Irritation brought quite a pretty color into her cheeks, he reflected, as he followed her outside.

"Yet another evil as a result of Eustace's greed!" she commented bitterly as he closed the door behind them. "We'll probably be well into the New Year 'ere I can trust my household to conduct themselves with circumspection!"

Wisely, Raoul said nothing. He eyed the tall gray walls rising on every side of the broad enclosure, wondering what it would look like in the spring. Several of the trees were grown enough to bear fruit, he thought. Blossoms would soften the view.

Dead leaves crunched under their feet as they followed the garden path. "I'll have this raked on the morrow," Judith promised. "Mary Mother, I'm surprised to find the walls still standing after such lax governance! Almost nothing has been done to maintain even a semblance of order! You should have seen the dust on the window ledges!"

"I cannot send Lady Agnes to the hangman," said Raoul abruptly. "She's with child."

Judith spat out an epithet which raised her husband's eyebrows. "None of our babes is safe while she lives, she's convinced me of that!" she snapped.

"Oh, I don't know," returned Hawk calmly. "What if we put her in that top chamber in the guard tower? She'd be behind stout bars and a thick oaken door; not much she could do from up there."

"Bah!" his lady returned. "And who'd have the key, my lord? The jailor, that's who. He's a man like any other, and loyal to his lord though he may be, she'd seduce him or one of the guards into acting for her. By the Blessed Virgin, I should have killed her when I'd the chance!"

Raoul pondered this as they turned and retraced their steps. After a while, his eyes began to sparkle. "I don't believe t'would be as you say if I made a slight change in the plans," he announced earnestly. "Look you, I will confine the regular jailor's activities to the donjon below, where Eustace'll be. I'll set Jean-Paul and Rollo Red-Hair over Lady Agnes. They've no interest in women, those two. Only in each other. What think you of that? Myself, I'm positive t'would work."

"Jean-Paul and Rollo are lovers?" she inquired, surprised. "I'd not have thought it!"

"'Tis not likely they'd display their practices before you, my lady," he replied with a grin. "All know how you view public display. Think how unseemly!"

Judith rolled her eyes at him.

Raoul continued in a serious vein. "They're good men, as they've proven in their care of you the while I was away. With them to guard her, Lady Agnes'd have no opportunity for mischief, however seductive she was."

Judith bit her lip. "It *sounds* good. What about Rudolf?"

"He's to have no traffic with his lady mother. I've already given orders to that effect, wife, and I expect to be obeyed in the matter. No softening later as you are wont to do when the edge of your anger is gone. There's a threat, since he's Eustace's son. He may have some loyalty toward his father, however misplaced. Still, I believe he is young enough to overcome the disadvantages of his breeding. We'll train him our way and give him the same affection and advantages we give our own. I've half a mind to give him over to the Church when he's of age. T'would be a goodly move and give the lad a chance in life. Also, it would keep him from producing heirs to challenge our sons. Well, how say you?"

"Brilliant!" she exclaimed. "I'll speak to Brother Plegmund this eventide. Our nephew seems a bright lad and biddable. Why, in time he might become an archbishop! With your influence behind him, there's no telling how far he might rise!"

"Perhaps, perhaps," he temporized, amused by her enthusiasm. "But now, we've other matters to discuss."

Judith smiled. "Yes, of course, How fared you at Ely? Is Hereward the Wake taken at last?"

He frowned and bent to pick up an acorn at his feet, wondering from whence it had come. "No, he's free somewhere in England. Disappeared like a damned evil spirit!" He flung the unoffending acorn high over the garden wall. "T'was a badly mismanaged business, first to last!"

"Well, what happened?" she demanded.

"Did not the clerk write you the whole of it?"

"Bits and pieces only, or I'd not have asked. What occurred? Are you trying to keep something from me? Were you wounded more seriously than I'd thought?" She eyed him narrowly, trying to recall if she'd noticed any new scars when they'd been in the bath. She thought not, but she'd had her eyes closed a good part of the time.

"Now, what purpose would I have in trying to keep wounds from you? You'd talk to Humphrey and ferret out the truth regardless of anything I might say." He shrugged. "As for what took place, there was no great deed of arms. Swein of Denmark took Peterborough Abbey. When the new Abbot, Turold, arrived with his men, t'was no more than a smoking ruin. The Norseman had moved on to York by then. We reached York to find it sacked. Not that there was much worth taking after the last trouble there, but t'was still standing, and the Vikings had gone on to Ely with Hereward and Morekere.

"Aye, the clerk wrote us about Morkere," said Judith, shaking her skirts to rid them of clinging leaves.

Raoul shook his head. "Not a pleasant end for the lad, hacked to death like that by his own. Still, what other kind of death can a traitor expect?"

"It was deserved," she agreed, thinking briefly of Eustace and Agnes.

Hawk grunted. "At Ely, the King paid Swein danegeld to be rid of the menace. And before you say aught in his dispraise," he added hastily, "t'was King Edward's custom as well, and that of other kings before him. There's no shame in it!"

Judith hid a smile. Obviously, Raoul was not best pleased that his liege lord paid tribute rather than offer battle to see the Viking host safely from their shores. "As you say, my lord. But do go on. What befall Hereward?"

"After Swein left, William found all the boats could be brought to use and laid siege to Ely. We finally took the isle, but Hereward escaped somewhere in the Fens with a goodly portion of his men. We searched for days, but he'd lost himself so well that there was not a trace of his passing."

He grinned suddenly. "I heard one of the other barons declare that Hereward must be in league with the Devil to have disappeared so, but that's nonsense. T'was only that we could find no clues to his route of escape, and that particular baron was given the likeliest area to search. He looked uncommonly bad when he had to report no results, so blamed it on demonic intervention. I think myself that Hereward's merely an exceptionally good solider."

"Well, 'tis a pity there's not an end to it," she commented. "I wish no harm to come to him, but I suppose he'll raise another army in Lincoln, and you'll have all to do again in the spring. So many deaths!" she sighed.

Raoul shook his head. "No, Hereward caused enough trouble in Lincoln, and the folk have not forgot what befell the rebels in York. If he's wise, Hereward'll make for the north parts where he may live out his life in safety. There's no room for rebels in the more settled regions, and the folk have had more than enough of fighting."

"I suspect that many a Saxon lord has taken refuge in the north," said Judith thoughtfully.

Raoul grunted.

"Then, how was it you were wounded?" she asked, seeing he was not interested in the political ramifications of the late rebellion.

"Oh, a graze from a spent arrow, little girl, as I told you. Scarcely bled at all and hasn't even left a scar."

"How paltry!" she sympathized. "What did you do to pass away the long hours, sit beside the fire and tell tales of old battles?"

"Actually, yes, we did. Disappointed?"

"Very. You must have yawned 'til your jaws cracked!"

"And yet," mused her husband, "I believe much was accomplished. I had several offers for Richard."

Judith stiffened. Her blood ran cold. "Offers for Richard? Who? When?" she was frightened.

"Come, little girl, this is no great matter," he soothed. "They are betrothal offers I speak of. There is nothing so serious you must take alarm of it."

"But he's yet a babe!" she protested. "'Tis far too soon to be planning for his wedding!"

"I am become a powerful man, Judith. I told you it would be so, do you not remember?"

She nodded, silent, eyes intent on his face.

"There are many these days would ally themselves with me," he told her, glancing at her sideling. "There were one or two offers, also, to foster the lad in other households, but I refused."

She let out a sigh of relief. "I feared you might decide to send him away," she confessed shakily. "I know it is the custom to do so, especially to increase the standing of one's family among the great."

"He stays." Raoul pulled her to him and held her close. "Richard is ours, sweet lady. I'll not give him over to another's careless tutelage. I was raised thus myself and might have died more than once through neglect, or been crippled."

"You were? I did not know of that." She raised her hand and placed it on his cheek. "Was it so very bad for you?"

Hawk grimaced. "Oh, they fed us well enough, and we'd clothes on our backs. I admit, too, that I learned to wield a sword well enough and better than most, but that was hardly the baron's doing. Rather I'd lessons from a man had been a mercenary all his life. He agreed to teach me in exchange for the gold chain, which was my father's only inheritance for me." He grinned. "Actually, it wasn't a bad bargain. His lessons saved my life more than once in later years. And as great a fool as I was in those days, I'd likely have given the chain to some wench or other after a night of pleasure." He sighed, taking her hand from his cheek and kissing the palm. "As I said, there were worse places. T'was hard to leave my mother, God rest her soul. The baron, Roger, his name was, left us lads to our own devices as often as not, with no supervision and little guidance. We were like a litter of pups, roaming about and looking for trouble. It generally found us," he added, "often in the form of the older menservants, who abused the younger lads shamefully. I was stronger than most boys my age, thanks to my lessons, and a few cuts and bruises taught them to leave me alone. Others were less fortunate."

"Why did you not complain of your mistreatment?"

"To whom? I had no coins to bribe a messenger to take word to my father, and 'tis doubtful he'd have cared had he known. My lady mother died the year I was sent away. Baron Roger thought it good training to suffer adversity, although I've no idea whether he knew just how much suffering there was, or of what sort. I'd not have any son of mine so treated."

"Poor little boy!" murmured Judith, soothing his sleeve with a comforting hand. "Had I been there, I'd have seen to it that you had all needful for your happiness."

Raoul chucked her under the chin. "My lady, you can have no notion how that pleases me! The fact is, I've made some few friends amongst all the nobles at court, for all I've not attended upon William at Christmastide these past few years."

Judith stared at him, comprehending and aghast. "Raoul! You *didn't*!"

"Of course I did! What would you? The new pages and maids arrive sometime in the spring. One of them, I forget which, is the second son of Hugh d'Avranches. And one of the girls is William FitzOsbern's youngest daughter."

With a strong effort, Judith managed to control herself. "Exactly how many children have you agreed to foster here at Oakwood, my lord?" she asked in a dangerous voice.

He read her expression correctly, and with great presence of mind moved away to the protection of a spindly pear tree. "'Er, eight in all, I believe."

"Eight!" she cried. "Eight?!"

"Yes, I'm sure that's the number. Four lads and four maids. Eight." His face carried the smugness of a man who had executed an impressive social coup. There was an infuriating twinkle in his brown eyes.

"*Eight*!" she cast him a look that should have withered the flesh from his bones. "What in God's Holy Name am I to do with eight more children?!"

"Oh, the usual things," replied the Hawk, keeping the tree between them for safety's sake as she moved to flank him. "You know, sewing and the like for the maids. Shouldn't be too difficult."

Judith clenched her hands and glared. "Are you mad?" she demanded furiously. "There're not enough hours in the day as it is! Dear Heaven, I'll have to find a woman to set over them, and where will they sleep? Not in the nursery, that's certain. There wouldn't be room enough, even if they weren't too old for such quartering." Her eyes shifted to a point over his shoulder, and her expression grew thoughtful.

"Mayhap I'll put them in the ladies' dormer," she murmured. "The women of the bower will have to bed down in the solar. It is a nuisance, but with a woman to watch over the girls and a maidservant to do for them, they should fare well."

"See?" said Raoul with a grin. "Nothing to it!"

Her eyes returned to his face. Now that she had begun to accept the situation, Judith could see why he was amused, but she refused to give in. "And the boys, my lord?" she demanded in a grumpy tone. "What will I do with them?"

"I'll see to most of their training," he replied easily. "You need only teach them manners, look to their clothing, and have Brother Plegmund show 'em how to put their names to parchment."

Judith advanced upon him. "Were I not hampered by these skirts, my Lord Baron," she informed him roundly, "I'd give you a kick in the shin you'd not soon forget! In fact, I may forget all sense of propriety and raise them enough to kick you anyway!"

"I have no doubt of that," he turned, grinning broadly. "That's why I choose to keep this tree between us!"

"Coward!" she mocked, her eyes daring him.

"I believe the word 'prudent' is closer to the mark," corrected Raoul, trying and failing to control his amusement.

She stopped circling about the tree, knowing that she would never catch him, as he moved when she did. She tapped her foot. "Come out from behind that tree!"

"Um, not yet, I think." His eyes laughed, and he made a face, eyes crossed and tongue lolling comically out of the corner of his mouth.

Judith was surprised into a giggle, hastily suppressed. "Come out from there!"

"No." Raoul crossed his arms over his chest. "Not until you swear upon your honor not to hurt me."

"Very well, I promise I won't hurt you," she said, suddenly amiable.

Raoul's eyes narrowed in suspicion. "One moment, my lady." She looked exactly like one of the village urchins bent on mischief. "You seem to have your hands behind you back. You wouldn't have crossed your fingers, by some chance, would you?"

"I might."

"Just as I thought!" he declared. He threw up his hands, disgusted. "You won't give me your parole, so I'm not coming out!"

She put her own hands on her hips and cocked her head to one side. "Has it occurred to you, my lord Hawk, that when you are with the King's forces come the spring, t'will be all upon my shoulders, this training of your new pages?" Her tone was dry in the extreme.

Raoul's eyes danced. "Yes, that has crossed my mind."

"Of all the beastly, selfish, ignoble men!" she cried, beside herself with his self-satisfied expression. "Ooooooh!"

The Hawk shook his head sadly. "Never seen you so shrewish, my lady," he remarked provocatively. "If I didn't know better, I'd say t'was that time of the month!"

Judith shrieked and lunged at him, but Raoul dodged her and caught her wrists. Laughing, he pushed her arms gently behind her back and pressed her hard against his chest. Then he kissed her 'til she softened and sighed.

Of a sudden, Judith jerked back her head. "Raoul!" she hissed, shocked. "You must loose me! Merciful Savior, what if someone comes!"

He gave her a slow, sleepy smile. "Hmmmm." Then he kissed her again. "You taste good. Care to retire to our chamber, my lady?"

"Where all *know* what we go to do?" she gasped. "'Tis not decent! How can you even suggest such a thing?"

He kissed her once more. "One day, woman, I'll get you alone in broad daylight and tumble you in a meadow like a peasant wench!"

"Raoul! You would not!"

He slapped her on the backside and led her toward the garden door. "I would, you know. And you'd love it!"

‡‡‡

GLOSSARY

Banns - Public announcement in church of a proposed marriage, commonly read on three successive Sundays

Bantam - Small fowl, the male of which is aggressive and a good fighter

Bier - Wooden frame with handles at each end, to support a corpse or coffin

Bower - Normally referring to ladies of the bower, or upper female servants and dependent well-born ladies

Byre - Cow barn

Chandler - A merchant who sells supplies and groceries, usually to ships

Cochineal Paste - A cosmetic made of crushed cochineal beetles (the females), found in warm regions of the world; it was once used for dyes due to its rich, red color

Danegeld - Tribute demanded by Vikings to quit English shores in peace

Demesne - A lord's house and attached land, as well as the farms supporting it

Destrier - Warhorse, either a stallion or gelding

Doddard - An old man or woman, usually trembling or shaking from age

Donjon - Heavily fortified inner tower or keep of a castle

Dormer - Sleeping quarters for single well-born ladies or ladies of the bower

Ewer - Pitcher

Fief - Land held from an overlord, in return for service

Fyrd - Militia who were called up to fight for the English king in times of danger

Gaiters – Cloth or leather straps used to hold up men's hose, worn criss-crossed from the instep to the top of the hose

Gateaux - Cakes (French)

Geldhide – Unit of measurement at the time of the Domesdei survey; each geldhide was approximately 120 acres; the measurement was used for taxation under the Saxons and Normans, and to determine how many men were provided to the fyrd, 20 men were required for every 100 hides

Gemot - A judicial public meeting in Anglo-Saxon England

Girdle - A belt, usually of metal for the nobles, hanging down slightly in front or slightly to one side

Groat - An English coin of small value

Heriot - A tribute paid to the lord on the demise of the owner, usually of the best beast or other chattel

Hauberk - A covering of the head and neck for protection, usually of chain mail, worn under the helm for extra protection

Helm - A metal helmet in Norman times with a long front piece to protect the nose

Housecarls - Trained, full-time soldiers who were paid for their service, under Saxon rule

Jongleur - A singer or minstrel who composed his own songs

Kinepox - Cow pox; a contagious disease of cows; people who had contracted kinepox were not susceptible to smallpox

Levant - Area of the eastern Mediterranean and Aegean, to include Greece, Egypt, and the rest of today's Middle East

Men-at-arms - Lord's trained soldier, also a cavalryman

Milch - Milk

Monger - Seller

Nithing - A coward, a dastard

Oubliette - Concealed dungeon with a trap door at the top; Usually used for persons condemned to life imprisonment or hidden death

Panniers - Wicker baskets for carrying loads on the back; for animals there are two panniers connected in the middle so that they are balanced on either side of the animal

Parole - One's word of honor, not given or taken lightly

Piggin - A wooden dipper

Puling - Whining, whimpering

Quern - A primitive grinding mill for grains; in this time period consisting of a flat stone on the bottom, and a rounded stone used to crush the dried grains by hand

Quintain - An object supported by a crosspiece on a wooden frame, used as a target

Raiment - Clothing

Reliquary - A small chest, box, shrine, or casket in which religious relics are kept and shown

Retting - Separating the fiber of the flax stem from the wood by soaking in water or dew

Slattern - A woman careless and untidy in her work, dress, appearance, etc.

Sufferance - The condition of remaining 'On Sufferance', that is, tolerated until one proves oneself worthy of acceptance and/or is forgiven

Suzerain - A lord paramount in position or power

Swill-tub - A large barrel in which garbage was kept or laundry washed, usually the former

Thane - An Anglo-Saxon noble who holds lands for military service to the king, corresponding to the later Norman baron

Trull - A rough tunic, usually knee-length, worn by serfs during the middle ages

Twitted - Teased

Vassal - One who holds land from a lord, does homage and pledges loyalty to the overlord by performing military or other duties in exchange

Viand - Foods, especially meats

Vill - Short term for 'village'

Villeins - Any member of a class of serfs or peasants, tied by law to the land, and "owned" by the lord to whom they owe fealty

Whitsuntide - The 5th Sunday after Easter.

Witan - A group of advisors or counselors to the Anglo-Saxon King

ACKNOWLEDGEMENTS

Novels are not created in a vacuum. Thanks are due to my husband for my inspiration, to my children for the fascinating experience of motherhood, and to my dogs for their companionship and their understanding when I couldn't play. Most of all I am grateful to my daughter, Danielle, the best editor, critic, and friend a woman could have.

Thanks, all of you.

JAI ROSE has loved historical fiction since her teens, when she discovered *The Tudor Wench* by Elswyth Thane. Life having an impact on women – and women having an impact on life. Such a revelation! She has been married to the man she loves for more than 50 years. They have two grown children, numerous grandchildren, and three great-grandchildren. They also have an adorable black Labrador retriever. People are her focus. While Jai Rose loves the historical aspect of her work, especially its accuracy, it's the story that draws her. She likes the similarities of people then and now, and the differences.

www.ingramcontent.com/pod-product-compliance
Lightning Source LLC
Chambersburg PA
CBHW030546310726
48979CB00010B/2047/J

* 9 7 8 1 9 4 3 4 9 2 8 2 4 *